THE JURY MASTER

"...hriller of the first order, delivered in high-octane
...rose . . . a winner."   —John Lescroart

"...eminiscent of the early John Grisham and should easily
...nd its way onto the bestsellers lists."   —*Library Journal*

"...ooking for a distinctive new voice? Robert Dugoni's
...ebut won't soon be forgotten. THE JURY MASTER is
a confident, complex, expansive thriller—part legal,
...art political, but always relentlessly paced and exciting."
                   —Stephen White, *New York Times*
                        bestselling author of *Missing Persons*

"[As] fast-paced and arguably more extensive than anything
...Grisham has written in the past few years."
                                        —*Tampa Tribune*

"...apid-fire fictional debut . . . The action keeps coming."
                                        —*Booklist*

"...ilarating ride . . . interesting . . . a great cast of
...ters who are sure to capture your interest. Be sure to
...s one to your reading list . . . highly recommended."
                                        —*Bestsellersworld.com*

more . . .

"A writer to watch." —*Kirkus Reviews*

"An exhilarating thriller about heroes who won't take 'no' for an answer—from the government or anyone else. This novel will make you wish you were brave. I could not put it down." —Tess Gerritsen, *New York Times* bestselling author of *Body Double*

"The finest legal thriller I have read in years. I became immersed in Dugoni's story from page one and quickly grew to care about the characters and what happened to them. The ending had me gasping for air." —Michael Palmer, *New York Times* bestselling author of *Society*

"Dugoni keeps THE JURY MASTER moving quickly . . . in one book, he can create enough memorable characters and action scenes to fill three. You can't ask for much more than that." —*BookReporter.com*

"An unusual and gripping thriller." —*BookLoons.com*

"Wonderful . . . powerful . . . action-packed . . . a ter[ri]ic thriller." —*HarrietKlausner.www[.]om*

The JURY MASTER

ALSO BY ROBERT DUGONI

The Cyanide Canary

The JURY MASTER

Robert Dugoni

WARNER BOOKS

NEW YORK   BOSTON

Copyright © 2006 by La Mesa Fiction, LLC
Excerpt from *Damage Control* Copyright © 2006
by La Mesa Fiction, LLC
All rights reserved. Except as permitted under U.S. Copyright Act of 1976, no part of this publication may be reproduced, distributed, or transmitted in any form or by any means, or stored in a database or retrieval system, without the prior written permission of the publisher.

Warner Books and the "W" logo are trademarks of Time Warner Inc. or an affiliated company. Used under license by Hachette Book Group USA, which is not affiliated with Time Warner Inc.

Warner Books
Hachette Book Group USA
1271 Avenue of the Americas, New York, NY 10020
Visit our Web site at www.HachetteBookGroupUSA.com.

Originally published in hardcover by Warner Books
First Mass Market Edition: January 2007

Printed in the United States of America

10 9 8 7 6 5 4 3 2 1

For my father, Bill, the best man I know;
my mother, Patty, who inspired me; and
my dear friend Ed Venditti—
God took a good man too soon

Acknowledgments

❧

A S WITH ANY PROJECT, there are many to thank. To all I am eternally grateful for your time and your talents. Your insight helped to make *The Jury Master* better. To any I forget to mention here, you know who you are, and your work is reflected within these pages. Any mistakes are mine and mine alone.

In particular, I am, as always, grateful to Jennifer McCord, Pacific Northwest publishing consultant and good friend, who helped me to find a home for my writing and who continues to promote my career. To Redwood City Sheriff Pat Moran and EPA Special Agent and former FBI agent Joseph Hilldorfer for their help with police procedure and for letting me hang out and bug them. To James Fick, gun enthusiast, for his fascination with weapons in particular, and knowledge of just about everything. You are a valuable resource. To Robert Kapela, M.D., for his thirty-plus years of experience in pathology and with autopsies and generally helping me to think of interesting and creative ways to do people in. To Bernadette Kramer, clinical pharmacist, for her help with drugs and their effects on the body, hospitals in general, and psychiatric wards in particular. I never knew my sister was that smart. And to the numerous librarians who pointed me in the right direction to find answers to every question.

To my good friends and former colleagues at Gordon & Rees in San Francisco, particularly Doug Harvey, who taught me the subtle and not-so-subtle practice of law during our twelve years together, my thanks. To my new good friends and colleagues in Seattle at Schiffrin, Olsen, Schlemlein and Hopkins, and to Theresa Goetz, terrific lawyers and friends whose flexibility has helped me to keep the lights on and the water running while encouraging me to write my novels and nonfiction books, my wife and children especially thank you.

To Sam Goldman, the wildest journalism teacher in the West. You taught me how to write and to love doing it.

To my agents, Jane Rotrosen, Donald Cleary, and everyone at the Jane Rotrosen Agency, but especially to Meg Ruley. You are better than advertised. I've said it before: You possess the three best qualities any writer could want— always available, always interested, and always helpful. I owe you all much. Meg, dinner is on me my next trip to New York.

I am extremely grateful to the talented people at Time Warner Book Group. My special thanks to publisher Jamie Raab for making me feel so welcome and giving my writing a home. To Becka Oliver for working so hard and so successfully to ensure that *The Jury Master* will be read in countries all over the world. To art director Anne Twomey for a classy and interesting cover, to production editor Penina Sacks and Michael Carr who copyedited the manuscript and made me look smarter than I am, and to Tina Andreadis, in publicity. And to my editor, Colin Fox, thanks for being in my corner and taking such good care of me and *The Jury Master.* We need to have that beer together, and soon.

As wonderful as you all have been, I tried to ensure that you only saw my good side. I saved most of the lamenting and self-doubt for my wife, Cristina. Through it all, she never wavered in her faith or patience. She believed in me more than I believed in myself. I am your biggest fan.

I once was lost, but now am found.
Was blind but now I see.

"AMAZING GRACE"
John Newton, 1779

1

San Francisco

THEY SHUFFLED into the courtroom like twelve of San Francisco's homeless, shoulders hunched and heads bowed as if searching the sidewalk for spare change. David Sloane sat with his elbows propped on the stout oak table, hands forming a small pyramid with its apex at his lips. It gave the impression of a man in deep meditation, but Sloane was keenly aware of the jurors' every movement. The seven men and five women returned to their designated places in the elevated mahogany jury box, bent to retrieve their notebooks from their padded chairs, and sat with chins tucked to their chests. When they lifted their heads, their gazes swept past Sloane to the distinguished gentleman sitting at the adjacent counsel's table, Kevin Steiner. A lack of eye contact from jurors could be an ominous sign for an attorney and his client. When they looked directly at the opposing counsel it was a certain death knell.

With each of Sloane's fourteen consecutive trial victories and his growing notoriety, the plaintiffs' firms had rolled out progressively better trial lawyers to oppose him.

None had been better than Kevin Steiner. One of the finest lawyers to ever grace a San Francisco courtroom, Steiner had a head of thinning silver hair, a smile that could melt butter, and oratory skills honed studying Shakespeare as a college thespian. His closing argument had been nothing short of brilliant.

Despite Sloane's prior admonition not to react when the jurors reentered the courtroom, he sensed Paul Abbott leaning toward him until Abbott's Hickey-Freeman suit nudged the shoulder of Sloane's off-the-rack blue blazer. His client compounded his mistake by raising a Styrofoam cup of water in a poor attempt to conceal his lips.

"We're dead," Abbott whispered, as if reading Sloane's mind. "They're not looking at us. Not one of them."

Sloane remained statuesque, a man seemingly in tune with everything going on around him and not the slightest bit concerned. Abbott, however, was not to be ignored. He lowered the cup, dropping all pretenses.

"I'm not paying you and that firm of yours four hundred dollars an hour to lose, Mr. Sloane." Abbott's breath smelled of the cheap glass of red wine he had drunk at lunch. The vein in his neck—the one that bulged when he became angry—protruded above the collar of his starched white shirt like a swollen river. "The only reason I hired you is because Bob Foster told my grandfather you never lose. For your sake you better have something good to blow that son of a bitch out of the water." Threat delivered, Abbott finished the remnants of water in his cup and sat back, smoothing his silk tie to a point in his lap.

Again Sloane did not react. He had visions of a well-placed elbow knocking Abbott over the back of his chair, and walking calmly from the courtroom, but that wasn't about to happen. You didn't bloody and abandon the grandson of Frank Abbott, personal friend and Saturday morning golf partner of Bob Foster, Foster & Bane's managing director. Pedigree and circumstance had made Paul Abbott the twenty-nine-year-old successor to the multi-million-dollar Abbott Security Company, and Sloane's worst type of client.

Abbott had conveniently forgotten that he now sat in a San Francisco courtroom because, in the brief period he had served as the CEO of Abbott Security, his incompetence had eroded much of what it took his grandfather forty years to build. An Abbott security guard, convicted of three DUIs that a simple background check would have revealed, had sat drunk at the security desk in the lobby of a San Francisco high-rise. Half asleep, the guard never stopped Carl Sandal for identification, allowing the twice-convicted sex offender access to the building elevators. Sandal prowled the hallways late that night until he found Emily Scott alone in her law office. There he viciously beat, raped, and strangled her. A year to the day after that tragedy, Scott's husband and six-year-old son had filed a wrongful-death civil suit against Abbott Security, seeking $6 million in damages. Sloane had urged Abbott to settle the case, especially after pretrial discovery revealed a number of failed background checks on other security guards, but Abbott refused, calling Brian Scott an "opportunistic whore."

From the corner of his eye, Sloane watched Steiner acknowledge the jurors' gaze with a nearly imperceptible nod of the head. Though too much of a professional to smile, Steiner gently closed his binder and slid it into a trial bag creased and nicked with the scars of a thirty-year career. Steiner's job was finished, and both he and Sloane knew it. Abbott Security had lost on both the evidence and the law—and for no other reason than that its CEO was an arrogant ass who had ignored all of Sloane's advice, including his pretrial admonitions against wearing two-thousand-dollar hand-tailored suits into a sweltering courtroom of blue-collar jurors just looking to find a reason to give away his grandfather's money.

From her perch beneath the large gold seal of the State of California, Superior Court Judge Sandra Brown set aside a stack of papers and wiped her brow with a handkerchief hidden in the sleeve of her black robe. The elaborate climate control system in the recently constructed state-of-the-art courthouse had crashed under the weight of a weeklong heat wave gripping the city, causing a pack of maintenance men to scurry through the hallways lugging bright orange extension cords and portable fans. In an act of mercy, Judge Brown had taken a ten-minute recess after Steiner's closing argument. To Sloane it felt like a temporary reprieve from the governor. That reprieve was about to be rescinded.

"Mr. Sloane, you may give your closing."

Sloane acknowledged Judge Brown, then briefly reconsidered the scrawled blue ink on his yellow legal pad.

It was all an act.

His closing argument wasn't on the pad. Following Steiner's summation Sloane had slipped his own closing into his briefcase. He had nothing to rebut Steiner's emphatic appeal and horrific description of the last moments of Emily Scott's life, or the security guard's wanton negligence. He had nothing with which to "blow the son of a bitch out of the water."

His mind was blank.

Behind him the spectators sitting in the gallery continued to fan the air like a summer congregation in the pews of a Southern Baptist church, a blur of oscillating white sheets of paper. The persistent drone of the portable fans sounded like a swarm of invisible insects.

Sloane pushed back his chair and stood.

The light flashed—a blinding white that sent a lightning bolt of pain shooting from the base of his skull to a dagger point behind his eyes. He gripped the edge of the table as the now familiar image pulsed in and out of clarity: a woman lying on a dirt floor, her broken body surrounded by a bloodred lake, tributaries forging crimson paths. Struggling not to grimace, Sloane forced the image back into the darkness and pried open his eyes.

Judge Brown rocked in her chair with a rhythmic creaking, as if ticking off the seconds. Steiner, too, remained indifferent. In the front row of the gallery, Patricia Hansen, Emily Scott's mother, sat between her two surviving daughters, arms interlocked and hands clasped, like protesters at the front of a picket line. For the moment her steel-blue eyes ignored Sloane, locking instead on the jurors.

Sloane willed his six-foot-two frame erect. At a muscled 185 pounds, he was ten pounds lighter than when he'd stood to give his opening statement, but his attire revealed no sign of the mental and physical deterioration inevitable after five weeks of fast-food dinners, insufficient sleep, and persistent stress. He kept a closet full of suits sized for the weight fluctuations. The jurors would not detect it. He buttoned his jacket and approached the jury, but they now refused to acknowledge him and left him standing at the railing like an unwelcome relative—hoping that if they ignored him long enough he would just go away.

Sloane waited. Around him the courtroom ticked and creaked, the air ripe with body odor.

Juror four, the accountant from Noe Valley, a copious note taker throughout the trial, was first. Juror five, the blonde transit worker, followed. Juror nine, the African-American construction worker, was next to raise his eyes, though his arms remained folded defiantly across his chest. Juror ten followed juror nine, who followed juror three, then juror seven. They fell like dominoes, curiosity forcing their chins from their chests until the last of the twelve had raised her head. Sloane's hands opened in front of him and swept slowly to his side, palms raised like a priest greeting his congregation. Foreign at first, the gesture then made sense—he stood before them empty-handed, without props or theatrics.

His mouth opened, and he trusted that words would follow, as they always did, stringing themselves together like beads on a necklace, one after another, seamless.

"This," he said, "is everyone's nightmare." His hands folded at his midsection. "You're at home, washing the dishes in the kitchen, giving your child a bath, sitting in the den watching the ball game on television—routine, ordinary tasks you do every day." He paced to his left. Their heads turned.

"There's a knock at your door." He paused. "You dry your hands on a dish towel, tell your son not to turn on the hot water, walk to the front door with your eyes on the television."

He paced to his right, stopped, and made a connection with juror seven, the middle school teacher from the Sunset District, who, he knew, would be his client's harshest critic.

"You open the door."

Her Adam's apple bobbed.

"Two men stand on your porch in drab gray suits, a uniformed officer behind them. They ask for you by your full name. You've seen it too many times on television not to know."

She nodded almost imperceptibly.

He moved down the row. The tip of the accountant's pen rested motionless on the pad. The construction worker uncrossed his arms.

"You assume there's been an accident, a car crash. You plead with them to tell you she's all right, but the expressions on their faces, the fact that they are standing on your porch, tell you she is not all right."

The white sheets of paper stilled. Steiner uncrossed his legs and sat forward with a confused, bewildered expression. Patricia Hansen unclasped her daughters' arms and put a hand on the railing like someone at a wedding who is about to stand and object.

"Their words are harsh, matter-of-fact. Direct. 'Your wife's been murdered.' Your shock turns to disbelief and confusion. You feel a moment of absurd relief. It's a mistake. They're at the wrong house.

" 'There's been a mistake,' you say.

"They lower their eyes. 'We're sorry. There's been no mistake.'

"You step onto your porch. 'No. Not my wife. Look at my house. Look at my car in the driveway.' You point up and down the block at your middle-class neighborhood. 'Look at my neighbors. Look at my neighborhood. People don't get murdered here. It's why we live here. It's safe. Our children ride their bikes in the street. We sleep with the windows open. No!' you plead. 'There's been a mistake!' "

He paused, sensing it now, seeing it in their hollow eyes, pleading for him to continue, yearning to hear the soothing comfort of his voice, taking in his words like drugs from a syringe.

"But there hasn't been a mistake. There hasn't been an accident. No. It was a deliberate, calculated act by a sick and depraved sociopath who, on that particular night, at that particular moment, was intent on killing. And there was absolutely nothing anyone could have done to prevent him from doing that."

He spread his arms, offering to shelter them from their pain, acknowledging the difficult task that awaited them.

"I wish the question before you was whether Emily Scott's death was a horrific, senseless killing." It was a subtle reference to Steiner's closing argument. "On that we would certainly all agree."

Heads nodded.

"I wish the question *was* whether her husband and their young son have suffered and will continue to suffer because of Carl Sandal's indecent act." His eyes scanned their faces. "More than any of us could imagine." His words blended with the drone of the fans in a hypnotic cadence. "But those are not the questions you must answer, that you swore an oath to answer. And deep within, each and every one of you knows that. That's what makes this so difficult. That's why you feel so pained. The question before you can't be answered by emotion. You must answer it with reason, in a case that has no reason. There is no good reason for what Carl Sandal did. There never will be."

Tears streamed unchecked down the blonde transit worker's face.

He looked to juror five, the auto mechanic from the Richmond district, and at that moment knew somehow that the man would be elected the jury foreman.

"I wish to God there was a way to prevent senseless, violent acts by predators intent on committing them. I wish to God we could do something here today to prevent anyone from ever opening his front door again and receiving the news Brian Scott received. I wish to God we could have prevented Carl Sandal from doing what he did." He felt them now; he felt the part of them that had once resisted his words welcoming him. "But we can't. Short of living in fear, barring our doors and windows and living in cages like animals . . . we can't."

He dropped his gaze, releasing them. They had opened their doors; they had greeted him into their homes. And at that precise moment, Sloane knew. He did not need to say another word. Abbott Security had not lost.

And he wished to God he could have prevented that, too.

2

~

Bloomberry,
West Virginia

PARKED BENEATH THE cover of an aspen tree, Charles Town, West Virginia, Police Officer Bert Cooperman pinched the dial of the scanner between his thumb and index finger like a fisherman feeling a nibble. Try as he might, he couldn't set the hook, and he sensed he was about to lose whatever played at the end of his line.

It wasn't dispatch. Kay was on duty, and no red-blooded American with a pecker would confuse Kay's come-hither West Virginia drawl with the man's voice that Cooperman's scanner was intermittently picking up. It could be park police; the switchback road, nestled in the foothills of the Blue Ridge Mountains, bordered the edge of the Black Bear National Park, which was within the park police's jurisdiction, but the dial wasn't close to the park police's frequency. It was tweaked just a hair past 37.280 MHz, which was damn near Charles Town's frequency. And that was what puzzled him.

Cooperman cocked his head toward the radio and

continued to massage the dial, a fraction to the right, left, back again.

"Come on. Give me something." Hell, he'd take anything at this point. Ten hours into a twelve-hour shift, he was already working on his sixth thermos cap of black coffee, and his eyelids still felt like garage doors wanting to roll shut. The damned full moon had given him false hope. Bullshit superstition or not, the crazies usually came out with full moons. When the crazies came out twelve hours passed like twelve minutes.

Not tonight.

Tonight it felt like twelve days. At least he had the weekend off, and with his wife and newborn baby boy in South Carolina to visit her family, that gave him a real chance to get in some uninterrupted sleep and some long overdue hunting. That thought—and the voice teasing him on the scanner—was the only thing keeping him awake. The voice had come out of nowhere, as Cooperman sat parked on the side of the road munching on an egg salad sandwich that was now stinking up the inside of the car.

". . . fire roa . . . eight miles ou . . . just about . . . iver."

There it was again—faint, breaking up, but still biting. Damned if he was going to let it get away.

". . . underneath a bush . . . emban . . . abo . . . waist."

Definitely a man. Sounded as if he'd found something in the bushes. Cooperman strained to listen.

". . . no question . . . dead."

"Damn." Cooperman sat back, slapping the steering wheel. "Animal fucking control." They were likely calling in a road kill. Wasn't that just his luck? He dropped the Chevy into drive and pulled from the gravel turnout.

The scanner crackled.

"—He's dead—"

Cooperman hit the brakes. Coffee broke over the rim of the thermos cap, scalding his leg. He lifted himself from the seat and threw napkins and newspaper under him, then quickly regripped the dial—left, right.

Nothing.

"No . . . no . . . no. Come back! Come back!"

He dumped the remnants of coffee out the window and sat back, the moon taunting him. The thought hit him like his father's hand slapping him in the back of the head when he'd done something stupid.

What if the guy isn't dead, Coop? What if he's still alive?

Anxiety and caffeine surged through him. He sat up. "Shit."

What if he's out there dying?

He hit the gas, but another thought caused him to hit the brake again. "Hell, he could be anywhere out there." Finding a man dying of a gunshot wound would be like searching for a needle in a haystack.

That's not good enough.

"I know, goddamn it. I know."

What the hell did the man say? Think! What did your tired-ass mind hear, Coop?

"I'm thinking. I'm thinking." But he wasn't. He couldn't. His mind was going over all the ways he'd screwed up, and the inevitable confrontation with J. Rayburn Franklin, Charles Town's chief of police. He'd be on graveyard forever, doomed to roam the night like a damned vampire.

Fire road.

Cooperman sat up. "Fire road. Right. He definitely said 'fire road.' "

Which could be nearly anywhere in the mountains, idiot.
He rubbed the back of his neck. "What else? What else!"
Eight miles.
"That's right, he said 'eight miles.'" The conversation
filtered back.
Where the rivers meet.
"Where the rivers meet."
The Shenandoah and Potomac.
Cooperman grabbed the shift, stopped.
No. Not the Shenandoah and Potomac. Too far.
"Has to be closer. What's closer?"
Evitt's Run.
The thought burst like an overfilled balloon.
"The fire trail. Shit, he's on the fire trail. Got to be.
Bingo."

He tossed the remnants of the egg salad out the window and hit the switch, sending strobes of blue and white
light pulsating against the trunks and branches of the
trees. He pulled a U-turn from the gravel shoulder onto
the pavement and punched the accelerator.

FOUR MINUTES LATER, Cooperman maneuvered the
switchbacks with one hand on the wheel and returned the
speaker to its clip. He'd given his position as north on
County Road 27. Procedure required that he call for
backup, but he knew it would take time for Operations to
contact the park police, and more time for them to get an
officer out to the scene.

This was his call—possibly his first dead body.

The cobwebs and burning eyes had been replaced by a
burst of energy as if he'd just completed a set of ten on the

bench press. Damn, he liked the rush! He looked up at the sky and howled.

"Full moons, baby!"

He punched the accelerator some more, leaning into a horseshoe turn, unafraid of overshooting the fire trail, which he could find with his eyes closed. Evitt's Run meandered in a somewhat perpendicular line until it merged with the Shenandoah. In February and October, when Fish and Game stocked the river with trout and bass, the fire trail became a regular thoroughfare. The rest of the year it was mostly deserted, with a rare hiker or hunter seeking access to the Blue Ridge Mountains. Every year one or two of them blew off a toe or hit a buddy in the back with buckshot. This was likely one of those occasions, though it sounded serious. Cooperman figured the voice must have been calling 911, which was how his scanner picked it up. It was just like Tom Molia said. The Charles Town detective had the department in a lather with a story about his scanner picking up a man and woman screwing over the telephone, telling each other to do all kinds of crazy shit. It sounded like pure Mole bullshit—the Mole liked to stir the pot—but damned if he didn't bring in an article from the *Post* talking about a glitch in the wireless technology that was causing scanners to pick up telephone calls like antennas picking up radio signals.

Cooperman grinned. "Well, it may not be two people humping, Mole, but wait till the boys hear my story."

He might even save a life, be a hero. J. Rayburn Franklin would call it "Damn fine police work," the kind of attentiveness he liked to see in a young officer. They'd probably write Cooperman up in the *Spirit of Jefferson,* the local weekly. Hell, he could get a mention in the *Post*, for that matter.

The car fishtailed, its back tires catching loose gravel at the edge of the road and sending it close to the embankment. Cooperman accelerated, then braked and corrected the wheel into the next turn. "Just like at the academy, Coop." He maneuvered another switchback, saw the familiar triangular sign reflecting yellow in the car's headlights, braked hard into a right turn, and corrected the wheel to bring the rear end in line. The car bounced and pitched on the unpaved road, dirt and gravel pinging beneath it. Its tires caught air cresting the bluff, and the car landed with a bump, headlights shimmering on the white ash and maple. Cooperman swung it to the right and stopped when the headlights illuminated a bearded red-haired man standing outside the cab of a beat-up white pickup truck.

He looked like a deer caught in headlights. "That's right, Red, the cavalry has arrived."

Cooperman threw the car into park and jumped from behind the wheel slapping his billy club into his utility belt while pulling the flashlight from its clip in two quick, rehearsed motions. The adrenaline pushed him forward, though somewhere in the recesses of his mind his instructors at the academy were yelling for him to slow down and think it through. His feet weren't listening.

He called out as he approached. "You the one who made the call?" The man raised a hand to deflect the light. Cooperman lowered the beam. "You call about a body?"

Red turned to the truck. Cooperman followed his gaze with the flashlight, illuminating the back of a head framed by a gun rack holding two high-powered rifles. The short hairs on the back of his neck twitched, enough for him to instinctively unsnap the Smith & Wesson on his hip, though he resisted the urge to draw.

Think it through. Use your head. Always.

Red wore jeans, boots, and a denim jacket—appropriate hunting attire. Check. The two men wouldn't have much luck without rifles. Two men. Two rifles. Check. The license plate on the truck was the rolling West Virginia hills at dusk below the familiar words "Wild, Wonderful." Check again. Just a couple of good old boys sneaking off into the mountains to do a little hunting.

The passenger door of the truck swung open, and a stocky dark-haired man stepped down from the cab. Cooperman directed the beam of light toward him.

"I'm Officer Bert Cooperman, Charles Town Police. You call nine-one-one about a dead body?"

The man nodded, approaching with a cell phone in hand. It was just as the Mole said.

"Yes, Officer, I just made the call. Damn, you gave us a start getting here so quick and all. Surprised the hell out of us." The man spoke with a distinct West Virginia accent. He sounded winded.

"I picked up the call on the scanner. I was patrolling nearby."

The man pointed toward a thicket of Scotch broom that looked to have partly swallowed a black Lexus. "Thought it odd, the way it was parked and all," he said as he walked toward the car. "Thought maybe it rolled. Nobody in it. Just a suit jacket. Thought that weird, too, so we took a look around, just out of curiosity, you know?" The man pointed to the edge of the embankment, changing direction as he spoke. "The body's just down the bluff. We didn't hear nothin', but it looks to me like he just done it."

Cooperman followed at a quick pace. "Just done it?"

The man stopped at the edge of a steep slope. At the bottom the Shenandoah flowed as dark as a tarred road at night. "Shot hisself in the head. Looks that way, anyway."

"Dead?" Cooperman asked.

"Body's still warm. I mean, we ain't doctors or nothin', but . . ."

Cooperman looked over the edge. "You think he could still be alive?"

The man pointed. "You can just see the legs right there, just to the left of that big bush—about twenty yards there. You see 'em?"

Cooperman swept the beam of light over bubby brush and red buckeye, then brought it back quickly and settled on something grotesquely out of place: a pant leg protruding from the shrubbery. A body. Goddamn, it *was* an honest-to-God body. Of course that was what he expected, but seeing it . . . his first one . . .

Things started moving fast again, thoughts rushing at him like objects in a kid's video game. Cooperman started down the bluff, stopped.

Call it in. He could still be alive. The body's still warm.

He started, stopped again.

Even if he's alive, he'll need more than you can give him. Call for an ambulance.

He climbed to the top of the bluff, started for the car, then turned to let the two men know what was going to happen. "I'm going to—"

Cooperman dropped the flashlight, the beam rolling across the ground and coming to a stop on the black toe of the hunter's boot. The veterans said it looked big as a sewer pipe and was something you hoped never to see.

"My backup will be here any minute," Cooperman said.

The dark-haired man smiled. "Thank you for that important bit of information, Officer." The accent was gone. So was the cell phone. In his hand the man held a large-caliber handgun.

Cooperman stood staring down the barrel.

3

Yosemite National Park,
California

THE CRY ECHOED off the granite walls like ghosts wailing. Sloane struggled to sit up, the sleeping bag cocooned tightly around him. He freed a hand from the twisted fabric, swept the ground for the rubberized handle, and unsheathed the serrated steel blade as he kicked free of the bag and jumped to his feet, crouching, eyes wide. His pulse rushed in his ears. His chest heaved for each breath.

The echo faded, retreating across the Sierras, leaving the sound of the mountains at night—crickets chirping, a symphony of insects, and the hushed din of a distant waterfall. A chill washed over him, bringing a trail of goose bumps and a numbing, harsh reality.

He was alone. The echoing cry was his own.

Sloane dropped the knife and ran his fingers through his hair. As his eyes adjusted to the dark, the threatening shadows became the trees and rocks by which he had made his camp.

Following the jurors' verdict, he had been determined to get far away from the courthouse, to forget, to let the mountains comfort him as they always had. He had left Paul Abbott in the courthouse and his cell phone on the counter in his apartment along with his laptop computer and trial bag. He had driven through the San Joaquin Valley with the windows down, Springsteen's "Born to Run" blasting from the speakers, the hundred-degree-plus heat whipping the smell of onions and cow manure from the pastures through the car. With each mile he put between himself and Emily Scott, his optimism had grown that he was moving forward and, in doing so, leaving the nightmare behind.

But he was wrong. The nightmare had followed him.

He should have known. His optimism had not been born of fact or reason, but of desperation. So encumbered by his need to forget, he had chosen to ignore the flaws in his reasoning, to invent facts that did not exist—a dangerous mistake for a trial lawyer. Now, like the dying embers of his campfire, his optimism had been suffocated, leaving only irrepressible frustration.

The pain spiked like an abrupt fever and spiderwebbed across his forehead and scalp. The headache always followed the nightmare, the way thunder followed lightning. Sloane grabbed his headlamp and stumbled across the blanket of pine needles and pebbles gouging the bottoms of his feet. His backpack was suspended from a tree branch, beyond the reach of animals. The daggers of pain spread like tentacles; a black-and-white discotheque of shimmering light blurred his vision. He bent to retrieve the stick he'd used to push the backpack high out of reach, and felt his stomach cramp, the pain driving him to one knee and forcing up his freeze-dried meal in a series of violent convulsions. The migraine would get worse, even temporarily blind him. That thought pushed him to his feet. He retrieved his backpack, pulled the small plastic container from the front pouch, and swallowed two of the light blue tablets with a squirt of water. The Fiorinal would dull the pain; it would not dull his frustration.

"Enough," he said, looking up at a full moon in a star-pocked sky. "Enough, goddamn it."

SLOANE CROUCHED ON his haunches in the rim of light emanating from the rebuilt fire and poked a stick at the flames, adding dry twigs. Pine needles crackled in a burst of yellow. He had broken camp, and his need to leave was now waging a battle with the voice of reason, telling him to wait for daylight. At the moment, his rational side wasn't listening. Though he had never ventured far from the catacomb of developments that sprawled cookie-cutter homes across the San Gabriel Valley in Southern California, Sloane had come to find the Sierra Nevada an unlikely escape from work and the problems that plagued him.

Not anymore.

Whatever haunted his sleep would not be cloaked like furniture in an abandoned home. It existed independent of the Emily Scott trial, fluid and unpredictable, alive. He looked out into the darkness and felt it, something, a presence. Whatever it was, it was not going away, and he could not hide from it. It was coming for him, relentless and determined.

He stood and kicked dirt over the fire, smothering it.

It was time to move.

4

Black Bear National Park,
West Virginia

DETECTIVE TOM MOLIA pulled back the shrubbery and fought that moment of revulsion when any normal person with a normal job would have tossed up the Italian sausage he had slapped between two slices of bread and called breakfast as he rushed out the door to his car. The body lay on its side, presumably as it had fallen— a well-built man, his white shirt and tie splattered in burgundy-red and gray brain matter. Near the curled fingers of the right hand, partially obscured by the tall grass and Scotch broom, protruded the ventilated-rib barrel of a Colt Python .357.

Serious shit.

Molia crouched to take a closer look. The bullet, a .357 Magnum or .38-caliber Special, had ripped through the man's temple like a runaway freight train, taking with it a substantial portion of the top of his head.

"I hope I never get used to this," he said.

He warded off a fly with the back of his hand. With the temperature quickly warming, it hadn't taken them long to find the body. Molia pulled a wood leek from the ground and stuck the root in his mouth, spitting bits of dirt off the tip of his tongue. The sharp onion taste would temper the smell of death, but it wouldn't keep it from clinging to the linings of his nostrils and clothes long after he'd left the scene.

"Colt Python. Probably a three fifty-seven. Serious piece. He meant business."

He might as well have been talking to the dead man. West Virginia Park Police Officer John Thorpe stood above the detective on the sloped ground, whacking at the tall grass with his flashlight; he had the personality of a lamppost.

Molia stood from his crouch and considered the terrain. "The grass will hide a lot. With an exit wound that big, the bullet could be just about anywhere around here—doubt we'll find it. But . . ." He paused, and if Thorpe ever learned the art of communication, he just missed another golden opportunity to show it.

Molia wiped a handkerchief across his brow and looked back up the steep bluff. Though he couldn't see them, he knew that a horde of park police investigators and FBI agents were converging on the black Lexus like ants on candy—and just one step behind the press. Thorpe had failed to cover the car license plate, and it hadn't taken long for the identity of the victim to be broadcast across the newswires. By the time Molia drove up the fire trail two uniformed sheriffs were already stringing a rope across the road to keep the reporters at bay.

Molia slipped off his sport coat and draped it over his shoulder, continuing to blot his brow. Maybe it was the exertion from climbing up and down the bluff, but the morning sun, already a white beacon in a cloudless blue sky, seemed intent to beat on him especially hard. Given the weather forecast, ninety degrees with 90 percent humidity, he figured to be dripping the rest of the day.

"It's not the heat that gets you, it's the humidity," he said. Born and raised in Northern California's comparatively mild climate, he found it one of the things about West Virginia he'd just never get used to. "Well, whoever said that never stood in ninety-degree heat sweating his ass off, did he, John? Hot is hot, humidity or not."

Thorpe looked out over the bluff as if stricken by gas. If Molia had twenty more like him, he could start a vegetable garden.

He loosened his tie and lowered it three buttons; his shirt was already wrinkled. Maggie always said she could send him out the door dressed in fine linen and he'd look like a rumpled bed before he made it to the end of the driveway. It was big-man's syndrome. At six feet he had never been what they called svelte, though as a younger man he had carried his weight like an athlete, in his shoulders, legs, and chest. But come forty, gravity had taken over, and everything seemed to be slipping to his midsection and butt, enough extra flesh for Maggie to grab and refer to as "love handles." Love, nothing. It was a spare tire, and it was inflating. Dieting was out of the question— he loved to eat too much, which was a part of the joy of being Italian. And if getting up at the crack of dawn to jog was his alternative, well, then, he'd rather be fat. When he stepped on the scale butt naked this morning he was forty-three years old and 228 pounds.

He stuffed the handkerchief into the back pocket of his khakis and found one of the tiny Confederate soldiers from the Gettysburg Museum that he had purchased for his son, T.J. "They'll have to go with powder burns," he said, assuming they'd never find a bullet for ballistics. "You sure you didn't see one of our guys, huh?"

Thorpe shrugged. "Look around."

Molia had. According to Operations, Bert Cooperman called in just after 3:30 a.m. to say he was rolling on a report of a dead body. That had been Cooperman's last transmission. Operations contacted the park police, and Kay got Molia's ass out of bed with that Southern twang that gave him butterflies in places that could get a married man hit over the head. But Kay wasn't calling out of love. Molia was the detective on call. It was all standard procedure, except that when Molia reached the site he found Thorpe, not Coop, claiming to be the responding officer and walking around like Alexander Haig at the White House. Thorpe directed Molia to the black Lexus, which was where he had found the blue and white laminated card that set off all the bells and whistles and was responsible for the federal agents in dark blue windbreakers with bright yellow lettering buzzing around the bluff like bumblebees from a disturbed hive. The dead man was Joe Branick, personal friend and White House confidant of United States President Robert M. Peak.

Thorpe shrugged. "Well, he was out of his jurisdiction; this is a federal park, Detective."

Molia bit his tongue. He hated the territorial bullshit between law enforcement agencies. J. Rayburn Franklin, Charles Town's chief of police, had told him more than once to play nice with the other boys, that they were all on the same team and all that other law enforcement bullshit. But Molia just wasn't the tongue-biting type, and at the moment he had that acidic fire burning in his gut that had nothing to do with the Italian sausage and everything to do with twenty years of experience. Something wasn't right.

"No doubt, John, except we also have a possible homicide."

"Homicide?" Thorpe smirked. "This doesn't look like a homicide to me, Detective. This looks like an old-fashioned suicide."

The smirk was not a good idea. Along with his love of food, Molia had inherited an Italian temper, which was like mercury in a thermometer—hard to keep down once it started rising. Molia took the smirk as the "big boys" taking a shot at the country bumpkin detective.

"Maybe, John, but Cooperman wouldn't have known that until he got here, now, would he?"

"Well . . ."

"And if it is a homicide, it's the jurisdiction of both park police and local, and local beat you boys hands down."

"Hands down?"

"Makes Cooperman the responding officer."

Thorpe whacked at the tall grass with continued disinterest, but Molia could see the look already forming in his eye. Thorpe hadn't climbed back down the bluff and stood in the sun because he wanted to strike up a friendship. He was worried he was about to lose the big buck he'd bagged, and was standing over it like a proud hunter not about to give it up.

"I don't know what he responded to, but he ain't here, Detective. We are," he said, referring to the park police. "At least you can take the rest of the morning off." Thorpe rubbed the palm of his hand over the top of his head.

"Lucky you. You won't be standing around here baking your brains."

"Afraid not," Molia said, rejecting the olive branch. He was about to drop his bomb, and when he did, no one was going to like him much, particularly not the bumblebees at the top of the hill. It wouldn't be the first time, not that Tom Molia cared. What he cared about was his gut, which the roll of Tums in the Chevy glove compartment wasn't going to soothe.

"I'm going to have to take jurisdiction of the body."

Thorpe stopped whacking the grass. "You're going to what?"

"Take jurisdiction of the body. Responding officer takes jurisdiction, John."

"You're looking at the responding officer."

"Nope. Bert Cooperman was the responding officer. Charles Town Police. Body goes to the county coroner."

Thorpe's face rounded to a dulled expression. "Cooperman isn't here. You're looking at the responding officer, Detective."

"Who called you, John?"

"Who?"

"Park dispatch called you, didn't it?"

"Yeah—"

"And how did they get the call?" He let the question sink in.

"Well . . ." Thorpe stuttered, seeing his buck being dragged deeper into the underbrush.

"Well, the body goes to the county coroner. It's procedure."

"Procedure?" Thorpe pointed up the hill, smirking again. "You going to tell *them* that?"

"No," Molia said, shaking his head.

"I didn't think so." Thorpe turned.

"You are."

Thorpe wheeled. "What!"

"You're going to tell them."

"The hell I am!"

"The hell you aren't. You got the call from dispatch. Dispatch got the call from a Charles Town police officer. The body goes to the county coroner. If the feds want to go through the proper channels to have it released, so be it. Until then, we follow procedure. You're obligated to enforce it. This is your site. You secured it." Molia smiled.

"Are you serious?"

"As a heart attack."

Thorpe had a habit of shutting his eyes, like a child who thought it would make everything bad go away. When he did his eyelids fluttered. At the moment they looked like two big monarch butterflies.

"Come on, John. It's not that big a deal. With a buck this big you want to make a mistake? The press will pick this thing apart like my brothers on a Thanksgiving turkey. And don't get me started on the feds. You break procedure, they're going to want to know why. They'll load you up with about two dozen questions and a stack of paperwork that'll keep you buried from here to Tuesday."

Thorpe's mouth pinched as if swallowing a hundred different things he wanted to say, none of which was "you're wrong." Without uttering a word, he turned abruptly and started up the bluff. Molia followed. He might go back to the station and find Bert Cooperman in the locker room lifting weights, which Coop liked to do after his shift. The rookie officer might even tell him he spooked when he realized he was out of his jurisdiction—a rookie mistake. Sure, those were possible explanations. And the autopsy might also reveal that Joe Branick, special assistant and personal friend of the president of the United States, decided to put a gun to his head and blow away half his skull. At the moment, however, Molia's gut was telling him that the likelihood of either scenario was less than that of his mother admitting that the Pope was fallible.

At the top of the bluff, out of breath, he looked up at the sky to curse the sun and noticed the trace outline still visible in the pale morning sky.

A full moon.

5

~

Pacifica,
California

A MOIST FOG had rolled off the Pacific Ocean in thorough disregard for summer and hung over the coastal town like a wet wool blanket, shading the streetlamps to a dull orange glow, the only color in an otherwise gunmetal-gray world that spread to the horizon—a monochrome that revealed no hint of the time of day. If the coldest winter Mark Twain ever spent was a summer in San Francisco, it was only because Twain had not had the courage to venture thirty miles south along the coast to the town of Pacifica. The fog in summer could chill so deep it made your bones hurt.

The windshield wipers hummed a steady beat across the glass. Wisps of the fog blew thick and thin, shrouding the two-story apartment building like something in a horror film. Like most things in Sloane's life, the building had been neglected and was in need of repair. The relentless moisture and salt air stained the cedar shingles with a white residue. Rust pitted the aluminum windows, which needed to be replaced. The exterior deck coatings were peeling, and there was evidence of dry rot in the carport overhang. Eight years earlier, Sloane had taken a real estate agent's advice and used his growing wealth to purchase the eight-unit apartment building and the adjacent vacant lot. Developers were paying handsome prices to turn the apartments along the coast into condominiums, but then the economy crashed with the precipitous drop in interest rates, leaving Sloane holding a white elephant. When an apartment became vacant he moved in to save money, not expecting to be happy about it. But in the intervening years he had grown fond of the building, like a mangy old dog that he couldn't consider getting rid of. He slept with the sliding glass door to his bedroom open, drifting off to the sound of waves crashing on the shore, finding comfort in the rhythmic roll and thumping beat of nature's eternal clock, a reminder of time passing.

Sloane turned off the ignition and sat back, numb.

"That is some gift you have . . . what you did to those jurors."

Patricia Hansen's words in the courtroom continued to haunt him. With practice, he had developed the fine art of stalling following a jury verdict, methodically packing his notebooks and exhibits, determined to be the last person out of the courtroom. He refrained from any backslapping and handshakes. For the family of the deceased, a defense verdict was like reliving their loved one's death, and right or wrong, that made Sloane the Grim Reaper. He preferred to leave quietly, alone. Emily Scott's mother had not been about to allow him that comfort.

When he turned to leave the courtroom Patricia Hansen remained seated in the gallery, a newspaper clutched to her chest. When Sloane stepped through the swinging gate she stood and stepped into the aisle.

"Mrs. Hansen—"

She raised a hand. "Don't. Don't you dare tell me how sorry you are for my loss." She spoke barely above a whisper, more tired than confrontational. "You don't know my loss. If you did, you would never have done what you just did." She paused, but she was clearly not finished. "What Carl Sandal did? I can almost . . ." She swallowed tears, fighting not to let Sloane see the depth of her pain. "What he did I can almost understand. A sociopath. A crazed lunatic. Isn't that what you called him? But what he did pales in comparison to what you did to my Emily in this courtroom . . . to our family, to the word 'justice.' You knew better, Mr. Sloane. You *know* better."

"I only did my job, Mrs. Hansen."

Patricia Hansen snatched the words like an actor given the perfect cue. "Your job?" She scoffed, looking around the courtroom with disdain before fixing him again with her steel-blue eyes. "You just keep telling yourself that, Mr. Sloane, and maybe, if you hear it often enough, someday you might actually start to believe that makes it all right." She unfolded the newspaper and compared the man who stood before her with the photograph. "That is some gift you have, Mr. Sloane . . . what you did to those jurors. I don't know how you did it, how you convinced them. They didn't want to believe you. I saw it when they came back. They had their minds made up." A tear rolled down her cheek; she disregarded it. "Well, consider this, Mr. Sloane. My Emily is dead, and my grandson will never have his mother. That is something you can't change with your words."

She slapped the newspaper against his chest. With both hands holding trial bags, Sloane watched it fall to the ground, his photograph staring up at him from the tile floor.

During Sloane's run of victories, all on behalf of defendants in wrongful-death civil trials, what began as a simple premonition that the jurors would find for his client, sometimes against his own judgment, had become unmistakable knowledge. Sloane *knew* before he stood to give his closing argument that he had lost. He knew that the jury considered Abbott Security culpable. He knew they believed the guard was negligent. He knew they hated his client. He knew, as did all good trial lawyers, that you did not win cases in closing argument—a television gimmick for the dramatic. He knew that there should have been nothing he could say to change their minds.

And yet he had.

They had returned a verdict for Abbott Security in less than two hours. He had convinced them all, every single juror, of something even *he* did not believe. What was more troubling was that when he had stood to give his closing he had no idea what he would say to convince them, and yet he had said the very words they *needed* to hear to assuage their doubts and erase their concerns. Only they weren't his words. It was his voice, but it was as if the words were being spoken through him by someone else.

Not wanting to linger on that thought, he pushed open the car door into a strong wind that carried a distant, whistling howl and the briny smell of the ocean. As he stepped from the Jeep he felt a shock of pain in his right ankle. He'd rolled it during his descent down the mountain trail in the dark, and it had swollen and stiffened on the drive home. He retrieved his backpack, slung the strap over his shoulder, and limped toward the building. The familiar light in the first-floor apartment window farthest to the right glowed like a beacon welcoming a ship, but he did not see the top of Melda's head. Melda rose at 4:30 every morning of the week, a disciplined habit from working in the fields growing up in the Ukraine. She'd be concerned to hear someone in the apartment above her. Sloane was not supposed to be home for two more days. He'd dump his backpack in his apartment and visit for a cup of tea. Drinking tea with Melda was like sitting in a soothing bath, and he could use one at the moment.

He fumbled with a cluster of keys that would have made a high school janitor blanch, found the key to his mailbox, and reached to insert it where the lock should have been but where now existed a small hole. He put the key in the hole and pulled open the metal door, finding the lock at the bottom. The doors to the seven other mailboxes mounted to the building remained closed, locks in place. Sloane picked up the lock and considered it. It had likely worked its way loose and fallen when Melda collected his mail—one more project on his growing checklist.

He put the lock in his pocket, adjusted the backpack on his shoulder, and ascended the two flights of concrete stairs, holding on to the railing for support. As he limped down the landing he noticed a wedge of light on the asphalt. The door to his apartment was ajar. Melda had a spare key, and it was possible she was inside, even at this early hour, but she would have shut the door to keep in the heat. It was also possible she had failed to shut the door fully on leaving, and the wind, gusting off the ocean, had blown it open. Possible, but also not likely. Melda was careful. She would have shaken the handle.

Sloane slid the backpack from his shoulder, reached to push open the door, and snatched back his hand at the sound of something shattering inside the apartment. Fighting the impulse to rush in, he listened a beat, then gently pushed the door. The hinges creaked like bad knees. He stepped over the threshold and leaned inside.

It looked as if a hurricane had touched down in his living room.

The wall-to-wall carpet was strewn with debris: paperback books, CDs, papers, clothes, and toppled furniture. The cushions of the couch had been shredded, the stuffing scattered about the room like large cotton balls. His stereo and television lay in ruins, the insides spilled on the carpet like gutted fish.

A glass shattered in the kitchen.

Sloane stepped over the toppled hall table, pressed his back against the wall that ran parallel with the kitchen, and slid silently forward. He paused at the wall's edge, gathered himself, and whirled around the corner. Glass shattered at his feet. A shadow bolted across the kitchen counter and leaped into the darkness of the living room.

Bud, his cat.

Sloane looked down at the broken plate at his feet, which a moment earlier had been on the leaning stack amid the contents of his cupboards. Bud had apparently been standing on the stack, licking at a puddle of syrup that had overflowed the counter. That explained the shattered glass. It didn't explain the destruction. That thought came simultaneously with the sound.

Soft footsteps behind him.

Too slow to turn, Sloane felt something hard slam against the back of his head.

6

~

The West Wing,
Washington, D.C.

PARKER MADSEN CONSIDERED the polish on a black wingtip shoe in his hand. Three other pairs waited atop their original boxes, each aligned against the wainscoting like soldiers at inspection. Madsen wore the fifth pair—a different pair for each day of the week, sturdy shoes built more for durability than appearance. According to a military doctor, Madsen pronated when he walked. He thought that by examining the wear on the rubber heels he could determine his most demanding day of the week. So far, he had noticed no correlation.

On the second and fourth Thursdays of each month, a staff assistant took the shoes to a stand on New York Avenue where a Vietnam veteran understood the term "spit-polished to shine." Madsen's assistant brought back the shoes Friday morning, along with Madsen's dry cleaning: button-down white dress shirts and three-button navy-blue suits. The Washington press corps was fond of saying the retired three-star general had traded his olive green for navy blue, a sarcastic dig that Madsen took as a compliment. He had little time for, or interest in, things like dress and decor. Uniforms saved time that could then be devoted to more worthy matters. The military understood this. So, too, had Einstein.

Madsen placed the shoe back atop the box, beside its partner, removed the .45 from the holster concealed beneath his suit coat, placed it on the top shelf of the lower cabinet, and closed the door. He sidestepped his red Doberman, Exeter, curled in a ball on a felt-covered beanbag, and walked to his desk, where eight neatly aligned newspapers awaited his attention. His staff stripped the papers of the sections that served only to give them bulk—sports, entertainment, culinary tips, and advertising—and underlined articles of interest. Then his secretary arranged the papers on his desk in the order he preferred: the *Washington Post* first, of course, then the *Washington Times,* the *Wall Street Journal,* the *New York Times* (which he considered a liberal rag), the *Los Angeles Times* (to get a flavor of the West Coast), the *Chicago Tribune,* the *Dallas Morning News,* and the *Boston Globe.* Normally Madsen had skimmed the articles before nine a.m. Today would not be normal.

He pressed the intercom on his telephone. "Ms. Beck, you may send in the assistant United States attorney," he said. Then he sat back, picking a piece of lint from the sleeve of his coat. It floated in the stream of light tunneling through the multipaned French windows behind him. Madsen chose to sit with his back to the view of the South Lawn, though he had lobbied hard for this particular office. It had nothing to do with the view. Traditionally, the White House chief of staff kept an office across the street in the Old Executive

Office Building, just fifty yards from the West Wing in distance, but miles in terms of prestige and power. The big boys worked in the West Wing. Madsen got an office two doors removed from the Oval Office.

When the door to the office opened, Exeter raised his head. Madsen snapped his fingers before the dog could bark, but Exeter's eyes remained focused on the assistant United States attorney walking across the carpeted floor. Rivers Jones had the gait of a circus performer on stilts, a robotic flow of rough angles and determined elbows and knees that seemed to add two to three inches to his six-foot frame. Jones's plain gray suit, white shirt, and burgundy paisley tie matched his demeanor: lifeless and devoid of color or interest.

Madsen stood as Jones entered. "Thank you for being prompt, Rivers. Please have a seat."

"General," Jones said, reaching across the desk to shake hands before unbuttoning his jacket and falling into the chair across the desk, looking like a schoolboy seated before the principal. Madsen had had the legs on the chair shortened by two inches. No one sat higher than the five-foot-eight chief of staff in his own office.

"You saw my press conference?" Madsen asked, getting to the point.

Jones nodded, struggling to get comfortable. "I watched it this morning as I dressed."

"I'm sure it made some editors' mornings. Not every day you can replace a business-section filler with a White House death. Joe Branick will sell a lot of newspapers."

Jones shook his head. With a sharp nose and fine hair, whose strands stood as if electrified, he looked like a Midwestern scarecrow. "A cowardly act."

Madsen looked down at him. "Have you ever fired a weapon, Rivers?"

Jones hesitated, the question unexpected. "No . . ."

"Well, I have. And it is my personal opinion that putting a loaded gun to one's head and pulling the trigger takes a hell of a lot of balls." Madsen put a hand to his lips and softened his tone. "Why does anyone do the things they do, Rivers? If I knew, I'd have a couch in here and a diploma on the wall."

As it was, Madsen had nothing on his walls. They displayed no artwork, no family photographs, no diplomas, though he was a third-generation graduate of West Point. There was no leaded-glass case displaying the impressive number of medals he'd received in battles from Vietnam to Desert Storm, nothing to distract focus from the present tasks at hand. Possessions encumbered a man.

"Unfortunately, I don't have time to consider it. As you well know, hell broke loose around here this morning and the timing is very, very bad. I cannot disclose details at the moment, but this is another crack in the levee, and I've already got my fingers in eight holes. I'm running out of fingers, Rivers."

"I'm here to help, General."

Madsen walked to the front of the desk, leaning on the edge, arms crossed, the fabric of his suit stretching taut along his back and arms. He considered Jones with hazel eyes the color of wood chips, and a face tanned and lined like worn leather gloves.

"This thing needs to be handled competently and efficiently. As hard as it may be, the president must put this behind him and do the job the people of this country elected him to do, the sooner the better. The press loves this kind of garbage; hell, you know that. Some nut will start spreading rumors faster than a summer fire in a field of dry grass. The next thing you know, they'll be calling this 'another Vincent Foster.' I need someone who understands that."

"It won't be a problem, General."

Madsen raised an eyebrow. "When a special assistant to the president of the United States kills himself it *is* a problem, Rivers. When the special assistant is also a friend of the president it is one hell of a *fucking* problem." Ordinarily Madsen did not use or appreciate profanity. He considered it indicative of a limited vocabulary, but he was making a point. "May I be direct with you?"

"By all means."

"The more people who are involved in an investigation, the greater the potential for error, and in this case every error will be magnified. Are you familiar with military procedure, Rivers?"

"Sir?"

"The military operates in teams of three. Do you know why? Because research proves three is an optimum number to produce maximum efficiency. More than three causes a blurring of responsibilities. Less than three does not provide adequate resources. I want a team of three, Rivers. You're my choice for third, and I've pulled some strings to get you."

Jones sat a little higher in his seat. "You won't be disappointed, General."

It sounded neither forced nor rehearsed, though, of course, it was. Madsen knew that Rivers Jones was the right choice, because he knew everything there was to know about the man, including his preference for briefs over boxer shorts. Thirty-nine, married with no children,

Jones cheated regularly on his wife with a high-priced escort in McLean. Though born a Catholic, he professed to be a Protestant for political reasons—he did not intend to be employed by the Department of Justice forever. Like everyone else in Washington, Jones had political ambitions. He wanted a career in the United States Senate or House of Representatives so he could live the rest of his life off the American tit and well-financed lobbyists. Fully aware of the importance of political allies in a town of politicians, Jones had married the daughter of Michael Carpenter, the Speaker of the House. It wasn't love. In short, crass terms, Jones was a kiss-ass, and he knew whose ass to kiss.

Madsen straightened and walked around the desk to his chair. "You've spoken with the park police?"

The White House Security Office had received the call at 5:45 a.m. They reached Madsen at home. He had been on the treadmill for exactly forty-two minutes. After hanging up, Madsen contacted the attorney general and requested Jones. He called Jones at his home, awakening him with the news that he would lead the DOJ investigation into Joe Branick's death. Because Branick was a member of the White House staff and a federal employee, and because his body was found in a national park, the federal government in general, and the United States Department of Justice in particular, had jurisdiction over any investigation. It was Jones's job to advise the park police of this fact. They were to stand down.

"I spoke to them first thing this morning, after you and I hung up," Jones assured him.

"And they agreed to transfer their files?" Madsen asked.

"They agreed, but they don't have jurisdiction, General."

Madsen pressed down a cowlick with the palm of his hand. The military had cropped the stubborn tuft of hair, but it had returned when his publicist recommended that he grow his hair longer as his political career took shape. "What do you mean, they don't have jurisdiction?"

"It seems that a Charles Town police officer was first on the scene, and one of their detectives took jurisdiction. Apparently he was rather stubborn about it." Jones pulled a small pad from his coat pocket and considered his notes. "A Detective Tom Molia. He had the body delivered to the county coroner." He looked up from his notes. "Technically, he's correct."

Madsen did not try to hide his displeasure with the unforeseen turn of events. "Contact the county coroner and tell him he is to relinquish the body without inquiry."

"Without inquiry?"

"An autopsy will be done at the Justice Department."

Jones gave him an inquisitive look. "Sir?"

Madsen eyed Jones's notepad and pen until Jones closed the pad, clicked his pen, and placed both in the inside pocket of his jacket. "I am not one to sully a dead man's reputation, Rivers"—Madsen walked around the corner of his desk and opened the drawer—"but as I said, I want there to be full disclosure between us." He handed Jones a packet and spoke while Jones opened the envelope and pulled out the contents. "I assumed you would subpoena Mr. Branick's telephone records as part of your investigation, and took the liberty of obtaining them. You will find a telephone call to the White House at 9:13 p.m. Joe Branick called the president night before last. The president related to me that Mr. Branick did not sound well, that he had been drinking. There were rumors of excess, but the president does not want unsubstantiated rumors repeated in the newspapers. Understandably concerned about his friend's well-being, the president offered to meet with him in private. Joe Branick arrived at the White House at ten-twelve p.m. You will find records of his arrival and departure."

Madsen waited while Jones shuffled through the papers. "Statements taken from the two uniformed security officers at the West Gate confirm Mr. Branick's agitated appearance. The president met with him in the first family's private quarters, alone. He has since related to me that Joe Branick did not look well. He was foul-tempered."

"Did he say what he was upset about?"

Madsen paced in the slatted light from the French windows and the motes of dust it illuminated, giving him the appearance of an old black-and-white movie. "The White House operates on late-night dinners and handshakes at cocktail receptions; you know that, Rivers. It's not the way I choose to do business, but when in Rome you do as the Romans do." He shrugged. "If my Olivia had lived, I'm not sure she would have understood, either."

"Understood, sir?"

Madsen stopped pacing and faced the assistant U.S. attorney. "Joe Branick's wife despised these affairs, Rivers. She rarely attended. She chose to live in the country. According to the president, their marriage was strained as a result, and Mr. Branick, unhappy. Depressed." Madsen walked to his desk, picked up a single piece of paper, and handed it to Jones. "Four weeks ago Joe Branick completed an application for a permit to carry a firearm. I took the liberty of obtaining a copy of that permit for you as well."

Jones studied the application.

"In short, Rivers, these are private matters. The president does not want his friend's reputation trampled in the newspapers. I agree, but for different reasons." Madsen returned to the front of the desk and stood over Jones. "What reflects poorly on Joe Branick will reflect poorly on the president, Rivers, which means it will reflect poorly on this administration. As callous as it may sound to some, I won't have it. As Joe Branick's friend, the president will feel great guilt. He will question whether he could have stopped him. I can't be troubled with guilt. I've lost a lot of men, good men, under my command. We honor them and we move on, not because we have forgotten them but because we have *not* forgotten them. We have a job to do. The president has a job to do, Rivers. The best way to honor his friend is to do that job and to do it well. I'm going to see that he does—six more years, God willing."

Jones stood. "I understand."

"Good." He turned for his chair again, speaking over his shoulder. "I'd suggest you start your investigation with Mr. Branick's office. I've ordered it sealed."

"Sealed? May I ask why?"

Madsen turned back to him. "Because I do not know what could be in there that could be sensitive to this administration or national security. Mr. Branick was a White House confidant, Rivers." Madsen paused. "But I assure you, from this moment forward, this is your investigation."

7

DARKNESS GAVE WAY to blurred light. Images pulsed and spiraled above him. Sloane lay on his back, staring up at the bank of fluorescent lights on his kitchen ceiling. Instinctively he struggled to sit up, but a wave of nausea caused the room to tilt violently off-kilter, like an amusement park ride, and he slumped back to the floor. He felt a hand on his chest. The face circling above him slowed and came to a stop.

Melda.

"Mr. David?" She slapped his cheeks and wiped his forehead with a damp cloth, stammering in rushed sentences. "I am so sorry, Mr. David. I was so scared. I hear the noises and think you were not to be home. You say, 'Melda, I will see you Sunday night!'" She put her hand to her mouth, fighting tears.

Sloane sat up and ran a hand over a tender spot on the back of his head. A cast-iron skillet lay on the floor near Melda's knees. It wasn't difficult to put the rest together. As sweet as the apple pie she baked, Melda was a tough old bird and had never lost the bloodlines of the girl on the farm. She took her duties watching the building seriously.

In the dark, with his back to her, she had swung first and asked questions later. Thankfully, Melda was in her sixties and not quite five feet, which limited the amount of force she'd been able to generate. The blow knocked him off balance; the condiments on the floor did the rest. He remembered barely getting his hands up in time as he slipped and fell forward, bumping his forehead on the kitchen counter.

He squeezed her hand. "It's okay, Melda. You're right; I came home early. I'm sorry I startled you."

Widowed with no children, Melda had adopted Sloane. She cared for him when he was home, and cared for the building when he left on business. She collected his mail, fed Bud, the stray he'd found eating out of the Dumpster behind the building, and sprinkled food in the fish tank. She also took to doing his laundry, cleaning his apartment, and leaving plastic bowls of food in his refrigerator—tasks for which Sloane had tried to pay her. It had only upset her. In eight years he'd never raised her rent. What she paid, he invested in a money market account, and each Christmas he presented her with a cashier's check, telling her it was a dividend from a computer stock he'd bought her.

He considered the open cabinet doors and empty shelves; their contents were spilled everywhere, dried goods mixed with plates, cups, and silverware. The pungent smell of balsamic vinegar filled the room. "What happened here?"

She continued to dab at his forehead with the washcloth. "You have been burgled," she said, eyes widening. "The horrible mess, Mr. David."

He gripped the edge of the tiled counter and pulled himself to his feet, his shoes slipping on the floor.

Melda stood. "I am going to call for you a doctor."

"No. I'm okay. Just give me a second to get my bearings."

She dried her hands on a dish towel. "The mess. Mr. David, it is everywhere."

He walked into the living room holding on to the counter for balance and flicked on the lights. Melda was right. The mess was everywhere. Glass showered the carpet. The television tube had literally exploded. A paperback floated in the fish tank. Even the heating vent covers had been pried from the walls. Melda sobbed behind him.

Sloane turned and hugged her, feeling her tiny frame tremble. "It's okay, Melda. Everything is going to be okay." He spoke softly until she stopped shaking. "Why don't you make us a pot of tea," he suggested.

"I'll make for you some tea." She said it as if the idea had been her own, and walked into the kitchen to retrieve the kettle.

Sloane walked through the apartment, not knowing where to begin.

"Did you hear anything, Melda? Did you see anyone?" Sloane found it hard to believe, given the level of destruction, that it could have gone on unnoticed or unheard.

She filled the pot under the faucet. "I hear nothing, but I am out on the Thursdays . . . my dancing night." She belonged to a seniors group through a local Catholic church. "This morning I come to clean and I find this," she said. "I go back down the stairs and call the police. Now I come back and you are in the kitchen, but it is dark and my eyes . . . Oh, Mr. David, I am so sorry."

Sloane stood in the center of the room considering his destroyed possessions, mentally replacing them where he

last recalled them. Curious, he walked through the living
room to the bedroom and turned on the light. His mattress
had been torn apart like the couch, his closet emptied. But
that was not of immediate concern. His immediate concern sat in plain view on the nightstand next to his bed, a
gift from an appreciative client.

His Rolex watch.

8

The Department of Justice,
Washington, D.C.

RIVERS JONES RECLINED against the cream-colored leather, rocking rhythmically and twisting a bent paper clip along his thumb and index finger while waiting for his call to be connected. He dropped the brown-bag lunch his wife had made for him into the waste can, along with a cold cup of coffee, and picked at a half-eaten bran muffin. He fixed his gaze on the ornately framed diplomas hanging in his drab government office: S. RIVERS JONES IV.

He had long since dropped the "S," which few knew stood for Sherman, and the Roman numeral, which stood for "pretentious" if you were anywhere but in the Deep South. Well, he was no longer riding with the good old boys, driving their trucks with mud flaps and spittin' Skoal through the gap in their two front teeth, and he wasn't going back. Not ever. He longed for the day when he would never again have to look at the two oversize pieces of paper on his wall, reminders of a career choice his father had dictated. If not for the massive heart attack that killed the son of a bitch, Jones had no doubt he'd be admiring his diplomas right now in an office with a view of downtown Baton Rouge, Louisiana.

Jones picked off another piece of the muffin and tilted back his head to avoid getting crumbs on his suit. Parker Madsen's call had awoken him from a sound sleep. Unlike the general, he was not one for getting up at the crack of dawn for calisthenics and reveille. He had just enough time to shower and shave—the shit had to wait—to get to the West Wing on time. Madsen demanded punctuality. The guy was a trip, with his "yes sirs" and "no sirs" and all that crap, but the inside word in Washington was that Madsen would be on the Republican party ticket as Robert Peak's next running mate. That put Madsen directly in line for a presidential bid. No wonder he had his butt cheeks pinched tight over Joe Branick's death. With the economy continuing to spiral down the toilet, unemployment and inflation going in the opposite direction, and terrorism against U.S. interests escalating, the unexpected suicide of a man supposed to be the president's closest confidant couldn't help matters. The general was looking out for number one, which was fine with Jones. He didn't care who he hitched his wagon to, as long as he was taken along for the ride.

Jones had just hung up after a chat with the Jefferson County coroner. Dr. Peter Ho had offered no resistance. Not surprising. Most county employees were lazy. Ho was likely relieved he wouldn't have to do an autopsy over the weekend. In a moment Jones would make things just as clear to the Charles Town detective, and he, too, would undoubtedly be relieved to have a file off his desk. The matter would be as good as closed, and Jones would have another powerful ally in his corner.

Jones's secretary interrupted his thoughts to tell him that she had placed his call. He sat forward, wondering how the title "Congressman" or "Senator" would look on a framed piece of paper.

CLAY BALDWIN SCOOTED forward, the legs of the stool scraping on the linoleum. He drummed the counter a little faster with each unanswered ring. The assistant United States attorney's secretary had made it clear he did not want to be put into voice mail. Baldwin rotated to consider the white eraser board on which he had printed the name of every member of the department. Ordinarily an orange magnet beneath the word "In" indicated the officer should answer his damn phone, but it didn't mean squat if the name on the board was Molia. Tom Molia forgot about the board coming and going, and Baldwin was starting to get the feeling the detective's memory lapses were intentional.

Baldwin stood, braced for the shock of pain that shot down his leg to his numbed right foot, and grimaced as he stretched the telephone cord to look through the venetian blinds covering the wire-mesh window. Sure enough, Molia stood in the middle of the room, entertaining Marty Banto and a couple of uniformed officers with more hand gestures and facial expressions than a teenage girl.

Baldwin yelled through the glass, "Hey, Mole!"

Tom Molia paused, looked up at Baldwin, and waved.

Baldwin pointed to the phone. "I . . . have . . . a . . . call . . . for . . . you."

Molia held his hands to his heart and mouthed back, "I . . . love . . . you . . . too . . . Clay."

Banto and the officers burst out in silent laughter.

Son of a bitch. "Pick up the goddamn phone, Mole!" Baldwin watched Molia walk to his desk and lift the receiver. "Damn it, Mole. I'm not playing grab-ass out here. Answer your damn phone."

"Wasn't sure what you were doing, Clay. I thought you were doing a little Irish jig out there. You got that foot-stomping thing going again."

Baldwin stopped stomping his foot. "My foot fell asleep . . . and I'm English, not Irish. What do you think I'm doing? I have a call for you."

"A call. Well, for God's sake, Baldy, who is it, the queen herself?"

Baldwin let out a slow hiss. He knew that cops liked to abbreviate last names, but the nickname Tom Molia had bestowed on him also happened to accurately describe the number of hairs on his head, which continued to dwindle daily.

"It's a U.S. attorney from the Department of Justice."

"Well, hell, Baldy, why didn't you say so? Enough of the chitchat. Don't keep the person waiting. Put him through."

"I told you—"

"Time's a-wasting, Clay."

Remembering the assistant U.S. attorney's admonition, Baldwin hurried back to the counter and transferred the call.

Tom Molia gave Clay Baldwin a thumbs-up as he answered the phone. "This is Detective Tom Molia."

"Detective Molia," a woman responded, "are you available to take a call from Assistant United States Attorney Rivers Jones?"

It was one of those strange Southern names, which was perhaps the reason for the pretentious formality. Molia was half tempted to tell the woman, "Sure, have him call me," and hang up, but decided against it. "Put him through," he said, and sat down at a desk that looked as though it hadn't been cleaned in years.

"Detective Molia?"

"How you guys doing over there at Justice this morning, Rivers? You keeping cool or sweating buckets like us?" Molia leaned back in his chair and placed his feet on the corner of the desk, knocking papers and manila folders onto the worn linoleum. A small portable fan oscillated on an antiquated metal filing cabinet in an office that could have held two desks comfortably but into which three had been squeezed. Paperwork obscured framed pictures of wives and children, and the walls were an assortment of wanted posters, memos, and other oddities. A black silhouette torso from the shooting range with a bullet hole directly in the forehead was tacked in the center of the wall, with multiple dart holes. Two darts pierced it. A third dart lay on the floor near the detective's desk.

"We're fine, Detective. I'm in an air-conditioned office."

"Well, be grateful for that, 'cause it's going to be hot again today, I'm told."

"You handled the Joe Branick matter, Detective?"

"You mean the suicide?"

"Yes, Detective Molia, I mean the suicide." Jones spoke in a deliberate, put-you-to-sleep drone.

"No formal report yet, but it's mine. My luck. I've been busier than a jackrabbit in heat the last week. I mean work, you know?" Molia lowered his legs, picked up the dart from the floor, and tossed it at the target, hitting the figure in the shoulder. He shuffled through papers on his desk. "At least this one looks pretty cut-and-dried. They found the guy a couple hundred yards from his car. Single bullet wound to the temple. Gun in his hand. Spent casing. Fired at close range. Probably not going to find the bullet, given the terrain. Powder burns on right hand and temple . . . yadda yadda yadda. I've ordered a ballistics test. Doesn't get much simpler than this."

Simple, except that no one had yet heard from Bert Cooperman, and despite assurances that Coop had put in for a vacation leave, there was no answer at his home, the cruiser was not parked out in front of Cooperman's house, and now the Justice Department was taking notice of an open-and-shut suicide. The ache in Molia's gut had become a pain that the roll of Tums and two swallows of the Pepto-Bismol he kept in his desk drawer hadn't dampened.

"On whose authority did you order a ballistics test, Detective?"

Molia laughed. "On whose authority? What, are you kidding, Rivers? I got a dead man. I got a gun. I got a dead man *holding* a gun. I order a ballistics test. Don't need any authority for that." He heard Jones take a deep breath. "You got asthma, Rivers? I get a touch of hay fever this time of year myself."

"I'm sure you followed normal procedure, Detective Molia—"

"Mole."

"Excuse me?" Jones asked, his tone annoyed.

"Call me Mole. I haven't heard 'Detective Molia' in years. You keep calling me Detective Molia and I'm liable to start looking around the room for my father. Love to see him, though it would scare the crap out of me—he's been dead going on six years."

"Yes, Detective, Molia," Jones said. "As I was saying, I'm sure the ballistics test is routine, but this death . . . This man . . . was a White House staff member and a personal friend of the president."

"Yeah, I think I read that somewhere."

"That's right."

"Well, you tell the president he doesn't need to sweat this one, Rivers. I'll see to it personally."

There was a pause. "I'm sure you would handle the matter adequately, Detective."

Molia heard a "but" coming, and as his son T.J. liked to say, it was a *big butt*. The assistant U.S. attorney did not disappoint him.

"But not this time. The Department of Justice will handle this matter. You are to cease any further work and transfer your files to me."

"All due respect to you and the president, Riv, but the body—"

"Detective Molia, did you just call me Riv? Let me explain something. I don't have a nickname. I have a title. I am an assistant United States attorney. That's with the Department of Justice. And that is where you will send your file. Do I make myself clear?"

Molia had been willing to give Jones the benefit of the doubt, to assume he was overworked and stressed like most government types and had simply left his manners at home, but he really hated it when people dropped authority on him. His father had been fond of saying that titles were like assholes—everyone had one. In Washington, some people had two, which usually made them twice the asshole.

"Well, that *is* a mouthful, isn't it?" he said. "You sure you're in an air-conditioned office, Rivers? You're sounding a little hot under the collar this morning."

"As I was saying—"

"Actually, I was the one talking, Rivers. You interrupted me. Not the first time, either, I might add. And what I was saying was, all due respect to you and the president, but the body was found in West Virginia by a Charles Town police officer. That makes it a local police problem—or, more specifically, since I was the lucky son of a gun to get up at the crack of dawn and leave my comfy bed to drive out there, it makes it my problem."

"Not any longer," Jones hissed. "The Department of Justice's jurisdiction supersedes your jurisdiction, and the White House has personally requested that this office handle the investigation. Any attempt by you to interfere will be met with harsh penalties. Do I make myself clear, Detective?"

"What investigation?"

What followed was what some people liked to call a "pregnant pause," but what Molia called "bullshit time." Rivers Jones, assistant United States attorney with the Department of Justice, was pulling his tongue out of the back of his throat, buying bullshit time, stalling for an answer.

"Excuse me?"

"You said '*investigation*,' Rivers. What *investigation* are you talking about?"

"If I said 'investigation,' I misspoke. Force of habit. I meant to say 'matter.' We will handle this matter."

Not good enough. "You didn't misspeak. You said the White House has asked you to conduct an *investigation*. Clearly, I might add."

There was another pause. Now Jones was about to get angry, which was also predictable. When you pushed a person who didn't have a good answer, they either crumbled or got angry. Again the assistant United States attorney did not disappoint him.

"Detective Molia, are you fucking with me? Because if you are, I want you to know I don't find it the least bit amusing. I don't have the time. My orders come from the president of the United fucking States. If those orders are good enough for me, I sure as hell know they are good enough for you."

Molia removed the pencil from behind his ear and sat forward, sticking the pencil in a half-eaten hamburger on a piece of grease-stained yellow wax paper. He'd pushed a button, as intended, and Jones didn't have the brains or temperament to talk his way out of it. People with something to hide were either evasive or aggressive. Jones was both. In the process he'd likely made two mistakes, letting Molia know there was an investigation *and* that the White House was involved. His stomach was never wrong.

"Well, Assistant United States Attorney Rivers Jones, I'm just a police detective trying to do the job I swore to do to the best of my abilities twenty years ago. So until I receive the proper authority from *my* superiors, I will conduct *my investigation* in the interest that is best for the people of Jefferson . . . fucking . . . County."

"Who is your authority, Detective Molia?"

"That would be Police Chief J. Rayburn Franklin . . . the Third," he said, and heard Rivers Jones hang up.

9

~

Law Offices of Foster & Bane,
San Francisco

SLOANE STEPPED FROM the elevator and hurried through a reception area of Italian marble, Persian throw rugs, leather furniture, and artwork secured to the walls. Similarly furnished reception areas greeted clients on each of Foster & Bane's five floors: expensive decor befitting a firm of nearly a thousand lawyers generating $330 million in annual revenues in offices scattered throughout the United States, Europe, and Hong Kong.

Sloane was behind schedule; the police had taken their time getting to his apartment. Once there, they appeared less than interested, asking the obligatory questions, which was as far as their investigation would go. Sloane had no clue who had trashed his apartment, or why, and since nothing of value was taken, not even the Rolex, he figured pawnshops wouldn't be of any help, either. He suffered through the exercise because he knew enough about insurance companies to know that his insurer's first question would be whether he had filed a police report. Now that the report was out of the way, he needed to file the claim, and he kept his insurance information at the office.

At just before eleven o'clock, the office would be in full swing, which meant answering questions about why a man who was supposed to be on his first vacation in five years was at the office. He decided to keep his answer simple. He was just tying up a loose end before leaving town.

He strode past the receptionist on the nineteenth floor, framed by a panoramic view of the San Francisco Bay stretching from Angel Island to the Bay Bridge, and leaned around the corner. The hallway was empty, though he heard voices spilling from the offices—associates toiling to secure "billable hours." More precious than gold, billable hours were the means big law firms used to measure associate productivity and commitment to the firm—not to mention to bill their clients for their services.

Tina Scoccolo did a double take as he strode past her glass-enclosed cubicle. There would be no getting past her unnoticed.

"What the hell are you doing here?" She sounded more annoyed than curious.

Sloane put a finger to his lips, not breaking stride, keeping his focus on the finish line at the end of the hall: the door to his northwest corner office. "I'm not. You don't see me."

She stepped from behind the glass as he blew past her. "Then I take it we're not having this conversation?" Her question chased him down the hallway.

"We're not. Hold my calls."

"You're limping."

He pushed open his office door, took a half step forward, and stopped suddenly, like a tourist behind a red rope at a museum. His eyes shifted to the nameplate on the wall: MR. DAVID SLOANE.

He didn't recognize his own office. The clutter from nearly fourteen years of practice had miraculously disappeared. Two potted ficus trees had replaced the stacks of pleadings, yellow notepads, and trial exhibits that had stood teetering for years in the corners of his office. He noticed that the maroon carpet had a bluish-gray diamond pattern. A modest pile of mail sat neatly arranged on the desk pad next to his in-box, which was empty. The last time he recalled seeing the bottom of the tray was his first day at the firm. He felt both violated and liberated. Like most attorneys, he found comfort in clutter, and Sloane wrapped himself in it like a quilt. But now he couldn't recall why all the papers had been so important, and felt as if a great weight had been lifted from his shoulders.

He called down the hall, "Tina?"

"Sorry," she yelled back. "Can't hear you. You're not here."

He smiled, stepped across the threshold, and ran a finger across his desk, detecting a wood-treatment product and a hint of lemon. She had even straightened the abstract painting above his credenza, just next to his diplomas on the ego wall, which was where he spotted it. They had framed the article and hung it amid the diplomas to try to hide it, for some as yet unknown purpose. The headline shouted arrogance: SAN FRANCISCO'S TOP GUN.

And below it his photograph, the one Patricia Hansen had slapped against his chest, was worse than the headline, if that was possible. The photographer had positioned

Sloane against the edge of a conference room table, leaning him like the Tower of Pisa. A recent haircut had caused stubborn strands of hair to stand like porcupine quills, and the heavy dose of gel he applied as a last-minute solution had colored his dark brown hair a shoeshine black and molded it like a plastic Halloween mask. The light through the tinted windows cast shadows like ruts in a road across his prominent jaw and cheekbones, aging him ten years. He looked forty-seven. His olive complexion, thick eyebrows, and full lips ordinarily softened his appearance, but with the sinister shadows and sculpted hair he looked like a smug comic book villain.

Befitting the headline and the photograph, the article was a pompous-sounding sketch on "the best wrongful-death lawyer in San Francisco." Bob Foster had insisted that Sloane talk to the reporter—something Sloane was loath to do—then added to the ego piece by providing the reporter with quotes that were all about getting the firm more clients and nothing about saving any semblance of modesty Sloane possessed. Since the article's publication, Sloane felt like a man with a bull's-eye on his back. His active cases had doubled in number, and any hope he harbored of settling some of them evaporated with the article. His clients were now emboldened about their chances of success, and opposing counsel saw it as a challenge to be the lawyer who knocked his ego from its perch.

Sloane removed the frame from the wall, turning to slide it in his desk drawer, when the door to his office burst open and a parade of attorneys, paralegals, and staff marched in behind Tina, shouting "Surprise!" and slinging confetti. Someone blew a party horn in his ear. Tina carried a half-eaten cake with two candles on top, a "1" and a "5," though upon closer inspection the "1" had been crudely carved from a "3." The six associates who worked for Sloane jockeyed for position like kids in a school play wanting to be seen, and those still lobbying to be part of the "Sloane trial machine," as it was now being called, made sure to shake his hand.

Tina held out the cake to him. Sloane put the framed article on his desk and brushed blue and gold stars from his shoulders and pulled streamers from his hair. The frosting letters looked like part of an unfinished crossword puzzle:

> PY
> THDAY

"Whose birthday cake?"

Tina ignored the question. "Blow out the candles," she instructed. She put the cake on his desk and began cutting slices. "I planned to have a victory party on Monday, when you *said* you were coming back. Sorry, but this was the best I could do on short notice." She handed him a paper plate with a square of chocolate.

"What is all this goddamned noise?"

Bob Foster, his voice rough from a two-pack-a-day habit, sounded like a tired engine turning over on a cold morning. He entered Sloane's office resplendent in a tailored blue shirt with white collar, onyx cuff links, and hand-painted tie, a stubborn holdout against the casual-dress craze made popular by the tech industry and to which San Francisco law firms had reluctantly conceded. The crowd parted for him like the Red Sea before Moses.

Foster confronted Sloane. "Two hours? You kept the jury out two hours, Sloane? Didn't I teach you better than that?"

he asked with mock indignity that brought laughter from the group. He gripped Sloane's hand. "Nice work. I didn't think you'd pull our ass out of the fire on this one. Frank Abbott called me first thing this morning. He's very happy. I might even beat him at golf this weekend."

Sloane forced a smile. "Great."

Foster leaned forward conspiratorially. "I know the little prick is a major pain in the ass. Everyone knows it, but it's his grandson, and believe me, with Paul Abbott at the helm, Abbott Security will be sued more than pigs on a farm, which is good business for us. He fired all his other counsel. He's sending over seven active files."

Sloane felt sick.

"Let's just hope this Scott episode doesn't change company procedures *too* much." Foster leaned back and released Sloane's hand. He eyed Sloane's windbreaker, San Francisco Giants baseball cap, and blue jeans as if just noticing them. "What the hell are you doing here anyway? You haven't taken a vacation since my hair was brown. I thought you were supposed to be climbing a rock somewhere."

"Just came in to take care of a few loose ends."

Foster arched an eyebrow. "Don't bullshit a bullshitter, Sloane. One or two loose ends on a Friday becomes half the day; then you decide you might as well complete the day to keep your weekend free, but you don't get to the first thing on your short list of loose ends because the phone is ringing off the hook, your associates spend more time in your office than their own, and you don't have time to take a piss. The next thing you know, it's Sunday night and your wife's on the phone telling you she wants a goddamned divorce and half your income—I know."

The room laughed, though there was more truth than humor in Foster's routine. Half the partners at Foster & Bane had divorced at least once, Foster twice. He eyed his watch. "Fifteen minutes. Then I'm personally kicking your ass out of here." He turned to the rest of the group. "All right, you people, eat your cake and get back to work so the man can go on his vacation." He rolled a large slice onto a plate, licked the chocolate from his fingertips, and turned the corner, barking down the hall at a ringing telephone, "I'm coming for Christ's sake."

The group dissipated with final handshakes and thumbs-up, until only Tina remained.

"I thought you said you were taking today off. I thought you were going rock climbing," she said.

Sloane walked behind his desk and picked up a letter at the top of the stack. "I wanted to clear my desk so I wouldn't worry about it. Guess I didn't need to. Thanks for cleaning up in here."

"Me and two bulldozers."

He nodded to the ficus plants. "The plants are a nice touch."

"I thought you needed more oxygen."

"In here or in general?"

"I plead the Fifth."

"What's the smell?"

"Fresh air."

She turned and closed the door. At thirty-three, Tina Scoccolo was four years younger than Sloane, but at times she treated him like a mother would, perhaps because she was one. She had a nine-year-old son, Jake, from a failed marriage that had left her a single parent at the ripe old age of twenty-four, an experience that had apparently hardened her. Sloane had never known her to date, though not from a lack of opportunity. At the firm's parties, when the attorneys drank too much and mingled too casually, she was the plum in the bowl of fruit. At five feet eight inches, she had a runner's build: lean legs and strong shoulders that tapered to a narrow waist. And though not what some might call beautiful, she had a natural attractiveness. Shoulder-length auburn hair framed fair skin, with a trace of freckles spotting the bridge of her nose giving her a youthful appearance. Her blue eyes sparkled when she laughed, and became stone-cold gray when she was unhappy. She either ignored the unsolicited advances, put the attorney in his place with a deft comment—often about his spouse—or left the party early before the alcohol loosened tongues.

"Are you all right?" She crossed her arms like a school principal expecting a truthful answer.

"I'm fine," he said.

"You look tired."

"I am tired. That's what trials do; they make you tired."

"You're not sick?"

"You're not that lucky."

She stepped closer, considering his face. "What's with the bump on your forehead?"

He pulled down the brim of his cap. "Just a bump. Hit my head."

"Rock climbing?" she asked with disapproval.

"Not yet."

He took off his windbreaker and slid into the leather chair, but Tina remained resolute. After so many years together she knew his bullshit, and God knew she never hesitated to call him on it.

He sat back. "Okay. Someone broke into my apartment and trashed it pretty well. I've been up most of the morning dealing with it."

"That's horrible. Did you—"

"Call the police? Yes. And they came and took a report and that's as far as it will go because they have no suspects and it does not appear anything of value was taken."

"Are you going to—"

"File a claim with my insurance company? Yes. It's another one of the reasons I came in."

"Do you—"

"Have any idea who did it? No, just the usual suspects who hate me."

She frowned at him. "Fine, be that way." She turned to leave.

He put down the stack of mail. "Tina?"

She turned back to him.

"I'm sorry. I'm just a bit tired and frustrated. I didn't mean to take it out on you."

"Apology accepted. Is there anything I can do?"

"How are you at picking out furniture from catalogues?"

"They wrecked your furniture?"

"I need a sofa and a matching chair. Leather. Basic colors. Just a place to sit. I'll also need a television, a stereo, and a new mattress."

"They stole your mattress?"

"Just ripped it open."

"Why?"

He shrugged. "That is the question. Find some place that will deliver. Put it on my credit card."

"Do I have carte blanche?"

"Don't empty my account. Oh, and would you bring my personal insurance file on the building?"

He waited for her to close the door behind her. Then he swiveled his chair toward an expansive view of a crystal-blue, cloudless sky above the slate-gray waters of the San Francisco Bay. An airplane had left a small white streak, like a painter's errant brush on a blue canvas.

Five minutes later Tina walked back in. "David—what are you looking at?"

He turned from the window. "Just thought I'd admire the view for a moment."

She walked to the window. "Why?"

"What do you mean, why? Why not?"

"Because in the ten years I've been here I've never seen you do it before." She handed him three pink message slips and four unsigned letters. "I forwarded the rest of your messages to your voice mail."

With his success she had started screening his calls and his e-mails. He recognized the first two messages and categorized them as "not urgent." He did not recognize the third name.

"Who's Joe Branick?"

10

~

Charles Town,
West Virginia

MOLE!"
J. Rayburn Franklin's voice rumbled down the hall like an avalanche, spilling coffee cups and papers from desks. Marty Banto jerked in his chair, banged his knee on a drawer, and swore. "Damn. Here we go again."

Franklin's appearance was always a letdown. He was the only man Tom Molia had ever met who couldn't compete with his own voice. The voice belonged to an overweight, cigar-smoking politician or a high school football coach. With round, wire-rimmed glasses on a thin, perpetually strained face, Franklin looked like a constipated accountant during tax season. The deep baritone had to have been a gift from God, a weapon in what appeared to be an otherwise empty arsenal.

Assistant United States Attorney Rivers Jones had been fast.

Franklin ripped the glasses from his face, getting one of the wires caught behind his ear and bending it as he struggled to pull it free, which only added to his frustration. He was out of breath, though the walk from his office was perhaps twenty yards.

"Do you want to explain to me how, in the course of a five-minute conversation, you can manage to piss off an assistant U.S. attorney *and* insult the president of the United States?"

"Hell, Rayburn, all I said—"

Franklin raised a hand. "I'm not interested in what you said or have to say. What I am interested in is what he had to say you had to say. Do you get some perverse pleasure out of making my life miserable?"

"Rayburn—"

"Don't you have any other hobbies to keep you busy?"

"Chief—"

"Because if you don't, I would strongly suggest you find some." Franklin held his index finger and thumb a fraction of an inch apart and leaned well into Molia's personal space. "I am this close to involuntary retirement, and if I go, I guarantee you I'm taking you with me."

"The guy was a horse's ass, Ray. Hell, I was looking out for you."

Franklin smiled, but it looked more like a grimace. "You were looking out for me?" He stood back and waved his arms, the glasses dangling from his hand. "Well, hell, why didn't you just say so? I guess I made a mistake. I guess I should be thanking you."

"You're being sarcastic, aren't you?"

"No, Mole, why would you think that? It's not like you just told off a U.S. attorney calling on behalf of the president of the United States—"

"—United *fucking* States."

"What?"

"He called it the 'United *fucking* States.'"

"I don't give a shit what he called it. I just got my ass chewed out so bad I may not sit for a week in my *fucking* office." Franklin delivered the final sentence inches from Molia's face; strands of his thinning hair, which he parted in the middle and slicked straight back, fell in front of his eyes.

"You *are* being sarcastic."

Franklin pulled back. "Come on, Mole. Christ. Quit fucking around here."

Molia spoke softly, as he did when pacifying his children. "He called it an *investigation*, Ray. Why do you think he would call a routine suicide an investigation?"

Franklin blinked one long blink. It could have been an incredulous blink, as if he could not believe what he had just heard, or it could have been a pause to regain his composure, but Molia suspected it was neither. He suspected that it was a blink of frustration, but with a hint of curiosity. As much as Molia frustrated the crap out of J. Rayburn Franklin, he was also his best detective, and his instincts were rarely wrong.

"I don't care what he called it," Franklin said. "I don't care if he called it Christ's Last Supper. What I care about is keeping my job. And I assume you do, too, or are you independently wealthy and I didn't know?"

"I don't like this one, Ray. My stomach's bothering me."

"With your diet, I don't doubt it. You eat crap a billy goat wouldn't touch." He put his glasses back on, pushed the hair back from his forehead, and smoothed the sides with his palms, calming. After a moment he asked, "Okay, so what's bothering you?"

"We still haven't heard from Coop."

"Coop's got the weekend off. He put in for it two weeks ago."

"There's no answer—"

"At his home. I know. That's because his wife is in South Carolina showing off the baby to her family, and Coop's using the time to get in some hunting and fishing. She took the car, so he put in to use the cruiser for the weekend. I okayed it. Said he was taking off immediately after his shift. Would you or I leave immediately after pulling the twelve-hour graveyard? No, but we aren't twenty-five years old anymore, either, Mole."

"What about the park? Why would he just take off, Ray, just leave the scene?"

"Coop's a rookie, Mole. Rookies do stupid things; you know that. He probably spooked when he realized he was out of his jurisdiction, and didn't feel like coming back here to get his ass bit and lose vacation time filling out the paperwork. You of all people know the saying about 'better to ask forgiveness than permission.' Hell, I think you *invented* it. Coop will come crawling in here Monday asking forgiveness. I'll chew on his ass then. Until then, as for this Branick thing, last I checked, the Justice Department was pretty well staffed, okay? So that there is no misunderstanding, I'm going to say this slowly. Close . . . your . . . file. If you have anything in the works, call it off."

"What am I supposed to do with it?" Molia liked to let Franklin have the last dig. It soothed his ego.

Franklin didn't disappoint him. "Take the file, put it on your chair . . . and sit . . . on . . . it." Franklin started out of the office, then turned in the doorway. "I'm serious, Mole. I don't want to hear even *rumors* you're working on that file."

Molia raised his hands as if under arrest. "No problem. I got enough to keep me busy."

"Sometimes I'm not so sure," Franklin said, the sound of his shoes slapping against the linoleum as he walked down the hallway. When he rounded the corner he looked back through the wire-mesh window. Molia stood, closed the manila file, placed it neatly on his chair, and sat on it.

11

~

Tina plucked the message slip from Sloane's hand and eyed it as if suspicious of her own handwriting, then handed it back. "I don't know."

Sloane laughed. "I take it he didn't leave a message?"

She took the slip again, considered it ~~further~~, gave it back. "Does it say he left a message?"

"So who is he?"

"How should I know? Probably the latest twenty-three-year-old go-getter with the hot stock tip of the week. You get about five a week now."

He smiled. "Maybe we could find out for sure?"

"Call the number."

He raised his eyebrows.

"Oh, I get it. 'We' means 'me.'" She plucked the slip from his hand with a roll of the eyes and walked out the door, talking under her breath.

A minute later she walked back in.

"That was fast."

"Maybe not fast enough. Dianne just called. His Highness wants to talk with you about your meeting with Transamerican Insurance Monday morning. You want me to block out the next three hours of your day for that blowhard?"

Sloane was in no mood for a meeting with Bob Foster. "What did you tell her?"

"I gave her the runaround, said you were in the bathroom. If she calls again, I'll tell her you slipped out before I could give you the message." She gave him a smug smile.

He grabbed his windbreaker off the back of his chair. "You're a genius."

"Talk's cheap. I want a raise."

"I'd stop and put in a request for you, but I don't want to make a liar out of you to Dianne. Have a nice weekend."

She put a hand on his chest like a school crossing guard, handed him the file with his insurance papers, and stuck three letters under his nose, along with a pen. "Hold on a minute, Mr. Top Gun. I need your autograph."

He scribbled his name, handing each letter to her. "What am I signing here?"

"Nothing important. Pay raise for Tina. Paid vacation for Tina. My annual review. I took the liberty of filling it out for you."

He handed her the pen. "How did you do this year?"

"Great as always."

"Good for you." He slipped the folded pink message slip into his pocket, knocked the painting on the wall crooked, and gave her a wink as he stepped past her, disappearing into the hallway.

12

❧

TOM MOLIA WAITED until late afternoon, when Clay Baldwin wouldn't perceive it as anything more than the simple act of getting an early jump on the weekend. He even slid the damn magnet from the IN to the OUT column, which always grated on his derriere. He suspected the board to be the brainchild of Franklin, Baldwin's brother-in-law. Franklin liked to keep track of his officers, especially Molia. After twenty years of coming and going as he pleased, Molia didn't like the idea of someone keeping tabs on him, except maybe his wife, who had earned the right by enduring him for twenty-two years of marriage. He had declared war on the board.

Inside his 1969 emerald-green Chevy he replayed his conversation with Assistant United States Attorney Rivers Jones. He'd set out to tweak Jones and see if anything shook free. It had, like leaves in autumn. Jones's use of the word "investigation" wasn't a slip of the tongue. The Department of Justice was investigating an open-and-shut suicide, and that request apparently had come from the White House. Why? The only logical explanation was that someone wasn't convinced it was a suicide, which made it a possible homicide, which made it Tom Molia's business.

He turned right on Sixth Avenue, pulled into the alley, parked behind the two-story brick-and-stucco building with smoked-glass windows, and stepped out. Waves of heat rose from the parking lot blacktop in ghostlike shimmers. He was sweating before he pulled open the unlocked metal security door and climbed the rear stairwell. The staff would be gone. At the top of the stairs he pushed open an interior door to an air-conditioned office and the blasting beat of U2. He cut through the receptionist's area, down a narrow hallway, and detected the visceral smell of an autopsy in progress, which reminded him of the way liver tasted.

Dr. Peter Ho sat on a wheeled stool, hunched over a body still partially wrapped in a dark green body bag. He bit the end of a high-powered laser light with his teeth, freeing his hands to manipulate clamps and forceps to hold back flaps of skin. Ho was the picture of concentration, except that every few seconds he would beat the stainless steel medical instruments on the edge of a nearby pan to the rhythm of his favorite band.

Molia slowed his approach, stepping lightly, and reached out and gripped Ho's shoulder.

The county coroner sprang to his feet as if the stool had ejected him, shooting it halfway across the linoleum floor. He spit the laser light into the open chest cavity. The reflector on his forehead shifted off-kilter, and his glasses, perched on the bridge of his nose, fell dangling by a chain around his neck.

Ho gasped, catching his breath, his face flushed. "Damn it, Mole. I've asked you not to do that."

Molia retrieved the stool, laughing. "Didn't think I was

one of your patients sneaking up on you, did you, Peter?"
He would have tired of the gag but for Peter Ho's animated reaction. A portly Asian man with a fleshy face, Ho
would never admit it, but Molia was convinced that the
Jefferson County Coroner was afraid of the dead. It was
like a mechanic being afraid of cars.

"You keep doing that and you'll *be* one of my patients."
He exhaled again. "You're going to give me a fucking
heart attack."

"Can't a guy just drop by to say hello?"

"You want to drop by? Drop by through the front door
like a normal person so I can hear the damn bell ring." Ho
readjusted the reflector back to center.

Molia raised a hand to deflect the glare of light. "Back
door is closer to the parking lot. Besides, you couldn't
hear the bell over this noise, and we both know I'm not
normal."

"U2 is not noise, and I agree—you are far from normal."

Molia sat on the stool and slid next to the corpse's covered head. "You should really lock the back door, Peter. It
could be a real security issue. People could sneak in here
on you." He picked up a sharp-looking two-pronged instrument and pointed it for emphasis.

Ho took the forceps. "Funny. Thanks, that was sterilized." He dropped the tool into a metal tray. "From now
on, I'm going to personally see that Betty locks that damn
door every night before she goes home."

"I'm sure she will," Molia said. Betty never did. He
raised the cloth draped over the corpse's head. "This guy
don't look too good, Pete. I think you lost him."

Ho pulled the cloth back. "Little respect for the dead.

And you wouldn't look too good either if someone plugged you with a twelve-gauge."

"Hunting accident?"

"Kitchen accident. That's the wife's story anyway, and so far she's sticking to it. Apparently it's just a coincidence she shot him the same afternoon she learned he was sneaking out with the grocery clerk at the local Winn-Dixie."

Molia tilted his head to the side and made a clicking noise with his tongue. "Ah! Bagging a grocery clerk. That's a switch."

Ho did a drum roll on a nearby metal pan. "Bud-dum-bum. Don't quit your day job. You'd starve. Sheriff says she walked into the house and dropped him right on his sandwich." Ho pointed to the man's shirt. "Still had mayonnaise on his shirt when they brought him in." Ho removed the latex gloves and wiped his hands on the rubber apron. "Thanks for the body this morning, pal. Maybe I can return the favor—inject you with hepatitis or something."

When Molia delivered the body of Joe Branick earlier that morning Ho had not yet arrived at the office. "Something going on?"

Ho mimicked him. "Something going on? . . . Like I said, you'd starve." He walked to a white porcelain sink to wash his hands. "People are bugging the crap out of me; that's what's going on. And don't tell me you don't know what I'm talking about."

"The Justice Department?"

"For one. Family. Reporters." He dried his hands with a paper towel, threw it in the garbage, and reached behind his back to untie the apron, draping it on a hook by a door before disappearing into his office. A few seconds later the music stopped, and Ho returned with a manila file, wearing a black T-shirt with the image of U2's lead singer, Bono. "Hand-delivered." He held up stationery faxed by the Department of Justice and lifted the half-lens glasses onto the bridge of his nose. "Branick, Joe. He is to be released without inquiry by the medical examiner. Etcetera, etcetera, etcetera." He closed the file and looked at Molia over the top of his lenses. "That means me. That means no autopsy. That means I get to go home and watch Jason pitch tonight."

"They have a game tonight?"

"Maggie asked me to remind you. Why don't you at least get a calendar?"

"You think the guy killed himself?" Molia asked.

"Wouldn't know. Haven't gone near the body. Now I don't have to."

"But he's still here?"

Ho pointed over his shoulder with disinterest at a stainless steel cold box with multiple drawers. "In the reefer. They're coming for him first thing in the morning. The papers are all signed." He walked to a table beneath shelves filled with thick textbooks on pathology, anatomy, toxicology, and forensic medicine.

"If you knew they were going to shut you down, why did you start the paperwork?"

"Wasn't going to, but the sister called from Boston. High-powered lawyer type barking out orders. Said she wanted to know the exact cause of death, and she meant exact. So I started the paperwork. Then I got the call from Mr. Jones telling me to apply the brakes. The fax followed. I assume you got one as well since you were next on his list of friends to spread his charm and warmth."

"Wait a minute." Molia got off the stool. "The sister said she wanted the results pronto; did she say why?"

"Nope."

"Then the Justice Department tells you to stop?"

"Yep."

"But offers no explanation."

"Nope." Ho turned off the lights to his office. "Guess they didn't have confidence in this country doctor, y'all."

Ho was from Philadelphia, and as "country" as Molia. "Did you call her back?"

"The sister? What for?" Ho walked across the room and turned off the overhead light above a metal tray table. "I don't care. Let somebody else do the carving."

"Why is the Justice Department involved, Peter?"

Ho shrugged. "He was a friend of the president."

"Yeah, that's what they're saying. But they're handling this one like he didn't kill himself. Jones lost his composure with me—"

"There's a surprise."

"And started throwing words around like 'investigation.' Why would they be investigating a routine suicide?"

Ho turned off the light and walked past him. "Don't know."

"And Jones said his orders came from the president."

Ho paused. "Really?"

"Yeah, really."

Ho dismissed it with a wave of the hand. "They were friends. The president has a personal interest in this one, and the family never wants to believe a relative killed himself. You know that."

"My gut's bothering me."

"Your gut is bothering you because you eat garbage. I hope I never have to cut you open. Probably find tin cans and a license plate."

"There was no call from dispatch that night, Peter. There was no nine-one-one reporting a dead body. I checked."

Ho thought about that for a moment. "So how did Coop find out about it?"

"Good question. And I have a theory, but let's assume for a moment that he wasn't supposed to find out about it. Let's say he stumbled onto something he wasn't supposed to stumble onto. That changes our conversation with Jones considerably, doesn't it?"

Ho's face strained as if he were computing a mathematics equation and disliking every minute of it. Then he shook his head as if to erase the whole thought. "You're jumping to a conclusion. There are no facts . . . Come on, the Justice Department? Why the hell would they be involved in something . . . This is ridiculous."

"That's my point. They wouldn't be involved if it *was* a suicide." Molia let the inference pique Ho's interest. The only way to find out if it was a suicide was to do an autopsy.

"Easy way to find out."

"Yeah?"

"*If* I were to do anything, which I'm *not*." Ho slipped on a lightweight windbreaker with "Charles Town Little League" stenciled across the chest above the word "Dodgers."

"You're not curious?" Molia asked.

Ho moved to the table and zipped up the bag, preparing to put the body back into the reefer for the night. "Not enough to get my tit in a wringer over it. I received my walking papers, Mole. So did you. Let the Justice Department figure it out. If he didn't kill himself, they'll know soon enough."

Molia spoke to Ho's back. "You're probably right. It's probably nothing. Just one big coincidence—like the Winn-Dixie guy and the baggage checker." He turned and started down the hall. "I'm around this weekend. Give me a call. We can take the boys fishing."

Ho let out a burst of air, like a whale purging its blow-hole. "Son of a . . . Why do you do this to me? You know I'm going to have to try to find out now."

Molia smiled. Ho was the kind of guy who picked up a novel and read the last page first. "Can it be done without someone knowing about it, Peter?"

"You that worried?"

"I just see no reason to arouse suspicion."

He thought for a moment. "To a degree. It wouldn't be too difficult with a gunshot wound—take a small piece of skin with powder burns from the temple, cross it with the burns on the fingers and powder residue under the nails, check the trajectory of the bullet, take a little blood to check for chemicals. It's not foolproof by any means, but it's safe. No one would know anything had been done."

"How long would it take? *If* you were to do it."

"They're coming for the body in the morning. Is it really that important, Tom?"

"It might be."

Ho removed his windbreaker and walked back to the sink to retrieve his apron, swearing under his breath, though it was halfhearted and forced. "You explain it to Jason." He lathered his hands with soap, like a man trying to take off his own skin. "He's going to be mad at me for missing his game."

"I'll have Maggie videotape the game. How long are we talking until we get something?"

Ho grabbed more paper towels. "I'll drop the samples off at the lab tomorrow. The residue check will take at least a couple of days. Blood tests could take ten days or longer. You want me to put a rush on it?"

Molia shook his head. "No. I'll just have to wait. Patience is a virtue, right?"

"Not for you."

"Thanks, Peter." He started again for the hallway but stopped at another thought. "What name will you use for the lab tests? You can't run them under his name."

Ho snapped on gloves, opened the green body bag covering the corpse on which he had been working, and flipped over a yellow tag attached to the toe. "Dunbar, John."

He looked up at Molia. "I'm going to need the ballistics test. Without it the powder burns won't be much help."

"See what I can do." Molia walked down the hall.

"And use the front door from now on!" Ho yelled.

Then he walked back into his office, cranked the music, and went to the stainless steel reefer to pull out the body inside the door labeled "Branick, Joe."

13

〜

SLOANE LEANED AGAINST the cedar siding outside his apartment door, struggling to catch his breath. Perspiration ringed his sweatshirt and dripped from his forehead and temples. Two doors down, the locksmith's drill hummed as he installed a dead bolt on Unit 6, working his way toward Sloane's apartment at the west end of the building. Word of the break-in had spread, and Sloane's older tenants had expressed concern.

He pushed open the door, dropped his MP3 and miniature headphones on the tile counter that separated the kitchen from the living room, and pulled a jug of cold water from the refrigerator, drinking from it in gulps, the overflow spilling from the corners of his mouth. Outside the kitchen window, seagulls swarmed a man and woman walking along the beach, tossing bread scraps in the air. Sloane heard the birds cawing through the open sliding glass door in the living room.

After leaving the office he felt the need to exercise. His ankle remained sore, but mostly if he moved laterally. It seemed to loosen up as he jogged along the coastline, Mick Jagger and the Rolling Stones moaning in his ears. He thought of people he hadn't seen or talked to in years;

faces from his childhood and school years flashed at him like a slide show put to music. He was so preoccupied that by the time he stopped to turn around he had run nearly five miles, with only one way back.

He popped the cap back on the jug of water and returned it to the fridge. Melda had left a plastic bowl sitting atop a handwritten note:

For you to be home. So glad.
Melda

He unsealed the bowl and scooped two fingers of chicken in mushroom sauce over rice into his mouth as Bud jumped onto the tile counter. Sloane held out his fingers. The cat sniffed them, then turned with disinterest and walked off.

"Typical. A year ago you would have eaten it out of the Dumpster. Now you're a connoisseur."

He resealed the lid and replaced the bowl in the fridge. Then he grabbed an ice bag from the freezer and rummaged in a drawer under the counter for the roll of duct tape. In the living room he sprinkled fish food in the tank and watched the grouper dart ahead of the angelfish to get at the tiny shrimp. Sloane had bought the tank on impulse; fish seemed the right pet for a bachelor living near the ocean. He set down the ice bag, tore a strip of tape with his teeth, and set to the task of salvaging a seat cushion so he'd at least have a place to sit and ice his ankle when he heard the familiar three soft knocks on his door.

Melda stood on the landing holding a bundle of envelopes. "I bring for you your mail, Mr. David. This time, it is not too much. Just the bills and the junk."

He had spent a year asking her to call him David, but it was a habit not meant to be broken. The mail reminded him of his mailbox. "Did you happen to notice that my mailbox was broken, Melda?"

She looked puzzled. "Broken? In what way is broken?"

"The door was open. The lock . . ." He tried to explain. "The lock was punched through."

She made a fist. "Punched?"

"Missing. The lock was missing." He could tell from the expression on her face that she didn't know what he was talking about. "Never mind. Do you want to come in and have a cup of tea?"

She shook her head. A smile creased her face. "I make apple pie. Tonight I bring for you a piece after my bingo."

Melda made apple pie for therapy. Sloane knew that the morning had unnerved her. He patted his stomach, still tight if no longer as hard as it once had been. "You must have a sixth sense, Melda. Whenever I get motivated to burn a few calories you bake an apple pie."

"You don't want me to?" she asked, disappointed.

"Have I ever said no to your apple pie?"

The smile returned. "Tonight, then. I go to my bingo, then I bring for you pie." She started down the landing, stopped, and put a hand to her temple. "I'm sorry. I not remember so well anymore."

"Something else?"

"The telephones—they have been fixed?"

"Fixed? Was there something wrong with your phone?"

She shook her head. "No. Your phone."

"My phone? What was wrong with my phone?"

She shrugged. "A man comes while you are gone and explains that the phones, they have broken and are in need of fixing."

"Did he say what was wrong?"

She shook her head. "I don't understand these things. Trans . . . something is problem. I just show him your phone."

"Inside my apartment?"

The storage closet off the carport housed the telephone equipment for the building. Sloane knew enough about the system to know that a problem would not have been limited to an individual apartment—especially not his, since he had not been home to report it.

"He says something about testing your phones. I watched him."

Sloane picked up the phone from its cradle on the kitchen counter. It had a dial tone. "It seems to be working okay. Did anyone complain about problems with their phone?"

She shook her head. "No. No problems."

"Did this man ask to go into the storage closet?"

"No," she said, more hesitant.

"Did he test other phones?"

"No. Just yours." Melda looked startled. "I do something wrong?"

The lawyer in him was already connecting the break-in of his apartment with the telephone repairman. If he was right, it eliminated the hypothesis that the break-in had been a random one.

"Mr. David? I do something wrong?"

Sloane shook his head. "No. I'm sure it's fine, Melda. You're sure it was the telephone company?"

She nodded.

"Did this man leave a card or some paperwork?"

She shook her head.

"How about a name?"

"No name . . . He was nice man. Very pleasing."

"I'm sure it's fine." He made a mental note to call the telephone company Monday morning and ask if they had a record of a service call, though he suspected he already knew the answer. He wondered if the man could be a relative of one of the victims from his cases, someone with an ax to grind. "Can you describe this man for me? What did he look like?"

She thought for a moment. "Smaller than you." She flexed her arms and hunched her shoulders. "Thick muscles."

"What about his face? What did his face look like?" She ran a hand across the top of her head. "Short hair. Flat on top . . . Oh! He has bird on his arm."

"A bird?"

"Eagle. You know." Melda grimaced. "What is word? Colors . . ." She pointed to the inside of her forearm. "With needle."

"A tattoo?"

"Yes. Tattoo. An eagle."

As if on cue, the telephone rang. "Well, I guess it's fixed," he said.

She smiled. "I see you tonight."

"I won't forget." He closed the door and answered the phone.

"David? Jesus, you scared the crap out of me." It was Tina. "What are you doing home? I thought you were going on vacation."

"I had a change of plans," he said. "Why are you calling if you didn't think I'd be home?" he asked, then realized it was after five o'clock on a Friday night. "You really are bucking for a raise."

"Keep the money. Nothing's worth this."

He heard more than her usual sarcasm. "What's wrong?"

"I was going to leave you a message in case you called in. I didn't want to blindside you first thing Monday morning."

"That doesn't sound promising."

"It's not. The proverbial shit is hitting the proverbial fan. Abbott Security sent over seven files this afternoon. Paul Abbott fired all of his other lawyers and wants you to handle them. Lucky you."

"I know. Bob Foster gave me the good news this morning."

"Really? Well, did His Majesty also tell you that one of the cases is set for trial—Monday?"

"*This* Monday?"

"This Monday."

Sloane laughed out of frustration. "We'll get a continuance."

"No, we won't. Amy Dawson rushed down ex parte to San Mateo Superior this afternoon, and Judge Margolis flat-out denied her. Apparently it's Abbott's third change of counsel. He sounds like a hell of a guy. Remind me to lose his address for the client Christmas party. And Judge Margolis made some vague reference to a top-gun lawyer being prepared, so you better be on top of your game. Abbott's called three times to talk to you, and the last time he wanted your cell phone and your home number and wasn't being polite about it."

"How bad is the file?"

"Amy said it's not great. One of Abbott's security guards apparently robbed the jewelry store he was supposed to be guarding. The guy was a convicted burglar. They hire only the best, don't they?"

Sloane would have bitched, but bitching to Tina could be like preaching to the choir, and the law was like a marriage: for better or for worse—it was his job. "I better find out how deep the water is. Tell Amy I'm on my way in. Order us some Hunan, will you?"

He hung up and began to prepare mentally for a long evening. Then he tossed his mail into his briefcase—with the amount of time he spent at the office, most of his bills were delivered there anyway—pulled his sodden sweatshirt over his head, and hurried into the bathroom for a quick shower.

14

Camano Island,
Western Washington

CHARLES JENKINS SAT back on the heels of his muddied boots, pulled the leather glove from his hand, and wiped a forearm across his brow, leaving flecks of dirt to mix with beads of perspiration. Though the weather was cool, sweat discolored the front and back of his sweatshirt beneath the bib of his overalls. Overhead, a flock of Canada geese flew in formation across the Northwest summer sky, a V backlit by the fading light of a dying sun. On the southern horizon Mount Rainier loomed, the glaciers a golden glow.

Jenkins slid his hand back into the glove and continued to pull weeds from a row of tomato plants, sifting through the pungent mulch of coffee-brown soil, horse manure, and yard waste, picking out twigs and rocks. In the pasture behind him the white Arabians galloped, kicking their hind legs and snorting as they lowered their heads and charged Lou and Arnold. Next to eating, his dogs' greatest pleasure in life was annoying the nine-hundred-pound animals. Their persistent barking was tolerable only because there were no neighbors for them to disturb. A thick forest of old-growth cedar, hemlock, and maple bordered Jenkins's ten-acre pasture to the west and north. A dairy farm bordered the east, an expanse of green lawn that lay like a blanket over soft rolling hills. Puget Sound was a quarter mile to the south, with only the white clapboard Presbyterian church and the two-lane road that circled Camano Island in between.

Sensing a moment of rare silence, Jenkins sat up and looked over his shoulder to see if the Arabians' hooves had finally found their mark, but Lou and Arnold remained upright, their sleek bodies rigid, ears perked, noses sniffing at the air.

Jenkins's senses remained just as sharp, though he'd had a bit of help. When he ventured into Stanwood that afternoon for bird netting to protect his prized vegetables, Gus at the hardware store told him someone had been around asking for him by name. That was also when Jenkins spotted the front page of the *Seattle Post-Intelligencer.*

The car came from the east, slowing as it neared the church, an obvious landmark someone had given the driver. He lost it momentarily as it passed behind the clapboard building, and picked it up again as it emerged on the far side and turned onto the dirt and gravel easement. The car slowed as it made its way up the road, then disappeared again behind the thick blackberry brush that marked the surveyor's line between the church's property and his own. No matter. He knew the path like the lines of his own hand. The gravel would end, giving way to a dirt road pocked with potholes. At the fork, just beyond another tangle of blackberry bushes threatening to overwhelm his dilapidated toolshed, the driver would turn right because the path appeared wider and, therefore, used more often. He would drive until he reached the creek, a dead end, and have to carefully back the car out. The left fork was so narrow the brush would scrape the sides of the car and not clear until the carport, a questionable wooden structure attached to the three-room caretaker's cottage. The more adventurous visitors would actually get out of their car and knock on the front door. Tonight the knock would go unanswered. The owner knelt in the garden pulling weeds from a row of his tomato plants.

At the sound of the car door shutting with a thud, Lou and Arnold bounded through the thigh-high brush nipping and jumping at each other. Their sudden appearance and sheer size—two Rhodesian ridgebacks each weighing 130 pounds, with a natural Mohawk of hair along their backs—would cause instant alarm. But their wagging tails and slobbering would reveal them to be harmless. Jenkins questioned their pedigree. Said to have been bred in South Africa to track and hunt lions, his dogs wouldn't hunt a squirrel.

Jenkins bent down and continued mixing the compost with the native soil. Minutes later he heard Lou and Arnold ripping through the tall grass at a frantic pace and sensed from their stops and starts that they were bringing someone to him. Reaching him, they circled, tongues hanging from the sides of their mouths. Jenkins removed his gloves, picked up the garden hoe, and stood, his six-foot-five-inch, 230-pound frame stretching from the ground like the stalk in the "Jack and the Beanstalk" fable. He wiped the dirt from his right hand onto his left pant leg, moved as if to repeat the motion, but spun instead to his right with a grip on the handle of the garden hoe, the blade whipping backhand through the air.

15

∽

SLOANE SLID THE binder back onto its shelf, closed his
eyes, and pinched the bridge of his nose. His optometrist
had said he'd likely need reading glasses by forty, but the
strain indicated that he was a couple of years ahead of schedule. The good news, however, was that, as with most legal
fires, the forest fire Tina had painted over the telephone
turned out to be a brush fire. Sloane's instincts were correct:
Judge Margolis wanted to force a settlement, and rightly so.
The case should not be tried. After an hour on the telephone
with Abbott, Sloane finally convinced him to fund the settlement and be done with it, but not before he had to threaten to
refuse to represent Abbott Security if he did not. Abbott
made threats of his own but, in the end, agreed.

Ordinarily it would have taken Sloane half the time to
get through the file. Over the years he had forged the ability to block out everything that could distract from a task
at hand. Work was his therapy—avoidance therapy, perhaps, but it had helped him to cope.

Not this time.

His mind kept wandering, slipping back to the break-in
at his apartment, and Melda's subsequent revelation of a

telephone repairman at the building beforehand. His legal training mandated that he see them as related, if for no other reason than that neither could be logically explained and that Sloane's apartment was the focus of both. He sat down at his desk and manipulated chopsticks to pick at the remnants of a carton of spicy beef that filled the room with the aroma of red peppers, green onions, and garlic, and washed down the final bite with a bottle of Tsingtao beer. He had no hard evidence that the two incidents were related; still, he had the persistent feeling he was missing something, some crucial fact that would put the two oddities together. It was the curse of being a lawyer: No two facts were unrelated; there was always a thread. There was always a conspiracy. No wonder lawyers were the most persecuted people he'd ever met—the persecution was of their own doing.

Do you have any enemies, Mr. Sloane?

In his mind's eye, Sloane saw and heard the police officer who came to his apartment to investigate the burglary. He had asked Sloane that question as they surveyed the damage.

"It looks to me like you pissed someone off," he'd said. "Do you have any enemies, Mr. Sloane?"

Sloane told him it could be any number of people, given his occupation. "Why do you ask?"

The officer led him to the front door of the apartment and pointed to the lock. "The lock was disengaged, not broken."

"Is that significant?"

"It means there was no forced entry. Nobody broke the door down. They either had a key or picked the lock; someone who knew what he was doing. Any ideas?"

"None," Sloane said to his empty office. He dropped the chopsticks into the empty carton and threw both in the garbage can by his desk, then pulled his mail from his briefcase, flipping through it until coming to the 9 × 12 rust-colored envelope. His name and address were hand-printed on the front.

Tina knocked, opened his door, and walked in.

"You're still here?" He put the envelope down as she handed him a draft of the settlement agreement he had dictated to put on the record Monday morning.

"In body only," she said. "My mind departed at five."

"I didn't expect you to do this tonight."

"Now you tell me." She brushed an errant hair from her cheek and tugged at the sleeves of the Irish-knit cardigan draped over her shoulders. "What? Do I have something on my face?" She wiped the side of her mouth in the reflection in the window.

He had been staring at her. He had thought Tina attractive the moment she was introduced as his assistant, but had really noticed her when she walked unescorted into the firm's twenty-five-year anniversary party wearing a black backless gown and a strand of pearls. They had sat together, each without spouse or date, and danced more than once. But then the clock struck midnight, and Tina left quickly. It was just as well. There could be nothing between them. She was his employee; a relationship would only lead to disaster, like all his relationships, a convoy of failures. But unlike those women, who were eager to be married, Tina gave no indication that that was something in her future. Sloane had come to respect her as intelligent and mature beyond her years, always putting the well-being of her son, Jake, first.

"I was just wondering who's watching Jake."

She turned from the window. "Would you believe his father? I called to see if hell had also frozen over." She put up a hand. "My mother says I shouldn't say those things, that I need to be more diplomatic. 'Frank's not a bad man. He's just not a very good father.'" She rolled her eyes, then nodded to the beer. "You got any more of those, or did you drink them all?"

Sloane popped open a beer and handed it across the desk. "You want some Chinese? I have an unopened carton of garlic chicken."

"I ordered for myself. You paid." She held up the bottle. "Cheers, here's to a rip-roaring Friday night." They tapped bottles, and she sat in a chair across his desk. "So where were you going?"

"What's that?"

"On your vacation, where were you going?"

"Oh, just up to the mountains for a few days. Yosemite."

"Rock climbing?"

"Nothing serious. I'm not in shape for it. I just like the mental challenge and the exercise."

"You're going to get yourself killed."

"I appreciate you sticking around tonight. I hope I didn't ruin any plans."

"Yeah, I had a hot date—my mother really loves the *Antiques Road Show* . . . Don't worry about it. It gave me a chance to study, and it gave Jake a chance to spend time with the man supposed to be his father. Oops, there I go again."

Sloane chuckled. "Studying?"

"Don't say it like you're shocked."

"I was laughing at your comment. Are you going to school or something?"

"Or something." She laughed, toying with him. "You are shocked."

"Give me a break here; you've never said anything. Are you taking classes?"

She smiled, coy, and took another drink of beer.

"What are you studying?"

"Architecture."

"Seriously, what are you studying?"

She lowered the beer and stared at him. "How does it taste?" she asked.

"What?"

"Your foot."

She was serious. He had expected her to say she was taking an art class.

"For your information, I've been taking classes for three years. When Jake was born I had to drop out of college, but I promised myself I'd go back and finish. Then Frank decided being a father crimped his life too much, and I had to wait. I wanted to make sure I could do it before I said anything to anybody."

"Do what?"

"I graduate the end of the summer."

He felt a sudden hollow ache in his stomach. "Graduate? Then what?"

She drank from the bottle. "We can talk about that later."

"Are you thinking about leaving?"

She hesitated. "I was going to talk to you about it earlier, but with the Scott trial I didn't want it to be a distraction."

He felt as if he'd been kicked in the gut. "You're leaving."

"I'll be giving my formal notice August first," she said.

"Two weeks?"

"You'll have a month to replace me, David. This opportunity came up unexpectedly. I need time to get Jake situated in school for the fall and to find us a place to live."

He felt as if the room were spinning. "A place to live . . . Where are you going?"

"Seattle. A friend offered me a job doing drafting. It's a good job. Better pay. Better benefits. I can afford a house. I can spend more time with Jake, and my mother can have her life again, too."

He didn't know what to say. He had never contemplated the possibility that Tina would leave. He had pictured the two of them receiving their gold company watches together.

"This isn't what I intended for my life, David. This is better for me—I mean, there's nothing here for me . . . Is there?"

"You could find a job here."

"Forget it." She turned and looked out the window, then looked back at him. "Why are you here?"

"It's a good firm, Tina—"

"No. Why are you here now, tonight? You haven't taken a vacation in years, and when you finally get one you seem to be avoiding going. And pardon me for saying so, but you do look tired."

Maybe it was because she was leaving, or maybe it was the beer. Whatever the reason, he was talking before he could stop himself.

"I haven't been sleeping much."

"You work too hard."

"It isn't work. I've been having a nightmare."

"A nightmare?"

"And I get these searing headaches and I can't get back to sleep."

She lowered her beer. "How long has this been going on?"

"Every morning since the Scott trial started."

"David, you should see a doctor."

He chuckled. "You mean I should have my head examined."

"That's not what I mean."

"The law is still an old-boys' network, Tina. You don't want word getting out you might be a little nuts."

"You're stubborn," she said. "See a doctor, David." She took a drink of beer. "What's the nightmare about?"

"You don't want to hear this, Tina."

"Why not? The longer I'm here the more time Jake gets to spend with the man who's supposed—oops—I mean, with his dad." She put her empty bottle on the desk. "Crack me another one." He handed her a second beer. "Besides, I shared my secret with you. I expect some reciprocity. Maybe you'll find that it actually helps to talk to someone about these things."

Keeping it to himself certainly hadn't helped. "What the hell." He started matter-of-factly, as if reciting facts to a jury. "I'm in a room—I don't know where exactly; the details are sketchy and it's very stark. There's a woman there." He closed his eyes, seeing her. "Sometimes she's working at a desk. Sometimes she's just standing . . . dressed in white, backlit, like an outline. And I'm not sure why, but I have this feeling . . ." He opened his eyes. "More than a feeling. I know something is going to happen to her, something bad, and I can't stop it."

"Why not?"

He struggled to find the right words. "I can't move. It's like my arms and legs are bound. When I try to call out to her, my voice . . . Nothing comes out."

She sat forward. "So what happens?"

"I don't know exactly. There's this blinding flash of light and an explosion." He put a hand to his ear as if hearing it. "Then people are rushing into the room, shouting."

"Who are they?"

He shook his head. "Everything is a blur. I can't see or breathe."

"What happens to the woman?"

He took another drink.

"David?"

He lowered his eyes. "They rape her," he said softly. "Then they kill her."

16

⌒

SHE NEVER FLINCHED.

The blade end of a garden hoe stopped two inches from her throat, and she never moved.

Remarkable.

She considered him as one might, on first sight, an old-growth redwood, marveling at its sheer size. Her eyes took in his overalls, from the taut straps across his thick shoulders and chest to the rolled cuffs above his mud-caked work boots. Charles Jenkins did not recognize the face, though it seemed to tweak a place in his memory, but her face would have been a particularly difficult one to forget. She was as stunning as she was composed. Her hair cascaded like spilled ink over her shoulders, the same indigo-blue color as her eyes. Her nose was thin and perfect, perhaps surgically altered, and though he detected no makeup, the cool weather—or the rush of adrenaline—had brought a blush to her cheeks. Otherwise, her bronze-colored complexion was unblemished. He estimated her to be five feet ten—most of it legs wrapped in straight-legged jeans—with perhaps an extra inch from the spit-shined ankle boots, the spiked heel sinking into the moist ground. She wore a waist-length leather jacket over a white blouse.

And behind the beauty was someone with remarkable training.

"Charles Jenkins?" she asked.

HE LEFT THE garden hoe on the ground and led her across the pasture to the cottage. At the back door he removed his boots and stepped inside. He passed through the kitchen to the main room, did not hear her follow, and turned to find her standing in the doorway, considering the kitchen with the same measured curiosity with which she had considered him. Pots, pans, and ladles overflowed the sink onto the worn Formica counter and buried all but a single burner on the stove. Dozens of mason jars, some with the lids wax-sealed tight, lined the counter like glass soldiers. Freshly picked blackberries and raspberries filled strainers, waiting to be washed and boiled. The supermarket in town sold his jam in a section for the locals—a hobby, like the Arabians. His parents had left him with a modest estate that, invested prudently and spent wisely, would sustain him into his old age.

"You're letting the heat out," he said, though it was cool inside the cottage.

She closed the door behind her and stepped lightly around a maze of tomato plants, fledgling squash, corn, sweet peas, and lettuce sprouting in black plastic containers to join him in the main room.

He dropped his work gloves on stacks of newspapers and grabbed a handful of the unopened mail addressed to "Resident"—a mountainous pile that spilled across the round table, a six-inch-thick piece of cedar he had cut from the base of an old-growth tree felled by the winter storms of 1998. Sanded and varnished, it served as a one-of-a-kind dining room table. He tossed all but one of the envelopes into a river-rock fireplace, struck a match on one of the stones, lit the envelope in his hand, and dropped it onto the pile. Then he knelt to add kindling, keeping his back to her, listening to the heels of her boots click on the plank floor. She walked about the bookcases that lined the walls like a country library and held an impressive collection of books and videotapes of classic movies. Fruit crates contained additional books he had not yet read and movies he was eager to watch again.

He looked over his shoulder and watched her flip through the canvases near a paint-splattered easel.

"They're not bad." She sounded more surprised than complimentary, which was honest. Van Gogh he was not.

Lou and Arnold crashed through the flap of plastic covering the dog door and jockeyed through the doorway. They rumbled into the room and took up their customary positions: Lou on the plaid couch with the nub-worn armrests, Arnold on the La-Z-Boy recliner facing the fireplace. The floor was not good enough. He had spoiled them. They sat upright, ears perked, eyes darting between Jenkins and this unexpected visitor who had interrupted their daily routine. Jenkins added the split maple, which crackled and popped and filled the room with a sweet, syrupy smell, and replaced the screen. He stood and scratched Lou behind the ears, which caused the dog's face to wrinkle like that of a ninety-year-old man.

She walked to the plate-glass window and cradled the bloom of an orchid plant, one of a dozen aligned on a wood plank. The flowers gave the room the feel and smell of a garden hothouse. Then she looked out over the pasture. "Arabians. Temperamental and high-strung."

"You know horses."

"My mother's family had a farm. Thoroughbreds, Arabians, a few mules." She turned from the window and walked toward him, extending a hand as if they were meeting in the supermarket checkout. Her fingers were chilled and soft, though the calluses revealed that she did not push paper for a living. "Alex Hart."

"Well, Ms. Hart, I haven't seen or talked to Joe Branick in thirty years."

"I'm not surprised. You don't have a phone."

He took out a cellular from a pocket in the front of his overalls. "I'm unlisted. I don't get a lot of calls. I also don't get a lot of visitors. People who need to find me ask for the black man. You asked for me by name."

"Word travels fast."

She picked up her briefcase, put it on one of the two peeled ash-wood chairs he'd made, and pulled out a copy of the *Washington Post*. The Associated Press article he had seen in the *Post-Intelligencer* was positioned below the fold with the same photograph of Joe Branick. Joe looked older, which was to be expected after thirty years. Traces of distinguished gray flagged his temples; otherwise, his tanned, weathered face still gave him the rugged outdoor appearance of someone living in the Sunbelt. Jenkins hadn't bothered to read the article in town and wouldn't now. The headline told him everything he needed to know. Joe Branick was not the type of man to kill himself. Thirty years wasn't going to change that.

He dropped the paper on the table. "I didn't know the *Washington Post* personally delivered their newspaper. Is there a special this month?"

She smiled and flipped her hair from her shoulder, folding it behind her ear. He caught the aroma of her perfume. It put the orchids to shame. Arnold moaned. She reached inside her briefcase and pulled out a thick manila envelope, handing it to him. "Joe said if anything were to happen to him, I was to deliver this to you."

He felt its weight. "What is it?"

"I don't know."

He considered her eyes, but if she was holding back information, she was good at it. Keeping his eyes on her, he turned over the envelope, conscious that she stood watching him, perhaps gauging his reaction. He tore open the tab, reached inside, and pulled out the contents.

The worn manila file staggered him—he felt like a parent seeing an estranged child after thirty years.

17

❧

TINA CRINGED, THOUGH not at the brutality of Sloane's gruesome revelation but at the fact that he had to relive it every morning.

"David, I'm so sorry," she said quietly.

"The worst part about it," he said, "is I feel like what's happening to her is my fault."

"You mean because you can't help her?"

"It's more than that." He paused to consider how best to explain it, running a finger over his lips before settling for "I feel like I'm responsible for what's happening to her."

"David, it's only a dream."

"I know," he said, but in his mind he watched the shadow grab the woman by her hair and lift her from the floor, her body dangling limp and lifeless, the light flickering—the polished blade catching the glint of the moon before cutting through the night as if through a blackened canvas.

She sat back. "It's no wonder you're not sleeping. What a horrible thing to go through every night, David! Do you have any idea who this woman could be?"

The question perplexed him. "You mean Emily Scott?"

Her eyes widened and her eyebrows arched. "You didn't say it was Emily Scott. Is it?"

He had assumed so, but now, put to the question, he realized he did not know. "I thought so."

Tina put her half-empty bottle on the desk. "Can I ask you something else?"

He smiled, knowing she would. "This seems to be the night, doesn't it? Fire away."

"How did it make you feel when the jury found Paul Abbott not liable?"

"You mean, how did I feel keeping an obnoxious son of a bitch from having to pay a large bill he was morally obligated to pay? It's not a perfect system, Tina, but it's not for me to judge my clients. That's the jury's job."

"Then forget about Paul Abbott for a moment. Forget about the jury. Forget about defending the system. Just tell me how winning made you feel *this* time."

"What are you getting at?"

She playfully chided him. "You always get to ask the questions. Let me play lawyer this once. How did it make you feel?"

"It's impossible to divorce your ego from it entirely. Nobody likes to lose."

"Blah, blah, blah. You're giving me textbook answers. I want to know how it made you *feel*. Were you happy, sad? Did you feel any guilt?"

The word hung over his head like a guillotine blade.

"Why would you ask me that?"

"Did you?"

He stretched the muscles of his neck, tilting his head from side to side, uncomfortable. "None of these are easy, Tina, and none are particularly satisfying, but I can't dwell on that. No matter how sorry I might feel for the family, it's my job to defend my clients, whether I personally like them or not."

She sat silently.

He rubbed a hand across his mouth. "If you're human, you feel compassion. That's what makes these cases so hard. Jurors want to find a reason to give the family money, but it doesn't change the fact that I'm hired to do a job."

In his mind he saw the photograph of Emily Scott's battered face on the courtroom easel. The homicide detective had used it to describe what he called "the most horrific act of violence I've witnessed in twenty-six years." Steiner had neglected to remove the exhibit after the investigator testified. Emily Scott's young son had been brought into the courtroom for a portion of the closing argument and sat in the front row, feet dangling above the floor, eyes regarding what would be the last image of his mother. Realizing this, Sloane had stood in the middle of Steiner's closing argument, ordinarily an intolerable act, walked to the easel, and turned the photograph around.

No one took offense. Not Steiner. Not the judge.

Sloane looked across the desk at Tina.

"Yes," he said, hearing the low whistle of the guillotine blade sliding down the rack and hitting the wood stump with a dull thud. "I felt guilt."

18

❧

PARKER MADSEN STOOD in his wood-paneled den looking out the leaded-glass panes, sipping tea from a mug embossed with a picture of a large deer—his Christmas gift from his secretary. Above the animal's proud antlers were the words THE BUCK STOPS HERE. On a manicured green lawn lit by sporadic Japanese landscape lanterns, Exeter gnawed a deflated basketball. Madsen's grandson would not be happy, but dogs often taught children valuable lessons. This one would be about leaving toys unattended.

Madsen turned from the window and reconsidered the sheet of paper in his hand beneath the muted light of a green and gold desk lamp. The log of telephone calls indicated that the last three calls had been made within two minutes of one another, two to an area code in the San Francisco Bay Area. The first number belonged to a San Francisco law firm, the second to a private residence in Pacifica, California. Both had the same thing in common: David Allen Sloane.

According to the San Francisco Bar Association, Sloane worked as an attorney at Foster & Bane. A lawyer. Madsen found that interesting. Each call was also charged as exactly one minute, which indicated that they were actually less than a minute—just enough time to leave a message or instruct the recipient to call back on another line.

Madsen returned the sheet of paper to the three-ring binder, snapped it closed, and flipped a tab. Sloane's date of birth was February 17, 1968. He had never married and had no children. A search of Social Security records in Baltimore revealed a California prefix, 573. According to the State Department of Public Health and Vital Statistics, Sloane's birth certificate had a reissue date of 1974. No reason was provided for why the certificate had been reissued, but Madsen reasoned that it was related to Sloane's parents' dying in a car accident in Southern California when he was a child. A clipping from the *Los Angeles Times* included a picture of the car wrapped around a telephone pole like an accordion. At six years old Sloane was NPG—"no parent or guardian." He was shipped to a series of foster homes as a ward of the state until, at seventeen, he enlisted in the United States Marine Corps. It was not uncommon for underage men to enlist. Some lied about their age; others obtained a parental signature. The records did not reveal that Sloane had done either. Somehow he'd talked his way past the marine recruiter. When he obtained the highest score that year on his Marine Corps aptitude test, one of the highest scores ever, no one was about to question his age. Madsen put on his bifocals and reconsidered the number. He had not misread it. Further military testing indicated that David Sloane had an IQ of 173. Near genius. And he wasn't just smart. Though he was the youngest member of his platoon, Sloane's commanding officers saw enough in the young marine to elevate him to platoon leader—First Marine Division, Second Battalion, Echo Company. Over the course of his four years of service, Sloane had compiled an impressive record, earning citations for marksmanship and a Silver Star for gallantry in Grenada. Madsen considered a medical report. Sloane took a Cuban bullet in the shoulder after removing his flak jacket during an engagement. That act explained the report that followed the medical report, which Madsen recognized immediately—a psychological profile. He adjusted the lamp.

> This Marine has unquestioned intelligence, skills, and leadership qualities. The men in his platoon show a unique willingness to follow his command and a loyalty and confidence in his abilities, which, given this Marine's young age I find remarkable. Nevertheless, I do not recommend this Marine for Officer Candidate School. This Marine's only explanation for removing his flak jacket during a hostile engagement is that he felt "weighted" and desired to "move faster." On the surface it appears to be a careless act not in keeping with a man of his intellect or abilities, a clear disregard for his own well-being. Further interviews, however, reveal it to be consistent with a pattern of impulsive behavior. He describes his decision to join the Marine Corps as one made while passing a Marine recruitment center while walking to a hardware store to buy bolts. "It seemed like something to do."
>
> It is my opinion the Corps became something heretofore lacking in his life—stability in a daily routine, and a brotherhood and family with his

fellow recruits. That he embraced the Corps, excelled, and developed strong bonds with the men with whom he serves is, therefore, not surprising. Nevertheless, his spontaneous decision to join the Corps is consistent with his spontaneous decision to remove his flak jacket. It is indicative of a man dissatisfied with his life and therefore prone to making rash decisions to change it. Such decisions could, in the future, endanger not only himself but also the men for whom he is responsible.

Madsen put down the report and pressed a finger to his lips, the ends of which lifted upward into a grin. Sloane was not unlike the soldiers he recruited: men without family, skilled and determined, but raw and in need of guidance and discipline. Commanding them was not unlike training a dog. Madsen broke them down and rebuilt them, dispensing enough discipline to control them without breaking their spirit and natural instinct to fight. Throw a carcass of meat into a pack of dogs, and all the training in the world went to hell. Mayhem replaced order. Instincts replaced training. Men were no different. Madsen had seen it in Vietnam more times than he could remember: the dark side of the human psyche that caused men to discharge a hundred rounds into a hooch of women and children, then burn it to the ground. His men did as ordered, without regard for the moral or ethical consequences of their actions. They were men who got things done. And they were men, like dogs, that you did not turn your back on. Ever.

Madsen closed the binder. The NSA was assisting in breaking down Sloane's telephone records for the past six months, as well as his credit card transactions. That was all well and good, but Madsen did not have the luxury of time. While there appeared to be no connection between Joe Branick and David Sloane, there most certainly was one. Branick saw fit to call Sloane twice and to mail him a package.

Exeter padded into the room, claws clicking on the hardwood, head shaking his new chew toy. After his wife died, Madsen had had all the Persian rugs in the house removed. Carpet muffled sounds, and Parker Madsen did not like to be surprised.

19

❧

TINA SUPPRESSED A smile, though not very well, and wiped a tear from the corner of her eye. "The beer," she said.

"Beer makes you cry?"

She gave him the empty bottle. "Shut up and give me another one." He opened a bottle and handed it across the desk. "You're human, David. The fact that you felt guilt only means you're human."

He chuckled. "Was there some doubt about that?"

"Sometimes I wondered," she said with sarcasm.

"Boy, I guess it's better not to know what people think about you."

"Don't start getting sensitive on me now."

"It's my human side coming out." They laughed. Then he became contemplative. "I'm sorry to see you go, Tina, but I'm happy for you."

She looked down at her beer. "They'll find you another good secretary. The firm won't want to slow down the Sloane trial machine."

"You've taken care of me for ten years and been a good friend. I appreciate it."

She looked up at him. "I have to think of Jake."

"I know," he said. "That's what makes you such a good mother."

She seemed to blush at the comment, then stood to look out the floor-to-ceiling windows. "You know, I can't recall the last time I had a Friday night free. My mother's always harping . . ." She stopped. "Well, you know how mothers can be."

Sloane didn't. But that was not for this conversation. "Why didn't you ever remarry?" The question seemed to catch her off guard, and he was just as surprised that he had asked it. "I'm sorry. That's none of my business."

She spoke to the glass. "A couple reasons, I guess. First, it would have to be the right situation." She looked at Sloane. "Not just for me, but for Jake, too." Then she looked back out the window. "Not having a father around is hard, but having a bad one would be worse. He's been disappointed too many times . . . So it would have to be someone good to him, someone who would spend time with him, someone who would learn to love him."

"That shouldn't be hard. Jake's a great kid. He's the only reason I go to the company picnic every year."

She turned from the window and walked back to the chair. "Yeah, he still talks about playing catch with you," she said.

"And what about you?" he asked.

She shrugged. "Practicalities."

"Such as?"

"I don't get out much, and the pool of appealing, single, heterosexual men is rather limited in this city."

"What about the guy in Seattle?"

"Who?"

"The guy with the architectural firm in Seattle?"

She laughed. "I don't think that would work."

"Someone here?"

"Maybe." She seemed to consider this for a moment, then looked back out the window. "But he's still searching to find himself. And until he does, I can't expect him to find me." She put her beer on the edge of his desk.

He was about to ask her if she wanted to get a cup of coffee when he remembered Melda and looked at his watch. "I'm late. I forgot I have a date."

Her expression went blank.

"When you're seventy years old and bake an apple pie, you expect the person to be there to eat it."

"Melda."

"Come on, I'll give you a ride."

"It's too far out of your way. You'll be really late."

She was right. "I'll pay for a cab."

"You bet your ass you will. I'm not taking the bus this time of night."

He tossed the empty carton of Chinese in the garbage, grabbed a pile of work from his desk, and reached to stuff it in his briefcase.

Tina grabbed his hand, stopping him. "You're supposed to be on vacation. Take at least a day off, David."

20

~

HE RAN HIS hand over the cover as if he were feeling fine silk. The edges had worn, the cover yellowed with time, and the word "Classified," stamped in red at odd angles, had faded to pink, but there was no mistaking it. Charles Jenkins started to open the cover, then closed it like the door to a closet filled with bad memories. His chest tightened to the point that he ran a hand over it and pulled back his shoulders. He felt suddenly out of breath.

"Are you all right?" Alex Hart asked.

No, he wasn't all right. He felt as if he were having a heart attack, and if he ever was going to have one, this was the moment. He looked down at the table. The file still existed. Absurd. All these years he'd thought it had been destroyed. It hadn't. Joe had taken it. The thought snapped him back to reality, and the reality was, if Joe had gone to the trouble of hiding the file for thirty years, he would not have entrusted it to just anyone. That put the stranger standing in his living room in a completely different light.

"How did you know him?" he asked.

"Joe? He was a friend of my father."

"Who's your . . ." The place in his memory that her face had tweaked in the garden flew open like an unlatched door in a strong wind; the resemblance was remarkable.

"Robert Hart," he whispered.

She looked surprised. "You knew my father, also?"

During their two years in Mexico City together, Jenkins and Joe Branick had visited Professor Robert Hart's home several times. Hart was an American married to a Mexican national. He taught at the National Autonomous University of Mexico and had homes near the Mexican Golf Club and in a suburb outside Washington, D.C.—a lavish lifestyle for a university professor. But it was not Robert Hart's face that Jenkins now saw so clearly. It was the face of the beautiful *criolla* woman who had greeted him and Joe at the door to her home. Her straight dark hair reached to the middle of her back, green eyes revealing her Spanish descent. Alex Hart was the spitting image of her mother, except for her height and the curl in her hair. Both came from her father. The past, one Jenkins had worked so hard to bury, had now been thrust in his face in the form of a woman he last saw riding a bike in the front yard of her family home.

"I need a drink," he said.

He walked into the kitchen and rummaged in the cabinets, finding it at the back of a shelf. Back in the main room he set the bottle of Jack Daniel's and two mason jars on the table, poured two fingers in each, handed one to her, and downed his shot, feeling the raw burn that caused his eyes to water. When the sting passed he poured a second shot.

"How old are you, Alex?" His voice was rough from the alcohol, like Clint Eastwood's in *The Good, the Bad and the Ugly*.

She laughed. "I'm well past twenty-one, but thanks for the compliment." She had her mother's easy way about her.

"You look like your mother."

She lowered the jar. "Thank you. She died a little over two years ago."

"I'm sorry. Your father—is he still alive?"

"No. He died six months later. The doctors said it was a heart attack. I think it was a broken heart. He loved her so."

"Yes, he did. He was a good man." Jenkins sat down and offered her the second chair. This time she sat. "I take it you know he worked for us?"

Robert Hart had for many years been a well-paid CIA consultant on South American affairs. His specialty was right-wing Mexican revolutionary groups.

"Not until I was older. My mother explained it to me." She downed her shot, grimaced, and put the mason jar on a stack of envelopes.

They considered the file between them like something that might bite. "Do you know how Joe got it?"

She shook her head.

"You were working with him, though." He rubbed his hands together, a habit when he thought. Then he said, "Oil. Nonreligious oil."

It was not a great leap of intellect. To the contrary, Robert Peak's election platform had played on American frustration and anger at rising gas prices dictated by OPEC, and on the surging resentment at the loss of American lives fighting oil wars. Americans were tired of Muslim terrorists holding them hostage. Much like Richard Nixon's promise during his presidential campaign to end the war in Vietnam—without revealing how—Peak had promised to end America's dependence on Middle East oil. Political pundits called it a campaign ruse. Peak had always been well financed by the oil companies, and as long as they remained the largest shareholders in American car manufacturing companies, the likelihood of Peak doing anything that affected their bottom line was slim to none. Others speculated that Peak intended to lobby Congress to pass a bill that would require increased research of alternative fuel sources and increase the percentage of automobiles required to run on those fuels. That, however, would affect the oil companies, and so long as the automobile manufacturers remained the major shareholders in those corporations, that scenario was also unlikely. With the economy continuing to spiral into the toilet, Peak was in no position to alienate his biggest political support structure. There were several Latin American possibilities: Venezuela, though the government was teetering on the brink of chaos, and Mexico, with its over 75-billion-barrel oil reserve, but only if he could get at the oil, literally, and with current technology. Neither was likely.

"How does he do it?"

She studied him for a moment. "A reopening of the Mexican oil market to American oil companies and related manufacturing industries."

Jenkins shook his head. The nationalization of Mexico's oil market was as sacrosanct to Mexicans as the Virgin of Guadalupe. In 1938, after an audit revealed that United States' and other foreign oil companies were robbing Mexico blind, Mexico's President, Lázaro Cárdenas, expelled them and nationalized Mexico's oil. Cárdenas had then forced Franklin Delano Roosevelt and John D. Rockefeller to back down from the confrontation, threatening to sell Mexico's oil to Germany during World War II if the United

States did not. Mexican history books proclaimed Cárdenas a hero, and Mexico continued to celebrate March 18 as a "day of national dignity."

"They'll never do it."

"Members of the administration have been meeting with representatives of Castañeda," she said, referring to Alberto Castañeda, Mexico's recently elected young president, who was being likened to John F. Kennedy.

Jenkins remained skeptical. "Why? What's in it for Mexico?"

"An increased percentage of the American oil market at a fixed per-barrel cost tied to the world market. That's tens of billions of dollars."

Jenkins thought about the information for a moment. "How high up are the talks?"

"The president wasn't going to South America to talk about global warming."

"And they wouldn't risk the confidentiality of the talks by bringing in Peak unless they were close to cutting a deal." He stood and paced, the wood planks groaning as he transferred his weight. Castañeda was known to be a right-wing conservative, publicly opposed to any foreign intervention into Mexican affairs, including subsurface mineral rights. "It's counterintuitive for him to be engaging in these discussions."

"You're thinking like an American. In Mexico the president is elected for a single six-year term. He doesn't have to worry about being reelected."

"It will ruin any chance his party has of staying in power. It makes no sense."

"Or it makes perfect sense."

He stopped pacing. "Tell me how?"

"Peak has him over a barrel—no pun intended. Mexico's oil fields were put up as collateral for the last financial aid package after the collapse of Mexico's private banks."

"Okay."

"If Mexico fails to repay that debt, they could lose control of the oil anyway. Castañeda's not exactly negotiating from a position of strength. He can blame the prior administration for getting Mexico into NAFTA; it was a bad deal. This allows him to cut Mexico's losses and negotiate a better deal. On its face it will help Mexican laborers to work in the United States, create better-paying jobs for the poor, expand Mexico's economic market, and bring money for social improvements."

"His primary support groups. He can paint himself as a hero," Jenkins said, picking up on her train of thought.

"He said he would be a president of the people, for the people. It's too good an offer to let pass."

Jenkins looked out the plate-glass windows to where the Arabians grazed in peace. "That's the problem. There is no such thing as 'too good an offer' if Robert Peak is involved."

21

Financial District, San Francisco

THEY STOOD SHIVERING, the collars of their coats turned up against a cold wind funneling through the canyon of high-rise buildings. It moaned softly as it passed, and brought the smell of the bay from a week of ninety-degree temperatures that spoiled the plant life and left a metallic taste in the air. The heat wave had ended.

Sloane found the financial district at night eerily quiet; it was like standing in the courtyard of an enormous, suddenly deserted apartment complex. The sheer immensity of the buildings played tricks on the mind, making one expect to hear all kinds of noise: people talking, car engines, sirens. Instead it was only the hum of the wind, an occasional car engine, and the scraping of an errant paper blowing up the sidewalk and gutters. San Franciscans fled the downtown business area at sunset, migrating to their homes, to the restaurants in North Beach and Chinatown, and to the trendy nightclubs south of Market.

It left the financial district feeling like a ghost town from a Hollywood set.

"You don't have to wait with me, David. I know you're worried about being late."

He pulled out his cell phone. "I'll let her know I'm running a bit behind."

Melda's phone rang three times before her answering machine picked up. Sloane left a message, flipped his phone closed, and looked at his watch again.

"Everything okay?" Tina asked.

"I'm just surprised she's not home yet."

"Go ahead. I'll be fine."

"No. It's all right." He put his hands in the pockets of his jacket and hunched his shoulders to protect his neck from the cold. "She probably stayed to have a cup of coffee with a certain gentleman she's been talking about."

"Another man? She stood you up!"

Tina grinned, turning her head slightly to allow the breeze down Battery Street to blow the hair from her face. He had always thought her eyes blue, but now, in the ambient light from the building lobby, they were more the color of a high summer sky, with flecks of gray and yellow. She leaned toward him, as if being pulled by an invisible string, and for a moment he thought she was going to kiss him. But she stepped past him to the newspaper bin behind him, studying the paper through the plastic casing.

"Do you have that message slip? The one I gave you earlier about the twenty-three-year-old stockbroker with the hot stock tip of the week?"

He reached into his pocket but had changed shirts.

"What was the name?" she asked. "The name on the slip?"

"I think it was Joe Branick—why?"

She spoke as if talking to herself. "Not the latest go-getter with the hot stock tip of the week," she said.

"What?" He walked to where she stood. The photograph was just above the fold, with the name typed beneath it. Sloane looked at her, disbelieving, then rummaged in his pocket for a quarter. He deposited the coin in the slot and took a copy of the paper, reading the headline out loud.

"President grieves friend's death."

She leaned over his shoulder, and they read the copy down the right side of the page.

The Associated Press

WASHINGTON—At an early morning White House press conference at which President Robert Peak was expected to discuss his participation in a South American environmental conference focusing on global warming, White House Chief of Staff Parker Madsen confirmed that Joe Branick, Special Assistant to the President, was dead.

West Virginia Park Police discovered Branick's body just after 5:30 a.m. near a deserted fire trail in Black Bear National Park. The single gunshot wound to the head was apparently self-inflicted. Madsen said no further details would be forthcoming from the White House and directed all questions to the Department of Justice. He described the President and the West Wing as "stunned."

Boyhood friends and college roommates at Georgetown, Peak and Branick had remained close

personal friends. The President, who was to leave
this morning for South America to attend the
summit, has canceled that trip. In a written statement
released by the White House, the President was said
to have delivered the news personally to Branick's
wife and three adult children.

Sloane lowered the paper and reconsidered his recollection of the name. "It has to be a coincidence," he said softly.

Her cab pulled to the curb.

"He's dead; the paper says he killed himself. Why would he call you?"

He looked at her. "We don't even know it was him."

"Of course it's him. Who else would it be? Do you know him?"

"I . . ." He considered the photograph in the newspaper. Something about the eyes. "No," he said. "I'm sure I don't."

The cabdriver, a reed-thin black man, leaned over, impatient. Sloane opened the cab door and handed him thirty dollars through the window slot. "Take her home. Keep the change."

Tina protested. "David, you're not paying for my cab." Despite her humor, he knew her to be fiercely independent.

"You bet your ass I'm not," he said. "I'll bill it to Paul Abbott."

"In that case I'll take the long way home." She smiled and slid into the backseat. "If nothing else it would make for an interesting story," she said, nodding to the paper in his hand.

He wondered.

"You okay?"

"I'm still in shock that you're leaving."

"Maybe not." She reached for the door handle. "I told you I'd stay for the right guy. You just have to find him for me."

She pulled the door closed, leaving him standing alone on the sidewalk.

SLOANE'S BODY PERFORMED the rote act of driving. His mind was elsewhere, working a puzzle that was increasing in its number of pieces and holes. The photograph in the newspaper stared up at him from the passenger seat.

Why did you pause? Why did you pause when Tina asked if you knew him?

He reconsidered the face, but his mind would not focus.

Click.

The image in his mind changed. He stood looking at the hole in his mailbox where the lock had once been. The doors on the other seven mailboxes remained shut. Locked.

Click.

He stood in his apartment with the police officer.

The lock was disengaged, not broken, the police officer had said.

Disengaged?

Someone knew what they were doing.

Click.

Sloane stood holding the lock to his mailbox, turning it over in his hand. It was unscratched.

The police officer had been talking about the lock on the front door to Sloane's apartment, but now Sloane realized he could have just as easily been talking about the lock on the mailbox. It, too, had been disengaged. It wasn't deferred maintenance. And that brought a whole other set of facts to consider. Whoever broke into his apartment had also broken into his mailbox. The two events were too similar, too close in time, to be coincidence. And if that was true, then that changed the motive, changed it completely. It wasn't some-one upset with him, someone looking to inflict as much damage as possible to his personal belongings.

Click.

In his mind's eye he stood amid the mess in his living room. The heating duct covers had been removed from the walls, the furniture torn open. They were looking for something.

Click.

He was holding the lock to his mailbox, the box empty. Something they thought would be in his mail.

Click.

Melda stood on his landing, handing him the bundle of envelopes. *Not too much this time. Just the bills and the junk.*

Click.

He sat in his office, flipping through the mail, stopping on the rust-orange package, the address handwritten. It was not all bills and junk.

Instinctively he looked to the floor of the passenger seat, then remembered that he'd left his briefcase in his office, after stuffing it with his mail. He looked for an exit, then stopped himself.

You're letting your imagination run wild. You don't know that it's anything but more junk mail. Probably one of those certificates for a free stay in Las Vegas or Palm Springs if you sit through a ninety-minute harangue about why owning a time-share is such a good deal.

He turned on the radio, but the music did not stop the thoughts that continued to turn each of the puzzle pieces, fitting the ends together, trying to create a coherent picture. Melda had not noticed the broken lock, which meant she'd emptied his mailbox before whoever broke it got there.

A terrible feeling flowered in the pit of his stomach. He looked at his watch, picked up his cell phone from the center console, and hit the speed dial. The telephone rang.

No answer.

It rang a second time.

No answer.

Third ring.

The answering machine clicked. He ended the call and looked at the time on the dashboard clock: 10:00. Bingo had been over for an hour. Melda should have been home.

MELDA DEMANJUK TURNED the key and pushed the handle. The door remained stubborn. The dead bolt. Frustrated, she removed the key and reinserted it in the newly installed lock, turned it, and listened for the click, as David had shown her. Then she slipped the key back into the door handle lock and jiggled it. Sometimes the teeth stuck. This time the doorknob turned freely.

She thought she had locked the dead bolt when she left for bingo, but her memory seemed to be getting worse each day. She must have forgotten. Now, returning home, she must have used the key to lock the bolt instead of unlocking it. She sighed. So much trouble because of others, so much aggravation.

Still, she managed a smile. She would not let it dampen her inner spirit. Not tonight. She'd won! Bingo. Her first time. When they called "B-5" she was so excited that "Bingo!" came out sounding like the yelp of a small dog someone had stepped on. The church gymnasium erupted in laughter, then applause, as she stood to collect the grand prize, $262.00. She cradled it in her purse like a small fortune. She already knew what she would buy with it. She would buy David the sweater she had seen in the store window in the mall. He had been so good to her, as good as any son.

She pushed open the door and flipped the light switch. The purse dropped at her feet. Both hands rose to cover her mouth in a silent scream. The mess pulled her across the threshold. Her collection of ceramic angels lay pulverized on the beige carpet. Pictures had been separated from their frames, her furniture ripped and torn. The destruction spilled into the kitchen; plates and cups scattered amid pots and pans and the contents of her refrigerator. Her freshly baked pie oozed cinnamon-spiced apples on the linoleum.

Her legs buckled, rubbery. She teetered against the kitchen counter, shaking as if struck by a sudden burst of cold air.

What to do? Dear God, what to do?

Fear engulfed her. She grabbed the heavy frying pan from the stove, clutching it to her chest like a priceless heirloom.

David. Get David.

She walked backward, stumbling on the debris until reaching the landing, turned and hurried to the stairs, climbing them a suddenly arduous task, like walking through deep snow. At the top landing she held on to the railing, winded, gasping for air, unable even to call out David's name as she pushed open his apartment door and stepped inside. He stood in the kitchen with his back to her. She caught her breath, about to speak.

Then he turned.

"You," she gasped.

22

CHARLES JENKINS KICKED the car door closed with the heel of his boot while juggling three bags of groceries and a fifty-pound sack of dog food. After putting the Arabians in the barn stalls for the night he had ventured into Stanwood for supplies. His kitchen wasn't exactly stocked for company, and Alex Hart might be here a while, at least until he figured out what was going on. If Joe Branick had instructed her to bring Jenkins the file, he had some indication that his life was in danger. Branick's death confirmed that suspicion. It also meant that both Hart and Jenkins were now in danger. Jenkins had lived the past thirty years in tranquillity because he and others believed the file had been destroyed. Its sudden reemergence changed things—for everyone.

The limbs of the cedars and hemlocks swayed overhead, a sure sign the wind on the island was kicking up, blowing off the sound in gusts as it frequently did at dusk this time of year. Neither Lou nor Arnold bothered to greet him. Man's best friend, my ass. Throw a woman in the mix and any sensible dog would desert quicker than an Iraqi soldier. No doubt he would find them following Alex Hart around the cottage like love-struck teenagers.

He didn't blame them.

The women he brought home usually smelled of Jim Beam and Marlboros and stayed just one night. Most were only curious. He remained an anomaly on the island, and not just because he was black and muscled and the stereotype persisted that such a big man must be hung like a donkey. When he had arrived on the island the community was tighter-knit than a family of Irish brothers. Rumors circulated about the black man who had bought the Wilcox farm. When Jenkins subsequently kept to himself the rumors became embellished. On those rare occasions when he did venture into town most people steered clear, though some of the local boys, fueled by a couple of bottles of courage, looked at him as a hunter might a prize buck. He walked away when he could, and ended it quickly when he couldn't. Word spread. He was let be, like an ornery old bull.

Before going into town he had showered and changed into a pair of black jeans, a button-down flannel shirt, and cowboy boots, the only pair of shoes he owned that weren't caked in mud. He even found a splash of aftershave.

He pushed open the back door with the heel of his boot, stepped into the kitchen, and dropped a bag. Fruit tumbled across the linoleum without obstruction—the plants were gone. The counter had also been cleared; the mason jars were neatly stacked in a corner, the blackberries and strawberries likely in the refrigerator. The salmon he had caught in the sound the day before lay gutted on a platter, stuffed with fresh vegetables from his garden.

He set the second bag of groceries on the counter, dropped the dog food on the floor, and walked into the living room.

"You didn't need to go to the store."

She had cleared the table of debris, covered it with a white sheet, and now stood setting plates and silverware around a bowl of green salad and tomatoes. The fire in the fireplace crackled, giving off the smell of fresh maple. Books had been replaced on shelves, the paintings neatly arranged. She had done more in an hour to make the place feel like home than he had done in thirty years.

"I'm sorry. I straightened up a bit. I shouldn't have." She stood gauging his reaction.

Unable to think of anything to say, he handed her the bottle of cabernet. "I didn't know we were having fish."

She put the bottle on the table, next to the bowl. "Everything is fresh. I can't believe the size of the tomatoes. What's your secret?"

"Huh?"

"The tomatoes—what's your secret?"

"A gardener never tells his secrets," he said, recovering slightly.

"I thought that was a magician."

"Could anyone but a magician grow tomatoes like that?"

She smiled, and her face lit up like a child watching fireworks on the Fourth of July. Jenkins walked back into the kitchen and held the corner of the tiled counter.

"I'm sorry. It wasn't my place to straighten up." She stood behind him in the doorway.

When he turned he could smell her breath, and it reminded him of the smell of warm caramel. He stepped back, bumped into the counter, and ended up doing an awkward pirouette, as if it had been intended, toward Lou and Arnold's dog bowls. "I better feed the hounds."

She leaned against the door frame, her head tilted slightly. "You seem to have a lot of secrets."

"Just because a man doesn't tell everyone his life story doesn't mean he's hiding anything, Alex." He spoke over the sound of pellets pinging in the aluminum dog bowls.

"I meant the tomatoes."

He put the sack down. "Oh."

"But now that you mention it, the IRS wouldn't be too happy with you."

"You going to report me?"

"I just might."

He picked up the dog bowls and tried to step past her, but the doorway was narrow and she made no effort to get out of his way. The light from the fire touched her cheek in a glow like a Midwest wheat field at sunset. He noticed the way her hair followed the curve of her jaw and flowed unimpeded to her shoulders. He had been wrong. She was not as beautiful as her mother. She was more beautiful. Was she flirting with him? It had been so long, he didn't know. The women in the bars usually had their hands on his crotch before they put down their long-neck Buds, yanking on him as if it were a rip cord to a life raft. He was out of practice in the art of subtlety, and—

And she was Robert Hart's daughter, the gangly kid riding her bicycle in front of the house.

"I better get Lou and Arnold some food."

She smiled. "I think you just did."

He looked down at the bowls. "Then I better find them. They're liable to start chewing on the furniture." He stepped past her.

Normally the pinging of the dog pellets in the bowls was like a call to arms, the two beasts nearly trampling each other and running over him in their rush. But not only weren't they stampeding, he did not find them in their customary spots or lying next to the fire.

"I thought you took them with you," she said.

He shook his head. "The two of them and food in the backseat of a car is not a good combination. They must be outside."

"I'll open the wine," she said.

He opened the front door and walked onto the small porch that looked across his property to the dairy farm. Sometimes when the Arabians ignored them, Lou and Arnold would slide under the barbed wire to bother the cows. Jenkins could make out the last of the herd heading undisturbed back to the barn. He put the bowls down and used two fingers to whistle a shrill cry, but the wind had picked up, a howling gust that swallowed the whistle before it left the porch. He walked out into the swaying stalks of tall grass, calling out their names. At nine-thirty on a Northwest summer night, the light of day was still fading, a blue-gray dusk that turned the grass into a sea of shadows. He saw no sign of either dog. That meant they were likely making a mess of themselves in the creek out the back door and, with the wind gusting, hadn't heard his car. He turned and started up the porch steps.

She had run his name through the IRS. How else could she have found him?

His past and present collided a split second before he heard the small crack—a snap like a dry tree limb that awakened his slumbering instincts. He dropped as if a trapdoor had opened beneath him, the aluminum bowls clattering, dog food spilling.

The first bullet broke past his right ear, splintering the door frame.

23

SLOANE EXITED from Highway 1 at Palmetto Avenue at an absurd seventy-five miles per hour and descended blind into the wall of pea-soup fog. Red lights flashed in front of him, and he hit the brakes hard, sending the Jeep skidding on the moist pavement. He corrected around the back of a car stopped at the intersection, checked for cross traffic, and punched the gas onto Beach Boulevard. A minute later he made a hard right into his building's gravel parking lot, stopping near a van parked parallel with the laurel hedge that separated the parking lot from the vacant lot. Road-weary travelers sometimes used the lot to save on a hotel bill. Sloane didn't care as long as they were quiet and didn't leave a mess. Tonight he didn't stop to lay down the ground rules.

He pushed out of the car and started across the lot in a light jog, his ankle sore from his extended run. The light was on in Melda's kitchen, but he did not see the top of her head. She was probably inside, cutting him a slice of pie. He took the stairs at the back of the building two at a time, feeling the pressure on his ankle, and hobbled down the landing. The door to her apartment was open, a bad sign. It got worse.

He stepped over the threshold, turning and spinning amid the mess and debris, feeling lost, panicked, and afraid.

The ceiling shook, and he looked up, the thought not immediately registering that it was his apartment. Someone was in his apartment. Someone on the move. Someone with footsteps too heavy to be a five-foot, hundred-pound old woman. He followed the sound across the ceiling, stepped out onto the landing, and leaned over the railing. The man on the second-floor landing walked purposefully away from Sloane's apartment. He wore navy-blue coveralls with an oblong patch on the back.

Pacific Bell. The telephone company.

"Hey! You!"

The man stopped, turned, his movements robotic. The gun materialized as if from thin air, surreal and foreign. Sloane froze as the gun swiveled across the man's body, and it registered that he was taking aim. Then instinct and training kicked in. He ducked beneath the landing, pressing his back against the wall, listening to the man's movements on the landing above him. There were staircases at each end of the building; the man could get to his van from either. Sloane heard him moving toward the staircase at the front of the building and slid down the landing toward the staircase at the back. He looked over his shoulder and watched the man quickly descend the first flight of stairs, grip the railing, and propel himself around the corner. Except that he didn't continue down the stairs. He wasn't going to the van. He was coming down the landing.

Sloane turned and hurried down the stairs, jumping the final four steps. His right ankle buckled on impact and he felt it roll, the searing pain instantaneous. He pulled himself to his feet. The landing above him shook. He swallowed the pain and hobbled through the darkened carport and the corridor that led to the back of the building.

He felt the wind and moisture of the fog blowing in off the ocean as he stepped from the back of the building. He paused and turned to look back down the corridor. The man's silhouette appeared as if at the other end of a tunnel. Then the shakes near Sloane's head exploded in splinters of wood that hit his face like a dozen needles. Sloane plunged into the fog and the darkness, his ankle turning on the uneven ground and ice plants, each step bringing pain. He changed direction frequently, crouching low, searching for a place to hide, finding none.

He kept moving away from the back of the building until his foot slipped and he fell to one knee. Somewhere beneath a thick layer of fog he heard the roar of the ocean breaking against rocks and felt the wind and spray on his face.

The ice plants had come to an abrupt end.

24

HE HURLED HIS body through the front door, shouting at her.

"Get down!"

Alex had been standing near the table, the bottle of wine in one hand, the corkscrew in the cork, when the plate-glass window exploded, the wine bottle shattered, and the potted orchids began flying like targets rung in a shooting gallery. The room swirled—glass and wood chunks caught in a tornado, books being blown off shelves, the wood paneling exploding with holes, rock dust spewing from the fire-place. They'd brought one hell of a lot of firepower, and they seemed determined not to go home with an unspent shell casing.

Jenkins slithered across the floor and pressed his back against the toppled table. Bullets chipped at it like a ticker tape gone haywire. Alex had her back pressed up against the wood, her white shirt a deep red, almost purple color, but the fact that she had managed to upend the table and pull a 9mm Glock from her briefcase was a pretty good indication that it was wine and not blood.

"Are you all right?" he shouted.

It was like yelling into the teeth of a storm.

"Can we get out the back?" She was as poised as she had been in the garden with a blade at her throat.

"They *want* us to go out the back. That's why they're hitting us from the front."

"Any locals likely to call it in?" she shouted back.

"With the wind blowing in off the sound, no one's close enough to hear it."

"Any idea who's out there?"

"I'm no rocket scientist, but I'd guess the same guys who killed Joe."

"So they want the file?" She nodded across the room, where she had moved the file to the chair near the fireplace.

"Again, no Stanford degree, but that would be my guess. Give me some cover?"

"What for?"

He nodded to the file.

"Leave it."

He shook his head. "Not this time, Alex." He got to his feet, crouching behind the table.

"Shit!" Alex got to one knee, realizing he was going with or without her. She got into a position to shoot. "My call," she said. Then, when the barrage paused: "Go!"

He broke for the chair as she rose up and squeezed off three shots, left to right, where the window had once been. It held them off for a second or two; then came another fury of bullets. The La-Z-Boy would provide Jenkins with little cover. From a prone position on the floor, file in hand, he looked back over his shoulder at her, waited until she rose up again, and dashed back across the floor as she fired three more well-placed shots.

"I am seriously low on bullets." She pressed her back against the wood as the barrage started again. "What the hell is it?"

"If we make it out of here, I'll tell you over dinner and another bottle of cabernet."

"Can't drink it," she said. "The sulfates give me a headache."

"Hope I have the chance to remember that. We'll drink good Scotch, in honor of your father."

"You buying?" Alex asked.

"Unless you tell me chivalry died during the last thirty years." He nodded to the door to the hallway. "My guns are in the bedroom."

She shook her head. "You can't get to it. It's too far, and I don't have enough bullets to cover you. Better to stay down."

"Don't have a choice," he said. "You can't hold them off forever. They'll tear this house apart quicker than termites. Besides, if they have that much firepower—"

The flash erupted, followed by a percussive blast that ripped the front door off its hinges and sent it flying across the room, knocking over bookcases. Thick smoke billowed from a canister rolling across the room. Jenkins scurried across the floor and shuffled it back out the gaping hole, burning his hand in the process, then used the cloud of smoke and the maze of books as the cover he needed to get to his bedroom. He flung open the closet door, grabbed the shotgun in the corner, and broke the barrel. One round in one of the barrels. He grabbed for the box of shells on the shelf, but it collapsed in his hand. Empty. He hurled clothes and shoes, looking for errant shells, and found one more. At a momentary lull in the fireworks he heard Alex again return fire—well-spaced shots to conserve ammunition but continue to give whoever was in the field further pause before rushing the house.

He slid on the floor to his nightstand and retrieved his Smith & Wesson. The clip was empty. He looked for the extra magazines, did not immediately find them, then recalled last seeing them in the trunk of his car, when he'd driven into the woods for some target practice. He found four loose .40-caliber bullets in the back of the nightstand drawer.

That was it.

A blast shattered the window over his bed, and the room quickly filled with the same acrid ammonia smell. He grabbed a shirt from the floor and crawled into the bathroom, holding his breath. He turned on the faucet. It was dry. They had cut off the water. He dipped the cloth in the toilet bowl and held it over his mouth and nose, trying to breathe. His throat was constricting, and his eyes burned as if they were on fire. He crawled back into the living room, ripped the dampened shirt, and handed half to Alex. She tied it over her nose and mouth.

"Any other exits?" she asked.

"You mean like a secret passage under the property?"

"That would be convenient."

"Sorry."

"You have any ideas?"

"Try not to breathe."

Flames burst in the hallway; the gas had reached the furnace pilot light. They didn't have much time. Loaded with the old newspapers and books, the cottage would go up like balsa wood. Flames leaped from the bedroom.

He handed her the shotgun. She shoved the Glock in her pants at the small of her back. He loosened the belt on his jeans and shoved the file in the front of his pants, covering it with his shirt. "When we get outside, head to your left. There's a path through the woods. It leads to a barn. It's about fifty yards, but the woods and brush are thick and will provide some cover."

"What are you going to do?"

"Clear us a path."

"Okay, but tell me how we're going to get outside if they're waiting by the back door."

"We're not going out the back door."

She looked at him as if he were crazy.

"You ever see *Butch Cassidy and the Sundance Kid*, Alex?"

"No."

He leaned his back against the table, pulled out the bullets from his pocket, released the clip on the pistol, and pushed in the .40-caliber slugs. "You've never seen *Butch Cassidy and the Sundance Kid*? It's a classic."

She looked at the spreading flames. "Can we critique my knowledge of movie trivia some other time?"

"There's a scene where Butch and Sundance are holed up in a barn in South America. They don't know it, but about ten thousand *federales* have amassed out front, waiting to kill them."

"You're not giving me any comfort."

"The point is, they go right out the front door because it's the least likely exit they expect them to take."

"Do they make it?"

Jenkins slapped the magazine in the handle. "The ending's not important. I just like the reasoning."

"Terrific. What are we going to use for cover?"

"Good question—a tree."

He shoved the .40 into his pants, spit into his hands, and gripped the base of the table. "Move on three."

"You can't lift that."

"Who do you think carried it in—Lou and Arnold? When we reach the window put a blast straight out, dead center. Let it rip. Give 'em something to consider."

He squatted like a weight lifter in a dead lift. "Three."

The muscles in his legs pressed his jeans taut, and he grunted like an angry bear. The table slowly rose from the floor, and he plunged forward, bull-rushing the gaping hole in the wall where the window had been. Alex shot a blast from the 12-gauge, turned left, and ran into the woods. Jenkins dropped the table, rolled, raised up with the pistol, and fired two shots at points where he thought the shooters had been before, then followed her into the thick grove of trees. The fifty yards to the barn looked to be a mile . . . 150 feet . . . 120 feet . . . Behind him he heard the rush and howl of the wind. Something buzzed his ear; it wasn't a mosquito. He caught her at a hundred feet, the two running side by side, hurdling branches, picking up their feet on the uneven ground like soldiers doing an exaggerated march. Damned if they weren't going to make it—

His foot caught. His body pitched forward. He hit the ground, yelling at her to keep running, rolled to a sitting position, and shot twice in the direction of the caretaker's shack, though it was too dark to see anyone coming. Scrambling to his knees, he put his hand down to stand and felt the thin, warm coat.

Lou.

The dog's tongue hung from his mouth in a frothy foam, his face a frozen mask of anguish and pain. His eyes had rolled to their whites, his lips stretched as if baring his teeth. His stomach had bloated to grotesque proportions. Next to him, partially hidden in thistle bushes and blackberry bramble, lay Arnold.

Jenkins crawled to his dogs, cradling their heads to his chest. "Oh, no. No, no, no."

"Come on. Come on." Alex stood over him, pulling him. "There's nothing you can do."

He looked up from the ground, screaming into the wind. "Goddamn it, Joe! Goddamn them!"

"Come on, Charlie."

A branch snapped. A chunk of wood ripped from the trunk inches from his head. Alex cried out and dropped like a bag of flour. Jenkins shook the memory, grabbed the shotgun, and shot the final blast at an approaching shadow. Then he scrambled to his feet, threw Alex over his shoulder, and started for the barn, carrying her like a fifty-pound sack of dog food. Thirty feet . . . He waited to get hit in the back . . . His legs churned. Twenty feet . . . He braced for the bullet . . . ten feet . . . He pulled open the barn door and ducked inside, chunks of wood flying as he did. He lowered Alex behind bales of hay, catching his breath. The chickens clucked and flew about in a blur of feathers. The Arabians thumped at their stall doors, shaking their heads in wild snorts.

Jenkins examined her shirt. The splattered wine stains made it difficult to determine where she had been hit, but he saw the rip in the cloth by her right arm.

"Can you grip my waist?"

"What?"

"Can you hold on to me?"

"I think so. Why?"

He tried to smile. "I don't imagine you ever saw John Wayne in *True Grit*?"

"No, but tell me it ended better for him than Butch and Sundance."

He grabbed a rope from a hook on a post, fashioned a loop through the slipknot, and opened a stall door. The white Arabian whinnied and reared, wild-eyed. Jenkins slipped the rope over its nose and around its neck, then managed to slip a halter over the horse's head. He threw the lead over its neck and clipped it to the other side to make reins. It would have to do.

Alex got to her feet, holding her arm. Jenkins led the horse from the stall, letting it prance, turning it in tight circles to calm it. He stepped onto a stump and swung his leg over the animal's back. Confused and agitated, it kicked and shook its head, but he squeezed with all the strength in his legs and continued to jerk it in a tight circle while ducking beneath the overhead support beams.

"Step up," he said.

Alex stepped up onto the stump, and he pulled her up behind him.

"So what happened?" she asked.

"What?"

"In *True Grit*—what happened?"

"Just keep your head down and hold on."

"I knew I wasn't going to like this."

He put the rope in his teeth, grabbed the Smith & Wesson with his right hand and the Glock in his left, and kicked the horse hard toward the barn door.

25

DIRT CASCADED OVER the top of Sloane's head and trickled down the collar of his shirt. He lowered his chin to his chest and closed his eyes, letting the tiny avalanche pass over him. He clung to the side of the cliff, perhaps twenty-five feet from the top. Above him, the man walked the edge.

The pounding surf had chipped away at the sandstone and rock like the mother of all jackhammers, leaving the upper half hanging out like a bad overbite. It and the thick fog became Sloane's refuge. Even if the man were to lie on his stomach to look out over the edge, he would not be able to see Sloane. Whoever he was, he'd have to assume that Sloane had taken his chances in the icy waters of the Pacific Ocean or evaded him in the dark. The immediate question was how long the man would wait to be certain. Sloane couldn't hang on forever. His ankle burned with a cold fire, and the muscles in his legs and arms, no longer as strong or durable as they had been when he climbed regularly, were already beginning to twitch—the first sign of muscle fatigue. Failure imminent. He did his best to shift his weight and alternate his grip to give the muscles respite while trying to maintain three points of contact with the wall. Beads of sweat, mixed with the damp salt air, trickled into his eyes, stinging them.

More dirt fell from above.

And even if his arms and legs held out, there was no guarantee the ledge would. The crevices he gripped had the consistency of chalk. With the ocean's persistent pounding, the sandstone was known to give way suddenly. Winter storms led to dramatic television footage of entire backyards slipping into the Pacific in a matter of seconds.

Sloane counted to himself: keeping track of the minutes, a trick he'd learned to keep his mind focused. When he reached seven minutes he knew it was as long as he could wait and still have enough strength to climb back up. In the dark, with a bad ankle, the wind howling, and his body chilled from the moist cold, the process would be laborious. He had to be certain of each hold before transferring his full weight. The potential consequences of a mistake demanded that he not rush.

He gripped a branch, found a notch for his foot, tested it, and stepped out. The notch gave way—his right foot dangling. He kicked at the wall until feeling another toehold, then took a moment. His chest beat furiously against his rib cage. Below him the rhythmic hush of the ocean inhaled and exhaled with each powerful surge, like a dying man sucking on a respirator.

Sloane shifted his weight, found another hold, and stepped up. His ankle pulsed, but he willed himself to ignore it, concentrating, like a chess player, on two and three moves ahead. Going back was not an option.

After twenty minutes he had reached the edge. If he was wrong and the man remained, he was dead. He paused and reached up, expecting a pair of shoes to step on his fingers and send him falling backward into the foam and fog. When they didn't, he lifted his head over the side and pulled himself over the edge, keeping low to the ground. He searched the shadows and wind-blown fog for anything out of place. Seeing nothing, he rose to his feet and limped back to the building and through the corridor, emerging in the carport with a view of the gravel parking lot.

The van was gone.

His thoughts turned to Melda.

Why wasn't she in her apartment? If she had come home from bingo to find her apartment destroyed, she would have gone only to one person. Sloane.

And that was where the man had been.

He leaned on the metal railing, using it like a cane to pull himself up the staircase, and hobbled down the landing. The door to his apartment remained open.

"Melda?"

Her cast-iron skillet lay on the counter.

"Melda?"

She was not in the kitchen or the main room. He hurried into the bedroom, stumbling over debris, and turned on the light. The shoe lay on its side, outside the closed bathroom door. White, soft-soled. Melda's shoe.

"Melda?"

Sloane never closed the bathroom door. His immediate neighbor was the ocean. With his pulse beating in his ears, he reached for the handle of the door. If there was a God, let the room be empty. He turned the handle, pushed open the door. The wedge of light swept over the linoleum, widening like the sun passing over a sundial, and came to a stop on the figure slumped against the porcelain tub. It was an almost serene image. Then Sloane flipped the switch, and the light brought unspeakable horror. Melda lay in a pool of blood, her head pitched backward, her throat a gaping hole.

Sloane's feet felt anchored to the floor; his hands twisted with anger, despair, and uncertainty.

"No," he cried softly. Then the agony burst from his throat in a torrent of rage. "Noooooooo!"

He stumbled forward to his knees, crawling to her, clutching her to his chest.

No. No. No.

"Breathe," he pleaded. "Please breathe."

Please. Breathe. Please breathe.

He lowered her to the floor, tilted her head back, and cupped her mouth with his own, blowing, pressing on her chest, all reason now lost and buried.

"One, two, three, four, five."

One breath, five thrusts.

His breath escaped through her neck like air from a hole in a tire.

"Three, four, five."

No. God, no . . .

Again. Blow. "Three, four, five."

Again. Again. The room blurred in white flickering lights.

"Two, three, four . . ."

The voice grew faint.

Darkness enveloped him, pulling on him like a weight tied to his ankles. He sank. The light faded. Pain exploded across his forehead and temples, plunging him further into darkness, alone, the only sound the fading of his own voice, a tape running low on batteries. "One . . . two . . . three . . ."

Then it, too, faded. And he was gone.

26

❧

HIS DESIRE TO punish those who had killed his dogs urged him to steer the horse down the narrow path, guns blazing like Rooster Cogburn—John Wayne—riding across the open field in the climax to *True Grit*. But this was not a movie, and in real life the good guys died. Jenkins turned the horse away from the barn and kicked it hard up the path, using one arm to protect his face from low-hanging branches. Behind him he felt Alex Hart's head against his back. She kept a tight grip around his waist. The brush cleared at the asphalt road. He stopped in the trees, considering the road for a moment, hoping that their attackers had not anticipated this path of retreat. Then he urged the horse across it, deeper into the darkness on the other side.

After ten minutes of hard riding, with the Arabian snorting white puffs in the cool night air, Jenkins slowed the animal to cross a small creek bed that emptied into the sound a mile downstream. He pushed the horse up a steep hillside, letting it find its footing, and looked down on the cottage, a tepee of fire. Dismounting, he tethered the animal to a tree and eased Alex to the ground, putting her back against a tree. She grimaced when he ripped the sleeve off her blouse to examine her arm.

She'd been lucky. The bullet had ricocheted off the tree and grazed her biceps. She'd have a scar, but she'd live. The wound was already clotting.

He used his teeth to tear strips of cloth. "We need to get you to a doctor," he said between clenched teeth.

"You going to ride the horse in?"

He ripped another strip and wrapped her arm. "This doesn't involve you, Alex."

"It does now."

He made a knot and applied another strip. "This is a surface wound. These wounds cut a lot deeper and have been bleeding since you were riding your bike in the front yard of your parents' home."

She pushed him away and struggled to her feet. "Well, I'm not riding my bike anymore. And I'm not a little girl, Charlie. So why don't you just let *me* take care of me."

She was stubborn, like her father. He stood from his crouch. "You make it personal, Alex, and you'll end up getting killed."

"What are *you* going to make it?"

He turned, looking down at the farm. From the distance it looked as peaceful as a campfire. "They killed my dogs," he said, the realization sinking in. "I was willing to let it all go. They took my career, my life, but I was willing to let it go." He turned his head to look at her, his voice taut with emotion, anger. "They made it personal."

"We're both in this now; neither of us has a choice. We need to be smart."

For a long moment they sat in silence, hearing the stream in the distance and the occasional gust of wind through the trees.

"Where did you go, Charlie? Where did you go back there? You looked up at me like you were a million miles away."

He didn't answer her.

"You called me 'Joe.'"

For the first few years the image of the woman had haunted him every night. Jack Daniel's and Southern Comfort helped pass the days. If he got drunk enough he could make it through a night, sometimes a week, but the memories of what had happened, of what he had been a participant in, were always there, as permanent as Mount Rainier on the southern horizon—dormant, but capable of erupting any moment. When the booze no longer helped him to forget, he quit cold turkey. He didn't need intervention or crisis counseling. He didn't need AA. He wasn't an alcoholic. He was just a man trying to forget a nightmare. He didn't even pour the whiskey down the drain to avoid temptation. It had sat in his cabinet, untouched—until tonight.

"What's in that file, Charlie?"

He looked at her, then back to the fires burning in the valley below. "A lot of bad memories," he said. "Too many."

27

The burst of light blinded him, the door exploding in a shower of needled splinters, shaking the room. The percussive blast propelled him from the bed like a man being tossed from a boat in a storm. Slipping over the side, he clutched at the covers, pulling them over him as he fell into the gap, his body wedged between the wall and the heavy wood frame. He couldn't move. Smoke tormented his lungs, burned his eyes, blurred his vision. The blast had deadened all sounds but for the ringing in his ears.

The floor beneath him shook again, people running into the room.

She fell to the ground, her face parallel with his own. A spray of blood spattered the dirt floor. He watched, helpless, as she flailed at the arms striking her, as if warding off a swarm of bees, until pain and instinct forced her to a fetal position. When the blows slowed the woman pushed to her knees, gasping, her body convulsing. Blood trickled from the corner of her mouth and one nostril. She raised her head, contemplating those who stood over her, then spat at their boots.

The beating began again. They ripped the clothes from her body, leaving her naked and exposed, and forced her onto her back. One after the next they climbed on top of her until she no longer fought them, no longer resisted. A gloved hand pulled her from the floor by a tuft of hair, her body dangling limp as a rag doll, her right eye swollen shut, her lip split. Her left eye shifted, finding him for one brief moment beneath the bed.

The blade arced, catching the flickering light of the moon before it sliced the darkness like a sickle through wheat.

No!"

This time no echo rang in his ears. No ghostly wail haunted him. Sloane struggled to sit up, felt pressure across his chest, and realized he could not move his arms or legs. A bright light blinded him, an orb of white. He started to panic, then heard someone calling to him by name.

"Mr. Sloane. Mr. Sloane, can you hear me?"

The light receded, leaving an aura of black and white spots that gave way to blurred images. He sensed someone standing over him, calling to him.

"Mr. Sloane?"

The images came into focus. A woman leaned over him, her face unfamiliar, round and flat, like a puffer fish when provoked, her eyes set behind thick plastic-framed glasses— a strange octagon shape and too large for her face.

"Mr. Sloane?"

The room was foreign, stark white but for a mauve drape that muted light from a window. A chair the color of the drape sat unused in the corner. He looked down at a red nylon strap across his chest. Similar straps bound his wrists. Though he could not see his ankles beneath the thin white sheet, the pressure told him they, too, were bound. A clear plastic tube ran from an IV bag suspended on a metal stand, to a needle in the crook of his right arm.

This was not his apartment . . . not his room.

"You all right?"

Now a different voice, a man's voice. Sloane turned his head. The images blurred and slid like time-lapse photography, coming to a stop on a black man standing in the room, one hand holding open the door. Fluorescent lights glistened off his shaved pate. He wore a plain tie and a gray suit.

"I thought I heard a scream."

The woman walked toward him. "I'm fine, Detective. Please wait outside."

"Is he awake?"

"I'm evaluating him. I'll advise you when I feel he's capable of talking."

"He looks alert to me."

"Detective Gordon, I'll be the judge of that."

The man shrugged, resigned. "I'll get another cup of coffee," he said, and let the door shut behind him.

The woman returned to the foot of the bed. "Mr. Sloane? Can you hear me?"

Sloane nodded. Her face shifted up and down until he squeezed his eyes shut and reopened them.

"Are you having trouble with your vision?"

"Blurry."

"I'm Dr. Brenda Knight. Do you know where you are?"

He shook his head, and her image bounced like a television picture that had lost its vertical hold.

"You're in the hospital," she said.

His mind connected the room's sparse furnishings, but things remained disproportionate, off-kilter, like a bad *Alice in Wonderland* movie. "How . . ." His throat felt as if it had been rubbed raw with sandpaper. Dr. Knight picked up a plastic cup from a side table and lifted the straw to his mouth. Tepid water burned the back of his throat. He winced, and she pulled the straw from his lips. His head fell back against the pillows.

"What happened to me? How did I get here?" he asked. The words pulsed in his forehead.

"An ambulance brought you in last night."

"Last night?"

"It's morning, Mr. Sloane."

He looked again to the mauve drape and realized that the muted light was daylight. Morning. The last thing he remembered was standing on the sidewalk with Tina, waiting for a cab to take her home.

"Was I in some sort of accident? What happened to me? Why am I strapped down?"

The doctor pulled an ophthalmoscope from her coat, clicked it on, and pulled back one of his eyelids, talking to him as she did. The light shot daggers of pain across the top of his skull. He grimaced and shook free.

She clicked off the light, snapped it to the front pocket of her coat, and folded her arms, studying him.

"Do you remember anything about last night, Mr. Sloane?"

"Not really."

"Try. Tell me what you can remember."

He focused on the wall across the room, his mind blank. He started to say, "Nothing," when the images began to flip like cards in a deck, slowly at first, then more quickly. He saw the mug shot in the newspaper. Joe Branick. Tina handed him the pink message slip, the name scrawled in ink. Joe Branick. His mailbox, the metal door swinging open. The mess in his apartment. The man walking on the landing, turning to him. The gun in his hand. Running. Stumbling across the ice plants, slipping at the edge of the cliff. Dirt cascading over him.

Melda. He remembered, something had happened to Melda. His apartment. Melda's skillet. Her shoe on the floor near . . . the bathroom door.

Melda.

"Oh, no." He closed his eyes.

"Mr. Sloane?"

The man held the woman upright by a tuft of hair, blood oozing from her nose and mouth.

"Mr. Sloane?"

The light flickered. The blade arced.

"Mr. Sloane . . . Mr. Sloane!"

A heavy weight dropped onto his chest, driving the breath from his lungs. He sank into the darkness. The voice above him grew distant. The light faded. "Mr. Sloane . . . Mr. . . . ."

He descended into darkness, to the woman now lying in a pool of blood. She was young. Her hair, a rich dark brown, covered a portion of her face. He knelt down and pushed the strands from her cheeks. It was not Melda. It was not Emily Scott. A sharp pain pierced his chest, a wound that radiated throughout his being.

Breathe. Please breathe.

Her legs were bent at the knees and tucked beneath her. Her head, twisted awkwardly over her shoulder, revealed a gaping wound. He pulled her to him. Tears flooded his eyes and flowed down his cheeks. His fault. It was his fault.

He sensed that he was no longer alone, and looked up to find two men towering over him: a black man, as tall and big as anyone he'd ever seen, stood beside a white man, hair dripping water down his face, breathing heavily, though not like one might after running a long distance. It was labored, choking back emotion, anger. Sloane looked into the man's face, and though it was a contorted mask of grief, it was somehow familiar.

He felt himself slipping away again, looking down at the two men and at himself as he floated above them, rising to the surface like a diver who has slipped from his weight belt, struggling against the buoyancy, unable to stay down. The dark depths gave way to flickering light. The voice returned.

"Mr. Sloane?"

He breached the surface, gasping for air, unable to catch his breath, heart thumping.

"Mr. Sloane? Can you hear me?"

He closed his eyes, wanting to go back down, to see the two men again, unable to descend.

"Mr. Sloane?"

Then, just as suddenly as Sloane had sunk to a place he did not know, the man who had been at the bottom, the one somehow familiar to him, breached the surface of Sloane's reality, bringing a startling revelation.

28

Highway 5,
Brownsville, Oregon

A SHARP PAIN radiated a trail of fire down his spine
from his neck to a searing point between his shoulder
blades. After six hours of driving, Jenkins felt like a pretzel.
His lower back ached. His left knee cracked when he bent
it—arthritis from an injury he couldn't even recall. With his
mother's youthful looks and a body that showed no outward
sign of deserting him, Jenkins sometimes forgot that he was
fifty-two years old. When he looked in the mirror the face surprised him; he still felt thirty—except at moments like this.

For the first two hours he had watched the rear and side
mirrors, but there were few cars on the highway; he would
have detected anyone following them. No one was. Alex
remained asleep, her leather jacket serving as a pillow
against the passenger seat window, her body twitching
from an over-the-counter painkiller—two Motrin washed
down with two beers, picked up at a convenience store.
Her arm would be sore.

Jenkins drove through Oregon on a barren desert stretch of Highway 5. The horizon burned in the distance with the approach of dawn like a windswept fire. It colored the brick-red dirt a rust orange and caused the glacier-carved mountains to glow like huge bonfires. It made him think of his home, and of Lou and Arnold.

He and Alex had waited until the flames died. Someone on the island had seen the fire and called the fire department. It took them better than three hours to put out the blaze. Alex had urged him not to go back to the farm, but he would not leave the dogs to rot in the woods, food for the coyotes and other animals. He buried them near the creek. It felt like the right place—they liked to run through the water—but he had not had enough time to pick out all the twigs and rocks cluttering their graves, and that continued to bother him. He'd also had no time to mourn them. He grabbed a handful of dirt, doing his best to remember a prayer he had learned by sheer osmosis sitting for hours in a Baptist church Sunday mornings.

"From ashes you came. To ashes you shall return," he said, letting the soil sift through his fingers and scatter in the wind. "Ashes to ashes and dust to dust."

They deserved that much. They deserved more. Someday, if he ever returned, he'd stack stones there, plant a tree or a rhododendron, something to grow from their memories. The finality of the thought caused the sadness to well inside him. He pictured them bounding to their deaths, tails wagging, never suspecting the inhumanity that men could inflict. Charles Jenkins knew. He'd seen inhumanity firsthand, and thirty years wasn't going to erase that memory, either.

His blue nylon windbreaker captured the heat steaming off his body. His shirt clung to his skin like cellophane wrap. He wiped the sweat and moisture pouring from his hair into his eyes. Dawn brought broken slits of sunlight filtering through gaps in the thick canopy of trees and vines, along with an almost serene quiet.

Too quiet.

He sensed an uneasiness in the jungle, an unnatural silence that comes when a predator has scared away or killed every living thing capable of movement.

He pushed through the thick foliage into a clearing—and a horror he had witnessed just once before, in Vietnam.

Smoke and ash hung thick in the stagnant air, rising from the embers, burning his throat and nostrils with the smell of charcoal and a sweet odor he had hoped never to smell again. Small fires smoldered where shacks once stood, an occasional flame bursting from the destruction, crackling and hissing at him like an angry snake disturbed from its rest. It was the only sound beneath the deafening canopy. Even the animals mourned in silence.

Jenkins dropped to one knee from exhaustion and grief, sick with anger. Behind him he heard the rustle of the plants, the fall of footsteps, and the heavy breathing of a man struggling to catch up. Joe Branick came through the foliage and stopped as if approaching the edge of a cliff. Whatever words formed in his mind stopped just as suddenly. Mouth agape, Branick stared at the carnage of bodies—in the doorways where the structures no longer existed, and along the roads and hillsides to which the villagers had fled in a desperate and futile attempt to escape.

They had been hunted and shot like animals. Slaughtered. Men and women.

Children.

Jenkins bent over and threw up, a yellowish spew that became violent dry heaves. He sat up, wiping the spittle from the corners of his mouth, spitting, the acidic burn lingering in his throat.

"They killed the men first," he said, his voice a whisper. "Center-mass and head shots. Kill shots. They let them run and used them like targets."

"Jesus," Branick whispered. Then he made the sign of the cross.

Jenkins stood and walked forward into the carnage. "They bound the women, tortured some, certainly raped others. Some they killed still holding on to their children."

The pattern became clear to him. Those children still clutching their parents in a fierce embrace were young girls. "They separated the boys," he said, and turned and hurried through the village, Branick following.

The one-room building near the large, flat stone had been badly charred but somehow remained standing, saved perhaps by the heavy rain and sodden air, or by other forces he did not want to consider. The door had been blown from its hinges, an act designed not to gain entry—a decent kick would have splintered the cheap wood—but to cause confusion and panic.

Jenkins ducked below the threshold into the room. A single body lay in the dirt, and despite the slaughter outside, seeing the woman on the floor, hideously battered and disfigured, alone, separated from the others, made the horror more personal and inconceivable.

The confirmation of what Jenkins had suspected forced his hands into fists of rage. The anger lodged in his throat, choking him with fury, agony, and a guilt that beat him to his knees with the force of sledgehammer blows.

"Charlie. Come on. Come on." Joe Branick stood above him, urging him toward the door.

"Goddamn them, Joe!" he said. "Goddamn them."

ALEX STIRRED AND winced in pain, but she did not wake.

Jenkins studied her in the pale light of the dashboard, wondering again whether Joe would have endangered the daughter of Robert Hart. She said they had been tracking right-wing guerrilla organizations that could impede an agreement requiring Mexico to reopen its oil market to foreign interests. That was likely true, but that wasn't why Joe was dead. Joe had left the answer to that question in Charles Jenkins's file.

He was dead because of David Allen Sloane.

29

$\backsim$

D R. BRENDA KNIGHT had removed the straps that bound Sloane's chest and ankles but not the ones that kept his wrists six inches from the side of the bed. Hospital protocol would not allow it, she said, unless he was put into the locked ward, which he did not want. Sloane knew there was more to Knight's decision than protocol. She thought he was either nuts or dangerous. With the police continuing to hold a vigil outside his door, waiting to talk with him, it was a logical conclusion. He could think only of Melda, of holding her tiny frame, lifeless in his arms. Sadness overwhelmed him. Then he would grow angry.

Who would do such a thing? Who would kill a sweet old woman?

And what of his dream? Had it been a dream or had it been something more, some type of premonition? Had he seen Melda's death? Had he somehow predicted it? Was it like the power he felt in the courtroom?

Alone in his hospital room, he felt the same guilt, that he was somehow responsible. The thought made him numb, lethargic. Then he would think of the man who killed her, and the anger burned.

Despite her unwillingness to allow him to speak to the police, Dr. Knight had been extremely interested in Sloane's vital signs, and he sensed from her questioning that something there was unique and fascinated her. She told him the police had found him in his apartment, clinging to Melda's lifeless body, moaning in agony. When they approached, Sloane had ignored their commands. When they tried to separate him from Melda he resisted. Then, just as suddenly, in the midst of the ensuing struggle, he had collapsed, his limbs flaccid. When he did not respond the police had brought him to the emergency room. The doctor on call examined him, could find nothing physically wrong with him, but could not wake him. He called Knight at home, and she admitted him. He now sat in a private room.

Knight had given him a two-milliliter injection of Ativan in the arm, telling him it would help him to relax. The drug was beginning to make everything dull. His head felt heavy against the pillows. His arms and legs tingled, as if he were sinking into a too-hot bath. He closed his eyes and saw the face of the man he had pulled from the depths of his memory. The features were younger, more distinct, not yet softened by age, but it was the same face as the one in the newspaper.

Joe Branick.

Somehow, somewhere, they had met, and that meant that the woman whose death he suffered through every morning was neither a premonition nor a dream. She was real, and Joe Branick, a White House confidant, had been there, too. Branick had also left Sloane a telephone message just a day before someone broke into Sloane's mailbox and trashed his apartment and, according to the newspaper article, just hours before police found Branick dead in a national park in West Virginia, an apparent suicide. If there was any doubt these events were related, it was erased when the telephone repairman came back. There was no other reason to search Melda's apartment except to look for Sloane's mail. In his mind's eye Sloane saw the rust-orange envelope, his name handwritten on the front. Joe Branick had tried to call him. Was it any more absurd to conclude that he had also sent Sloane a package?

Sloane grew tired, the sedative increasing in intensity. He saw a duck, a yellow plastic duck, floating on the surface of a body of water—a kid's bathtub toy. He felt himself drifting, floating, eyes heavy . . . a sleeping duck . . . a sitting duck.

The man had not continued down the stairs to his van. He had not tried to get away. He had come down the landing, gun in hand.

He had come to kill Sloane.

Sloane opened his eyes. The foreboding sensation he had felt so strongly in the mountains, the knowing certainty that someone was stalking him, enveloped him. The man could have turned and left. He had chosen instead to come for Sloane.

And he would come again.

Sloane looked down at the red nylon straps binding his wrists.

A sitting duck.

30

～

Highway 5,
Dunsmuir, California

ALEX SLID ONTO the cherry-red vinyl seat in the booth at the back of the diner. They had driven through Washington and Oregon without stopping. After nine hours Jenkins had conceded to their bladders and hunger pangs when the roadside diner appeared like an oasis in a desert. At minutes after noon the temperature outside was approaching ninety-eight degrees. Having grown accustomed to the Pacific Northwest's mild climate, one that rarely exceeded eighty degrees, Jenkins felt as though he had driven into a furnace.

"Sore?" he asked.

She felt the bandage beneath her shirt. "My shoulder is fine. My head's killing me. I feel like I have a hangover. Where did you get that remedy, anyway?"

"My grandfather liked to say enough beer cured any ailment."

"I feel like someone hit me with a two-by-four." She let out a breath of air and shook the cobwebs from her head. Then she pointed to his hand. "Arthritis?"

He had been flexing his fingers to relieve the stiffness in the joints. It was worse the day after he worked in the garden.

"My hand just fell asleep." He folded them in his lap. He considered arthritis an old man's disease.

"My father used to do the same thing," she said, smiling.

A young woman in a pink-and-white-striped uniform set two Cokes in old-fashioned glasses on the table, along with two straws, the paper partly torn off. Jenkins ordered a sandwich; Hart, a salad to go. He ignored the straw, drinking from the glass. A rare deviation from his diet, the Coke tasted as sweet as maple syrup, but this morning he needed the sugar and the caffeine. He turned his head to stretch his neck and watched a young man dressed in a thick army fatigue jacket hitchhiking along the side of the road—perhaps another ghost from the 1960s, a decade no longer willing to let him be.

"Vietnam," he said to himself.

"Vietnam?"

He looked back at Alex. She had her hair pulled back with a tie, revealing the soft line of her neck, the straw in her mouth. He hesitated to think it, but she looked like a little girl.

"Little skirmish in Southeast Asia slightly before your time," he said.

She gave him a patronizing smile.

"I was just thinking I haven't been in weather this hot since Vietnam," he said.

She drank from the straw. "You don't look that old."

"Thanks."

She winked at him. "Were you drafted?"

"I volunteered," he said. "Seemed like the right thing at the time, fighting for my country. Too many of my friends didn't have that option. I was eighteen when I stepped off the plane in-country at Da Nang, and middle-aged when I stepped back on American soil thirteen months later. The last two days there were the scariest moments of my life. I was sure I was going to die. It took me thirty-eight hours of flying and driving to get back home to New Jersey, and I promptly fell asleep on my parents' couch smoking a cigarette and nearly burned to death."

"How did you end up working for the Agency?"

He put his hands on the table, playing with the paper from the straw, rolling it between his fingers into a ball. "Two months after I got home I could still feel the stares of the people on the street and in the mall. People I'd known most of my life suddenly were looking at me differently, and I saw them differently, too. Things were not the same, and they never would be again. I didn't fit in, and they didn't want me there, a visual reminder that young men— good young men—were dying over there and they were too busy going about their day to give a damn. Then two guys showed up on my porch, asking me if I might be interested in government service. I figured they weren't talking about the French Foreign Legion. Since I wasn't employed and had no immediate prospects, I thought, what the hell? I had to do something to get the hell out of there."

"Recruiters?"

"They'd already run a complete background check on me."

"Before you said yes—why?"

"They were in a hurry and they were looking for someone fluent in Spanish and tactically trained."

She nodded. *"Tu hablas español."*

"Not very well any longer."

"That's how you ended up in Mexico City."

"My first foreign assignment."

"And that's where you met Joe?"

"Yeah," he said, turning and watching the hitchhiker continue down the road, the asphalt shimmering ghostly waves all around him. "That's where I met Joe."

She seemed to consider this for a moment, then asked, "Why Mexico City?"

"Ironically, because of what was happening in the Middle East. That was right about the time that the Saudis were realizing that the value of their oil exceeded just billions of dollars and that they could use it to assert influence on the world political stage. The royal family began to make not-so-veiled threats that if the United States did not withdraw its support of Israel, Saudi Arabia would nationalize its petroleum industry, just like Mexico. That kind of talk makes a lot of wealthy stockholders nervous, and since they are largely responsible for putting presidents in office, things usually begin happening. Nixon tried a strong hand at first and told the Saudis to pound sand. No pun intended. The Saudis responded in kind, raising the price of a barrel of oil seventy percent. When that didn't end the standoff, they ordered Aramco to cut off all oil supplies to the U.S. military. With the cold war at its peak and Russia backing the Palestinians and working to establish a foothold in the region, we needed a response the Saudis would understand."

"We needed something to bargain with," she said, sipping Coke through the straw. "An alternative oil source."

"Exactly. We suspected that when push came to shove the royal family would be more committed to making billions of dollars than to supporting the Arab cause."

"And that was also right about the time Mexico started discovering vast reserves of hydrocarbons and natural gas beneath the lush savannas of Tabasco State and in the Campeche Sound of the Gulf of Mexico," she said.

"Very good. Initial estimates were upwards of sixty billion barrels, perhaps a hundred billion."

"The answer to Nixon's prayers."

"That's what we needed to find out. The oil was there. The question was whether we could develop the technology to get at it and whether Mexico would ever allow us to do so. Necessity being the mother of invention, we figured the technology part would take care of itself."

"We needed to find a way to convince Mexico to reopen its oil market to foreign interests."

"And you may also recall from your history books that Mexico was having its own share of problems at that same time. Student and labor uprisings were becoming more frequent and more violent. There were reports of communist insurgents from Cuba and the Soviet Union working to turn Mexico into another Vietnam. It was one thing to have that threat in Southeast Asia, Alex. It's a whole other ball game when it's in your own backyard."

"And you and Joe were trying to determine how legitimate the threat was," she said, the realization dawning on her. "You and Joe were monitoring these groups to determine those likely to cause civil unrest if the United States and Mexico entered serious discussions."

"Our job was to preserve the status quo in the event the Saudis didn't flinch."

"History repeats itself," she said.

"It always does." He sat back, an arm on the top of the seat. "So I need to know what you and Joe were working on, Alex. I need specifics to determine if it's related to what he and I were doing."

She took a breath and sat back, settling in. "We were working with Mexican intelligence to identify certain organizations, revolutionaries that could impede the current ongoing negotiations. Joe asked me if I would assist him. He said his Spanish was rusty after thirty years and he needed someone to interpret conversations and documents for him."

He laughed. "Joe's Spanish wasn't rusty—it was never any good. Tell me, did these organizations you were monitoring include el Frente de Liberación Mexicano?"

Her brow furrowed. "What's going on, Charlie?"

"Was it one of the organizations Branick had you look into?"

"Yes."

"What did you find?"

"You know what I found. The MLF is supposed to be extinct. Nobody has heard from it in thirty years, which is right about the time you and Joe were there." She raised her eyebrows in question.

Jenkins picked his words carefully. "The organizations die out, but not the philosophy, Alex. Splinter organizations rise from their ashes. We're getting a healthy dose of it now in the Middle East with the Islamic extremists. They call themselves something different, but their philosophies are the same—they want to take down Western culture."

She nodded. "It's been rumored that the National Labor Party has some historical connection to the MLF," she said.

Knowing Mexico's history, he had already suspected as much. The National Labor Party happened to be the party of Alberto Castañeda—the only political party in eighty years to overcome the corruption embedded in Mexican politics enough to defeat the PRI. Castañeda was referred to as the *destapado,* the uncovered one, because he had come out of obscurity to win the presidency. His primary support had come from Mexico's indigenous people and lower classes: union members, factory workers, farmers. It was normally the element of Mexican society least likely to vote. This time they had. They were also the same groups of people to whom the MLF had appealed in the 1970s, when it was causing considerable unrest, particularly in the southern region of the country.

"The leader of the MLF was a man known as el Profeta," Jenkins said.

"The Prophet?"

"He preached, primarily to the lower and middle class, that Mexico could not be free until its leaders were free of all outside influences, and that together they had the power to do it. He proclaimed that he had the power to deliver Mexico from centuries of bondage to outside forces, most notably the United States. At first no one in the government paid him much attention, but when the MLF started assassinating government officials and wealthy landowners for treason, the Mexican government took notice. The people, particularly those in the villages in southern Mexico, seemed emboldened and organized. Something had given them hope that a change was on the horizon. The government pulled out all stops to get him."

"Who was he?"

Jenkins shook his head.

"You never caught him?"

"No. Despite employing what were normally highly effective interrogation techniques, they had no success identifying him. Neither did we."

"So what happened to him?"

"Until you showed up at my door," he said, "I assumed he was dead."

31

~

DESPITE THE VIGOR of Sloane's pleas, Dr. Knight refused to allow him to speak to the police. She told him it was ill advised in his present condition. When he demanded that she release him from the hospital she quoted the law to him, calling his situation a "classic fifty-four fifty" and telling him she could hold him indefinitely. Rationalizing with her was pointless, and getting angry only made her want to increase the sedative, and he was having enough trouble fighting off its effects, struggling to stay alert.

Dr. Knight closed the file and held it against her chest. "We'll run a series of tests and talk afterward," she said. Then, before he could further protest, "Your wife is here to see you. I'll allow it, but only if it's brief. Right now what you need is to rest."

She opened the door to his room and spoke to someone in the hall. A moment later Tina stepped in.

"Keep it short," Knight said, one hand holding the door open. "Ten minutes at the most." Then she handed Tina a card from the front pocket of her smock. "When you're finished, I'd like to talk with you. My office is upstairs."

Tina walked to the foot of the bed as the door swung shut. She looked uncertain, worn out. Her hair was flat, her eyes hollow and bloodshot. "They wouldn't let me in unless I was a relative."

"How did you find out?"

"You have me down as your emergency contact, David. They called me in the middle of the night. All they would tell me was that you had been brought in by ambulance. I thought you'd been in a car accident. I expected to find you breathing on a ventilator. I've been outside, waiting all morning to see you."

When he had filled out the form at work he never thought his emergency contact would be an issue. He had chosen Tina by default. He had no one else. Melda could never have handled it.

"I'm sorry, Tina, I should have asked."

"I don't mind, David, it's just . . ."

He knew what she was about to say. This was his other secret, one he had not revealed to anyone but Melda. "I don't have any family. My parents died in a car accident when I was six or seven. I was raised in foster homes. There *is* no one else. Melda was the only family I had." The thought saddened him. His chest heaved.

"David, I'm sorry."

"The police think I killed her."

She sat in a chair near the bed, exhausted. "You loved Melda, David. I know that. I know you didn't do it." She let out a breath of air. "David, your dream. How did you know?"

He shook his head, uncertain how to explain it to her, certain he didn't have the time. The foreboding that the man was coming grew stronger.

"Tina, what I'm going to tell you is going to sound strange, crazy, but you have to believe me because you're all I have now."

She nodded, tentative. "Okay."

He told her of the man on the balcony, what had happened that night, and his theory that it was the same man who had broken into his apartment.

"That's why you couldn't reach Melda."

"Yes, that's why."

"Who is he? What does he want?"

He thought of Joe Branick. "He wants a package, something that was mailed to me. He didn't just break into my apartment, Tina. He tore it apart from top to bottom, looking for something. He also broke into my mailbox. I didn't see the two as related right away. That's the reason he went to Melda's apartment."

"She collects your mail when you're gone," she said.

"Exactly."

"What is it?"

"I don't know, but do you remember Joe Branick?"

"The guy who left the message—the guy in the newspaper?"

"Yes."

"You think he sent you a package?"

"Call the number and confirm it's him. I'm certain of it."

"How?"

"I don't have time to explain. You're going to have to trust me. I need to get out of here."

"David—"

"That man is still out there, and he's no longer content with getting the package back. That night on the balcony he could have got away. He could have just left, but he didn't.

He came down that landing, gun in hand. And he'll come again. I know that sounds crazy, but you're going to have to rely on everything we've been through for the past ten years when I tell you that I can feel it. I need to get out of here."

"But, David, how would he know you're here? And there's a guard outside the door. What could he do?"

He pulled on the straps to show her his predicament. "He'll kill me, Tina."

The door to the room pushed open. A pudgy male nurse entered. "Mrs. Sloane, I'm afraid it's time."

He spoke more quickly, with a sense of urgency. "He's short and stocky, with a crew cut. Melda said he had an eagle tattooed on his forearm. It was the same man I saw last night. There was a detective here earlier—"

"Frank Gordon. He's the detective I talked with." She pulled a card from the pocket of her jeans. "He gave me his card."

"Dr. Knight won't let me speak to him. I need you to give him the description of the man. Tell him about the break-in at my apartment. Tell him that I filled out a police report. And tell him to ask around the building to find out if anyone else saw this man. He drove a van. Someone might have written down the license plate."

"All right," she said.

The nurse stepped farther into the room. "Mrs. Sloane . . ."

"Have the detective ask the tenants if any of them saw or spoke to this man. Someone had to tell him that Melda manages the building for me. It's the only reason he would have searched her apartment. And tell him to call the telephone company. He'll find out there were no service calls. I'm sure there weren't."

"Mrs. Sloane, I'm sorry."

Tina turned to the nurse, then back to Sloane.

"You know the hall at the back of my building, off the carport? Tell Gordon to look in the wall."

"For what?"

"A bullet hole."

Her eyes widened.

"Tell him to look."

The pudgy nurse touched her elbow. She turned on him. "Hey, back off. I'm talking to my husband."

The nurse backed off.

Sloane smiled. "I need you to do me one more favor. I need you to get me my briefcase."

She looked puzzled. "Your briefcase?"

"I left it at the office under my desk, remember?"

"You put your mail in it," she said.

"I need you to get it for me. Will you bring it to me here?"

She nodded, started for the door, then stopped, as if struck by a thought, and turned back to him. She walked to the side of his bed and gripped his hand. Then she bent down and kissed him on the cheek, lingering for a moment before turning to leave.

32

⌒

Tina stood at the window, cradling a cup of herbal tea to her lips and staring at a snapshot view that tourists purchased from every sidewalk photographer at Fisherman's Wharf. Drenched in a bright morning sun, the towers of the Golden Gate Bridge sparkled as if made from the precious metal. The rest of the bridge, and the Marin Headlands to which it spanned, remained enveloped in a billowing white fog.

It was like looking at a painting, two-dimensional and devoid of substance. Her mind was elsewhere, going over the conversations she had just had with David and with the detective in the hall.

Frank Gordon was a big man and had a way of scowling when he looked at a person, as if he didn't even believe she was giving him her correct name—which she wasn't. Despite Gordon's skepticism, she persisted in telling him everything that Sloane had asked her to say. Gordon took notes, and when she had finished he paused, his nostrils flaring and his chest inflating with a deep breath. If he remained skeptical, he didn't say. Sloane had given him things, tangible things he could verify, and Tina knew that was what was bothering him. Gordon didn't want to believe the story, but he had no choice but to confirm whether what Sloane was telling him was true or not. He closed his notebook and called over a uniformed hospital security officer and told him to watch the door. Then he turned and left Tina standing in the hall.

The fatigue had burrowed into the muscles of her face and neck, making her head heavy, like a two-glasses-of-red-wine hangover, but the warmth of the tea on her face and hands, and the smell of orange spices, seemed to be helping revive her.

"I'm sorry. That took longer than I expected." Dr. Knight hung up the telephone. Tina turned from the window. Knight sat at a cluttered desk in a modest-sized office that appeared to be more of a place to put things than to actually work. There were diplomas on the wall and certificates on shelves, but no pictures of a husband or children or even a favorite pet. Manila files sat stacked on a small round table to the right. With her glasses removed, Knight's face looked strangely smaller and foreign, like when a man removed his hat to reveal a bald pate. The yellow legal pad on her desk was filled with notes and tiny blue dots she made with the tip of her ballpoint pen—a habit when she was speaking.

Tina took one of two seats across the desk, and they continued their conversation that had been interrupted by the telephone.

"I've been a psychiatrist for twenty-five years, Mrs. Sloane, and I've never seen or read about anything quite like this."

"What do you mean?"

"When the police brought your husband in he showed no signs of physical trauma, yet he was nonresponsive to external stimuli. Pinpricks on the bottoms of his feet and along the palms of his hands brought no response. His pupils were fully dilated with rapid eye movement, and his pulse fluctuated from a normal rate of seventy-two beats per minute to a high of a hundred, then would drop suddenly to the mid-sixties though he remained completely at rest. At other times his breathing became labored and his body temperature would drop to as low as 96 degrees, then shoot up to 101.5. His blood pressure was equally inconsistent."

"What does all that mean?"

"I don't know yet," she said, though Tina suspected that Knight had some idea and was obviously intrigued by it, which was why they were continuing their conversation. "As I said, I've never seen anything quite like it. If I had to come up with some sort of diagnosis I would say his state was dissociated, a defense system by the body to escape the reality of what the mind is experiencing."

"The reality?"

Knight rocked back in her chair. "The symptoms your husband is experiencing are very similar to what is referred to as body memory, Mrs. Sloane." Knight propped her elbows on the desk and held the pen between her hands as if she were trying to snap it in half. "You've heard of post-traumatic stress disorder?"

"Yes, in soldiers coming back from a war."

"Most people associate it with that, yes, and we have an entire encyclopedia of clinical information, thanks to the Vietnam War. Body memory is not unlike post-traumatic stress disorders that I have treated. With PTSD there's usually a delay in the onset of the disorder—'amnesia' might be a familiar word to describe it. The person can bury a memory for years and seem perfectly normal, completely unscarred. They lead normal lives, maintain good jobs, stable relationships, families."

"But then something happens?" Tina asked.

Knight lowered the pen. "There is considerable controversy in the profession about what can trigger a repressed memory, but there is little doubt they can be triggered. It's more common than most people realize. You do not have to have served in a war. Repressed instances of physical or sexual abuse are common."

"And you think this Emily Scott trial could have triggered something David has repressed?"

"Possibly. How old was your husband when his parents died?"

Tina thought about what David had told her. "He said he was a boy."

Knight gave a "Hmm," wrote a note, and continued to make the blue dots.

"Is that significant?"

"Amnesia can be more complicated in children. Children are normally nurtured through their traumatic experiences by an adult—usually a parent. In many cases that can be enough for the child, and the end of the matter. Your husband's situation is obviously complicated by the fact that he had no parents to fill that role, and from what you've told me, no close relative, either. It's fascinating from a clinical standpoint. I've never seen it before. Do you know what happened to him after his parents died, who raised him?"

"He was raised in foster homes."

Knight made a face. "After a traumatic event like that, without someone to nurture him . . . well, there's no opportunity for the child to understand why it happened. Children often feel that what happens is because of them, that they are somehow to blame."

Tina sat forward. "That's what he said. He said he felt like what was happening to her, to the woman in his dreams, was his 'fault.'"

Knight nodded. "A lot of children blame themselves for things in life they can't understand—parents divorcing, for instance. The only other option is not to deal with it, to bury it. The brain gets stuck in denial, and the event is pushed farther and farther below the surface—sometimes, as I said, for years." Knight sat staring, as if uncertain whether to continue.

"What is it?" Tina asked.

"We can't divorce the similarity of your husband's dream with the manner in which this woman died, Mrs. Sloane."

Tina shook her head. "He didn't kill her, Doctor, no matter the similarity. He loved Melda. She was like a mother to him."

"Well, there is another possibility, but I'm hesitant to mention it."

Tina waited.

Knight scratched a spot on her head. "This is entirely speculative at the moment."

"I understand."

"I'll admit, I'm intrigued. Despite the rather obvious similarities, you said your husband does not believe the woman in his dreams is the same woman who was killed in her office . . ." She checked her notes. "Emily Scott."

"He didn't equate the two when we talked about it, no."

"And it wasn't this woman, Melda."

"It couldn't have been. He's been having the nightmare for weeks. What does it mean?"

"Maybe nothing," Knight said, though in a tone indicating she thought it wasn't. "But nightmares are not the problem, Mrs. Sloane; they're the red flag that there *is* a problem. From what you've told me, it doesn't appear that your husband is repressing the car accident that killed his parents."

"I don't really know," Tina said.

"He recalls it?"

"Yes."

"Which could mean that your husband's nightmare is not about the car accident or the death of his parents."

"It might be something else," Tina said.

Knight nodded. "Something in his past. Something so horrible his mind has chosen to forget it completely. Until now."

33

～

SLOANE LEANED FORWARD to see the mirror on the inside of the bathroom door. It had been left open and angled so that it reflected the rectangular wire-mesh window of the outer door to his room. Every fifteen minutes, give or take half a minute, a uniformed guard looked through the exterior window into the room. That was a problem, but so was waiting for the telephone repairman to show up.

Sloane had counted twelve minutes since the guard last peered through the window. Counting was, at the moment, a complex function that kept him semialert. The guard would return in three minutes. The pudgy male nurse would follow seven minutes after the guard.

Five minutes passed.

The door to the room swung open with a burst, the nurse behind it. The guard was off schedule.

Sloane quickly contemplated his options. It was impossible to know if the guard had just gone to the bathroom, to return at any moment, or had left for good. That was something that would reveal itself down the road, if he got that far. *One move at a time,* he told himself. *Think ahead, but make just one move.* Rock climbing had conditioned his body and mind not to rush, to concentrate on the minutiae. He relied on that training now.

The nurse bounced to the side of Sloane's bed and grabbed his wrist. When he did, Sloane gripped the man's left wrist and held it to the side of the bed. At about the same moment the nurse saw the steady drip of the IV tube on the hospital floor, the needle pulled from Sloane's right arm, which was free of the restraint.

When she had leaned down to kiss him, Tina had positioned her body between the nurse and the bed and unsnapped the restraint.

The look in the nurse's eyes changed from confusion to fear. His mouth opened in alarm.

"I'm sorry," Sloane said. He hit the nurse flush with his right hand, buckling the man's legs and feeling his body drop like a weighted sack. He managed to keep the man from crashing to the floor and pulled him across the bed, keeping watch in the reflection in the mirror. He swung his legs over the side of the bed. The room spun like a merry-go-round. He gripped the edge of the bed, fighting centrifugal force with one foot dragging on the floor. When the room stopped spinning he rechecked the door.

No guard.

He stood and felt the cold burn in his ankle: another problem he'd have to deal with. He crossed the room, careful to duck below the window in the door, and pulled open the small closet near the bathroom. His wallet and college ring sat on a shelf, but his clothes were not there—another problem he hadn't counted on. He wouldn't get far in a hospital gown with his ass hanging out the back. He turned and reconsidered the nurse.

Working quickly, he switched his gown for the nurse's blue hospital shirt and pants. Both were tight, the pants too short. There was no hope for the man's shoes. Sloane threw them under the bed. Hopefully the guard would not look down. He slipped the nurse's hands and legs into the restraints and tightened them enough to keep the man in the bed. The nurse moaned. Sloane stuffed an end of the gown into the man's mouth and pulled the sheet up so it was just underneath his nose. Then he picked up the clipboard from the chair and turned for the door, catching sight of the guard's reflection peering through the wire-mesh window.

34

~

KNIGHT'S TELEPHONE INTERRUPTED them again.
Frustrated, she reached to answer it. "Excuse me. I'm
sorry. I thought I had forwarded my calls. This will just be a
second." She picked up the phone. "This is Dr. Knight."

Tina sat back in her chair, watching a black speck, a
bird, drifting and hovering on the wind currents above the
snow-white billowing fog that showed no sign of receding
back out to sea.

"David Sloane? Yes, he's my patient."

At the mention of David's name, Tina looked from the
view back to Brenda Knight. Knight made a face as if pained
and gave her a gesture as if to say, "Sorry," then went back to
tapping the point of her pen on the pad of paper. "Correct, he
should have no visitors. I thought I made that very clear on
his chart." Her voice rose with irritation. "Was it a Detective
Gordon? Well, who was it?" Her brow furrowed. "Hang on
a minute."

Knight covered the phone with the palm of her hand.

"Is there a problem?" Tina asked.

"It's the front desk. They say a visitor came to see your
husband and they inadvertently gave him the room number

before seeing my notation in his chart that he was to have no visitors."

"Who is it?" Tina asked.

"Well, that's the confusing part. Didn't you tell me your husband has no relatives?"

She felt a pang in her stomach, suddenly anxious. "That's what he said."

"Well, the front desk says a man just showed up and said he's your husband's brother."

Tina stood. "His *what*?"

"His brother from Indiana. He said he flew in—"

"He's not from Indiana. He grew up in Southern California." The tension exploded across her neck and shoulders. Sloane's voice echoed in her head.

Melda described a man. She said he was short and stocky, with a crew cut. She said he had an eagle tattooed on his forearm. I saw the same man at the apartment building last night. He was there when I got back from the office.

She pulled open the door to the office. "Call security!" she shouted, and ran into the hall.

35

SLOANE ANGLED HIS body to prevent the guard from getting a clear view of his face. The door to the room swung open.

"Everything okay in here?" the officer asked.

Sloane scribbled notes on the clipboard with the pen, sneaking a glance at the nurse and doing his best to imitate the man's singsong cadence. "Uh-huh. Everything is okey-doke. Sleeping like a baby."

He sensed the officer lingering.

Then the door swung shut.

Sloane exhaled but knew that his relief would be brief. Getting past the guard, down the hallway, and out of the building would be difficult. He sensed that the exits would be limited on a psychiatric ward, and because he had been unconscious when they brought him in, he had no perception of the floor layout. To avoid suspicion he couldn't stand in the hall turning in circles; he had to walk with a purpose. Where, exactly, that would take him he had no way of knowing.

He stepped to the door and looked through the window but did not see the guard. Opening the door a crack, he peered down the hall. The images were blurred from the sedative, but he could make out the guard leaning on the counter of a nurses' station, where two hallways intersected. That was also presumably where the elevators were located. He looked in the opposite direction. It was a dead end.

The nurse moaned louder. Sloane was out of time and options. He raised the clipboard, pulled open the door, and stepped out.

The pain shot from his ankle with each step, but he willed himself not to limp as he approached the nurses' station, where the guard talked with the reason he was off schedule: a blonde nurse.

"Just keep talking," Sloane whispered as he neared. "Don't look up. Don't look down."

The guard turned his head, but it was to look past Sloane down the hall. Then he resumed his flirtation. Sloane raised the clipboard as he walked past the station and approached the intersection.

Tina slid around the corner, head down, regained her balance, and ran past him down the hall. Steps behind her, white coat billowing, a winded and flushed Brenda Knight tried to keep pace. Knight stopped at the counter and spoke to the guard while pointing down the hall.

"You. Go with her; hurry."

The officer straightened. "Everything's fine; I just checked on him. He's sleeping. A nurse is with him."

Sloane turned the corner, found the bank of elevators, and pressed the call button as he searched the hall for a stairwell, not seeing one.

Knight spoke to the nurse as she and the officer started down the hall. "Has anyone else been in there?"

"No," the young woman said, flustered. "Michael was in there."

Sloane continued to search for an exit, no longer content to wait for the elevator. When he looked back at the counter the blonde nurse was staring at him with a confused "you don't belong" look in her eyes. Anxious voices echoed down the hallway. At the same moment the lightbulb clicked on, and the nurse at the counter started pointing and shouting.

"Hey! He's at the elevator. He's at the elevator!"

The elevator bell rang.

Footsteps. People running.

The elevator door slid open. Tina reached the nurses' station, the security guard behind her. She turned to the elevator. "David!"

A man stepped from the elevator as Sloane stepped on. *He is shorter than you. Thick muscles. Short hair. Flat on top.*

Recognition came simultaneously. The man grabbed Sloane by his shirt, and Sloane shoved the man backward into the elevator. The doors closed as they hit the back wall. The elevator shuddered. They wrestled from one side of the car to the other, Sloane gripping the arm holding the gun. The man's other hand seized Sloane's throat, his thumb digging into Sloane's larynx, cutting off his air supply. The drugs in his system had left him weak despite his anger and adrenaline rush, and he felt the man overpowering him, the arm holding the gun bending toward him. He felt like an arm wrestler losing strength, the barrel inching closer to his head.

Sloane whipped his head forward and heard the bridge of the man's nose shatter with a crack. Blood sprayed. At the same moment he planted on his good leg, pivoted, and bull-rushed the man into the railing on the opposite wall.

The elevator jerked violently, knocking them off balance, then came to an abrupt stop.

Sloane repeatedly slammed the hand holding the gun against the wall until the gun fell. He turned to retrieve it, but the elevator dropped again, then caught with a snag, throwing him off balance again. The elevator doors opened. Sloane grabbed the gun as a woman stepped onto the elevator. The man shoved her at him, then shoved others who also had stood waiting for the elevator. They fell into Sloane like bowling pins. The elevator doors rhythmically closed and opened, a loud buzz indicating an obstruction. Sloane scrambled over the bodies and rushed into the hallway. Hospital employees ducked for cover and fell to the floor. At the end of the hall he watched the man pull open a door and disappear into a stairwell. Limping after him, ankle burning, Sloane pulled open the door and leaned over the railing to see the gunman quickly descending. Even on two good legs Sloane would never catch him. Voices and footsteps echoed from above. More voices came from below. Sloane's own choice of exits was being rapidly reduced. He descended a single flight, put the gun in the waistband of his pants beneath the nurse's shirt, and exited onto a lower floor where a female nurse struggled with a patient bed and an IV stand on rollers. Sloane limped up behind her, grabbed the metal frame of the bed for support, and pushed.

"Let me give you a hand," he said.

"Thanks." She had her head down. "The wheels keep getting . . . my God, what happened to you?"

Sloane's shirt was splattered with blood. "Bloody nose," he said. "Just going to change my shirt. Where are you taking him?"

Twenty feet in front of him two young security guards exited from the stairwell running. Sloane turned his head and adjusted the sheet, timing his steps so that he would be obscured by the nurse on the other side of the bed, who now looked at him with greater suspicion.

"I haven't seen you before."

She looked down at his bare feet.

End of the ride.

Sloane spotted an exit sign, hit the door midstride, and disappeared into the stairwell, leaving the IV stand to drag.

AT THE BOTTOM of the stairs Sloane threw open a door to an empty service corridor and two swinging doors. He pushed through the doors and felt the rush of cool air as he stepped out onto a loading dock of large canvas laundry baskets. The dock, however, was empty of cars or vans. He pulled out a light blue top and matching pants and quickly slipped them over the nurse's uniform, stretched a blue cotton hat over his hair, and pulled hospital booties over his bare feet. Gravel dug into the bottoms of his feet as he crossed an asphalt drive. Halfway to the street he spotted a cab parked at the entrance to the hospital. It was a risk, but he would not get far without shoes, limping on a bad ankle. He turned and made his way to the cab and pulled open the back door.

"Dr. Ingman?" the driver asked.

"I'm in a hurry," Sloane said.

36

∽

IT LOOKED AS IF a carnival were in town. Tom Molia
parked behind a string of police cruisers and orange highway vehicles lining the edge of Highway 9, their lights marking the dusk in strobes of color. A news truck had arrived,
and reporters were hurrying to set up, dragging portable
cameras and lugging cable. Molia badged two uniformed
officers on crowd and traffic control, ducked underneath the
police tape, and walked toward a large crane taking up the
half of the road closer to the edge of the cliff. Thick cables
extended from its boom down the steep terrain to a portable
winch at the water's edge.

Despite the pang in his stomach, Molia still held out
hope it was a mistake, that Clay Baldwin was wrong. *God,
let him be wrong,* he thought.

Baldwin had called Molia at home, as he played catch
in the front yard with T.J. Maggie had come down the
porch steps and handed him the telephone. "It's Clay. Are
you on call again?"

He wasn't, and just hearing Baldwin's name caused his
gut to flare; he knew that Clay Baldwin wasn't making
a social call. By the time Molia hung up, his stomach was

burning like a furnace, but his body was chilled to the bone.

The captain of a charter fishing boat had picked up the detail on the boat's sonar—something he referred to with great pride as a Garmin Fishfinder 240. He'd been returning from a late afternoon charter, and professed to know every inch of the Shenandoah, which was why the dark image that filled his screen had given him momentary pause. He thought it might be the mother of all fish. A finer resolution confirmed that he was wrong.

"They think they found him. They think they found Cooperman," Baldwin said.

From that simple statement Molia knew they hadn't found Bert Cooperman at the local pub drinking a beer and shooting pool.

"Looks like he lost control on a turn," Baldwin said. "They found tire marks, like his tires spun on the loose gravel and he couldn't correct it in time. There's no guardrail, Mole. That's why nobody noticed it. He was there one moment and gone the next."

Molia looked down the steep embankment and felt the backs of his knees go weak and a cold sweat break out on his forehead. He stepped back from the edge. He was not good with heights—never had been. They gave him the willies. Though the ground sloped, at that moment his mind made it out to be a sheer cliff, with the final step a bottomless pit. He walked to the cab of the crane, where the operator sat talking on a handheld radio, presumably to the winch operator at the water's edge.

Molia held up his badge as he spoke. "What do you got?"

"Three divers in the water." The operator spoke over the hum of the machine, manipulating levers. "They're working to fix chains so we can lift it up the hillside." The man pointed over his shoulder with his thumb at a flatbed truck.

"What kind of car?" Molia asked.

"Tough to see down there. One person trapped inside behind the wheel, though."

Molia was horrified. "They didn't pull him out yet?"

"Couldn't." The man pushed another lever. "Apparently the car was banged up pretty bad." A call came over the man's handheld. "You're going to have to excuse me." The operator adjusted in his seat and got serious with the machinery. Several minutes later, after further instructions on the handheld, the cable line went taut. "Here she comes now!" he yelled down at Molia.

Molia walked forward, staying back from the edge, listening to the hum of the cable and the engine straining. When the car breached the surface, water poured from its battered body. A police cruiser. Bert Cooperman.

Molia spit over the edge; the pain in his gut had become a bitter taste in his mouth.

The operator shouted down to him. "He one of yours?"

"Yeah," Molia said, not turning around. "He's one of ours."

Somebody had killed a cop, and this time no fucking United States attorney with an attitude was going to take the body. This time Tom Molia was going to do the job he swore to do for the people of Jefferson *fucking* County. And he didn't give a good goddamn who he pissed off in the process.

37

A DOZEN BLACK-AND-WHITE police vehicles bunched together at the front entrance to U.C. San Francisco Hospital on Judah Street, lights flashing in the fading light of dusk, adding to nature's color scheme. The sunset had turned the clouds a mixture of purples and blues. Across the street, medical school students burdened with heavy backpacks stood shoulder to shoulder with hospital staff, watching the scene in animated discussion. Rumors continued to circulate. People inside the hospital were dead, lots of them. A deranged mental patient had managed to escape from his room and kill several of the staff and now held hostages as the police SWAT team searched floor to floor, room to room.

Detective Frank Gordon marveled at the crowd through the tinted glass doors of the hospital lobby. "You turn on the lights of a police car and it's like moths to a porch lamp," he said. "Doesn't matter how dangerous the situation could be, that they could get themselves killed, they just can't help but swarm to the lights." He turned to Tina. "Who are you, really—a girlfriend? I know you're not his wife." Gordon pointed to her left hand. "No ring. And I checked: Sloane isn't married."

"I'm his secretary, Tina Scoccolo."

Gordon leaned forward as if having problems with his hearing. "His secretary?"

She nodded. "We've worked together for ten years."

Gordon shook his head with a bemused "What next?" smile. "Twenty-four years on the force, and this is the craziest goddamn thing yet."

"But his story checks out, right? What he said about the man at the building is true."

Gordon sounded resigned and not very happy. "Yeah, the front desk's description of the guy claiming to be Sloane's brother fits the description Sloane gave you, and it fits the description we got from one of Sloane's tenants. I took a drive out there. The tenant said he directed a telephone repairman fitting that description to this Melda . . ." Gordon looked at his notes.

"Demanjuk," Tina said.

"Demanjuk. Right."

"But he wasn't with the phone company," Tina said.

"Apparently not. Sloane was right about that, also. There's no record of a service call to that building."

"So David was telling the truth about a burglary," she said.

"I don't know about a burglary. All I can tell you is, Mr. Sloane did file a police report like he said, and according to the two uniformed officers who took a ride out there, someone did tear up his apartment, just like someone tore up Ms. . . . ."

"Demanjuk."

"Ms. Demanjuk's apartment. Right. Anyway, yeah, that all checks out."

Tina let out a sigh of relief.

"But the officer also said the whole thing was peculiar."

"Peculiar?"

"As in, whoever broke into Sloane's apartment didn't take anything."

"I don't understand."

"Neither do I. Usually burglars steal." Gordon arched his eyebrows to make a point. "Whoever broke into Sloane's apartment apparently didn't take anything of value—not the stereo, not the television. They just trashed it. That would appear to rule out robbery as a motive." Tina thought of what David had told her about the man looking for a package. She played dumb. "Does Mr. Sloane have any vices you're aware of?"

"Vices?" she asked.

"Drugs, alcohol, gambling . . . women."

She shook her head. "He hardly even drinks, Detec—" She stopped in midsentence, remembering Sloane's request that she retrieve his briefcase from the office. The package from Joe Branick was in it.

"Ms. Scoccolo?"

"Huh?"

"Vices?"

"No," she said. "No, nothing I'm aware of." She no longer sounded confident, and the detective appeared to pick up on her hesitancy.

"Something that could get him into trouble, maybe get someone pissed off at him? Did he owe anyone any money?"

"No," she said, sounding less sure. "Not that I'm aware of." She crossed her arms. "I don't know everything about his personal life, Detective, but I can tell you he isn't addicted to anything . . . except maybe his work. I don't know where he'd even find the time. As for money, I deposit his paychecks for him and pay quite a few of his bills. I can tell you he isn't hurting. He rarely spends anything on himself. I order his suits and shirts from catalogues."

"What does he do with his money?"

"Invests it, or just lets it sit in his accounts. He gives a lot to children's charities."

Gordon rubbed his chin as if examining the closeness of his shave. "What about enemies?"

She shrugged. "He *is* a lawyer."

Gordon chuckled at that comment.

"What I meant," she said, "is that he usually wins, so I'm sure there are a few people who probably don't like him much, but specific enemies, no, not that I know of."

Gordon pulled out a plastic bag from his coat pocket and held it up for Tina to see. Inside was a bullet. "One of the officers spotted it. It was just where Sloane said it would be."

She felt another chill run through her body.

"Can you get a message to him?"

"I can try."

"I suggest you do. Tell him he needs to turn himself in."

"But you believe him," she said. "You said he's telling the truth."

"About everything? I don't know. No, it doesn't appear he's a suspect in Ms. Demanjuk's death, but unfortunately he doesn't know that."

"What do you mean?"

"I mean he's on the run, and according to witnesses, he's walking around with a loaded gun."

"He's not dangerous, Detective."

"Ordinarily I'd likely agree with you, Ms. Scoccolo, but this isn't ordinary. Desperate men can do desperate things. Sloane was desperate enough to get out of that hospital room, which I assume had something to do with the guy he popped in the elevator, though you said he was running before that guy made an appearance. That tells me Sloane knew the guy was coming or had some other burning reason to feel threatened. How and why are a couple questions I'd like to ask him at the moment, along with a few dozen others, but that's not my immediate concern at this time."

"What is?"

"The guy who came to the hospital. He's still out there, and I don't want to see a bad situation escalate."

38

⌒

METAL SHELVING UNITS filled with Melda's gardening tools and miscellaneous building supplies cluttered the cramped storage closet, which was no larger than a walk-in closet. Sloane sat on a five-gallon bucket of wood stain left over from the last application to the shingles. Overhead a bare lightbulb fixture he'd nailed to a wood joist and crudely wired emitted a low-wattage glow. He awoke feeling the lingering effects of the drugs in his system, fatigued and groggy, but at least he was no longer dizzy or wracked by chills. He had no idea how much time had passed.

He'd directed the cabdriver to drop him in the vacant lot, watched the building to be sure there was nothing out of the ordinary, then walked along the cliff's edge to the back of the building and the storage closet off the corridor. There he collapsed. As the adrenaline from his altercation in the hospital elevator subsided he began to feel more and more light-headed and nauseated. He needed a place to sit down and get his bearings—without his keys he would have to climb the balconies to get into his apartment. The last thing he remembered was resting his head against the concrete cinder-block wall to catch his breath.

He stood, pulled the string hanging from the bulb to turn off the light, and slowly pushed open the door into darkness. However long he'd slept, it was now night. He heard the crickets in the field and the muted crashing of the ocean. A cool breeze blew down the corridor. Ambient light from the moon filtered down the hallway. The fog had not rolled in. He let his eyes adjust before stepping out and making his way to the carport, staying below the roof of a big SUV to look through its windows into the gravel lot. The lights atop a police cruiser parked near the laurel hedge were silhouetted in the shadows.

This was not going to be easy.

He crept back to the storage closet, grabbed the five-gallon bucket of wood stain, and carried it to the back of the building. Standing on the bucket, he could reach the wrought-iron railing of Melda's deck. He pulled himself up, slipped his legs over the railing onto Melda's deck, then stood on her railing and reached up to grip the edge of the deck to his apartment and repeated the process. He slid open the glass door to his bedroom, listened for a moment to make sure he was alone, and stepped in, trying not to think about Melda or what had happened there. He exchanged the hospital scrubs for a pair of jeans, a T-shirt, and a plain gray sweatshirt, then retrieved the roll of duct tape from where he'd left it after bandaging the seat cushion. His ankle was black-and-blue, but he wasn't going to have any time soon to treat it. Sitting on the edge of his bed, he pulled on an athletic sock, wrapped the ankle in duct tape to give it support, and swallowed the anticipated pain as he forced his foot into a hiking boot, lacing it tight. He stood and tested the ankle. Sore, but the tape and boot gave it enough support so that he could walk without a perceptible limp or too much pain.

Sloane picked up the gun from the bed. He knew enough from his stint in the marines to know it was a Ruger MK2, a .22-caliber automatic. What the hell was going on? He felt as if he'd been suddenly thrust into a virtual-reality game, with forces he could not see or hear controlling and manipulating him. He stood, shaking off the thought, and chided himself to think linearly. Then he shoved the pistol in a gym bag from his closet and stuffed the bag with random clothes from his dresser and toiletries from the bathroom. Back in the bedroom, he knelt in the closet, tossed aside shoes and dirty clothes, and pulled back the carpet to reveal the small floor safe he had installed when he purchased the building. He used it as fireproof storage for important papers and rent payments—his older tenants still paid in cash. He pulled open the safe and counted $2,420.

He wanted to avoid using his credit cards or ATM as long as possible. He grabbed the Rolex from the nightstand, figuring he could pawn it. As he slipped the watch onto his wrist, he noticed a red number "1" flashing on the answering machine beside his bed. Feeling a strange compulsion, he pressed the button. The beep sounded like a car alarm. Sloane quickly lowered the volume.

"David? It's Tina." She sounded anxious. "If you get this message, please call me. I spoke to Detective Gordon. He said he talked to one of your tenants. You were right. The man who came to the hospital was at your building posing as a telephone repairman, and your tenant directed him to Melda. Detective Gordon checked. The telephone company has no record of a service call. The police also found a bullet in the siding of your building, David. Gordon wanted me to tell you that the man, whoever he is, is still out there . . ." Her voice paused. "I hope you get this message, David."

He felt a sense of relief. At the very least he had not been hallucinating everything that was happening to him. He was about to shut off the machine when, as if struck by an afterthought, Tina continued.

"I'm going to get your briefcase from the office tonight. Call me at home."

As the machine clicked off, the foreboding feeling washed over him again like a sudden rogue wave. His briefcase. He'd forgotten that he asked her to get it, and now realized it had been a horrible mistake. Sloane's office was the next logical choice to look for the package, and Sloane knew, as certainly as he had known that the man would come for him in the hospital, that he would go there. At that same moment another domino fell—something his mind had continued to work on subconsciously but had been unable to solve. If the man was skilled at picking locks, why bother to come as a telephone repairman, except perhaps to avoid attention?

Sloane hurried through the living room to the kitchen, pulled the telephone from its cradle on the counter, and snapped off the back. The tiny microphone, no larger than a watch battery, was wedged behind the battery pack.

He looked at his Rolex. He was at least thirty minutes away.

JACK CONNALLY LOOKED up at the sound of heels on the marble floor and folded the corner of the page in his novel to mark his spot. He pressed his palms flat on the counter, pushed back his chair, and stood. Tina smiled as she approached, one hand rummaging through her purse in search of her computerized access card to the building. With the Emily Scott episode and a less recent rampage by a client armed with military weaponry through his attorney's offices, most buildings had put in security systems that shut off the elevators in the lobby without computerized access, and had doors installed on each floor that locked the suite of offices from the exterior hallway. A computerized card was needed to gain after-hours access through both.

"Tina, what's a pretty young girl like you doing working this late on a weekend?" said Connally, who was a recent grandfather and old enough to be her father.

"Oh, you know, Jack, another trial."

"Well, I hope you won't be here too late again."

"Not tonight," she said, continuing to dig through her purse. "Just need to pick up some things."

"You should be out enjoying yourself on a Saturday night. You work too hard. You sure put in the hours."

"Have to pay the bills, Jack." She found her card. "Besides," she said, giving him a wink as she ran the card over the electronic sensor, "all the good guys like you are taken."

Connally smiled like an embarrassed schoolboy. The computer registered her checking into the building at 9:22 p.m.

"Nineteen is unlocked." Connally picked up his novel. "Janitor just went up."

Tina stepped into a waiting elevator, leaning back against the wall as the doors closed, and watched the floor numbers tick off as the car ascended. She had left messages for David at his home, office, and cell phone and hoped he'd get at least one of them. The elevator slowed and came to a stop, the doors separating. She stepped off, startled, and quickly jumped back, her hand to her chest.

"Oh, my God! You scared me."

The janitor stood in the lobby, cleaning an ashtray and looking nonplussed. "Sorry," he said. He pulled the garbage can to the side to allow her to pass.

Tina punched in the access code on the keypad mounted to the wall, just below the gold-embossed sign indicating "The Law Offices of Foster & Bane," and pulled open the door. She stepped into the darkened reception area, lit by a single overhead security light and the green glow of an exit sign above the double doors, and walked in sporadic light down the hall to David's office. She found his briefcase exactly where he had left it, picked it up, noticed the corner of a burnt-orange envelope protruding from the pocket, and wondered what it could possibly be.

A telephone rang down the hallway. She wondered who else would be working on a Saturday night. No wonder so many were divorced. She walked back down the hall and was about to turn the corner back to the reception area when she noticed the red light on her telephone blinking, indicating that she had a message. Given that she had worked until nearly ten Friday night, the message was unlikely to be business related. She could think of only two people who might know she was at the office late on a Saturday night: her mother . . . and David. She stepped into the cubicle and punched in the number for the systemwide voice mail, then her password. The computerized voice advised that she had two messages. The first message had been sent roughly twenty minutes earlier.

"Tina? Tina, are you there?"

She felt a rush of adrenaline at the sound of his voice, but the message ended abruptly. She quickly pressed "pound" to retrieve the second message, delivered four minutes after the first.

"Tina. It's David. I just spoke to your mother. Are you there?" He swore as if to himself. "Damn it. Tina, I got your message."

She could tell from the static that he was calling from his cell phone. He sounded out of breath, as if he was running.

"Forget about my briefcase. Do *not* get my briefcase. Leave it where it is. If you are there and you get this, just leave it and get out of the building. Damn."

His words hit her like a punch to the gut. She held the phone a moment, suddenly uncertain what to do, hung up, and quickly dialed the number from memory. It rang once before he answered.

"David."

"Tina, where are you?"

"I'm at the office—"

"Get out! Do you understand me? Get out as quickly as you can."

"What—" She heard the wheels of the janitor's cart on the marble floor in the lobby. Smoking was not allowed in the building. There was no reason for the janitor to be cleaning an ashtray by the elevator.

"Tina? Tina!"

She thought of Melda Demanjuk. Then she thought of Emily Scott.

HE MOVED QUICKLY through the carport, using the cars for cover and watching the parking lot through the windows. His Jeep was out of the question; the police were sitting on it. Melda's 1969 Barracuda was his only other option; Sloane kept a spare key for her. If he could get to it and get the engine to start, he had a chance. Melda had rarely driven after her husband died, and the car sat unused for long periods.

He had contemplated simply rushing out of his apartment to the two officers waiting in front of his building, but dismissed the idea. They were looking for an escapee from a psychiatric department who was armed and presumed dangerous. Under those circumstances, it was unlikely they'd believe Sloane's premonition that a woman in a downtown San Francisco high-rise was in danger, or even give him the time to explain it. He'd tried to reach the detective, Frank Gordon, at the Ingleside station, but he had not answered and the exchange wasn't about to give Sloane Gordon's home telephone number. They said they'd do their best to get him a message, but he couldn't count on the detective getting to the building before him.

He slid between the wall and the car and popped the lock. The driver's-side door groaned like a steamer trunk being opened after years sitting unused in an attic. He squeezed in, pushing back the driver's seat while watching the rearview and side mirrors, but did not see the officers. The car had the musty smell of an old person's closet, poorly camouflaged by a pine-scented air freshener that had long since lost its usefulness. The car was spotless—not a crack in the cherry-red seats or dashboard. Sloane hoped the engine was in as good shape. He was about to find out. He inserted the key, crossed his fingers, and turned the ignition. The engine strained, a hyena laughing. He played with the pedal, trying to coax the engine to kick over, but sensed the power in the battery quickly fading and turned it off. Keeping an eye on the rearview mirror, he forced himself to count to ten. Then he kicked the gas pedal once to set the automatic choke and turned the key again.

This time the engine whined and sputtered hopeful chokes of exhaust. He pushed it, working the pedal, urging it.

"Come on. Come on, kick over."

The car sputtered and spit like a drowned person coming back to life.

Then it died.

"Damn." He turned off the key, waiting, searching the parking lot in the mirrors, fighting the urge to rush, hoping there was enough juice left in the battery. He counted again but this time only reached five before he turned the key. The engine gave a quick burst of life and backfired—a shotgun blast that echoed loudly beneath the carport. Sloane heard voices, and the two officers appeared in the rearview mirror. All they had to do was follow the plume of smoke from the Barracuda's exhaust pipe.

Sloane closed his eyes. "Okay, Melda, if you're up there and you're still taking care of me, kick this son of a gun over."

He pumped the accelerator once, turned the key. The engine strained, sputtered, fired again. He played with the pedal, revving it, fighting to keep it from dying. A carbon-gray cloud obscured the view out the back window. He kept the rpm high, dropped the shifter into reverse, took his foot off the brake, and hoped the two officers standing somewhere in the smoke got the hell out of the way.

39

PETER HO'S NAVY BLUE Chevy Blazer, with JEF-
FERSON COUNTY MEDICAL EXAMINER stenciled in
white on the door panel, sat parked in the street at the
brick walkway to Tom Molia's colonial-style house.
Located at the end of a cul-de-sac, the pale yellow house
had blue shutters framing dormer windows. Roses and
azaleas bloomed in the garden, and the lawn was mostly
green but for patches of brown where the portable sprin-
kler didn't reach. Molia stopped the Chevy to consider his
suburban neighborhood of green lawns, mature trees, and
three-bedroom houses aglow beneath perfectly linear
streetlamps and an assortment of porch lights. It was the
type of house, in the type of neighborhood, that Bert
Cooperman had always talked about owning.

Not anymore.

Molia had personally delivered the news to Cooperman's
family. He had knocked on doors before, but nothing compared to this. Debbie Cooperman broke down the moment
she saw him. She knew. The family knew. They were all
there. Waiting. Hoping against hope. Cooperman's infant
son cried in his mother's arms. He had the right.

J. Rayburn Franklin reasoned that the accident explained why Cooperman had just disappeared, why the young officer hadn't radioed when he arrived at the site, why the park police did not find him waiting when they arrived. Coop had never made it. His car had skidded around the turn and plunged down the ravine into the Shenandoah. It was a logical explanation.

Except that Tom Molia wasn't buying it. Not any of it.

Bert Cooperman didn't misjudge a turn he had made hundreds of times in his life. He didn't miscalculate his speed because of fatigue. Somebody wanted it to look that way. Somebody wanted it to look like an accident, as if a tired young officer in a rush to get to where he was going had made a fatal error in judgment. They had done a pretty good job, too. They covered the physical evidence all the way to erasing the cruiser's tire tread at the bluff. They weren't run-of-the-mill, amateur killers. They were good. Real good.

But they didn't know Bert Cooperman the way Tom Molia did.

They didn't know that Coop was a country boy who had hunted the West Virginia mountains and fished its streams since he was old enough to sit on his father's lap and see over the top of the steering wheel. They didn't know what it was like to be a young police officer at the end of a shift, rolling to your first dead body. Cooperman would not have been tired. He would not have felt fatigued. He would have been wide-awake.

Molia parked in the street and pushed open the car door, trudging up the walkway and stopping to pick up his son's bike. He leaned the handlebars against the porch railing, but it pitched to the side and fell. He left it. He pulled open the screen door to the whir of an oscillating fan—they didn't like to use the air-conditioning at night because it was expensive and made the air stale. Peter Ho sat on the couch next to Maggie. She wore shorts and his Charles Town Police Department softball T-shirt and had pulled back her red hair into a ponytail. She had never looked more beautiful. His daughter, Beth, lay on the oval throw rug, trying to read a book while T.J., still in his Little League uniform, pressed the end of Ho's stethoscope against her head. She swatted at him like a bothersome fly, which only encouraged him.

Maggie got up from the couch and hugged Tom. "You okay?"

He fought back the tears that had flowed freely in Debbie Cooperman's living room.

Maggie stepped back. "Anything more?"

He shook his head and doubted there would be. The official report would conclude that Bert Cooperman's death had been a tragic accident. There was no physical evidence to refute it.

"I'll make you something to eat," Maggie said.

"I'm not hungry, thanks." He looked down at his children, who were now staring up at him, sensing that this had not been a routine day. Then he hugged them fiercely, pulling them both to him. When he let go, Maggie stepped in.

"Okay, come on, kids. It's bedtime." She ushered the children out of the room, Molia kissing each on the top of the head as they walked past. Maggie took the stethoscope from T.J. and handed it back to Ho. "Nice to talk with you, Peter."

Ho smiled, but it was halfhearted. "You, too, Maggie. Liza's been meaning to call you about the church retreat. Things have been hectic."

"I know the feeling. You sure you don't want to stay and have something to eat? It's no problem."

"I better not. I'm afraid I've ruined a few dinners this week. I'll be getting home in a minute. We won't be long." Ho waited for Maggie to leave the room, then turned to Molia. "A lot of bruises on the body. A contusion at the back of his head that likely knocked him out."

Molia had called Ho from the accident site and met him at his office with Cooperman's body. He left two armed police officers at the building while he went to deliver the news to Cooperman's family. "Can you—"

"Can I tell you whether the bruises were caused by the accident or a blunt trauma before it?" Ho shook his head in frustration. "I'm sorry, Tom. I wish I could, but at the speed he was traveling and the likely impact with the water . . . He would have been thrown around the car considerably. I'd be guessing. He had a linear skull fracture indicating impact with the windshield. He also had a basal skull fracture." Ho put his hand at the base of his skull. "I might not have even found it under ordinary circumstances, given the linear fracture."

Molia slumped onto the couch and rubbed his face. "And a basal skull fracture is consistent with someone hitting him in the back of the head with a blunt object like the butt of a rifle before they dumped him inside his car and pushed it over the edge."

Ho let the comment pass. "He had a subdural hematoma, also indicating a blunt trauma before he died. The problem, Tom, is that I can't differentiate what was caused from the accident and what might have occurred before it, though I'm pretty certain something did."

Molia gave him a look.

Ho picked up a manila envelope from the couch and tossed it onto his lap. "John Dunbar. The lab owed me a favor."

"John Dunbar?"

Ho pointed to the envelope. "Joe Branick. I asked them to push it without drawing attention to it."

Molia studied Ho's face. "He didn't kill himself either, did he?"

Ho shook his head. "Also inconclusive. But also a pretty damn good bet."

Molia opened the package and pulled out photographs and a ballistics test. "In your medical opinion?"

"In my medical opinion I'd say the percentages are better that he did not."

Molia studied the report. "Ballistics match."

"No bullet, Tom. The powder burns on the hand and skull match. Same gun. Specific pattern of powder burns on the scalp, head, and face indicates a single shot fired at very close range. There was trauma to the tissue at the temple, hemorrhaging—"

"Which indicates the muzzle of the gun was either pressed directly against the flesh or very close to it."

"Exactly, and the trajectory of the bullet through the skull is consistent with the reflex action one would expect to find in a self-inflicted wound. The bullet entered the temple and exited the rear, top portion of the skull." He pointed to the envelope. "You'll find some beautiful photographs in there, which I would suggest you commit to memory, then bury in your backyard."

Molia stood to look at the photos. He thought better when he paced. "Blood test turn up something?"

"Nothing. No sign of any needle marks on the body indicating a chemical injection. I assume his lab work will also reveal no sign of any heavy metals, toxic substances, therapeutic drugs, or narcotics in the blood or urine. But that will take a couple weeks."

"Then how can you be so sure it wasn't a suicide?"

Ho chugged his beer, wincing; his eyes watered from the carbonation. He pushed his hair back from his forehead, staring at the floor as if re-creating the events. "I'm about ready to wrap this thing up, put the body back in the locker, call and tell you your instincts and a quarter will buy you a cup of coffee. Then I notice a cut across the back of the hand, just above the knuckle of the middle finger. There's a beautiful picture." Ho retrieved the envelope and flipped through the photographs to a blowup of Joe Branick's hand. "You see?"

Molia remained unimpressed. "That's a scratch. It could be from anything. It could have happened when he fell."

"It probably did. The fact that there is a scrape is immaterial. What's important is there is no coagulation. No bleeding."

Molia knew enough about dead bodies to know it was of interest. "I'm listening, Peter."

"Okay. Crash course on the human circulatory system. When a person is alive, the blood circulates. That's why when a person is shot or suffers an acute injury red blood cells escape from the large and small vessels adjacent to the path of the trauma. In layman's terms, you expect to see free red blood cells throughout the wounded tissue— like Cooperman's hematoma at the base of his skull." Ho held up his hand and made a fist. "When a person dies, the blood stops circulating. The heart ceases to function and there is no loss of blood into the tissue. The lack of red blood cells along the path of injury is a very obvious sign the person was traumatized—in this instance—shot, after he was already dead. It's more difficult to determine when a high-caliber weapon is used, because the bullet does so much damage to the flesh and skull."

"So why do you think that to be the case this time?"

Ho paced an area near the glass coffee table. "That was my suspicion. So I decided to do a fine-needle aspiration. A small-gauge needle, five or six times the diameter of a hair, is inserted into the skin to recover tissue samples. I took a biopsy, made a paraffin block for a slide, stained it with hematoxylin and eosin, and confirmed the red blood cells were still within the tissue. They had not leaked out of the blood vessels."

Molia nodded. "He was already dead before they shot him."

40

Tina dropped the telephone, rushed across the hall into a darkened office, and quietly shut the door. She crouched behind the desk and pulled the telephone onto the floor, punching the red emergency button. It rang once. Jack Connally answered.

"Jack? This is Tina. Call the police."

"Tina? . . . I can hardly hear you."

"Jack, call the police," she said, speaking as loud as she dared. She no longer heard the wheels of the garbage can in the hallway. The "janitor" had likely abandoned it and was now searching the offices door to door.

"Are you all right? Tina? I can hardly hear you."

She pictured him dropping his paperback as her voice pulled him out of his chair.

"Jack, just call the police, turn off the elevators, pull the goddamn alarm, and lock yourself in the room behind your desk."

"Tina, what is it? Should I come up?"

"Damn it, Jack—"

The door to the office flung open, the light from the hallway flowing into the room.

"Jack, call—!" she yelled.

The janitor moved quickly, ripping the phone cord from the wall. He looked down at the briefcase in her hand, smiled, and advanced, wrapping the cord around the knuckles of both hands, leaving a two-foot-long piece between the two. Tina circled the desk, throwing anything she could find. He deflected them, keeping himself between her and the door. She saw the firm's fifteen-year anniversary present, a letter opener handed out to every employee, lying on the desk pad.

"The police are coming. They'll be here any minute," she said. "They know who you are."

He smiled.

She feinted, threw a book at him, and grabbed the opener as she rushed for the door. He grabbed her from behind, yanking her backward. She thrust the letter opener as hard as she could, felt it embed in the man's leg, and drove it five inches up to the blue and red Foster & Bane logo on the handle.

The janitor screamed through clenched jaws—a cry of pain. Tina wriggled free of her sweater and bolted out the door and down the hall for the emergency stairwell exit. She pulled open the emergency exit door and looked behind her. The man hobbled out of the office, a patch of blood quickly spreading on his right pant leg, a gun in his hand.

THE TIRES SPUN on the slick carport pavement, spewing white smoke to mix with the gray carbon spitting from the car's exhaust. Then the rubber gripped and the Barracuda lurched backward, fishtailing into the parking lot and kicking up gravel. The two officers dived out of the way, falling to the ground. Sloane kept the car in reverse, propelling it backward across the lot, through the laurel hedge, and over the sidewalk. Car horns blared. Tires screeched. He dropped the steering column gear into drive and punched the gas.

Three minutes later he merged the Barracuda onto Highway 1. With its V-8 engine and none of the modern smog-control gadgets that drain cars of their raw power, it was surprisingly fast. The speedometer pushed past eighty before the engine gave a shudder of displeasure. Sloane cut north over Highway 280, waiting to hear the sound of police cruisers coming up quickly behind him. None did.

He flipped open his cell phone and hit "Redial." The extension at Tina's desk rang, but she did not answer. Her voice mail picked up.

"Tina? Tina, are you there?"

He took the downtown interchange, exiting at Fourth Street, where the freeway came to an abrupt end. He blew the light at the bottom of the exit and gauged the progress of a multicar MUNI streetcar on his left. The tracks ran parallel with the road, and Sloane was going to have to make a left turn across the tracks at Sansome Street. He punched the accelerator, hesitated when he couldn't pull clear of the bus, then decided to go for it. He turned sharply, heard the sound of metal scraping and the hiss of air brakes, thought he'd made it, then felt the streetcar clip the back bumper, sending the back end of the Barracuda skidding sideways into a parked car. No time to leave a note—he accelerated and kept going. As he neared Battery Street he picked up the phone, and was about to push "Redial" again when it rang in his hand.

"Tina?"

"David."

"Where are you?"

"I'm at the office—"

"Get out. Do you understand me? Get out as quickly as you can. Tina? Tina!"

He tossed the phone onto the seat and grabbed the gun from the gym bag as he turned down the alley going the wrong way and lurched the Barracuda to a stop in a delivery zone at the back of the building. The back door was locked. He looked for police cars as he rushed up the alley to the front of the building, but saw none. Moving methodically left to right, he pulled progressively harder on the locked series of glass doors until the door on the far right flew open. He hurried across the lobby. The night security guard stood at a counter yelling into the telephone.

"Tina, are you all right? Tina?"

Jack Connally pushed buttons on the console, his movements jerky and uncertain. "Mr. Sloane," he said as Sloane reached the counter. Connally's eyes widened at the sight of the gun. He raised both hands shoulder high.

Sloane rushed past him, stepped inside an elevator, and hit the button for the nineteenth floor. The doors did not close. He hit the other buttons, but they, too, would not remain lit. *The computer.* The elevators were locked down. He needed his card.

He rushed back to the desk. "Jack, turn on the elevators."

"Take it easy—"

"Jack, turn on the damned elevators."

Connally hesitated.

"Turn the elevators back on. She's in trouble up there."

Connally shook his head, hands shaking. "I can't. It takes a minute after shutdown for the computers to start back up."

Sloane looked to the door at the end of the lobby. Nineteen floors, but he couldn't just stand here. Then the stairwell door flew open and Tina burst out, slipping on the marble floor, out of breath, yelling, "Jack, get down!"

He started for her, then stopped, everything slowing, moving as if through a pool of thick oil. Tina rushed past the security desk, and Connally stepped out as she did. The stairwell door crashed open again against the wall. Flashes of light and the *pop-pop-pop* of semiautomatic gunfire reverberated like applause. Connally's body jerked in spasmodic reflex from the bullets ripping through him, like a tin can being kept aloft, each hit redirecting him until the shots stopped and he fell.

With Connally no longer obstructing his aim, the gunman swung his arm like a pendulum and locked on Tina.

41

~

"YOU'RE CERTAIN?" Molia asked. "The biopsy is legitimate, I mean as far as evidence?"

Ho raised both hands. "Hold on, Tom. Nobody said anything about evidence. Remember, this guy was never supposed to come out of the reefer. Besides, the biopsy alone is pretty thin."

Molia leaned forward. "Which means you didn't stop there." Tom Molia knew Peter Ho; he knew that beneath the facade of the country doctor, Ho was a highly gifted coroner, tops in his class at Johns Hopkins, and a man as dedicated to his job as Molia was to his own.

Ho paused. "I decided to get more tissue. I went through the mouth, underneath the palate; it's the least likely place anyone would look . . . I recovered enough to confirm the fine-needle aspiration."

Molia thought through the information, talking out loud. "So, then, how did he die, Peter? You said he had no signs of physical trauma except the scratch on the hand. If there were no chemicals in his system, how did he die?"

"For certain?" Ho shook his head. "I don't know. But to a coroner this is type-one stuff, Tom. You don't see this every day. In fact, the closest I've ever come may have been when I was still back at Johns Hopkins. I worked on a couple of kids who drowned in a boating accident. Tragic. The father said they fell overboard while he was passed out drunk. The parents were estranged, and the district attorney thought the father had suffocated the kids and dumped them overboard—some sadistic act to get back at the ex-wife."

"Jesus."

"My job was to find out which it was. When a person suffocates, the blood stays in the vessels and the cause of death is from a general lack of oxygen, usually the brain failing first, then the heart. There's a circulatory collapse like what we're talking about here. That could explain the lack of blood leaking into the tissue, as with an acute injury, like a gunshot or stabbing."

"So you're saying our guy looks more like an asphyxiation than an acute injury," Molia said.

"Exactly."

"Someone suffocated him."

"No, I don't think so."

"You just—"

"The major findings in someone who dies slowly from a lack of oxygen, suffocation, are splinter hemorrhages visible over the surface of the heart, lungs, and thymus gland in the neck. A less prominent finding would be swelling of the brain. Given the condition of this guy's head, that would be pretty close to impossible to determine. To do that I'd have to cut him open—hello, autopsy . . ."

"Then—"

"I just think he died quicker than that."

"Why?"

"There's no indication of a struggle, Tom. You'd expect to see marks on the body, bruises, like Cooperman. This was not a small man. He was fit. Muscular. If he had been suffocated, you would expect to see something about the nose and mouth, broken blood vessels. Something. Cuts and scratches on his hands, bruises on his arms. Except for the hole in his head, this guy showed nothing. I know he was dead before he was shot. But I don't know how."

"Any guesses?"

Ho shook his head. "There are very few drugs I can think of that would not leave telltale signs and be detected viscerally or through chemical analysis."

"But there are some?" Molia asked.

"Some. Carbon dioxide for one. But what I'm getting at, Tom, is whoever did kill this guy—and Cooperman, if you're right—they were no amateurs. It's as close to perfect as I've ever seen. They knew what they were doing, and they did it extremely well."

They sat listening to the hum of the fan, like millions of mosquitoes in flight.

"I'm sorry I involved you in this, Peter," Molia said. "My ego."

"It's my job, too, Tom."

"Nobody is going to find out you did anything, Peter. I'll keep this under my hat."

"What are you going to do?"

"They killed a cop, Peter."

"But you have no evidence. You don't have anything."

"I know. But something always comes up. There's no such thing as a perfect crime. Something always falls through the cracks, Peter—you know that—and when it does, I'll be there to catch it."

"Just don't let them carry you into my office in a bag, Tom."

"I'll be all right."

Ho stood. "I'm going home to have dinner with my wife and kids. I suggest you go in there and do the same." He left the beer bottle on the coffee table, walked to the screen door, and pulled it open.

"Peter." Ho turned. "Thanks," Molia said.

Then Ho stepped out onto the porch; the screen door slammed shut behind him. Tom Molia stood in his living room watching his friend walk down the path, a blurry image in the screen mesh and dark of night.

42
〜

THE TRAINING RUSHED back to him like a river undammed, flooding him. Sloane didn't stop to remember the details; he went with the torrent. The world narrowed to a round tube of concentration that brought everything within it into sharp focus and certain clarity. His heartbeat pulsed in his head. His breathing rushed in and out of his chest cavity like the rush of the waves against the rocks, controlled and deliberate, a low whistle parting his lips. He spread his legs shoulder width, cupped a palm under the hand holding the gun, and locked on his target, exhaling half a breath and squeezing off two rounds.

The janitor's right shoulder jolted like a shaken rag doll, the automatic emitting an angry burst that sent bullets ricocheting sparks off the marble floor and walls. Sloane maintained focus, gun on target, waiting for the man to drop, waiting to secure his weapon. But the man did not drop; he stood, blood flowering a deep red bud, nearly black against the forest-green uniform, a stain to match the stain on his right pant leg. His right arm dangled limply at his side, but his hand refused to release the weapon. The pain alone should have dropped him like a bag of sand. Instead, he turned his head and locked eyes with Sloane, his facial expression a blank mask, his eyes two chunks of charcoal.

Sloane resisted the urge to pull the trigger again, to allow his anger and desire for revenge to control his actions. He didn't want to kill the man. That would do him no good. He needed him alive. He needed answers to his questions.

Noise sounded from outside the tunnel—footsteps and voices shouting. Shades of dark blue entered Sloane's peripheral vision— police officers dropping into crouches and sliding behind the security console.

"Drop your weapons. Now! Show me your hands. Hands! I want to see your hands."

Sloane kept the gun fixed on the janitor, who also did not move.

"Put it down! Put it down!"

The janitor, too, gave no indication that he saw or heard anything outside their tunnel of concentration. Apparently, he was willing to engage Sloane in a high-stakes game of chicken. Then his face twitched, an almost imperceptible movement, a muscle spasm that wasn't. His lips flattened, and the corners of his mouth extended into an "It doesn't get any better than this" grin just before he reached across his body with his left hand to grab the automatic.

And the officers opened fire.

43

～

THE DOOR TO the apartment was closed, which was to be expected at ten o'clock at night. What was of considerably more interest were the strands of yellow police tape crisscrossing the threshold. Jenkins pushed open the door and bent under the tape, snapping one as he did. The inside of the apartment had been straightened but still revealed signs of what had been a significant struggle, a search, or both. He looked for blood, did not immediately see any, and concluded that the disarray was more likely the result of a search, further confirmation that Joe Branick's research was correct.

Alex Hart stepped into the apartment behind him. "You two share the same cleaning service?"

Jenkins had decided to limit what he told her, still uncertain of her involvement. He told her only that they were going to find a guy who might be able to explain why Joe was dead.

"I'd say we've come to the right place," Alex said. "Just a little late."

"At least they didn't burn it to the ground."

Jenkins considered the room in detail. The telephone lay on the counter, the backing pulled off, the battery pulled out, revealing a tiny listening device. He walked about the main room, hearing the hushed rush of waves along with the occasional melancholy blast of a distant foghorn. He stepped into a bedroom. A curtain rippled in front of a sliding glass door, which led to a small balcony. He leaned over the railing and looked down at a five-gallon bucket on the ground. Then he walked back into the room, to a mirrored closet. There was a floor safe in the corner. He bent down and pulled out a life insurance policy and a will, briefly studying them. David Allen Sloane, being of sound mind and body, was leaving everything to a woman named Melda Demanjuk. If her death predated his, his estate was to be divided among several different children's charities and a woman named Tina Scoccolo.

David Sloane had no immediate family.

Jenkins stood, walked into the bathroom, and turned on the light.

"Oh, Christ," Alex said. She stood behind him eyeing the dried blood, the rust color of bricks smeared on the white linoleum. "We are too late."

Jenkins placed his steps carefully, opened the medicine cabinet, using a corner so as not to leave a print, and looked around the sink. Then he stepped past her to the bedroom and picked up an article of clothing on the floor, a blue hospital scrub. It, too, was covered with blood.

"He's alive," he said, dropping the garment.

"What are you, an eternal optimist?"

"He's alive, unless you want to tell me that a dead man has a use for toothbrushes and razors." He nodded at the bathroom. "He took his toiletries. No toothbrush. No toothpaste. No razor. With that much blood on the floor, I doubt that he would have been able to stand and change his clothes if it had been his. Dead men also don't normally concern themselves with clean clothes or money, and someone came back here for both—someone who knew the sliding glass door would be unlocked, and knew the combination to that safe." He indicated the sliding glass door. "He came in from that balcony. You'll find a bucket down there he used as a step to get up onto the lower balcony."

"Why?"

"Probably because he was worried someone was watching the building. The back of the building is concealed. You can't see it from the front."

"So how do you explain the blood?"

"Not certain. Someone likely bled to death here, but it wasn't him. He straightened the living room; the police aren't about to tape his seat cushion back together for him. That tells me he was alive after the search."

"The search?"

"Somebody did a significant number on this place."

"How do you know it didn't happen during a struggle?"

"Intuition."

"If he cleaned up, why didn't he clean up the blood in the bathroom or pick up the clothes on the floor?"

"That happened afterward." He pointed to the clothes on the bed. "Those and the toothbrush tell me he came back, probably for money and clothes. He was packing— in a hurry."

"Or he was packing when someone killed him," Alex said.

"Then we'd find the suitcase of packed clothes and toiletries and probably a body or a chalk outline of the body, wouldn't we? No reason for the killer or the police to take his suitcase and toiletries."

She was quiet.

"He's alive. And he's running."

She didn't sound convinced. "Well, if you're right, he'll be tough to find unless you tell me more about what his involvement in this is."

Jenkins walked around the bed to a nightstand and pressed the button on the answering machine, waiting for it to rewind. The machine beeped, followed by a female voice. He turned up the volume. When the message finished he opened the cover of the machine, pulled out the tape, and slipped it into his pocket.

"Maybe not," he said, "but then, I'm an eternal optimist."

44

⌒

JACK CONNALLY'S LIFELESS BODY lay covered beneath a white sheet. Across the street from the glass
doors of the building entrance, a police barricade held back
a crowd. The lights from mobile television units reflected
through the glass doors like artificial suns, illuminating uniformed officers, plainclothes detectives, paramedics, and
forensic specialists crowding the lobby. Near the security
guard console, a police officer who appeared barely old
enough to shave stood in a stunned state of disbelief and
relief. His shirt pulled open, he fingered the hole in his uniform and the small indentation in his Kevlar vest. Other
officers stood inspecting a deformed bullet encased in a
plastic evidence bag as if it were a hunting trophy.

In the corner, Detective Frank Gordon sat in a chair with
a notebook in his lap, a pen in his hand, and a scowl on his
face. His jacket and shirt were off, and a paramedic worked
to bandage Gordon's muscled shoulder—the detective was
unwilling to go to the hospital until he spoke with Sloane.
The errant shots from the gunman were a reflex to the
police officers' bullets ripping through his body, making it
shake and flop like a marionette. Gordon was the unlucky

recipient of one of the strays, though luckily it had only grazed him. Not that he acted particularly happy about it. At the moment he looked like a kid forced to sit in a barber chair and get his hair cut, annoyed at the world and everyone in it. Despite the pain in his shoulder, the detective had been interrogating Sloane for the better part of an hour.

Across the lobby, behind a screen to shield against the news cameras, paramedics lifted the stretcher carrying Connally's body. The legs unfolded like an accordion and snapped into place. Tina stepped back, wiping away tears, and watched as they wheeled Connally toward the glass doors and the glow of lights. News anchors no doubt waited in television studios for updates and live footage of another shooting in a San Francisco high-rise. It would be a dramatic story.

"Those people must think the fucking circus is in town. Twice in one day we've managed to spice up their dreary little lives," Gordon said. "You know, I could arrest you just for not having a permit for that gun. In fact, I'm not quite sure why I don't."

Gordon sounded convincing, but Sloane knew that the detective wasn't about to arrest him. Sloane had just saved Tina's life. His story checked out; the dead janitor was more proof than Gordon would need. And Gordon had too much going on at the moment to worry about a gun permit, including a trip to the hospital. It was frustrated bravado.

Gordon let out an agitated sigh. "You have no idea who he is?"

Sloane reconsidered the janitor, the body a gruesome mass of holes and blood that looked like something from a mob hit. One of the bullets had torn out his left eye. At Sloane's request the coroner had pulled up the man's shirtsleeve to reveal an eagle tattoo, talons extended, a knife in its beak. It was just as Melda had described it. Otherwise the body was treated like a sacred artifact. A lot of people stood near it; some took photographs, but no one touched it, and no one would until the forensic team had photographed the scene and drawn its diagrams of everything's precise placement.

Gordon had responded to Sloane's professed lack of knowledge of the man's identity with measured disbelief and did not try to hide it. "It was like watching someone jump off the side of a fucking cliff," he said. "Overpowered, outgunned, not a fucking snowball's chance in hell, and he reaches for his weapon. That's the scariest fucking thing of all. It was a goddamned suicide. He preferred to die." Gordon looked back at Sloane. "And you're telling me you have no idea what his beef was with you? Well, I'm having a hard fucking time believing that, Mr. Sloane. I truly am."

Sloane didn't blame Gordon. He was having a hard time with it, too. Unfortunately, with the man now dead, neither of them would get the answers they wanted to their questions: who the man was, what he wanted, and why. Sloane also suspected that the file in his briefcase, about which he hadn't told Gordon and didn't intend to, would also not answer all his questions. Not even close.

Gordon closed his notebook and pointed his pen at the automatic weapon near the janitor's body. "That's an AC556F submachine gun. Four years in the army sticks to you like well-chewed gum, and that son of a bitch has 'military' written all over him, and not just because of the tattoo. Regardless of who he turns out to be, he was a pro, and he meant business. These kinds of guys don't usually act alone, Sloane. You know what I mean?"

Sloane had reached the same conclusion. Four years in the marines was equally hard to get out of your system.

"Don't go far," Gordon said, giving in to the inevitable trip to the hospital. He stood and draped his jacket over his shoulder, the paramedics at his side. "I will be calling you, and we will be talking further. Count on it."

Sloane walked to where Tina stood, her arms wrapped around her body as if she was unable to get warm. "Are you all right?"

She nodded, then turned and buried her head in his chest, her shoulders shaking in silent heaves. Sloane let her cry. After a minute he put an arm around her and led her to the back of the lobby, toward the rear doors. A woman wearing protective glasses and gloves was bent over the janitor, carefully examining the body. Sloane heard her as they passed.

"Jesus in heaven. Look at this, Frank."

Gordon stopped walking and looked over. The woman held the gunman's palm up to reveal scarred lacerations across the tips of his fingers from some form of crude, self-inflicted surgery.

"He has no fingerprints," she said.

THE CORNER OF Eighth and Mission Streets, the fringe of San Francisco's Mission District, had not yet been swept away in the South of Market redevelopment craze that had started in the 1990s and brought a new baseball stadium, trendy restaurants, and self-contained chic condominium communities. It likely never would. The poor had to live and work somewhere. Graffiti decorated the walls of automobile repair shops, warehouses, pawnshops, and corner markets that sold more liquor than groceries. Most of the businesses were closed for the night, protected behind rolling metal doors—also covered with graffiti—and locked gates. Young men in oversize parkas, baggy jeans, and wool knit watch caps stood on the sidewalk, leaning against American-made cars sporting chrome hubcaps, lowered almost to the ground and parked defiantly beneath "No Parking" signs. Rap music busted a thumping beat.

On the third pass, taking a third different route to satisfy himself they had not been followed, Sloane pulled into the parking lot of the Quality Inn, a misnomer if ever there was one. Tina waited in the car while he went inside the office to get a room. Jake would stay with his grandmother for the night. The guy behind the counter wanted to know how long Sloane anticipated needing the room—guests using the room for an entire night were apparently a rarity. Sloane asked for a room as far from the street as possible and parked the Barracuda in a spot near the back. He and Tina walked up an outdoor staircase that shook like the Loma Prieta earthquake, then around a U-shaped landing that looked down on a half-full pool of brownish water in desperate need of a filter.

Despite the building's outward appearance, the room surprised him—clean and neat. The motif was cheap 1970s wood-laminate furniture, purple floral bedspreads on two queen-size beds, and a burnt-orange shag carpet. He closed the door and snapped the metal security latch. Gordon had taken the Ruger; he was unarmed.

"The Taj Mahal," he said, surveying their surroundings. He set his duffel bag and briefcase near the desk. The television was chained to an eyebolt. "Let's hope the hookers use the rooms with just one bed." Tina did not react. "Are you hungry? I saw a couple of fast-food places down the road—"

She shook her head.

They stood in silence for a moment; then he started past her. "I'll start a hot shower for you. It'll make you feel better."

"Hold me," she said, stepping to him.

He wrapped his arms around her and held her close. He considered her so physically strong, yet her back felt as narrow as a child's. He felt the warmth and curves of her body against him and smelled the floral fragrance of her hair.

"Tina, I'm sorry," he started, but she looked up at him, stood on her toes, and kissed him hard on the mouth.

He wanted to stop her. He wanted to tell her it was not a good thing, but she gave him no chance to speak, and he realized that he had no desire to do so. They worked quickly, undoing buttons, pulling clothes from each other. He laid her down on the bed, feeling the warmth of her body pressing up against his, yearning as she guided him, helping him inside her, the warmth overwhelming him.

SHE SLEPT ON the adjacent bed, her breathing deep and full. After making love, they had moved to the shower, the stream of water and the steam soothing them as they gasped for breath, their mouths groping, their hands searching and exploring, their minds wanting to leave the horror of the night behind them and find solace in something beautiful. When they had finished they went back to the bed, where she lay in his embrace until he felt her drift slowly to sleep, physically and mentally exhausted. Then he gently removed his arm and covered her with blankets, watching her sleep, her features small and delicate.

In the span of forty-eight hours Sloane had come to realize why he had never married, why the women he dated never satisfied him, why he could not commit to them. But as with everything else in his life, he had pushed his feelings for Tina into the black abyss and covered it with work. It was easier that way, not dealing with it. It was complicated. It could never have worked out between them. Then, as he stood outside the taxi, she told him that it could work if he was willing to take the chance. She told him that he was the guy she was waiting for, but first he had to find himself. He wanted to slip beneath the covers beside her, to have her hold him. He wanted to go with her to Seattle and leave the past—whatever it was—buried and forgotten, to start over fresh. He wanted to take care of her and Jake, the little boy he had come to know from the firm's picnics, to be the father Jake had never had—uncertain how he would do that, but certain that he would be everything Jake's father was not. He'd take him to ball games, help him with his homework—be there for him—the things Sloane wished he had had growing up, but did not. But he knew that couldn't happen if he continued to sleepwalk through life. Tina was right. He could not find her until he had found himself, and he knew in his heart that this meant finding out what was happening, and why. His dreams were not dreams—they were memories. The dead woman was not a figment of his imagination or some psychological creation of his mind. She was real. So was Joe Branick, and that meant that the enormous black man who stood beside Joe Branick in Sloane's memory was also real. Branick was dead; so, too, was the woman, but perhaps the black man, whoever he was, was still alive.

Sloane removed the package from his briefcase but did not immediately rip it open like a child tearing through presents on Christmas morning. Four people had died because of the package. They deserved reflection. Melda deserved reflection. Then, with the beat of the car stereos and din of the people on the street corner silent, it was time. He redirected the cone of the lamp so the light would not shine in Tina's eyes, and turned the switch. He held the package beneath the dull, somber light, studying the handwriting. Though thin, the envelope felt heavier than he recalled—weighted, perhaps, by sorrow and circumstance. With that thought he turned the package over, lifted the metal tabs, unsealed the flap, and pulled out the pages.

45

MIGUEL IBARÓN PLANTED the rubber tip of his gold-handled cane on the cracked and uneven stones and leaned into his next step. His face displayed no outward sign of the familiar pain splintering from his ankles, knees, and back and shooting through his bones like an electric current. He could do nothing to hide the physical effects of the tumors on his once muscular body, now withered like a flower in the hot sun, but he could will himself to control his emotions, silently enduring the pain.

The cancer had taken inches from his height and thinned his body and once full head of rich, dark hair, leaving it a bleak white, but it would not take what remained of the dignified statesman. Tall and light-skinned, likely the result of Spanish blood in his ancestry, Ibarón remained over six feet tall, with a broad-shouldered frame that had once comfortably carried 210 pounds but now held just 175.

The woman at the entrance to the museum greeted him with a smile, refusing his money as she did on each visit.

"*No sirve aquí*" (It is no good here), she said. "For me to take money from you would be a great dishonor. You honor us here with your presence."

It was the reception accorded a man who had devoted his entire life to Mexico and to its people. Since joining the PRI, the Partido Revolucionario Institucional, Ibarón had been the epitome of a Prista—a party member. During a thirty-year career he had served Mexico as a *diputado* in the lower chamber of congress and as a *senador* in the upper chamber. Twice he had been one of the *tapados*, the "veiled ones," picked by the party as a potential presidential successor, but on neither occasion had he been deemed *verdadero tapado*, "the real veiled one."

Midday on a Saturday, Ibarón shuffled through the museum's seventeen rooms, the cracked terra-cotta floor sloping beneath his feet. Like most of the buildings in Mexico City and its surrounding area, the museum sank millimeters each year as the city's twenty-five million residents sucked the water from the soft soil that had once been the bed of the great lake, Lago de Texcoco.

The Ex-Convento de Churubusco stood on a place of great honor, filled with artifacts of great disgrace. Constructed on the site where the Aztec warriors had offered throbbing human hearts to appease their war god, Hummingbird, the building had been a fortress from which Mexican soldiers fiercely battled the United States Army advancing from Veracruz to Mexico City in 1847. The soldiers had expended every bullet to keep U.S. General David Twiggs at bay. When Twiggs finally entered the fortress and demanded that General Pedro Anaya surrender the remainder of their ammunition, Anaya had replied, "*Si hubiera cualquiera, usted no estaría aquí.*" (If there were any, you wouldn't be here.)

And yet, on a site of such honor and dignity had arisen a museum of ignominy. The stucco walls and red-tiled corridors were lined with faded photographs, yellowed documents, and memorabilia chronicling each foreign invasion from the Spanish to the French, to the Norteamericanos.

Ibarón stopped to consider the Monroe Doctrine from behind the glass. As he did, a man approached, a rolled newspaper in his right hand. "The arrogance of those Republicans does not allow them to see us as equals but as inferiors." The man read the comments of José Manuel Zozaya, Mexico's first ambassador to Washington.

"With time they will become our sworn enemies," Ibarón said, finishing the statement, each man letting the other know he was free to talk.

Mexico's intelligence chief, Ignacio López Ruíz, adjusted the collar of his jacket and straightened his tie, a habit that made it look as if the piece of cloth were choking him. A taut ball of muscle, Ruíz stood no more than five feet five but had forearms as thick as anvils, and a barrel chest developed from working during his formative years in his father's rock quarries. He was balding, a fact he tried to hide by growing his hair long and combing it across his head. His face was flat from years of boxing, and as tough as shoe leather. What Ruíz lacked in height and beauty he made up for in energy, stamina, and initiative. It had propelled him quickly through the police ranks, his swift ascent aided in no small measure by Miguel Ibarón.

Ruíz patted the comb-over with his fingers in a futile attempt to cover the crown of his head. "I received a call from the CIA station chief. With the consent of the PFP and the director, I have been requested to provide a complete analysis of my files," he said, referring to the Federal Preventive Police and the head of the Directorate for Intelligence, the two organizations that had become the umbrella for Mexico's intelligence service. They intensively tracked the activities of guerrilla and revolutionary groups.

"I was asked about the Popular Revolutionary Army, EPRI, the Zapatistas, the Revolutionary Army of the People . . . and the Mexican Liberation Front."

Ibarón nodded, showing no outward sign of emotion.

"They said only that they wanted the information to be thorough," Ruíz continued. "I have called my most reliable sources. No one knows the purpose of this request, Miguel. Beto knows nothing, nor does Toño," he said, referring by nickname to Alberto Castañeda and to Antonio Martínez, Mexico's police minister.

Ibarón contemplated the information with no more emotion than he showed for the faded pieces of paper in the glass case. "Who made the request of the CIA station chief?" he asked.

"An American in Washington, Joseph Branick."

"Do you know why?"

"No, but I do know that this man is dead."

Ibarón turned his head. "Dead?"

"The American papers have reported it to be so."

Ibarón walked past an exhibit depicting General Antonio López de Santa Anna signing the Gadsden Purchase, the document that forced Mexico to sell what is now southern Arizona and New Mexico. "What do we know of him?"

"Joseph Branick?" Ruíz shook his head. "Nothing. There appears to be no reason to suspect anything out of the ordinary."

"How did he die?"

"He killed himself. Shot himself in the head."

Ibarón considered Ruíz out of the corner of his eye but otherwise showed no response. "And you do not consider a friend of the president taking his own life to be out of the ordinary?" He, too, had read the papers. "Has not the president canceled the meeting here this weekend and chosen to stay in Washington for this man's funeral?"

"We have been assured this will not affect the progress of the negotiations."

"We cannot take that chance," Ibarón said. "Determine all that you can about this man Joe Branick."

"And what of the negotiations?"

"If Robert Peak will not come to us, we will go to Robert Peak." Ibarón turned without further comment, retrieved his white straw hat from the woman at the entrance, and left the building, leaving Ruíz standing alone.

Outside, he replaced his hat to protect his head from the hot summer sun. The air was thick and heavy, sodden, but not from the layer of smog that hung over the valley and choked Mexico City and its people during the humid summer months.

Ibarón smelled a storm.

46

Berryville,
Virginia

LEAVING TINA AT the hotel was as difficult as anything Sloane had ever done, but he also knew she could not come with him. Aside from the danger, this was his life to figure out. He retrieved his laptop computer from his office, and holed up in a hotel under a false name. He spent the day searching the Internet, making airline, hotel, and rental car reservations, and calling Foster & Bane's Los Angeles office. His cases started much the same way. A client came to him with a problem. He needed to find a solution. Before he could decide on a course of action, he needed to know the facts—every detail, no matter how small or trivial. Those facts became puzzle pieces that, when put in the correct positions, revealed a story. The only difference was, this time he was both the lawyer and the client. He hoped the saying about the lawyer who represents himself having a fool for a client didn't hold true.

Joe Branick was the primary subject of his research, and Sloane found no shortage of information about the man. Branick had graduated from Georgetown University, where his freshman roommate was a political science major named Robert Peak, known to his friends as Rob. Over the next four years the two became close friends, sharing an apartment and an interest in politics and sports. Both graduated at the top of their class. Peak followed his father to the CIA, and with the elder Robert Peak in a position to help, Robert was groomed like a show poodle, serving as the youngest station director in England, Germany, and Mexico. He became deputy director for operations at forty-five, the deputy director of the Agency at forty-eight, and director under President George Marshall, in whose cabinet his father served. Robert Peak entered mainstream politics when Marshall lost his bid for reelection to Gordon Miller, putting Peak out of a job. Four years later Peak became the vice presidential running mate of Thomas McMillan in a successful campaign to unseat Miller. Peak succeeded McMillan after two terms.

Joe Branick's life had been less storied. An engineer, he married his high school sweetheart and went to work for a series of national and international oil companies. Married thirty-five years, he and his wife had two daughters and a son. After a three-year project between the American oil equipment manufacturer Entarco and Mexico's oil company, Pemex, Branick returned to the United States and moved the family back home to Boston to be near his eight siblings in an Irish Catholic enclave. He joined his four brothers in a family-owned and -operated import-export business. Life seemed set. Then his friend Robert Peak announced his intention to seek the presidency and asked—some say begged—Joe Branick to run his campaign. With his three children grown and in college, Branick accepted and was given considerable credit when Peak won. It was widely assumed that Branick would become White House chief of staff, but apparently politics intervened. The Republican party had its eye on retired three-star general Parker Madsen, a rapidly rising player in the Washington political arena. Word was, Madsen would join Peak on the Republican reelection ticket. Branick had decided to return home, but Peak again enticed him to stay, creating a position just for him: special consultant to the president. Branick was largely unheard from until park police found his body in a national park.

Conspicuously absent from any of Sloane's research was a rational explanation why such a seemingly well-adjusted, well-liked family man would put a loaded gun to his head and pull the trigger. Details were scarce. Branick was reported to have left his office shortly after three-thirty Thursday afternoon. No one, not even his secretary, knew where he went. His wife grew concerned when he did not call that evening, as was his routine. She was unable to reach him at an apartment he kept in Georgetown on nights he worked late and didn't want to commute. Shortly before dawn his body was found in Black Bear National Park, a gun in his hand. The Department of Justice had taken jurisdiction, though the *Washington Post* was reporting that local law enforcement was none too pleased, and intimating that the DOJ was keeping a tight lid on its investigation. The DOJ said little in its defense. Rivers Jones, the assistant U.S. attorney in charge of the investigation, declined comment and directed all inquiries to the DOJ press office, saying it would be inappropriate to make a statement while the investigation was ongoing. The White House had also been mum. The only statement came from Parker Madsen, who appeared in the East Wing the morning Branick's body was discovered, and read from a prepared statement that described the president and first lady as "shocked" and "deeply saddened" at the loss of a good friend and dedicated public servant. To Sloane it sounded neatly scripted and devoid of emotion for a man who had lost his lifelong friend, but that might also be the way a public figure with a job that could not be ignored, coped.

After getting as much information as he could from the Internet, Sloane found a men's store in a mall, bought additional clothes, then drove around the Bay Area picking up airline boarding passes. He called Tina's cell phone from a pay phone in the airport just before catching a red-eye to Dulles.

"I'm sorry I couldn't say good-bye," he said.

"Then don't. Tell me you're coming back."

"I'm coming back," he said, "after I find myself."

"David, I didn't mean that."

"You couldn't have been more right, Tina. Count on me."

"I will."

THREE MILES OUTSIDE Berryville, Sloane drove with the window of the rental car down. The air had a tranquil, undisturbed feel indicating that it would be hot, with little or no breeze. Thick groves of trees had given way to fields of summer-brown grass and a landscape of scattered farmhouses and grazing horses. After the slope in the road, a landmark, he slowed and turned onto a country road, then drove until he came to the string of mailboxes on wooden posts—his second landmark—and turned onto the dirt-and-gravel easement. Lush green lawn rolled out like carpet around a white two-story farmhouse with dormer windows, forest-green shutters, and a large wrap-around porch. A red barn loomed behind it, and chestnut and bay horses grazed in an expansive pasture.

Talking to surviving relatives was always delicate because their response could never be predicted, but Sloane hoped Joe Branick's family would share something in common with a stranger: a desire to know why he was dead. He considered the burnt-orange envelope on the passenger seat beside him. As he had suspected, the information it contained generated more questions than it answered.

A thick hedge blocked his view around a turn in the road, and he had to brake suddenly to keep from rear-ending a police cruiser parked in front of a freestanding garage. A golden retriever bounded off the porch to announce his arrival, barking, tail wagging. Sloane stuffed the package into his briefcase and turned to find the dog's paws on the window, head in the car, tongue panting.

"Well, how are you?" he asked. "How about letting me out?" The dog whined and got down from the window.

Sloane stepped out and bent to let the dog smell the back of his hand, then scratched her behind the ears and under the chin. She responded by jumping up and putting her paws on his hips. It never hurt to make friends with the family pet. At worst it was a topic of conversation.

A uniformed officer approached. "Can I help you?" he asked.

"That's all right, Officer." A distinguished-looking woman in khaki cotton slacks, a blue silk blouse, and flat shoes walked down from the porch. When she reached

Sloane she tugged once on the dog's collar. "Down, Sam. Sit." She looked at Sloane. "I'm sorry. She hasn't had much exercise lately." She spoke with a New England accent that rolled off her tongue, ignoring the letter "r."

"That's all right. She's a beautiful dog."

"She was my brother's. Are you David Sloane?"

Sloane held out a hand. "Call me David."

She gripped Sloane's hand with the firmness of a woman used to shaking men's hands. There was nothing feminine or conciliatory about it. "Aileen Blair."

Sloane guessed Blair to be in her early to mid-fifties. She had a tall, athletic build, with auburn hair cut naturally to lie just past her shoulders, a streak of gray just to the left of the part. Her face remained youthful, with just the trace of crow's-feet showing at the corners of her eyes. A strand of pearls circled her neck. She was an attractive woman.

"I have iced tea inside," she said.

Sloane followed Aileen Blair up two wooden steps that creaked under his weight. A porch swing hung motionless in the corner, near a wicker table. Clay pots lined the porch edge, the flowers beginning to wither. Sam followed them, but Blair would not allow her through the screen door.

"Stay," she directed, and the dog stopped. "She's really a good dog. It's a shame they can't keep her. Do you know anyone looking for a dog?"

"I'm afraid I don't," Sloane said. He followed Blair through the screen door. It was dark inside the house, mostly from the dark oak floor and patterned wallpaper. The house smelled of dough baking—cookies or a piecrust. He heard voices in other rooms of the house, but no one came into the hall to greet them. Blair slid apart two paneled doors and stepped into a den of green walls and white-shuttered windows. Two burgundy leather couches, a glass coffee table, and a forest-green wingback chair surrounded an oak entertainment console. Behind one of the couches was a green felt pool table and, standing near it, a life-size cardboard cutout of Larry Bird, the former Boston Celtics basketball player and living legend. A basketball junkie, Sloane gravitated toward it as Blair slid the doors behind him closed. This would be a private conversation.

"Joe loved the Celtics, especially Larry Bird," Blair said, adjusting the shutters to let in slatted light. "He bled Celtics green. He and his brothers considered the parquet that man walked on to be sacred. They went to every game at the Garden and cried like babies when they tore it down. I'm not sure how Joe got that thing, and even less sure how he convinced his wife to let him keep it, but my brother was pretty persuasive when he wanted something." She turned from the shutters. "So am I."

Sloane turned to her.

"You damn well better not be looking for a story, Mr. Sloane. I handle the family business matters." She looked up at a family photograph still mounted on the wall. Five grown men stood in mud-covered cleats and rugby uniforms with their arms locked around each other's shoulders, Joe Branick in the middle. "Joe's brothers handle the physical matters."

47

~

The Zona Rosa,
Mexico City

The telephone call startled him from a deep sleep. Joe Branick offered no pleasantries. "Get dressed. Be in front of your building in five minutes."

Charles Jenkins hung up, took seconds to clear his head, threw aside the covers, and stood. He took a moment to allow his body to adjust to being suddenly vertical instead of horizontal, then stepped across the room to the cold bathroom tile, splashed lukewarm water on his face, and relieved his bladder. He pulled on a pair of jeans and a button-down shirt he picked from a pile on the floor, and four minutes after hanging up the telephone he walked out the door, slipping into his blue windbreaker with "Entarco" embossed in gold letters across the right breast. He waited beneath the glow of a streetlamp. At not quite three in the morning, beads of perspiration were already forming on his forehead. It would be hot and humid in Mexico City—no surprise. The smog would be bad. By the end of days like this it hurt his chest to take a deep breath.

Jenkins rented a small apartment above a sidewalk café in the Zona Rosa, an affluent suburb of lively, colorful shops and restaurants he had come to enjoy for their vitality and for the women who frequented them. At the moment, the Zona Rosa remained asleep, the store windows dark, the streets uncluttered with the persistent flow of cars or the sound of taxis honking. He bit into a green apple and watched the headlights of a blue Ford racing toward him and pulling to the curb.

"I'll need directions," Branick said as Jenkins lowered himself into the passenger seat.

Jenkins spoke through a mouthful of apple. "Where are we going?"

Branick pulled from the curb and drove around the back of a VW Beetle taxi, the only other car on the street, ran a red light, and headed south. Wherever they were going, they were going in a hurry.

"The village," he said.

Jenkins stopped chewing. In the dark of early morning he had not noticed it, but now he saw the strain on Branick's face. He looked troubled, his expression grim. "What's the matter, Joe?"

Branick spoke softly, like whispering a prayer. "I think something happened there last night." He looked over at Jenkins. "Something bad. Something very bad."

Jenkins rolled down the window and tossed the apple out onto the street. In the past several weeks he, too, had sensed something happening, like a man whose body begins to ache with the first signs of a flu. Only it wasn't his body that ached, it was something inside him, something deep within the fabric of who he was, something that the years of sitting in a pew in a Baptist church had planted— his soul troubled him.

"Why?" he heard himself ask, though he knew he would have been more correct to ask, "What happened?" And that, too, troubled him.

"Because of your reports, Charlie," Branick said. "Your reports made people nervous."

Jenkins felt heat spreading from his gut, tension and anxiety flowing to his limbs. Branick glanced over at him, then turned back to the windshield as if speaking to a ghost on the highway. "They were so believable," he said. "You made them so damn believable."

CHARLES JENKINS SAT UP, momentarily disoriented. Something was ringing—his cell phone. He reached for it on the laminated nightstand in which someone had carved, "DS sucks dick," and flipped it open.

"Hello? Hello . . . *Damn* it."

He flipped the phone closed, stood, and paced the tiny room. His shirt was damp, his hands clammy. The joints of his fingers and the backs of his knees ached with a cold pain, as if his body temperature had dropped, leaving him numb. Feeling suddenly claustrophobic in the squalid motel room, he stuck his head out a window he'd managed to pry open despite several coats of paint. He breathed through his mouth to avoid the smell of rotting garbage and urine rising from the alley below.

After leaving Sloane's apartment he and Alex knocked on several of the other tenants' doors. Those willing to speak had a lot to say. What they said led them to a Detective Frank Gordon.

They found Gordon propped in a leather chair in his den, his arm in a sling and his mood foul. On a Sunday morning,

Gordon looked like it was five o'clock on a Friday afternoon. Red lines made his eyes look like a road map; they seemed to be begging for sleep. His face said "fatigue." The only things that seemed to keep him going were the pain pills he washed down with gulps of cold coffee; Alex's legs, which he eyeballed while rocking rhythmically; and the self-satisfaction that he had been right, that there was more to Sloane's story than Sloane was letting on. This last piece of information he inferred from the fact that the CIA was sitting in his den.

In Jenkins's experience, the only thing cops loved more than having a good story to tell was telling it. Gordon was no different. After an hour Jenkins had pried from him three important pieces of information: Sloane was alive, though where he was at that moment, Gordon didn't know. Someone had died in Sloane's apartment—the woman Sloane had named in his will, Melda Demanjuk—and apparently Sloane had found the body. When Gordon told them the woman's throat had been slit, Jenkins had to momentarily close his eyes and regain his composure. When the police arrived, Sloane was clutching the woman, crying, and unresponsive. That had led to his being hospitalized under the care of a psychiatrist by the name of Dr. Brenda Knight at UCSF Hospital. Knight apparently had experience with post-traumatic stress disorder and believed that Sloane was suffering from a similar condition. Finally, Gordon was holding a stiff in the county morgue—a man he said was likely ex-military and carrying enough firepower to keep a small platoon hunkered down for a week.

The cellular telephone in Jenkins's hand rang again. Only one person had the number. He flipped it open. "You've arrived?"

After leaving Gordon's home he had driven with Alex to the airport. They paid cash for one-way tickets to Washington. Even with false identifications the two of them would have been a difficult couple to miss. Besides, the conversation with Gordon had triggered one more thing that Jenkins wanted to do before he left town, and since a psychiatrist would not readily talk with him, he'd have to do it the old-fashioned way. Alex had called a friend in Langley who would meet her at the airport with a few of his buddies. In the interim she had asked him to look discreetly into David Sloane.

"No problem," she said.

"What do you know?"

"Sloane made eleven airline reservations to eight different destinations on six different airlines departing from the San Francisco, Oakland, and San Jose airports. In each city of arrival he made reservations at car rental agencies and local hotels. He used a credit card for each transaction so the reservations could be easily traced. Then he picked up at least three boarding passes, each to a different destination but leaving at roughly the same time."

"It's a shell game."

"Maybe, but you picked the right shell. One of the tickets was to Dulles. Are you going to tell me how you knew that?"

"What, and spoil the surprise?"

"I'll keep an eye on his credit cards and bank accounts, but my guess is, he'll use cash from here on out."

Jenkins was sure Sloane would, and that was a good thing. If Jenkins couldn't find Sloane, maybe nobody else would, either. "What about the tattoo Detective Gordon described?"

"I'm working on it, but it will take time if you want to keep it discreet."

"I do," Jenkins said. He looked down at the yellow pad with the scrawled notes and the small blue dots and doodles in the margin that he'd taken from Dr. Brenda Knight's office.

"You okay? You sound a million miles away," Alex said.

Jenkins thought of the village in the jungle and what he had seen there that morning. "You woke me. I was napping."

"Must be nice."

"I'll call you tomorrow when I get in. Keep your head down, Alex. I can't emphasize that enough."

He hung up, picked up the notepad, and studied Dr. Knight's scribbled handwriting detailing David Sloane's recurring nightmare—and his own.

48

⌒

AILEEN BLAIR DIRECTED Sloane to the couch and handed him a glass of iced tea with a slice of lemon. It was cool in his hand. Condensation clouded the outside of the glass. She took a seat in the wingback chair, shook a cigarette from a pack of Marlboros, studying him as she did so, then offered him the pack. Sloane declined.

"Good for you," she said.

She lit the cigarette, set the pack and lighter on the coffee table, and put a glass ashtray in her lap, blowing smoke at the ceiling as she talked. "One damn habit I've never been able to lick. I've quit more times than I can remember. My mother harangues me. My husband harangues me. My kids *really* harangue me. I stopped for about three weeks. Then I got the news of my brother's death."

"I'm very sorry," he said.

She flicked ashes as if flicking away his comment. "So who are you, Mr. Sloane?"

"Please, call me David." He handed her a business card from his shirt pocket.

She considered it for a moment with a bemused smile. "A lawyer."

"I'm not here looking for business, Ms. Blair." He recalled from the newspaper articles that Aileen Branick Blair was an attorney in Boston. He hoped it gave him credibility, and the two of them common ground.

"I hope not. It wouldn't say much about your practice if you had to come three thousand miles for business." She put the card on the table. "You said you have information that concerns my brother's death?"

"I believe I do."

She crossed her legs and smoothed her khakis. The family resemblance to her brother was strong, especially with her hair pulled back and tied in a ponytail: the prominent chin, Irish-fair skin, blue eyes. "All right, but let me be straight with you before you get started. I'm not even sure why you're sitting here. I've been asking myself why I said yes ever since you called. Next thing I knew, I was giving you directions. We've had dozens of telephone calls and I've said no to every single one of them. But there was something about you on the telephone, something in your voice, a sincerity I hadn't heard in the others, that convinced me to talk with you. I like to believe I have pretty good instincts." She stubbed the butt of the cigarette into the ashtray, picked up the pack, and tapped out another as she continued talking. "But let me tell you something before you get started and waste both our time: I've been hearing a lot of crap for three days now and not getting a lot of answers. My mother and father are too old for this, my brothers have a business to run, and Joe's wife . . . well, she's not emotionally capable of handling this right now. We sent her home to Boston with her kids to make the arrangements. I'm the youngest, but I'm also the family bulldog. I don't deny it. The responsibility falls to me. I've gone from shock to denial. According to my therapist, I'm supposed to be at reluctant acceptance by now, but I'm too goddamned pissed."

He smiled at her comment. "Fair enough."

She nodded. "So how did you know my brother?"

"I don't know."

She arched an eyebrow. "You told me on the telephone that Joe called you."

"He did call me. Your brother called my office in San Francisco and left a message for me Thursday evening, six-thirty San Francisco time." Sloane handed her the pink message slip. "Judging from what I've read in the newspapers, that's after anyone reported seeing him alive."

"That's his office number," she said.

"And I have to assume from the fact that he left that number and a message requesting that I call him back that your brother intended to go back to his office." The implication hung between them like the cigarette smoke. "So, cutting to the chase, it appears your brother expected to be alive. Not exactly the act of a man contemplating killing himself."

Blair studied him. "But you never talked to him?"

"No."

"And yet you say you didn't know my brother?"

"I said I don't think I knew him, Aileen. It gets more complicated after the phone call."

She nodded. "I thought it might. I didn't figure you flew three thousand miles to tell me your voice mail, either. I think you better start from the beginning, David."

He had considered where to begin on the drive to the house. "The night after your brother left his message, someone broke into my mailbox and my apartment. The strange thing about it was, they didn't take anything. They just tore it apart. I dismissed it as vandals."

"But not anymore."

"Whoever broke in was looking for something, something in particular. Something sent to me in the mail—by your brother." He reached into the briefcase, took out the envelope, and handed it to her.

She considered the envelope. "That's Joe's handwriting," she confirmed. She opened the tab, pulled out the papers, and studied them for several minutes. Then she looked up at Sloane, her brow furrowed. "Adoption papers?"

"Your brother sent me the paperwork for the release of those papers. He found them. I didn't. Before I received that package I had no idea I was adopted. I understood that my parents died in a car accident when I was a young boy."

"You had no idea?"

It had been an astonishing revelation, except that Sloane, on contemplating thoughts he had never before stopped to analyze, for fear of the answers, realized he did not feel pain or anger when he opened the package. He felt relief. He could not recall ever crying over the death of his parents or remember longing for a gentle touch, a guiding hand, or a consoling voice, and that had brought guilt. Why did he feel so little for two people he was supposed to love instinctively? The revelation in the package had lifted that burden from his shoulders, though in its place it had left an even heavier weight, one that made him feel even more like a rudderless boat in a storm.

He pointed to the papers in Blair's hands. "Edith and Ernest Sloane, the people I believed to be my parents, died in a car accident when I was six years old."

Aileen Blair shuffled through the file. "These are the papers to adopt you?"

"I thought so."

She stopped fingering through the pages and looked up at him. "Joe was wrong?"

"You'll see records in there from St. Andrews Hospital in Glendale, California. I had my law firm in Los Angeles obtain them for me. The woman on those forms, the one who supposedly gave me up for adoption, was named Dianna O'Leary. Eighteen years old, unmarried, living with a staunchly religious aunt and uncle."

"Jesus!" Blair said. She had come to the articles that Foster & Bane's Los Angeles office had obtained from the *Los Angeles Times* archives. Dianna O'Leary did not leave the hospital with a baby boy, and she had not given him up for adoption.

"She suffocated her own son," Blair said, startled.

"The district attorney didn't have any compassion for her. She did fifteen years for second-degree murder. When she got out she killed herself with an overdose of prescription painkillers."

Blair gave him a quizzical look. "But if that woman didn't give up her child for adoption, then these papers make no sense."

"No, they don't."

She looked up at him.

"Someone forged them to make it look like Edith and Ernest Sloane adopted that child and named him David."

"Who?"

"The only logical assumption is that it was your brother."

She lowered the papers. "Joe? Why would Joe forge these papers?"

"Again, I don't know for certain, but the only rational explanation I can think of, Aileen, was to hide me, my identity."

Now she leaned closer. "Why would you assume that?"

He took the papers from her hands, shuffling through them before handing one back to her. "Because Edith and Ernest Sloane did adopt a young boy, Aileen." He handed her a death certificate. "But David Allen Sloane, seven years old, died in that car accident with them."

49

$\sim$

EXETER ROSE FROM his beanbag to greet Parker Madsen as Madsen stepped into his office. He rubbed the crown of the dog's head, buzzed his secretary, and instructed her to admit his visitor.

"I apologize for disturbing you," Rivers Jones said on opening the door and entering the office. His gait was noticeably quicker. "You said you wanted to be completely briefed on the Branick investigation. We have a problem."

Madsen arched an eyebrow as he fed Exeter a dog treat and continued to rub his head.

"We've reviewed Joe Branick's telephone records for the past six months. There's a number that comes up repeatedly." Jones circled behind a chair, as if distance would soften the blow of the information he was about to impart. "The number is to a home in McLean. The calls were made at all hours of the day and night, sometimes one right after the other. Several the final day."

"A woman," Madsen said, still scratching the dog's head.

Jones leaned forward. "She's an escort, sir."

Madsen looked up. "A prostitute."

Jones cleared his throat. "In a manner of speaking."

"She gets paid to have sex with men?"

"Yes."

"A prostitute. A whore."

Jones propped his briefcase on the chair, took out a single sheet of paper encased in plastic, and handed it to Madsen. "And we found this."

Madsen snapped his fingers and pointed Exeter back to his beanbag before stepping forward and taking the document. He put on a pair of bifocal reading glasses. "Where?" he asked, lowering the page.

"In his briefcase."

"Who else knows about this?"

"Difficult to say. The briefcase was in his office when we went in to . . . check for things. The office was still sealed, so possibly no one, but I can't be sure."

"Be sure."

Jones nodded, taking back the letter. The sound of the air conditioner hummed above them. "Excuse me for saying so, General, but you don't appear surprised."

Madsen smirked. "Very little surprises me anymore about men and their character, Rivers. I've spent my life evaluating men. Unfortunately I've become a cynic. Few men are as they appear. I told you when I briefed you on the situation that I suspected more. I'm sure this is another reason the president wants this matter handled delicately." He turned and walked back behind his desk. "What are you going to do?"

Jones thought for a moment. "I intend to talk with this woman, Terri Lane, find out what she knows about this, when she last saw or spoke to Mr. Branick."

Madsen rubbed a hand across his lips, appearing deep in thought.

"Do you disagree?"

Madsen shrugged and put a hand in the air. "It is your investigation, Rivers."

Jones looked troubled. "I respect your opinion."

Madsen took a breath. "If this woman is interviewed, Rivers, this matter will leak. We both know that. The more stones you throw in a pond of water, the more ripples you create. The more ripples, the better the chance some will reach the shore. If one does, who knows what stories this woman is liable to start telling."

"Sir?"

"Given her chosen profession, Rivers, and the fact that these calls are to McLean, I have to assume she had a regular and well-paying clientele. Do you think the press would leave this with Joe Branick? They'd smell blood. They'd smell a scandal."

"You don't think she'd be discreet?"

Madsen found this amusing. "God knows how this woman recorded her clientele to protect herself, Rivers. If it is as I suspect, she'll be on *Oprah* and every other talk show across America." Madsen looked to his right, as if he could see Robert Peak sitting in the Oval Office. "You can imagine how something like this, if leaked to the press, would destroy Joe Branick's family." He circled behind his desk. "The president is clearly protecting a fallen comrade, Rivers. Unfortunately, I'm afraid others won't see it that way. After Watergate and Ken Starr, everyone wants the chance to take down a president."

Jones cleared his throat. "I've thought about that, and I think I may have a solution."

Madsen turned back to him.

"This information doesn't change the fact that Mr. Branick killed himself."

"I suppose it doesn't," Madsen said.

"The man committed suicide. We took this matter in-house to confirm that fact. Now we have. This is not a matter of national security or public interest."

Madsen nodded. "I agree. What's your point?"

"My point is, we can issue a statement to the press that the United States Department of Justice is satisfied that this was a horribly unfortunate, self-inflicted act, and direct that the matter be handled by the West Virginia park police to close."

"The press will want to know what convinced you."

"The autopsy." Jones smiled, apparently seeing a light at the end of his dark tunnel. "We obtained it yesterday." He pulled the report from his briefcase and handed it to Madsen. "The ballistics tests match. The powder burns are consistent with a self-inflicted wound. He shot himself."

Madsen looked up from the report. "What about the chemical analysis?"

"It's irrelevant," Jones said. "It has nothing to do with the question of whether he did or did not kill himself. It doesn't change the ultimate act. We'll issue a short statement that the autopsy confirms Joe Branick took his own life. It will be left to the local authorities to close the investigation. Since they won't find anything, it will end there."

Madsen shook his head as if unconvinced. "The press will still want to know why he did it, why he took his own life."

"Leave that to the family. If they want to besmirch his reputation, disclose that his marriage was in a shambles and he was drinking, let them."

Madsen nodded. "It sounds like a workable solution. But how do you intend to give this information to the family?"

Jones grimaced as if feeling the onset of a sudden pain. "That could be difficult. Mr. Branick's sister has been raising hell waiting for the autopsy results. She's scheduled to come to Washington tomorrow to clean out Mr. Branick's office, and she wants a status report."

"When are you meeting her?"

"Noon. I intended to break the news to her then. I could cancel—"

"No." Madsen considered this for a moment. "Keep your appointment. Meet her at Mr. Branick's office." He handed the autopsy report back to the assistant United States attorney. "Then tell her there's been a change of plans."

50

AILEEN BLAIR STARED, mouth agape. The ash on her burning cigarette looked precariously close to snapping off and falling in her lap. "But if that child died, as you say, then . . ."

"Then who am I?" Sloane was standing, hands in the pockets of his pants. "Right now I have no idea," he said. The words, which he had only been thinking since opening the package, sounded foreign and unnerving.

He had, in some respects, felt "different" all his life. Being raised in multiple foster families, some better than others, had separated him from his peers. His were not parents who sat on the PTA and volunteered their time in the classroom. So, despite how well he did in school academically, he remained branded as a result. He was the "foster" kid, which translated into the kid with "problems." He was the kid without parents, without family by which other parents could judge his respectability, character, and values. Not knowing anything about his background, about his makeup, unnerved other people more than it had ever unnerved him. He was like the stray dog found walking down the sidewalk that by all appearances looked friendly, but no matter how well it behaved, suspicion about its background always lingered, with the fear that something dark within that background would eventually force it to lash out. So, although at school he was not shunned or ignored, those who did take the time to get to know him kept that relationship within the safe confines of the school walls. Sloane didn't blame them or hold any resentment for it. There were always excuses why he could not be included in public functions, why he was not on the birthday party list, why girls chose other boys to take them to the school dance. As a result, he had turned inward, with a fierce desire to succeed and to find his own place in life. The marines had initially given him that opportunity, a sense of belonging, but in time he realized that it had been a false reality, a brotherhood created more from circumstance and the common bond of having nowhere else to go. He left the Corps because he would not accept then that he could not do better than that. Now he wondered whether he could.

"And there appears no way to trace it," he said. "Any paper trail ends before it ever starts."

The ash gave way, tumbling into her lap. Blair stood, brushed it from her pants, and stubbed out the cigarette. She started to look at her watch, then dismissed it. "To hell with the time; I need a drink and I don't think there's a person in the world who'd blame me. Join me, Mr. Sloane? If I know my brother, he has some good Scotch around here."

She found it in a cabinet beneath the mounted pool rack and poured them each a small glass over ice. "I don't have an answer for you, David, but I can tell you one thing about my brother Joe. He always did the right thing. If he did what you say, forged these papers, then it was the right thing to do."

"Let me ask you something, Aileen. Have you ever considered the possibility that your brother—"

"Didn't kill himself?" She handed him his glass. "My brother did not kill himself, David. That's as good a bet as any I know, and I've wagered a few in my day." She raised a finger as she made each point. "One, my brother was a Catholic. I know that sounds like a lot of religious crap to most people, but not to this family. Suicide is not acceptable. Two, my brother didn't just love his wife and kids; he adored them. He would not do this to them. He would not leave them this way. Three, my mother. She's Irish Catholic, David. She doesn't need any more reason than that to take all the credit for her children's accomplishments, and all the blame for their failures. Joe knew that. He was her favorite. I say that without bitterness. They had a special bond. He wouldn't do this to her. He wouldn't put this at her feet for the remainder of her life." She fixed Sloane with steel-blue eyes. "God knows I love my faith and my sister-in-law, but I won't have my mother blaming herself for Joe's death. Do you understand?"

He nodded. "I understand."

"Now, there's something more you're not telling me, David. You wouldn't be here otherwise. You already knew these papers were forged. You didn't need me to tell you that. There must be something else. You said you thought you didn't know my brother. Did you know him?"

"I've met your brother before, Aileen, though I don't remember where or when. But what happened that day is haunting me."

During the next forty-five minutes Sloane provided Aileen Blair the details of his nightmare and told her about seeing her brother standing in the room alongside a large African-American man. Blair sipped her Scotch, listened patiently, and asked few but pointed questions.

When Sloane finished she had an empty glass and an ashtray of cigarette butts.

"I'm not sure where all this is going to lead, but I would like to know more about your brother," he said. "I thought maybe it might lead to this other man. It's not much, but it's a start."

"I'd like to help you, David, but I haven't got very far myself. There's a wall up at the moment, and I haven't been able to get over it. I'm sure part of that is related to Joe's career."

"His career?"

She sat silently for a moment, and he sensed she was considering what to tell him. "You won't find it in any newspapers or on his résumé, David, but my brother worked for the CIA."

In his mind Sloane shuffled through the newspaper clippings he'd read earlier, his mind ticking off the facts. Branick had worked overseas in England, Germany, and Mexico. For some reason that had registered as significant, but he couldn't figure out why. Now it came to him. Each was a country where Robert Peak had served as a CIA station chief.

"He worked for Robert Peak. They were friends."

She nodded. "As I understand it, Joe was put on a company's payroll to make his presence in the country legitimate. Of course, we weren't supposed to know any of this, but secrets are hard to keep in this family. We were happy the day he quit and came back to Boston. None of us wanted him to go back to Washington."

"I don't imagine you would have any records, any checks that might tell me the companies he worked for?"

Blair shook her head as she looked around the room. "I'm sure we could dig up some of the names, but I haven't seen any records, David, and I doubt Joe would have kept any here. The most logical . . ." She stopped, seeming to study him for a moment.

"You could do it," she said.

"Do what?"

"You're a bit young, but not so much that I think anyone would notice. Jon has always been youthful in appearance."

Now Sloane was totally confused. "I'm sorry—Jon?"

"My husband. I thought it when I saw you get out of the car. How tall are you, David? Six one? Six two?"

"Six two."

"About a hundred and ninety pounds?"

"About. Why?"

Blair smiled. "You and he look very much alike, when he was a younger man and his hair dark. You're also the same size. Same build. Same complexion."

"You've lost me, Aileen."

"I'm supposed to clean out Joe's office tomorrow. I can't; a problem has developed getting his body home to Boston, and that takes priority. Before you arrived I was about to call and tell them I'd have to reschedule."

"And you think I could go."

"I can call and tell them I'm sending Jon in my place."

"I don't know, Aileen."

"It would get you in the door, get you a chance to look through Joe's office. That's the most likely place you'd find his personal papers, Rolodex, contacts."

Sloane shook his head. "I don't have any identification, Aileen."

"That's what I meant about your build. You can borrow Jon's license. He's one of those drivers who never gets a ticket; they renew his license in the mail. I think he was just about forty when he last had his picture taken. You two could be brothers. And I'll get you a couple of his business cards just in case."

"Is that enough?"

"You won't need anything else. I've raised Cain the past week. The assistant U.S. attorney handling this is scared to death of me. When I call I'll tell him I don't want you hassled with the usual Washington red-tape crap, that I want it expedited beforehand. I've been to Joe's office before. It's in the Old Executive Office Building just across from the White House. You have to pass through security, but they can put you on a VIP list to make it easier. They're mostly concerned about weapons."

"What about a secretary or somebody—"

"Who knows Jon? Jon's a homebody. He rarely ever leaves Boston." She smiled. "What could go wrong?"

51

CLAY BALDWIN SAT on a stool balancing his weight on his right leg while reading the front-page article in the *Spirit of Jefferson,* the local weekly. Late in the afternoon, the prolonged sitting aggravated his sciatic nerve, but that wasn't what, at the moment, was making him think of just calling it quits. Three months earlier he had begged his brother-in-law to rescue him from the "honey-do" list his wife had saved for Baldwin's retirement. J. Rayburn Franklin had given him a part-time job answering the phones and manning the front counter, and it had gotten him out of the house. But with the news of Bert Cooperman's death, Baldwin was thinking more and more about going home and spending time with his wife and grandchildren.

Cooperman's funeral had been that morning. The department remained subdued and would likely be that way for a while. They started a memorial fund, hoping to raise enough money to help with the baby's expenses and future education. It was a poor substitute for a father. Baldwin lifted the newspaper and considered the picture of Cooperman's battered patrol car hanging suspended from a crane. It made him think about how Coop had always wanted to see his picture and name in the paper.

"Christ," Baldwin said.

The glass door opened behind him, but Baldwin didn't bother to turn. He'd seen Tom Molia's emerald-green 1969 Chevy drive into the parking lot. "Board," he said.

Molia stopped in midstride, fighting the urge to tear the piece of cardboard from the wall and break it into tiny pieces. For the first time in his twenty years he hated being a cop. He hated the feeling that someone was getting the better of him, that someone had killed Coop and there would be no retribution. His inquiry into Cooperman's murder had led to a dead end. Ho couldn't do anything with the body. There was no way to determine the content of the telephone conversation Molia was convinced Cooperman overheard that had led him to drive to the bluff. The Branick investigation was out of his hands.

Dead end after dead end after dead end.

Molia slid the designated magnet from the "Out" to the "In" column as the telephone on the counter rang. Baldwin answered it.

"We're not handling that matter any longer; that's being handled by the Justice Department," Baldwin said. "I can't tell you that. You'll have to talk with the chief of police."

Molia looked back to the board and quickly slid the green magnet next to the name at the top. Baldwin turned and looked over his shoulder. "He's not in. I'll have to take a message and have him call you back." Baldwin wrote the message and a telephone number on a pad of paper, hung up the phone, and started off the stool. He grimaced and sat back down with a hand at the small of his back.

"Back hurtin' you, Clay?"

"Huh?" Baldwin turned, surprised to find Molia still standing there. "Just stiff. The wife had me pruning trees yesterday."

"Yard work's a bitch." Molia pointed to the note in Baldwin's hand. "I can drop that off for you. Where's it need to go?"

"Ray." Baldwin turned and looked again at the board. "I didn't see him leave."

"Must have snuck out while you were taking calls. Good thing you have the board."

Baldwin gave him a look. "Yeah, well, that's what it's there for."

Molia held out his hand. "I'll drop it off."

Baldwin hesitated, but what suspicion he had of Molia's motives faded with the increased pain in his back. He handed Molia the note. "Just leave it on his chair."

"No problem."

SLOANE HUNG UP the telephone, kicked off his shoes, and lay back on the motel bed. He had slept little in the past week, and his body and mind were both giving out. The Charles Town Police Department would not provide him with any information on the Joe Branick investigation, though he understood from a newspaper account that they had taken initial jurisdiction before the DOJ pulled the plug. He wasn't holding his breath that the chief of police would bother to call him back. If he did, it would undoubtedly be to refer him to the Department of Justice, which is where the Jefferson County coroner, a Dr. Peter Ho, had referred him when Sloane called to find out about the autopsy Aileen Blair had demanded.

He picked up the phone and called Aileen Blair. She confirmed his appointment at Joe Branick's office for noon the next day.

"There will be a pass waiting for you at the front desk," she said. "You're to meet a Beth Saroyan. She's some minion from the Justice Department I've been assured will get you through the security crap and take you to Joe's office. I'm leaving for Boston tomorrow. If they give you any trouble, call me on my cell phone." She gave Sloane the number. Then she hung up.

The telephone in the motel room rang, startling him as he dozed. He expected Aileen Blair, but the voice belonged to a man.

"Mr. Blair?"

"Yes."

"This is Detective Tom Molia with the Charles Town Police Department. I understand you called about the Joe Branick investigation?"

52

Bluemont,
Virginia

THE J&B PAWNSHOP was located in a one-story building just outside Bluemont, Virginia, off State Highway 734, wedged, ironically, between an ice-cream store and a miniatures doll shop. It was the fifth pawnshop Sloane had called. The local Yellow Pages listed it under the word "Guns" in a two-inch-square advertisement with the letters printed in red ink above a black handgun:

> Cash Paid for Used Guns
> We Buy, Sell, Trade

Sloane had focused on the words "cash" and "trade." The adoption of the Brady Bill, with its mandated restrictions and required criminal checks, meant a month's delay, minimum, to purchase any handgun. Sloane couldn't wait that long. His trick at the airports wouldn't fool whoever was pursuing him forever, and if they were CIA, as he now suspected, they had ready access to sophisticated equipment to locate him. A handgun might not help in the long run, but it wouldn't hurt, either. The J&B proprietor spoke with a Virginia lilt and provided Sloane directions over the phone. They chatted about what type of gun Sloane was looking for, and Sloane kept him on the phone long enough to learn that the man was a card-carrying member of the NRA and a Vietnam combat vet—a marine. When Sloane related that he, too, was a marine and had been wounded in Grenada it seemed to create an unspoken bond between them. It was that bond that Sloane would use.

Sloane had waited until the end of the day, just before closing, when it was less likely there would be anyone else in the shop. He walked in the front door to the jingle of hanging bells. Thirty minutes later the bells rang again and the J&B proprietor locked the door behind Sloane. He left without his Rolex, and lighter in the wallet. In a brown bag he carried an unregistered Colt Defender .45, an adaptation of the Colt Commander used in Vietnam, three clips, two boxes of Remington Golden Saber brass-jacketed hollow-points, and a Beltster holster, which the man had given him without asking.

Sitting inside his car, Sloane loaded the clips, slapped one in the handle, and examined the stainless steel and rubber stock, feeling the gun's weight and balance. It fit well in the palm of his hand. Before picking up the Ruger in the hospital elevator, he hadn't held a gun since the day he left the marines, and had sworn he never would again.

He switched his braided-leather belt for the holster, which had an extra-thick piece of leather sewn at the right hip to secure the gun tight against the body, then drove through a fast-food hamburger joint with a pay phone in the parking lot. He got change in quarters and plunked a handful into the slot. Tina answered her cell phone on the third ring.

"It's me. Don't use my name."

"Are you all right?"

"I'm fine. Are you doing okay?"

"We're fine. Listen, you need to be careful."

"I am."

"That's not what I mean. Dr. Knight called me. She said someone from the FBI came to her office asking to speak about you, but she declined. Over the weekend someone broke into her office. She couldn't for the life of her figure out what anyone could have possibly wanted until she noticed it missing."

"Noticed what missing?"

"Her yellow legal pad, the one with the notes she took of our conversation about you; the description I gave her about your nightmare. She said she checked with hospital security and they've determined that a man came to the counter to deliver a Federal Express package. It was the same man who came to the hospital and said he was with the FBI."

"How does she know that?"

"Because they described him to her and she said he wasn't easy to forget."

"Did she describe him to you?"

"Yes. She said he was African-American. Very tall and very big."

53

Tom Molia clenched half a pastrami sandwich between his teeth as he slipped into his sport coat and checked his watch: 10:00. Jon Blair was punctual. Molia hurried down the hall toward the building entrance, saw J. Rayburn Franklin turn the corner from the opposite direction with an "I'm looking for you" glare, and made a quick detour for the bathroom, slipping the sandwich into his coat pocket as he did.

"Don't even think about it," Franklin's voice boomed, bringing Molia to an abrupt stop.

Molia pulled his hand back from the door. Story of his life. So close . . . He turned to Franklin. "Think about what, Chief?"

"Think about ducking into the bathroom to avoid me, that's what. Because right about now I wouldn't think twice about following you into the stall."

Molia put a hand on his stomach. "I wouldn't do that, Chief. I'm not well."

"You don't return phone calls?" Franklin's breath was sour from the morning coffee.

"Were you trying to get a hold of me? Sorry, I haven't been at my desk. You know me and my stomach. I've been . . ." He motioned to the bathroom with his thumb. "I must have caught a flu bug from one of the kids." He coughed, causing Franklin to take a step back. "Though it could also be the Italian sausage coming back on me from last night. I shouldn't have had the second one. Still, I wouldn't get too close. That ain't pretty, either."

Molia pushed on the bathroom door, but Franklin stretched an arm across the doorway. "Then I suggest we cut the pastrami. Where's the note?"

Molia gave him a blank stare. "Note? What note?"

"Don't 'what note?' me, Mole. The note Clay gave you yesterday."

Molia rubbed a hand across his chin as if checking the closeness of his shave. "Clay gave me a note yesterday?"

Franklin smiled. "The guy who called about the Branick investigation. Ring any bells?"

"Oh, that note."

"Yeah, that note. Clay said you offered to personally deliver it to me. Now, why would you agree to do that?"

"Baldy's back was killing him—"

"And you decided to be a Good Samaritan because you and Clay are so close."

"Right." Molia stepped toward the door, but Franklin again stretched his arm across the entrance. They were close enough that Molia could see flecks of dust on Franklin's glasses. "Rayburn, you're really beginning to mess with the laws of nature here."

"I'd like to know what my senior detective has been doing to occupy his time."

"Working—and using the bathroom a lot."

"Working on what?"

"You know, Ray, various files. I'm busier than—"

"A rabbit in heat, I know. What files?"

"What files? Well, let me see. That house burglar, for one. Got some real good leads I've been following up."

"What house burglar?"

"You know, the house burglar, the guy that's been burglarizing houses."

Franklin smiled. "I know what a house burglar is, Mole. What I want to know is who he is."

"Well, that's what I'm trying to find out."

Franklin looked at him over the top of his glasses. "Then I can expect a report soon?"

"Before memories fade and fact becomes fiction," Molia said, repeating a Franklin mantra.

Franklin lowered his arm. They stood staring at each other, neither believing the other, both unwilling to call bullshit. Franklin held out his hand. "The note?"

Molia pulled out the crumpled message slip from his pocket, now smeared with mustard from the pastrami sandwich. "I got distracted yesterday—phone calls and files, you know."

Franklin took the note by an edge, regarding the mustard with disgust. He looked up and studied Molia for another moment. "I'd like to go over some of those files you're working on."

Molia looked at his watch. "No problem. How about this afternoon?"

"How about now?"

"Can't now, Ray." Molia motioned to the bathroom door.

"I'll wait for you."

"Could be a while, Ray. You know me. I can get through a whole sports page."

"I don't mind."

Molia checked his watch again. He was screwed. "Sure, come on, I have the files right on my desk." He turned and started for his office. When he didn't hear Franklin's shoes on the linoleum he turned around.

Franklin remained anchored in the hall. "Aren't you forgetting something?"

"Forgetting something?"

Franklin motioned to the door with his thumb.

"Right. There you go getting me distracted again, Ray—threw off my rhythm." Molia walked back down the hallway and pushed open the bathroom door, Franklin watching him. "Files are on my desk; I'll just be a minute."

SLOANE SAT IN a blue plastic seat bolted to the floor in the lobby of the Charles Town Police Department, flipping anxiously through a two-month-old copy of *Newsweek* and watching the clock on the wall. Detective Tom Molia had not hesitated at Sloane's request to meet. Unfortunately the detective wasn't as punctual as he was interested, and Sloane was now out of time. He was told the trip to D.C. was an hour and a half. He'd be cutting it close. He stood to leave. The metal door to his right swung open, and an athletic, slightly overweight man bulled into the room, fumbling in the pockets of a rumpled sport coat, the top button on his shirt unbuttoned, his tie loosened several inches. He extended his hand, mumbling a greeting through a sandwich clenched between his teeth. When Sloane reached to shake hands the man pulled his hand back and took the sandwich from his mouth.

"Sorry about that. Early lunch. You Jon Blair?"

"Yes, you're—"

Molia reached to take Sloane's hand, hesitated, stuffed the sandwich in his coat pocket, and shook Sloane's hand while ushering him out the door.

"Real sorry to keep you waiting. I got tied up with something."

They stepped into bright sunlight.

"Detective, I'm afraid we'll have to do this another time. I have another appointment. I won't have time for coffee."

Molia kept a hand on Sloane's back, walking him across the lot. "I'm sorry about that, Jon. Tell you what, where's your appointment?"

"It's in D.C."

"I'll give you a lift."

"To Washington? Isn't that a bit out of your way?"

The detective dismissed it. "Least I can do. Hate like hell for you to be late on my account." He kept the hand on Sloane's back.

"That's very kind of you—"

"Not a problem. I have some things I've been meaning to take care of anyway. I'll be killing two birds with one stone. Plus I can guarantee you won't be late, and I can park wherever I want. Job perk. You ever try to park in D.C., Jon? It's a bitch. We can talk on the way."

They reached an emerald-green unmarked Chevrolet. Tom Molia pulled open the passenger door and Sloane ducked to get in but felt the detective grab him by the shoulder, abruptly stopping him just before a blast of air hot as an oven shot out of the car.

"You got to let her air out a bit this time of year, Jon. You'll fry your tail off. Where you from?"

"Boston."

"Hot there, too, I saw on the news. All up and down the East Coast you can fry an egg on the sidewalk."

"Yes, it is," Sloane replied, feeling as though he'd failed a test. "Guess I'm just anxious to get going."

"We got time." The detective bent down and picked up old newspapers and food wrappers from the floorboard, discarding them in the backseat. "Sorry about the mess." He reached into his coat, pulled out the half-eaten pastrami sandwich, and stuck it back into his mouth, then continued to search his pockets.

Sloane pointed to the car keys. "They're in your hand."

Molia took the sandwich from his mouth. "Wife says these will be the death of me, but my cholesterol is as low now as when I was twenty." He shrugged. "Go figure." He held up the keys in front of Sloane, like a kid showing off a foul ball he'd just caught at a baseball game. "Okay, let's get going. Don't want you to be late."

THE DRIVE TO Washington was scenic but hot. The detective estimated the temperature outside the car at "screaming past ninety and knocking on a hundred," which was also an accurate description of how fast he drove. The Chevy did not have air-conditioning. With the windows down it was like being behind the prop blast of an airplane engine.

"It's not the heat that gets you; it's the humidity!" Molia shouted above the hum of the wind. "Can you explain that expression to me, Jon?"

Sloane smiled and shrugged.

"I never understood it till I moved to the East Coast. The heat I can handle, but feeling like I just got caught in the garden sprinklers gets old. Weighs you down. Then again, if it weren't for the summers I'd probably be ten pounds heavier. My wife no longer bothers listening to me. She says I keep the old Chevy here instead of getting something with air-conditioning just so I have something about West Virginia to bitch about." He smiled at the thought. "She's right, too."

"Where are you from, Detective?"

"Oakland, California," he said with noticeable pride. "And call me Mole. Everyone does."

"Okay."

He glanced over at Sloane. "Great name for a detective, huh?"

Up until that moment Sloane hadn't considered it. "Yes, it is."

"Maybe it's one of those predestined things, you know, like weathermen named Storm or Cloud. I don't know, but I'm third-generation cop. Got to be something to it."

"What brought you to West Virginia?"

"What else? A woman. Never thought I'd leave Northern California, but I fell in love with a West Virginia girl and she made living here a package deal." He shrugged. "What was I going to do? I loved her. It's a long way from home, and I get homesick once in a while, but it's a safe and beautiful place to raise a family. People sleep behind screen doors in my neighborhood. Still, you can take the boy out of Oakland, but . . . You ever been?"

"Oakland? No. Been to San Francisco, though."

"Night and day. San Francisco is wine and cheese; Oakland is beer and bratwurst. It stays with you like dirt under your nails. It's as much a part of me as the old Chevy." He ran a hand across the dash as if feeling the coat of a fine racehorse. "My dad bought it used and gave it to me on my sixteenth birthday because he said it was a reliable car. Right, too. Never let me down. We drove out to Virginia together and went back when my dad got sick—can't bring myself to get rid of it."

"You drove? Why didn't you fly?"

Molia shook his head. "I got this thing about heights— don't like 'em. The thought of being thirty thousand feet in the air gives me the willies. Got on a plane once, was going to conquer my fears and all that crap. I decided conquering your fears was overrated—never even made it to my seat."

"You've never flown?"

"Nope, and can't imagine a good enough reason to say I ever will." He knocked on the dash. "Chevy gets me where I need to go. Damn near thought I killed the engine the last trip, but I keep putting oil and gas in and she keeps running." He looked at the odometer. "Three hundred and twenty-eight thousand, four hundred and thirty-seven miles and counting."

The detective changed subjects the way he changed lanes: without pause. He had two children, a boy and a girl, joined the army like his father, and became a police officer when discharged. "Were you in the military, Jon?"

Sloane chose what he knew. "Marines."

"What do you do now?"

Sloane continued with the familiar. "I'm an attorney."

"Got a sister who's one of you."

"How long have you been a cop?" Sloane wanted to change the subject.

"Ten years on the street, eight years as a detective. Perfect job for me, except when I get cases like this one."

Sloane had been waiting for an opening; some crack that told him the detective wanted to talk about Joe Branick and the investigation, which, of course, he did. Molia wasn't driving Sloane to Washington, D.C., for the company. He was looking for information. Sloane probed, but not too forcefully. "Yeah? Why's that?"

Molia wiped a bead of perspiration from his temple with a finger. "When the Justice Department stepped in we were out."

"That's what I understood. Why *did* the Justice Department step in, Detective?"

Molia looked over at him. "Don't you know?"

"They said something about jurisdiction."

Molia nodded. "Law enforcement can be more territorial than wild dogs marking trees, you know what I mean? They found your brother-in-law's body in a national park so it's a federal problem."

"Thought I read somewhere your department took jurisdiction."

"Initially, that's true."

"Why was that, then?"

"Because the call came in from one of our patrolmen. Regulations require that the body go to the county coroner until everybody goes through the proper channels to get it released."

"I didn't know that. How'd the patrolman find out about it before everyone else?"

"Not sure," Molia said.

"You don't know?"

Molia looked over at him, one hand on the steering wheel, an elbow out the window. "The officer's dead, Jon."

Sloane's chest tightened. "Dead?"

"Seems his car went over a cliff, apparently en route to the site. He never made it, so we don't know."

Sloane picked up on the words "seems" and "apparently." "I'm sorry," he said, feeling the loss of another life. Then he had a thought. "I thought those kinds of calls were recorded."

"His call was, but we got nothing on anyone calling in a dead body, if that's what you mean. The only call came from Coop—the officer, Bert Cooperman."

"So how did he hear about it?"

Molia just shook his head in silence. "Dispatch called me at home. When I got there park police had claimed jurisdiction. And let me tell you, when I took issue I wasn't the most popular girl at the dance. But I insisted and had the body taken to the county coroner."

"Why'd you fight it?"

Molia took a moment before answering, nodding in silence. "Guess I'm just a stickler for details, Jon."

"What about the autopsy?"

"Never happened. Justice—"

"I understood his sister specifically asked the county coroner to perform an autopsy."

Molia looked over at him. "His sister?"

Sloane stumbled to correct his mistake. "Joe's sister. My wife. She asked for an autopsy."

Molia nodded. "Seems the Justice Department issued a cease-and-desist order. Said they would conduct the autopsy in-house. I'm surprised they didn't tell you that, Jon."

"They probably told my wife. I've been handling other matters."

"Cleaning out his office?"

"Cleaning out his office. So you're off the case?"

"That's what I've been told."

"But you still have a file open?"

Molia smiled like a kid caught with his hand in a cookie jar. "Let me tell you something about law enforcement, Jon. These things have a way of coming back on you like a bad lunch, know what I mean? After twenty years I've had my share of bad lunches. Here's how it's going to work: The Justice Department steps in because your brother-in-law is high profile, but after the publicity dies down the feds won't have the resources or the desire to devote to a suicide, which means it will get dumped back on my desk to close it out. So I keep a file open."

"That doesn't sound very encouraging." Sloane didn't buy the detective's explanation any more than he was buying the detective's willingness to take an hour-plus ride to Washington, or the bumbling, idle, get-to-know-you chitchat. He'd seen some of the best lawyers employ the same down-home tactic, stepping all over themselves in the courtroom while endearing themselves to the jury and getting every bit of information they needed from a witness. The local newspaper had quoted an anonymous source as saying local law enforcement was frustrated with the way the DOJ had handled the Branick matter. Sloane now had a pretty good guess who that anonymous source was.

"Well, what is it you hoped to learn, Jon?"

"The family is a bit frustrated, Detective. We're not getting a lot of answers."

Molia reached over and turned down the radio. Up until he did, Sloane hadn't even known it was on.

"What kind of questions are you asking, Jon?"

"My brother-in-law was not the type of man to kill himself, Detective. My wife asked the coroner to perform an autopsy for that reason, and he said he would. Now we're hearing that didn't happen and we've heard very little from the Justice Department. It's frustrating."

Molia nodded again, but this time a bemused smile creased his face. "I know that feeling."

54

Old Executive Office Building,
Washington, D.C.

THE OLD EXECUTIVE Office Building was a white granite structure with a blue slate roof and freestanding columns. It looked like something out of ancient Rome, but then, Sloane thought that about all of Washington, with its squat cement structures and monuments. When they parked in front of the building, Tom Molia asked if he could accompany Sloane inside. It didn't come as a complete surprise. Sloane knew that the detective hadn't left his file open to get back a bad lunch. He kept it open because he wasn't convinced Joe Branick's death was a suicide, or that the police officer had died in an accident. Molia likely was frustrated, as he said, because he, too, had questions and wasn't getting many answers. If he could befriend a member of Branick's family, that might be a start. For his part, Sloane couldn't think of a reason not to bring the detective with him. It couldn't hurt to have someone on the same side, and the fact that Molia was a cop and carried a gun didn't hurt, either, especially since Sloane had no choice but to leave the Colt Defender in the glove compartment of the rental car. He continued to have visions of the telephone repairman coming down the balcony, gun in hand. Sloane had to believe there were others out there with the same intent. Besides, he liked Tom Molia. The detective was like an old shoe, immediately comfortable.

They entered the building together, and Molia pulled at his shirt, fanning the air-conditioned air. As Aileen Blair had described, a security desk and metal detectors greeted them in the lobby. Sloane hoped she was also right about her ability to cut through the red tape. He watched a man in a suit ahead of them. The security guard gave the man's identification a cursory glance before he stepped through the metal detector.

Tom Molia flashed his badge, declared a 9mm Sig Sauer handgun, and walked around the machines, waiting for Sloane on the other side. Sloane announced himself as Jon Blair, as if it were supposed to mean something. Apparently it didn't. The guard, a no-nonsense-looking man who looked as if he could be a pit boss in Vegas, asked him for a picture ID and slid toward him a clipboard with a lined sheet of paper for visitors to sign in and out.

Sloane opened his wallet and flipped the license on the counter without taking it from the plastic—an old trick from his youth when he was underage trying to buy beer with a fake identification. He signed Jon Blair's name in the visitors' log. "You should have a pass. It's been arranged by Assistant United States Attorney Rivers Jones."

The guard picked up the wallet and examined the license, then looked at Sloane. "Could you take it out of the wallet, please?" he asked, handing it back to him.

Sloane tried to remain calm but felt as if heat were coming through the soles of his shoes. "Certainly."

He removed the license and held it across the counter, not smiling, since Jon Blair had not smiled in his picture.

The guard took the license and reconsidered it. Then his eyes lingered on Sloane's face. After a moment he said, "If you'll stand off to the side, please."

Sloane resisted the urge to ask if there was a problem, intent on acting as if were none. He stepped off to the side as instructed, and the guard picked up a phone on the console, dialed a number, and spoke into the receiver, though Sloane could not hear him. Sloane looked over at the detective. If he was interested in what was going on, he didn't show it. He had had a smile and comment for just about everyone entering the building, mostly about how much cooler it was inside.

Two minutes later Sloane watched a young woman bound down the hall toward them carrying several flat cardboard boxes under one arm. She put the boxes down and held out a hand, as eager as a teenage camp counselor. "Mr. Blair? I'm Beth Saroyan."

At the same time the guard behind the desk handed Sloane Jon Blair's license and a name tag encased in plastic with a clip on the back. "Here you go, Mr. Blair."

Saroyan shook Sloane's hand, then turned to Tom Molia, who had joined them. She apologized for not having set aside a pass for him.

Molia dismissed it with a smile. "Don't worry about it, kid. I'm a friend of Jon's."

They took an elevator, and Saroyan led them down a hall where a uniformed guard stood sentry outside a gold-leaf-covered door. It looked like the entrance to a mausoleum. Without prompting, the guard stood, unlocked the door, and peeled yellow police tape from the doorjamb. Sloane got the impression it was an act, the guard's actions orchestrated for his benefit. That feeling became stronger when he stepped into the office. It was neater than his office after Tina cleaned it. Joe Branick's desk reflected the recessed overhead lights. The books on the shelves were neatly arranged with family photographs and mementos. The carpeted floor was clear, not a scrap of paper on it. He watched Tom Molia walk to the wastepaper basket and casually glance down. Both it and the recycling container beside the desk were empty. Once again Sloane and the detective were on the same page. He had practiced law for too many years to believe that someone who reportedly left his office in a rush habitually kept it so clean. Someone had sanitized it.

It was another dead end.

HALF AN HOUR later Sloane slid the top on the last of the Bekins boxes. They now contained Joe Branick's personal effects, which he had promised Aileen Blair, but nothing that was going to help him identify the companies Branick had worked for or the identity of the black man in his memory. He looked up as a man with a stiff gait and narrow features entered the office and stretched out his arm as if they were old friends.

"Mr. Blair? I'm Assistant United States Attorney Rivers Jones."

At the mention of the name, Sloane watched Detective Molia's head snap to the side; then he walked out, striking up a conversation with the guard in the hallway.

With short, neatly parted hair, a muted premature gray that appeared artificial—and thin—Jones looked like a bureaucrat or a computer nerd. "My pleasure," Sloane said.

"I apologize if your wife and I got off on the wrong foot. I was hoping to meet her. I'd like to believe I make a better impression in person than over the telephone."

"No hard feelings. I'll let her know."

Jones turned to the young woman. "Ms. Saroyan has taken care of you?"

"Very well, thank you. In fact," he said, looking around the office, "I think I'm done."

"Good." Jones looked past him to Tom Molia and walked to the doorway. "I don't believe we've met," Jones said, offering his hand.

Molia did not respond.

Jones tapped him on the shoulder.

Molia turned.

"I don't believe we've met," Jones repeated.

"Oh, how'ya doing?" Molia gave Jones's hand a perfunctory shake before trying to return to his conversation with the guard, but Jones tapped him on the shoulder again.

"I'm fine. I'm Assistant United States Attorney Rivers Jones. I didn't catch your name."

The detective chuckled, feigning embarrassment. "Forgot my manners today," he said to the guard, then glanced at Sloane before looking back at Jones. "It's Jim," he said, muttering the name under his breath.

"Excuse me?" Jones said, leaning forward.

"Jim. Jim Plunkett," Molia said.

The detective, a native of Oakland, had just introduced himself to the assistant United States attorney as the former quarterback for the Oakland Raiders.

"It's nice to meet you, Mr. Plunkett," Jones said. "Were you a friend—"

"Of mine." Sloane stepped forward, eyes on the detective. "Mr. Plunkett is a friend of mine, Mr. Jones. Tell me, who made the decision to seal Joe's office?"

Jones nodded. "You saw the tape on the door."

"Yes, I did. When did that happen?"

"That decision was made by the White House chief of staff."

"The chief of staff?" Sloane asked. "Why would he make that decision?"

"Circumstances. The call that morning from the park police in West Virginia came to the White House Secret Service office. They found Mr. Branick's White House identification card. The security officers on duty contacted the chief of staff at his home. He instructed them to have the office immediately sealed. I concurred in his decision."

"Why?" Sloane asked.

Jones looked puzzled, and his response was patronizing. "To ensure no sensitive information was compromised or removed. It's fairly routine in a situation where a person decides to leave, or . . . well . . . in this type of situation."

Sloane looked around. "So no one has been in here since Mr. Branick left?"

"No one," Jones said. "Why? Is there something in particular you're not finding?"

Sloane shook his head. "No, no, everything appears to be in perfect order."

"Good. I'd like to—"

"Was it also the chief of staff who ordered that the investigation be taken in-house by the Justice Department?" Sloane interrupted.

The question caused Molia to lean forward.

Jones looked caught off guard. "I'm not sure how that decision was made."

"This is your investigation?"

"Absolutely. This was a Justice Department—"

"But you don't know who actually made the decision?"

Jones faltered. "It's not that . . . It's not that I don't know. It's—I believe it was a mutual decision between the attorney general and the White House. Actually there are some things I had hoped to discuss with your wife over lunch," he said, stumbling forward quickly. "If you're available?"

Sloane looked to Molia. "I'm sorry, Aileen didn't mention anything."

"No problem." Molia stepped back into the office, suddenly interested. "Lunch sounds good. I'm starving."

Jones smiled. "I'm sorry, Mr. Plunkett. I meant Mr. Blair . . . alone?"

"Whatever you have to say, you can say in front of Mr. Plunkett," Sloane said.

Jones shook his head. "It's nothing personal—"

"It's not a problem, Jon," Molia interrupted. "I don't want to be a fifth wheel or anything. You'll get home all right?"

"We'll have a car drive you wherever you need to go," Jones assured Sloane. "It will be no trouble. Ms. Saroyan will have the boxes labeled and shipped."

Saroyan stepped forward with pen and paper. Sloane had no clue where to send the boxes. "I'll have to get back to you with an address."

Jones looked surprised.

"Some of this is going to storage."

Saroyan handed him a business card.

"Very good, it's all settled." Jones put a hand on Sloane's shoulder and led him back into the hall, then stopped and turned back to the detective. "You seem familiar to me, Mr. Plunkett. Are you sure we haven't met before?"

Molia shrugged. "Rotary Club? I meet a lot of people there. And bowling. Do you bowl?"

Jones smiled. "No, I'm afraid I don't. Maybe you just remind me of someone I know."

"I have one of those faces," Molia said.

JONES TALKED WHILE he and Sloane waited for an elevator. "I apologize that your friend couldn't join us," he said. "It would have been no problem, except there's been a slight change of plans."

"Change of plans?"

The elevator arrived. Jones ushered Sloane inside and hit the button for the lobby. "I think you're going to see how committed we all are to making sure Mr. Branick's death is investigated to the fullest extent possible, Jon." He paused as if about to deliver the punch line to a joke.

The doors closed.

"The president has asked to speak with you personally."

55

Tom Molia fell in behind a sport utility vehicle as big as a tank, picked up a car phone that was a relic by modern standards, and punched the keypad with his thumb.

Marty Banto answered his direct line on the second ring. "Mole? Where are you? Franklin's busting my ass looking for you. Says you left for the bathroom hours ago and never came back. Thought you died on the can. We were about to draw straws to see who was the unlucky son of a bitch who had to go in to look for you."

"Nice to be loved. Any idea what Rayburn wants?"

"He wants to know where the fuck you are, is what he wants."

When J. Rayburn Franklin wanted to know Tom Molia's whereabouts, he asked Marty Banto. Molia and Banto covered for each other. Franklin knew it. He just wanted to get the word out that he was keeping tabs on them.

"No specifics?"

"Not that he's sharing, and I'm leaving so I don't have to listen to him bitch about you anymore."

"When are you going?"

"Now," Banto said, sounding adamant. "I'm leaving now, Mole. And if I wasn't in a hurry before, I sure as shit am now because I don't like the sound of that question."

"Just a question, Banto."

"Bullshit. I know that question. You need a favor. Look, Mole, the only one riding me harder than Franklin is Jeannie. I need to get home and spend time with my kids before the summer is completely over. She's not happy we worked all weekend."

"Blame me."

"I always blame you."

"No wonder she likes me so much."

"At the moment she likes you a lot better than she likes me."

"You know the routine, Banto. Ten minutes after you get home your son will ask to go to a friend's house to play video games and your daughter will get on the phone." He changed lanes. "Besides, this is an easy one."

"I knew it."

Molia thought he heard what sounded like a hand slapping the desk.

"I know you like a bad book. What am I, your personal secretary?"

"I just need you to run an ID," Molia said.

Banto picked up a pen. He could argue, but Molia would wear him down eventually. He always did. It was quicker just to do what he asked. "Go ahead," he said, sounding resigned.

"I owe you one."

"One? I'd have better odds playing the lottery than betting on you ever paying off."

"The name is Jon Blair, no 'h' in Jon." Molia spelled the name.

"The guy who called here yesterday?"

"Same guy."

"What's up?"

"I just spent a morning with him."

"The guy sitting in the lobby this morning?"

"You have brilliant deductive skills, Marty."

"Yeah, how about you deduce to do this ID on your own?"

"Sorry. Okay, look, I have a hunch. This guy says he did a tour of duty with the marines. Check military records for me and see if the name comes up. He also says he's an attorney in Boston. Check the Massachusetts Bar Association."

"Don't all felons have to register?"

Molia laughed. "Easy. My sister is one of them. And run a Department of Motor Vehicles check and see if we can get a picture of this guy. And I noticed a sticker on the bumper of his car in the lot. It's a rental but not from one of the big ones. Check and see if there's a reservation under the name Blair. I'll call you back in half an hour."

"Christ, Mole, anything else? How 'bout I make you a sandwich and hold your dick while you take a leak?"

"Sandwich would be nice," Molia said. "The dick thing is just sick."

56

⌇

THEY WALKED ACROSS Pennsylvania Avenue at a brisk pace, the heat of the day stifling and humid. Sloane was sweating, and his heart pounded like that of a condemned man taking his last walk. His mind had gone blank. He felt as if he were being swept along in a powerful current, unable to swim out, and with no plausible way to avoid the inevitable: a meeting with President Robert Peak.

Rivers Jones continued his soliloquy about the Department of Justice and its vast resources as they covered the fifty yards between the two buildings, making analogies to steam engines rolling. Sloane heard intermittent bits of the monologue but was focused on a different conversation: the one he'd had with Aileen Blair. Blair said her husband did not like political functions, that he was a homebody. Did that mean he didn't go, or that he didn't *like* going? She said he didn't like leaving Boston, but again, that could mean he didn't leave, or he didn't like leaving but did it anyway. A lot of husbands did things they didn't want to do. Aileen Blair said she had been to her brother's office before, but she hadn't mentioned the White House. Surely Joe Branick brought his family to the White House. What person with an opportunity to do so wouldn't? And Branick and Peak had been friends since college. Peak must have been present at Branick family events. Had Jon Blair been there? The chances were, he had been. Then again, Aileen Blair was the youngest, and by a good margin. Maybe by then her oldest brother had moved out of the house. Shit, Sloane didn't know what to think except that he needed to come up with something fast.

Jones facilitated their access through the West Gate. Uniformed Secret Service officers checked him for weapons but did not request any further identification, Jones apparently having orchestrated everything in advance. He handed Sloane a pass from the security officer, and Sloane dutifully clipped it to his sport coat as they continued toward the visitors' entrance on the north side of the West Wing. It was surreal. The West Wing. Sloane was on the White House grounds. He followed Jones up four steps, where two marines stood rigid beneath a portico. The marine on the left snapped sharply to the side and pulled open the door.

Jones led Sloane down a paneled hall adorned with a portrait of Robert Peak and other photographs of Peak meeting world leaders. They came to an officious-looking lobby with an American flag in each corner, a dark brown leather couch between them, matching chairs to the side. Sloane took a seat on the couch while Jones announced himself to a bevy of people working behind a counter. Then he sat beside Sloane to continue his one-sided conversation.

Sloane's mind remained blank, and he wouldn't get much time to fill it. Just a minute after Jones sat down, a middle-aged woman in a smart blue suit with a black brooch that looked like a huge bug stuck to her lapel suddenly loomed over them. "Mr. Jones. Mr. Blair. The president will see you now."

She led them through an interior door and down a hall. Men and women walked in and out of offices, the sounds of telephones and voices spilling into the hallway. The woman turned right and came to an abrupt stop. She gave three purposeful taps on the door before pushing it open. Then she walked in, holding the door open behind her.

Jones turned to Sloane and put out his left hand. "After you."

Sloane wanted to turn and run. He briefly considered feigning illness; the chances that he could throw up on Jones's shoes were good at the moment. But he steeled himself for the inevitable and willed himself to step inside.

President Robert Peak sat in profile behind an oversize ornate desk, the telephone pressed between his shoulder and ear. He was clearly trying to cut short the conversation. He faced a bronze sculpture of a fly fisherman, and a large rainbow trout mounted on the wall, its mouth open and head cocked to the side. Despite his inner turmoil, Sloane thought the room smaller than he envisioned. A round royal-blue area rug embossed with the presidential seal covered nearly every inch of the hardwood floor. The seating area in front of Peak's desk consisted of two couches with a marble coffee table between them, and a rocking chair. Sloane couldn't help but acknowledge the immensity of the history that had been made inside this room, and recalled the grainy black-and-white photographs of John and Robert Kennedy from history books, the two men huddled together, grave expressions on their faces during the showdown with the Russians. Sloane was about to have his own showdown, and he decided he wasn't going to go down without trying.

Practicing law taught lawyers to accept the inevitable. There were moments in a trial when nothing they could do or say could change their client's fate. They could be right and still be found wrong. They could win on the evidence and still have a jury rule against them. The thought brought Sloane a strange, comforting peace. If Robert Peak knew Jon Blair, Sloane was already screwed. There was nothing he could do about it now. Wasting energy worrying about it would not change the outcome. But if Peak and Blair had never met, then he still had a chance. Branick and Peak were reported to have been good friends. Peak would be comfortable talking to a perceived family member. Sloane's fortunes had taken a dramatic turn either for the worse or for the better. If he was going to get information about Joe Branick, there was no better place to get it.

Practicing law had also taught him much about reality and perception. The two were not the same. It was impossible for any lawyer, no matter how organized or capable, to be prepared always. Good lawyers acknowledged this and focused instead on *appearing* prepared. There were survival techniques in court: Speak only when asked a direct question; if you did not know the answer to a direct question, rephrase the question to fit your answer; talk in general terms rather than specifics; get what information possible, be thankful for it, and sit down and shut up. Get in and get out. The less time you spoke, the less chance you had of making a mistake.

Peak hung up the phone, seemed to pause to mentally change gears, then stood and came around the desk. He had the posture of a man with chronic back or knee pain, a former athlete paying the price for the pursuit of glory. Unlike the Oval Office, Peak appeared bigger than on television:

about Sloane's height, but with wide shoulders that carried more weight comfortably. With a full head of gray hair, his jacket off, his shirtsleeves rolled halfway up his forearms, Peak looked like the CEO of a Fortune 500 company about to put a shovel in the ground at some ceremonial ground-breaking. He extended a hand to Jones. Jones turned to introduce Sloane.

"Mr. President, allow me to introduce Jon Blair."

PARKER MADSEN HUNG up the telephone. When it did not immediately ring he used the moment of silence to catch his breath. He had fought more battles than he could remember—pushed his body beyond physical and mental exhaustion in the sweltering jungles of Vietnam and South America and through the oppressive sand of the Middle East—and when the battle was over he couldn't sleep, couldn't rest. Amped on adrenaline, his mind reworked each mission over and over, dissecting it, determining how the result could have been better, the effort more efficient. He loved the rush of seeing things go off according to plan, his plan, perfectly orchestrated, every man pulling his weight, doing exactly as ordered without question or hesitation. The pleasure it brought was better than sex, though nothing compared to the pleasure he felt during the engagement. Even as his rank steadily increased, Madsen never left his men—never let them go into combat without him, never sat in a tent looking at computer screens while his men risked their lives in the field. A soldier first, Madsen remained a soldier. God, he loved it.

But now he was tired. Alberto Castañeda, Mexico's president, had not stuck to the plan. The son of a bitch had strayed from it significantly, as the Mexicans were prone to do. It explained why a country of such immense size and natural resources, one that Henry Kissinger once said had the greatest potential to affect world politics, would always remain a bit player. Its leaders were just too damn disorganized and irresponsible. They had spent months arranging for meetings in clandestine locations to keep news of the negotiations from leaking—the last thing they needed was to piss off OPEC and the Arabs without a viable alternative in place—and what does the Mexican president do? He appears at a press conference in Mexico City to announce a tentative accord between Mexico and the United States to increase Mexico's oil production and corresponding sales to the United States. The press was now demanding specifics.

After the initial shock of Castañeda's blunder, the West Wing regrouped, raised the drawbridges, and hunkered down. Madsen gave strict orders to the White House press secretary that no confirmation of Castañeda's statement was to be released; the White House was to have no official comment. First they needed to find out exactly what Castañeda had and had not said. Calls to reach him had not been successful. Whatever Castañeda did say, Madsen feared it was premature. Mexico's chief negotiator, Miguel Ibarón, had hinted that Mexico was prepared to accept the most recent United States offer, which had precipitated the South American summit, but there had been no further confirmation. It was not that simple. Agreeing to assist the Mexicans to increase their oil production and actually being able to do it profitably were two entirely different things. It was not like the Middle East, which spewed oil from each hole punched in the ground. Madsen preached caution, but Robert Peak, more concerned that Castañeda had stolen the spotlight and desperately in need of a little illumination with his approval rating plummeting, compounded Madsen's problem by scheduling an evening address to the nation. It had only further stirred the news media pot.

Madsen stretched his neck and felt it pop. His legs ached for exercise, and his ear remained red and sore from the relentless telephone calls, one politician or bureaucrat after another. It was what he detested about Washington: the need for every decision to be considered, reconsidered, and considered again. Everyone had an interest. Everyone had a political chit to call in. No wonder nothing was ever accomplished. There were so many middlemen, so many t's to be crossed and i's to be dotted, you couldn't take a crap without needing presidential authorization to wipe your ass.

That would change. Madsen would be a commander in chief unlike any Washington had ever seen. He'd make decisions. His decisions would stand.

While he waited for a draft copy of the president's speech, Madsen picked up one of the newspapers on his desk. The stack remained untouched. He scanned the headlines and paragraphs his staff had underlined. After a quick twenty minutes he picked up the paper at the end of the stack, a copy of the *Boston Globe*. The double-column headline caught his attention immediately:

BRANICK FAMILY TO
HIRE PRIVATE INVESTIGATOR

He smirked. Let them. Let them spend their money. Maybe then they'd be satisfied. Their investigation would come up blank, and they'd be forced to back off their criticism of the DOJ. Death was another thing that separated civilians from soldiers. Soldiers understood that death was always a possibility. People lived and people died. Some died in service to their country, defending the principles on which it was founded. Others died of old age. But they died. It was their time. Soldiers came to accept death as a part of nature's cycle. Civilians never did. They grieved for years for deceased spouses, parents, and children. They made shrines to those who had gone before them, prayed to them for guidance and counseling. When his Olivia died Madsen had allowed himself forty-eight hours to get his affairs in order and move on. He had needed just thirty-six.

He read the article beneath the headline. The news conference had been held in Boston, outside the family home. The article reported little of substance. Madsen was about to put it down when his eyes shifted to the photograph accompanying it. A woman stood at a microphone, surrounded by a dozen people. It looked like a gathering of the fucking Kennedys. The caption identified the woman as Aileen Branick Blair, Rivers Jones's nemesis. That brought a wide smile to Madsen's face. Jones had sounded relieved to learn that Blair was heading back to Boston and sending her husband to clean out Joe Branick's office. Madsen looked at his watch. Jon Blair was likely meeting with Peak at this very moment. Then it would be over. The family wouldn't want to dig in the boneyard Madsen had created for them.

He looked again at the photograph. Joe Branick's family encircled Blair like a gospel revival group, the whole Irish Catholic clan present in a show of support, starting with the man directly at her side. Her husband.

Jon Blair.

* * *

PEAK REGARDED SLOANE with the doleful blue-gray eyes and measured smile that had become famous during the campaign, and which Washington satirists now exploited in political cartoons. Nothing in those eyes indicated either recognition or confusion.

"Jon. It's a pleasure. I only wish we could have met under different circumstances."

Sloane felt the collective weight of a thousand gorillas lifted off his shoulders. "Mr. President," he said, shaking Peak's hand. "Thank you for seeing me. I can only imagine how busy your schedule is. I hope I'm not taking up too much of your time."

"Call me Robert, please, and don't apologize. This was my idea, after all. I'm sorry Aileen could not be here. I haven't seen her for quite some time."

"She'll be disappointed," Sloane replied. He looked to Jones. "We didn't know . . ."

"I understand. I wanted to speak to you directly," Peak said. He looked to Jones. "Thank you, Rivers."

Jones turned to Sloane and shook his hand, all business. "There'll be a car waiting at the West Gate for you. You'll be escorted there." He handed Sloane a business card. "Please feel free to call me at any time, for any reason."

Sloane took the card. "You've been most accommodating, Mr. Jones. I'm very grateful to have had the chance to meet you and for all of your hard work. I'll be certain to pass it on to the rest of the family."

Jones beamed like a kid getting a compliment in front of the class, gripped Sloane's shoulder, and exited through the door where the woman with the bug jewelry stood waiting. The door closed behind her.

Peak guided Sloane to one of the two blue-and-beige striped couches. He sat in the rocking chair, taking a moment to pour himself a glass of water from a pitcher on a marble table. "I'm supposed to drink eight glasses a day for a thyroid condition. I use the bathroom more than I use the telephone." He held the pitcher up to Sloane.

Sloane nodded. "Please."

The glass would also serve as a prop, something to keep his hands occupied and to allow him to stall for time, if he needed it.

"How's Barbara doing?" Peak asked, as if on cue.

Sloane took the glass and sipped at the edge. He knew from the newspaper articles that Joe Branick's wife's name was Katherine. Branick had two daughters. It was unlikely Peak had singled out one over the other. By process of elimination he deduced that Peak's inquiry was about Branick's mother, but he couldn't take the chance he might be wrong.

"As well as can be expected. She's taking it hard. This is about the last thing any of us ever expected."

Peak's chest suddenly heaved and shuddered. He removed a handkerchief from his back pocket and blotted his eyes, which had quickly watered. The emotion seemed to come from nowhere. Sloane had not expected it.

"I'm sorry." Peak took a moment to regain his composure. "Other than Sherri, you're really the first person I've had the chance to talk with about this since I delivered the news to Katherine. I guess it overwhelmed me."

"I understand," Sloane said. Despite the sudden burst of emotion, he could not feel the depth of Robert Peak's pain. When he tried it was like a rock skipping across the surface of a body of water, deflected away.

"Joe and I have known each other for forty years. It seems like only yesterday we were at Georgetown. We had so much ambition." He smiled at the memory and cleared his throat. "We talked about this, you know? We talked about sitting in this very office. The first time we met here we had a drink and toasted to ambition and fulfilled dreams." Peak blew out a breath. "I can't believe he's gone. I get up every morning and I think it was just a bad dream, that it wasn't real. Then I see a story in the paper or I turn to ask him a question at a staff meeting, and he isn't there." He shook his head. "I relied on him heavily. I relied on his advice so heavily."

Sloane nodded in silence.

Peak continued. "I've known Katherine almost as long as I've known Joe. You know, I was the best man at their wedding?"

"Yes," Sloane said.

"The hardest part was talking with little Joe, seeing his pain. They were so close. I envied their relationship. God knows I love my daughters, but . . . well, when Joe asked me to be little Joe's godfather, that was a very proud moment for me."

"You've been a good friend, Mr. President. I know Joe felt the same way."

Peak shook his head. "Robert, please," he said again. "And I'm not so sure. If I had been a better friend, perhaps this would not have happened."

The door to the room opened. The woman with the killer brooch entered carrying a tray of sandwiches and fruit. She left it on the table between them. "Rivers indicated you had lunch plans. I thought you might be hungry," Peak said.

Sloane nodded. "I'm fine, but thank you."

There was a brief pause. Peak rubbed a hand across his chin, then sat forward, getting down to business. "I wanted to speak to you directly, Jon. I'm afraid the investigation has uncovered some troubling information."

Sloane put his glass of water on the table, crossed his legs, and folded his hands in his lap. "Troubling?"

Peak stood, walked to his desk to retrieve a manila file, and handed it to Sloane, sitting as Sloane opened it. "It was found in Joe's briefcase."

Sloane pulled out a handwritten letter sheathed in plastic. Evidence. The letter detailed how Joe Branick loved his wife and family and never meant to cause them any pain. It rambled, sometimes angry, sometimes confusing—the words of a man on the edge. There was a woman involved. Sloane read the letter carefully, then reread it, committing things to memory in case he needed to talk about them with Aileen Blair. Then he put it back in the plastic sleeve. This was one of those moments he was expected to say something, to express shock. He went with his instincts.

"I don't know what to say," he said after a pause.

Peak pushed away from the back of the rocking chair. "I'm sorry to have to be the one to break that to you, Jon, but it's one of the reasons I wanted this meeting. I didn't want the family to hear this from anyone else. I ordered Joe's office sealed and I had most of Joe's personal papers removed."

"That was your decision?"

"I suspected something like that," he said, pointing to the letter.

Sloane looked up at him. "You suspected this?"

"I was aware Joe was having an affair, Jon." Peak sat back down and leaned forward, elbows on knees, hands folded. "It went on for some time. Joe was discreet, but I won't lie and say I didn't know about it. Katherine, as you know, was not fond of Washington and all of the public events. Joe usually attended alone. We talked about it once, but he said it wasn't my place, and I respected that. He was my friend, not my son. It wasn't for me to judge him."

Sloane continued to study Robert Peak's eyes, but he remained unable to get past them, to feel anything about what Peak was thinking. Despite the gravity of the moment, and though Peak's tears appeared to have flowed freely, Sloane could feel no angst or inner turmoil emanating from the man. He saw Peak like Dan Rather at the CBS news desk: flat and devoid of emotion.

"I'll be honest. When it started I was more concerned with how it might reflect on my administration. I was concerned about a scandal." Peak shook his head. "It was shortsighted."

This was an unexpected turn of events, a surprise witness at trial. It was impossible to be fully prepared to respond. The key was to obtain as much information as possible without looking alarmed. "Who is the woman?" Sloane asked.

"She lives in McLean," Peak said. "None of us is innocent of wanting things we can't have. I can only imagine the pain and confusion Joe must have been experiencing when he realized his mistake, not to mention the guilt."

"Has anyone spoken to her?"

Peak shook his head, a grave expression on his face. "Not yet." He ran a hand across the back of his neck. "This is delicate, Jon. If the Justice Department starts hammering on her, she's liable to get an attorney and we'll have one hell of a circus. I'm not worried about covering my own ass anymore. I'm too damn angry for that. But I don't want this for your family, for Joe's family. I don't want the press kicking him around like a football, not after everything Katherine and the children have been through. I want them to remember the husband and father they loved and respected." He sat back, contemplative. "The last couple of days I've thought a lot about John F. Kennedy Jr. and that moment captured by thousands of cameras when he put his hand underneath the flag to touch his father's coffin. I thought of what he had to live through over the next thirty years. Wasn't it enough that he lost his father?" Peak used the handkerchief to wipe errant tears from the corners of his eyes.

Sloane's mind swirled with questions, but he knew he was already pushing the envelope, that it was time to wrap this up and make a graceful exit before making a mistake. He knew it instinctively. He knew it from experience. And yet he found himself pressing, because the voice of Aileen Branick Blair kept telling him not to believe it.

Let's get one thing straight before you get started and waste both of our time. My brother did not kill himself.

Sloane believed her. "May I ask how you know all of this? If no one has spoken to this woman, where did this information come from?"

Peak blew his nose into the handkerchief and wiped his upper lip, then took another drink of water. "Joe was here the night before he died. We spoke for about a half hour in my private quarters in the White House. It was all the time I could give him; I had a state dinner to attend." Peak refilled his glass and took a drink. "I tried to get him to stay but . . . Joe was agitated and upset, Jon. He wasn't himself. Still, I never suspected . . . Joe was not the type of man . . ." Peak's voice trailed. After a moment, when he had regained his composure, he said, "I tried to calm him. I tried to get him to drink some coffee and clear his head and spend the night at the White House. He wouldn't have it."

"Did he say where he'd been?"

Peak looked up, as if the question were somehow inappropriate. "Where he'd been?"

"The family's curious. We understand he left his office around three-thirty that afternoon, but nobody heard from him."

Peak nodded to the file. Sloane opened it. Inside was a log of what appeared to be telephone numbers.

"Joe called me from a bar in Georgetown on his cell phone. I had his telephone records pulled for that day." Sloane opened the file and considered the records. He noticed a number that kept repeating, presumably the woman's. Peak cleared his throat, changing gears again. "He apparently went to her house as well." He pointed to the pages. "Those records have been requested by the Justice Department, Jon. If they get them, they will follow up, and the documents will become fair game to the press."

Sloane put the log of phone calls back in the file. He knew the follow-up was to ask about handling the telephone records, but that wasn't what he was interested in. "Where did he go? When Joe left you that night, did he say where he was going?"

Peak put up his hands. "He said he was going home. That's the hardest part about this. He said he was going home to set things right. I don't know where he went. I assume he went to McLean. If I'd known he had a gun . . . Joe never carried a gun; never in all the years I knew him did he carry a gun." Peak rubbed the back of his neck and stretched the muscles as he spoke. "I'm very sorry to break this kind of news to you, Jon, very sorry."

"I'm sure this has been very difficult for you. I appreciate your honesty. The family appreciates your honesty. It answers a lot of questions." Only it didn't.

The voice in Sloane's head was now screaming at him to leave, but still he pressed.

"So how will this be handled?"

"The Department of Justice will hold a press conference late this afternoon. I wanted to get the family's approval," Peak said.

"Approval?"

Peak retrieved another document from his desk and handed it to Sloane. It was a prepared statement, innocuous. They would sanitize the autopsy just as they'd sanitized Joe's office. The Department of Justice would conclude that Joe Branick took his own life.

> The medical examiner has concluded that the powder marks on the decedent's hand and temple are consistent with a self-inflicted gunshot wound.

"It's conclusive," Peak said. "The rest is . . . well, unnecessary." He leaned forward. "The Justice Department will report that it found no evidence of foul play. It will make no reference to alcohol or other things irrelevant to the cause of death. The autopsy will be limited to the facts, the consistency between the powder marks and the weapon proving a self-inflicted wound. After the announcement, the Justice Department will close its investigation and this file."

Sloane put the statement in the file with the other documents. And there you had it, neat and clean, just like Joe Branick's office. It was just the type of information a family would not want to be made public, the type of information to make them go away quietly, and the Justice Department would help usher them on their way.

Tom Molia was about to get another bad lunch left on his desk.

And even if everything Robert Peak had just told Sloane was an elaborate lie intended to do just that—to get the family to end its inquiry into Joe Branick's death—Sloane could think of no way to disprove it. The autopsy report would be limited to the cause of death, the office had been sanitized, and Peak intimated that the telephone records and suicide note would be expunged. The only witness was a call girl who had little credibility but apparently a nuclear arsenal capable of blowing a lot of prominent men out of their comfortable homes—if Sloane could even find her. At the moment he did not even know her name. Peak had not mentioned it, and he couldn't ask without it appearing suspicious. He—

The telephone records!

He looked down at the file. He had her telephone number.

The door to the office opened. Peak turned to acknowledge the woman in the blue suit with the brooch.

"I'm sorry, Mr. President. You have your cabinet meeting."

Peak looked at his watch, stood, and walked the woman back to the door. "Please tell them I'm on my way."

Sloane opened the file and quickly removed the sheet of telephone numbers. Could he memorize it? Ordinarily he could, but with everything happening, he didn't trust that to be the case, and he couldn't take that chance. With one eye focused on Peak, he folded the sheet and casually slipped it in the inside pocket of his jacket. It felt like a lead anvil.

Peak turned. "I'm sorry, Jon."

Sloane casually removed his hand from his jacket pocket and stood. "I understand. You've been more than generous with your time, thank you." He handed Peak the file.

A corner of a sheet of paper had slid out.

Peak opened the file.

Sloane's heart skipped a beat. He put out his hand. "Thank you, Mr. President, for everything."

Peak straightened the pages, seemed to briefly consider them, then closed the file and put it on his desk. He walked Sloane toward the exit, shaking his hand. "I intend to make Joe's funeral."

"The family will appreciate it," he said.

His internal alarm was now shouting at him. *Shut up and walk out. Do not ask any more questions.*

But this was his chance, maybe his last chance. He couldn't just let it pass.

No. Get out. It's time to leave.

"That reminds me. We're trying to reach some people, friends and coworkers of Joe's. We were going through his things and, well, we'd like to get in touch with as many people as possible."

"How can I help?"

"We're looking for his work colleagues. For instance, Katherine recalled that Joe had an acquaintance, a black man he worked with."

Peak's eyes flickered, an almost imperceptible crack in the persona he had maintained throughout their meeting. He seemed to stall. "A black man, I'm sorry . . ."

"Apparently difficult to miss: very big, tall, well muscled. Katherine remembered him well, but not his name. She believed he and Joe worked together some time ago, but said they had been in recent contact."

Peak ran a hand across his mouth, but Sloane could not tell if it was acknowledgment or concern. "Do you know what about?"

"No." He had a hunch and decided to play it. "Just that Katherine indicated they worked for you. I know we're not supposed to know certain things, but—"

Peak nodded. "That's all right . . . I believe I know to whom Katherine might be referring, though that goes back many years . . . thirty years."

"You knew this man?"

"If it's the man I think she's referring to. His name was Charles Jenkins."

Bingo. Sloane had a name. "Charles Jenkins," he repeated.

"Yes, but I'm afraid Katherine must have been mistaken, Jon."

"Mistaken?"

"About the two of them being in recent contact."

"Really? Why is that?" Sloane asked, feeling suddenly deflated.

"Because Charles Jenkins did work for me. It was in the early seventies in Mexico City. Shortly after he started, however, we noticed some peculiar behavior, some problems."

"Problems?"

"Charles Jenkins was a Vietnam veteran, Jon . . . and, well, there are a lot of things that happened over there that we are not very proud of. Apparently he'd experienced some things that had a deep emotional impact on him. He became delusional and began to have a problem distinguishing present reality from what he had been through during the war. It began to weigh on him."

"I see. Do you know what happened to him?"

"Ultimately he was allowed to leave the agency."

"Where did he go?"

"I don't know exactly, but I heard some years back that he had died. I'm surprised Joe wouldn't have known that and advised Katherine."

"Well, thank you, anyway," Sloane said.

He turned to leave when the door pushed open suddenly, nearly hitting him. Behind it, White House Chief of Staff Parker Madsen stepped in.

57

~

TOM MOLIA CONFIRMED dinner at six o'clock sharp, promised Maggie he wouldn't be late, and scribbled a note on the palm of his hand to remind himself to pick up another gallon of milk.

"Milk, okay—"

"And a loaf of bread."

"Loaf of bread," he said, writing "bread" on his palm. "Got it. Okay, bye—"

"And you might want to get a few more potatoes."

"Tomatoes."

"Potatoes."

He changed the "T" to a "P." "Potatoes, right."

"And a new car."

"New—"

"Good-bye," Maggie said, hanging up first, as she always did when she knew he was rushing her off the phone.

Molia disconnected the call and immediately redialed Marty Banto's direct line.

"It's about fucking time."

"Nice mouth, Banto; you kiss your kids with that mouth?"

"What, you been watching *The Sopranos* while I've been waiting here half an hour?"

"Don't get your panties in a bunch; you'll be out of there in two minutes."

"No rush."

Molia laughed. "Let me guess: Matthew is spending the night at a friend's house, and Emily and Jeannie went shopping."

"Fuck you," Banto said. "You've been talking to Maggie. Matthew's spending the night at your house, and Jeannie called Maggie to go with them."

"I'm a genius, Banto. I've been meaning to talk to you about Jeannie not wearing a bra."

"I wish. They're shopping for Emily."

"Emily? She's just a kid."

"She's thirteen, Mole."

"Damn. Where does the time go, Banto?"

"I don't know, Mole. I'm too busy wiping your ass to find out."

"How's Franklin?"

"Raising the dead. Lazarus just walked by my desk."

"How'd he look?"

"Better than you're going to look if you don't call in and pacify him."

"He'll get over it. Deep down, he loves me."

"At least someone does."

"Maggie's cooking a pot roast. Come for dinner. I think the Orioles are probably on the tube. You can spend some quality time with your family."

Banto laughed. "You're such an asshole."

"We're eating at six, sharp. Don't be late. You know

Maggie. Hell hath no fury like my wife with an over-cooked pot roast. So what do you got for me?"

"Military service records have a match for a John Blair."

"No kidding. So I'm not a genius."

"Except *that* John Blair spelled his name with an 'h' and died in World War One."

"Probably *not* the same guy," Molia said.

"Not unless Franklin raised him from the dead, too, but I don't think so."

"You got more?"

"Don't I always? The Massachusetts State Bar has a listing for a Blair, but it's Aileen Branick Blair with a spouse named Jonathan, no 'h.' "

"Bingo."

"But he ain't licensed to practice law."

"No?"

"No. So I pulled up a photo from the Massachusetts DMV. It's close, scary close, from the brief glimpse I got around Baldy's fat head of the guy sitting in the lobby this morning, but I'd say it's likely not him. We're not playing horseshoes, are we?"

"No, we are not."

"So there's that, and the fact that the rental agreement in the glove compartment of the car in the parking lot says the car was rented to a guy named David Sloane."

"You broke into the car?"

"Hey, I'm in a hurry here. Besides, it's a rental. What's the worst that can happen? He loses his deposit. Since he paid cash, I'd guess he can afford it."

"Who pays cash for a rental car?"

"Somebody who doesn't want to use his credit cards. It

gets a whole lot more interesting from there, Mole. The guy's packing a Colt forty-five and more ammo than a bank robber. I ran a check. There is no gun registered to a David Sloane."

"Any criminal history?"

"Nothing in D.C. or California. National will take a while, but my buddy over at the FBI promised a—"

"California? Why'd you run him in California?"

"Because I did a DMV search, and this David Sloane is from a place called Pacifica. Apparently it's on the coast near San Francisco. He's one of you cherry-ass California assholes, Mole."

"Banto, I take back all the bad things I've said about you."

"Can't be half as bad as what I think about you."

"See you at six. And put a lock on that new bra. There are kids out there just like you and I used to be."

"I'm not worried. Emily and I have an agreement. She's not dating until she's married."

58

PARKER MADSEN STEPPED into the Oval Office, a folded newspaper under his arm. "Mr. President, I'm sorry to interrupt." Though he spoke to Peak, his attention shifted to Sloane, who sensed the situation getting bad, fast.

"I know, Parker. I'm on my way."

"Sir—"

"We were just finishing up, Parker. Jon, this is Parker Madsen, my chief of staff."

Sloane shook Madsen's hand and felt a sudden surge of energy, as if he'd stuck a fork in a light socket. He fought the urge to pull his hand back. The bulb flashed, followed by the clap of thunder. Sloane struggled against the descent into the darkness, a man digging in his heels as he slid feetfirst down a hill. He focused on Madsen's eyes—dark, lifeless spheres without pupil or iris.

Peak pulled open the door.

Sloane pulled back his hand. The descent stopped.

He stepped into the hall, forcing himself to look away from Madsen. The woman waited patiently.

"Sheila, please see that Mr. Blair is escorted to a staff car and driven wherever he needs to go."

Madsen again interrupted. "Mr. President—"

"I'll be right along, Parker."

Peak gripped Sloane's hand. "I only wish we could have met under better circumstances, Jon."

"Maybe someday." Sloane felt light-headed and nauseated. As if being pulled by an invisible force, a compulsion, he looked again at Madsen. Again the light flashed, this time bringing only darkness. Sloane shook free, smiled wanly, and followed the woman down the hall, feeling as if he had a rope tied around his waist, certain he'd be yanked and dragged back at any moment. He passed the Roosevelt Room, now nearly full, and followed the woman outside. They crossed the asphalt toward the West Gate. The tension on the rope became tighter with each step, but he maintained a casual pace, keeping stride with the woman's high-heeled steps. At the gate he thanked her. Then he stepped through it, though not before looking back over his shoulder.

No one was coming.

PEAK STEPPED BACK into the office and closed the door. He walked casually to the tray of sandwiches on the table and picked up half a chicken salad sandwich.

Madsen opened the newspaper and approached. "Mr. President—"

Peak raised his hand and walked around his desk to French doors that led to the Rose Garden. He stood eating the sandwich as if admiring his backyard garden. Swallowing a bite, he spoke.

"Do you want to explain to me," he asked, his voice even and calm, "how a man gets past the highest security in the world and walks into the Oval Office of the president of the

United States, Parker?" Peak turned. "I'm aware that was not Jon Blair. At least I suspect that to be so. He's a bit too young to be Aileen's husband, and there is no way that he or Aileen would have had any knowledge of Charles Jenkins. So what I want to know, General, is who is he, and how the hell did he make it in here?"

"I'm not certain, Mr. President."

"Well, you better get certain. I want to know everything about him. I want to know his name, how he knew Joe, how he is involved in this, and why he is interested in Charles Jenkins. I want to know where he's staying, who he's been talking to, and how he became Jon Blair. I want to know his family history, what he eats, when he sleeps, and when he takes a fucking piss. Do I make myself clear, General?"

Madsen nodded. "It will be taken care of."

"Really? Because I'm beginning to lose confidence in your ability to take care of things. This was supposed to be buttoned down and closed. Those were your words, were they not?"

"The matter is being handled, Mr. President. The investigation is coming to an end. The loose ends are being snipped."

"Well, let me tell you something, General, a very large loose end just walked out of my office. See that it is snipped." Peak took a breath, tossed the rest of the sandwich into a garbage can, and pulled open the door.

"And, Parker?"

Madsen had started for the door on the opposite side of the room. He stopped and turned. "Sir?"

"That man said Joe spoke with Charles Jenkins recently. I just told him Charles Jenkins is dead. Are you going to make a liar out of me as well as a fool?"

59

SLOANE STEPPED FROM the black Lincoln Town Car and started across the Charles Town Police Station parking lot. The heat of the afternoon rose from the pavement in ghostly wisps, like something from the African savanna—so hot it was painful to pull a deep breath into his lungs. He draped his coat over his shoulder, the list of phone numbers in the pocket. The migraine had never come, though he felt as if it had. His limbs felt weak, and he was nauseated. The encounter with Parker Madsen had unnerved him unlike any he had ever experienced. His right arm continued to tingle, and he couldn't shake the image of the dark, lifeless eyes. They lingered like something evil and unholy.

Sloane considered going inside the building and playing his cards with Detective Tom Molia. Neither of them was who he said he was, and Sloane had a good feeling about the detective. Tom Molia had been told to close his file and walk away. Most people would have jumped at the invitation, and hell, why not? The detective didn't know Joe Branick from a hole in the wall, and investigating a crime that others didn't want you snooping around was probably a whole lot more trouble than it was worth.

Yet the detective had clearly not given up on the file. In fact, he was doing things he wasn't supposed to be doing, which was the only explanation for giving a fake name to Rivers Jones. Sloane would know.

And if Sloane was wrong about all that . . . what did he have to lose?

Robert Peak was either lying or did not know that Charles Jenkins was alive. Either that or a very large apparition had walked into Dr. Brenda Knight's office and stolen Sloane's file. Sloane had no idea whose side Charles Jenkins was on. For all he knew, he was the person who had killed Joe Branick and was now intent on killing Sloane, though Sloane didn't think so. The fact was, Sloane didn't have a choice. He needed to find him, or be found by him, and he liked his chances of doing that a whole lot better with the kind of resources a police detective could provide.

He looked around the parking lot but saw no sign of the green Chevy. He'd check into a new hotel and call the detective from there. Reaching the rental car, he unlocked the door, pulled it open, and bent to lean inside. Startled, he jumped back suddenly, stumbling off balance and nearly falling.

"I warned you, Jon. You got to let it air out a bit this time of day. Otherwise you'll burn your ass."

Tom Molia sat in the passenger seat, the Colt .45 in his lap. Gray sweat stains ringed the collar and cuffs of his shirt, which he'd rolled up his forearms. He looked as if he'd been in a sauna with his clothes on.

"What the hell are you doing in there?"

"Waiting to talk to you." Molia looked chagrined. "Cooked this scheme up myself to keep you from driving off without us getting that cup of coffee together. Think I lost five pounds in the last twenty minutes. I really got to think these things through better. You always carry a gun and extra ammo when you travel, Jon?" Molia gave him a look that said they could both knock off the bullshit. "It's against the law to carry a concealed weapon without a permit, and I have my doubts you're going to show me one. I believe it's also illegal to practice law without a license in the State of Massachusetts, which shouldn't be too big a problem, since you live in California." He held up a photograph of Jon Blair's driver's license. "Not bad. Damn close, in fact, but this isn't horseshoes. No points for being close."

"What do you want?"

"I want to get the hell out of this oven before the buzzer goes off, is what I want. Come on. I'm starting to melt."

60

Lanham,
Maryland

THE CABDRIVER dropped him in front of an ornate cast-iron gate. Charles Jenkins pulled the piece of paper from his pocket, punched the numbers on the coded keypad, and heard the motor whine as the gates clattered, separating in unison, and disappeared behind a stone wall. He walked down the driveway past a lush green lawn and a small orchard of apple trees that he remembered being shorter. Overripe Braeburns littered the lawn leading to the Spanish Mediterranean house with orange roof tiles. The walls were covered with deep blue and lavender bougainvillea that he also did not recall. The wands of a weeping willow blew like the braids of a girl walking headlong into the wind. The wind was picking up, and Jenkins smelled an afternoon storm coming, though it would not be like on Camano, where the sky turned a funereal gray and the rain came in a steady mist. East Coast thunderstorms blew through differently, quick and powerful. The sky overhead remained clear, but darkness loomed on the horizon and looked to be coming this way fast.

The cell phone in his pocket rang.

"Where are you?" he asked.

"Still stuck in traffic," Alex said. "Maybe twenty-five minutes. The thunderstorm will make it worse. Heading your way."

"I can see it coming."

"You got past the gate okay?"

"Approaching the front door as we speak. Still looks like a Spanish garrison," he said, following a bricked path to a front door cut into an unfinished piece of wood adorned with brass rings and large square bolt heads. He punched in a second set of numbers on the keypad lock. "A lot of security for a university professor."

"You know my father. He was never unprepared or undercompensated."

"You going to live here?" he asked. Thunder rumbled low in the distance.

"On a government salary? I couldn't afford the property taxes."

"Glad to hear the government hasn't changed the way it pays its employees."

"Besides, it's too big for me. I'd get lost in there."

"What are you going to do, sell it?"

"You interested?"

He pushed open the door and stepped into a foyer with vaulted ceilings and thick wood-beam construction spanning a Spanish tiled entryway. A staircase swept down from the upper floor. The only thing different was the musty smell. He'd always remembered the wonderful smell of spices simmering. "Circumstances being what they are, I am in the market. Cut me a deal?"

"A million dollars, cash."

"A million is cheap for this place."

"Not in its current condition. It could get a little rustic tonight. I had the utilities turned off after Dad died. There's no heat or electricity at the moment."

"Now it's beginning to feel like home."

Jenkins stepped down into a carpeted sunken living room. He left his briefcase, which held his file, at the foot of the stairs. River rock formed a fireplace along the north wall from floor to ceiling. "Any word on our friend?"

"No, but I do have some news on the tattoo that will make the hair on your neck stand up."

Jenkins heard a dog bark somewhere down the block. It made him melancholy.

"The stiff that Detective Gordon is holding in the morgue in San Francisco is Andrew Fick. Service records identify him as a former Army Ranger known for taking trophies from dead Vietcong, but you won't find that in his official record."

Jenkins moved to the sliding glass doors, undid the lock, and stepped out onto a deck with a wrought-iron rail. It overlooked a substantial fall into a canyon of brush. There were similar decks above and below him. "Let me guess. His official record says he was a choirboy, just a GI Joe humping it in the jungle."

"You got it."

"So what was he really doing?"

"Mostly covert stuff, crossing over into Cambodia and Laos."

"Special Forces?"

"Not likely."

"No honorable discharge," Jenkins said.

"I'd bet no, but I wouldn't know. His file just ends. I ran it by a friend of mine at the Pentagon with some pull—top-level clearance. He called me back from a pay phone, wanting to know what kind of shit I'd got myself into, and unhappy I'd involved him."

"Sounds promising. Did he actually know anything?"

"He says the tattoo fits the description of a group that was known in Vietnam as Talon Force, though he said I'd find nothing official to confirm it, and that included him."

Jenkins didn't need anyone to confirm that such forces existed. He'd seen it for himself. These were forces so deep and dark they carried no identification, not even dog tags. Their uniforms were stripped of names, stripes, even manufacturing labels. They carried no cigarettes, no chewing gum, ate only the food of the country in which they were operating, even disguised their smell—nothing to identify them as American soldiers. They moved in anonymity and died that way. If they got hit across the border and their comrades couldn't carry the body back, the military would not claim it. Jenkins had walked into a village one morning and found it burned to the ground, most of the peasants with it. The men were shot in the head, execution style, or given a running start like startled deer trying to flee. Their bodies were scattered varying distances from the village, an indication that whoever shot them thought it sporting to give them more and more time before tagging them. They found the women and young girls dragged off into the bushes and raped, their throats slit. They'd even shot the dogs and pigs.

These weren't men. Some might call them animals, but Jenkins wouldn't denigrate an animal with the comparison.

Animals did not kill for sport. That was a wholly human failing. These men had no conscience, no morals—no governor that told them right from wrong. And scariest of all, they were exceptionally well trained.

"They don't exist," Alex said. "Apparently never have and never will."

"Just like the MLF," he said.

61

MERLE'S DINER LOOKED every bit the traditional small-town coffee shop, with the name and address stenciled in white on a maroon awning and across two picture windows facing the street. Inside, a half-dozen customers sat on stools at a counter that formed a horseshoe around a hooded grill. Two middle-aged women in uniforms the color of the awning attended to them like family in their own kitchen. Another half-dozen people sat in booths along the windows, drinking coffee and chatting without a care in the world. That is, until Tom Molia walked in. They all stood to greet him, acknowledging him as if he were the mayor.

"Come here often?" Sloane asked, sliding into a booth at the back.

Molia smiled. "Did I tell you it would be nice and cool?" He fanned his shirt as he slid into the booth. "Isn't this better?"

One of the women from behind the grill, middle-aged, with a head of thick, dark curls held back from her face by two clips that looked ready to spring open at any moment, walked up behind Molia and squeezed his shoulder. "What can I get you, darling?"

"Just tea, my love." He introduced her to Sloane. "This is Merle."

"Hi, gorgeous. Where on earth did the Mole dig you up? You're a hell of a lot better-looking than Banto."

"Hey, I'm a hell of a lot better-looking than Banto," Molia protested.

Merle leaned on Molia's shoulder but kept her smile on Sloane. "Yeah, but you're taken. He's not wearing a wedding ring."

"You're good," Molia said. "I didn't even notice."

Merle pushed his shoulder playfully and directed her question to Sloane. "All right, sugar, what can I get you?"

"Tea will be fine," Sloane said.

Merle put two porcelain mugs on the table, returned from the counter with a pot of hot water to fill them, and left two bags of Earl Grey.

Molia dunked the tea bag, then left it dangling until the mug of hot water was nearly black. "I think she likes you. That's the problem I'm having, David. I like you, too. I just don't know who you are, and that always makes me nervous."

"I'm Jim Plunkett."

Molia smiled. "Thanks for the help back there."

"Isn't he a bit dated?"

"Hell, I'm a bit dated. Spent many a Sunday sneaking into the Coliseum to watch Jim Plunkett play. He brought the pride back to 'Pride and Poise.'" Molia shrugged. "I always pick an athlete. First thing that comes to mind. Didn't expect you were a Californian. If I had, I might have picked someone else."

Sloane smiled. He thought of Joe Branick and his cutout of Larry Bird. Though he had never met the man,

Sloane had a sense that Joe Branick would also have liked Detective Tom Molia. "You like sports, Detective?"

"My wife says if there's a ball involved I'll watch it or play it, basketball more than football, but baseball—now, that's my passion. Plunkett was just the first person I thought of without hesitation, and when someone asks your name, you can't hesitate."

"Did you like Larry Bird?"

The detective sipped his tea. "Bird? He was okay. Slow white guy. I'm a slow white guy. Give me Tracy McGrady on a dunk. I like to dream." He sat back. "So tell me why an attorney from San Francisco is interested in a suicide in West Virginia, David. You a friend of the family?"

"You can say that."

"PI?"

"No. Tell me why a Charles Town detective is so interested in a case he was told to close. You guys don't have any other crime out here in West Virginia?"

"You sound like my boss." Molia put the mug on the table. "Another thing I'll never understand: drinking a hot drink to cool off." He shrugged. "Okay, David, here's my story. Consider it a show of good faith. I was ready to accept that Joe Branick put a slug in his head, even though my gut told me otherwise from the start, and let me tell you, I got a cast-iron stomach. If something's bothering me, it means something's wrong. You understand?"

"I understand."

"So it would have made my life a hell of a lot easier if I had just closed my file and let it go. I'd be home right now relaxing with my wife and kids, enjoying the summer. Except when I get out to the scene I find the park police claiming jurisdiction and can't find hide nor hair of the young police officer whose last radio contact says he's rolling on a dead body in a national park." Molia paused to make a point.

"You think someone killed him, that it wasn't an accident," Sloane said.

"Let's just say it wasn't sitting well with me, and that's before I get back to the station and get a call from a pompous ass named Rivers Jones who's using words like 'investigation' to describe what we're being told is an open-and-shut suicide. Well, I'm not the brightest bulb in the pack, David, but a light goes on in my dim cranium, and as you might have gathered by now, I'm subtle—like polyester at a country club—so I ask Jones why he's investigating an open-and-shut suicide. Next thing I know, he gets pissy on me and goes over my head. I get my ass chewed out by my boss. I get pulled from a case I never touched, and the case gets shut down before it gets started. All for a suicide." He sat back from the table and arched his eyebrows. "I got this thing, likely hereditary because my old man was the same way. Except for my wife—and God knows she's earned it—I don't like people telling me what to do and how to do it. Still, I might have let it go."

"Until the officer turned up in the river."

Molia nodded. "Until the officer turned up in the river. They made it look like an accident. Did a real good job of it." He spoke the words as if his jaw hurt just talking about it. "He had a wife and brand-new baby, and a whole life in front of him. Somebody took that away. I can't live with that. Understand?"

Sloane thought of Melda. "Yes, Detective. I understand."

62

Parker Madsen scribbled another note in the margin of the document and considered how the sentence read. The muscles of his face cut deep shadows along his jawbone, his eyes black pins of concentration. He told his secretary to hold his calls and cancel his afternoon appointments, then holed up in his office, working to meet a 6:00 p.m. deadline. That was when Robert Peak, against Parker Madsen's advice, would go on national television and address the nation with his plan to drastically reduce U.S. reliance on Middle Eastern oil. The term was "nonreligious oil," though it could not be found anywhere in the speech, so as not to offend Muslims. The draft of the speech, hastily pulled together by a team of the president's speechwriters, was bold and confident. Tonight Robert Peak would politely tell the Arabs to go to hell and take their oil with them. He would tell the American public that U.S. policy in the Middle East would no longer be influenced by threats of nationalization or increases in the price of a barrel of oil. America would no longer prostrate itself before military regimes that held out one hand for foreign aid and stabbed the United States in the back with the other. America would not be dictated to by sheikhs and kings with billion-dollar bank accounts. American families would not send their sons to die in the desert. Their tax dollars would go to increase homeland security.

And Robert Peak dared Congress to deny him the votes he needed to approve the pact.

It was all well and good. In fact, Madsen would have liked nothing better than to be the first in line to tell the Arabs to drown in their oil, but for one nagging fact: Peak and the Mexicans had yet to actually ink a deal. Castañeda was pushing for it. He wanted a summit in Washington, sooner rather than later, but Madsen was uncomfortable with the pace of things.

In between considering the speech, Madsen continued to receive reports on the man who had come to the White House, and was only mildly surprised to learn that it was David Sloane. The car had dropped Sloane off at the Charles Town Police Station, and Sloane had driven off with someone in the passenger seat. They both now sat in a booth in a diner, engaged in what looked to be an interesting conversation. Sloane was an anomaly, his involvement in the matter a complete mystery, as was his background. He seemed to have materialized from thin air. He had no wife, no children, no relatives. Madsen wondered if he was a spook. A man without attachments was a tough man to negotiate with. And that had been the problem. Without a family, Sloane had no readily accessible weakness, nothing he was unwilling to sacrifice.

That was about to change.

Madsen's men had found Sloane's Achilles' heel. Every man had one.

Exeter looked up from his beanbag a second before the knock on the door. Madsen didn't bother to put down the red pen in his hand. He knew who it was. "Enter."

Rivers Jones walked in as though dragging a ball and chain. "I'm sorry to disturb—"

"I don't have time for apologies, Mr. Jones."

"I think you'll find this important."

Jones's Hugo Boss appearance looked beaten: the collar on his shirt unbuttoned, the tie missing. His face sagged like dough left in the sun. Jones looked at Madsen with bloodshot eyes, and Madsen detected the lingering odor of alcohol. Stress weighed on some men like wet clothes, leaving them weighed down and drained. Madsen was not one of them. He relished it, fed off it—like drinking pure adrenaline. It was not something that could be taught or learned. It was genetic. He saw tough men cower and fold at the sound of a car backfiring, while others, equally well trained, could be pinned down in the middle of a firefight, wearing a shit-eating grin.

"I know who came to the office, and I know how we might find them," Jones said.

Madsen set the pen down and leaned back in his chair.

Jones took a breath, gathering himself like a condemned man making his final speech for clemency to the governor. "I spoke to the security guard at the desk in the Old Executive Office Building. He said one man signed in as Jon Blair. He had a license, which means he was there with the family's knowledge."

"You said you knew his identity," Madsen said, his patience dwindling.

"Not that man. The man he came with. Security said he had a badge. He's a Charles Town police detective named

Tom Molia. I had a run-in with him when I pulled the file. He's an arrogant son of a bitch. I'm not sure who Jon Blair is, but he's apparently working with this detective. I will call his superiors and haul his ass in here tomorrow and we'll get to the bottom of this."

Madsen said nothing.

"And there's something else. The pathologist who performed the autopsy on Joe Branick called and said there appeared to have been some work done on the body." Jones put a finger in his mouth, pointing to his palate and obstructing his speech. "A hole in the roof of the mouth. He said it was as if someone was trying to conceal a biopsy. It must have been the county coroner. I shut him down, too."

"Apparently not," Madsen said.

Jones cleared his throat. "I've already called and spoken to him, General. I'll have his license. Tomorrow I will personally call Detective Molia's superiors and get to the bottom of this. If he is working on this case, it will be the last case he ever works on. I'll have his badge."

Madsen stood, out of time and patience. "Thank you, Mr. Jones. However, you have been dismissed from further work on this matter."

"General, I assure you I will handle this—"

"You made a mistake, Mr. Jones. I do not tolerate or excuse mistakes. I advised you of that fact up front. In my profession there is no room for error. You're dismissed. If you make any further calls, this will be the last file you ever work on."

Jones gathered himself. "This is my investigation. I started it. I would like to complete it."

"That's not going to happen. If I find you are involved in this investigation, you will be out of a job."

"General, I don't want to say this, but I don't work for you. I work for the Justice Department. If I have to, I will go to my superiors, and I think they would be very interested to know that the White House has misrepresented the results of an autopsy and concealed relevant evidence. So I think we both need to cooperate with each other, or we *both* might find ourselves out of a job."

Madsen knew enough about men to know that Jones's bravado was born not of courage but of desperation and fear. Still, he had to give the man some credit. Maybe he did have a backbone. Good for him. He'd need it.

"I'll call the detective in the morning and get him in here," Jones stammered through Madsen's silence. "Once I do, I'll find out the identity of . . ."

Madsen opened the top drawer of his desk, removed a manila envelope, and unclasped the prongs.

". . . his companion. If I need to issue a subpoena, I . . ."

Madsen turned the envelope upside down, photographs spilling. Jones stood in stunned silence, mouth open, his naked image spread across the desk in various positions of submission, Terri Lane hovering over him dressed in black leather, a riding crop in her hand.

63

Sunset District,
San Francisco

TINA PULLED THE clear packing tape across the top of the box and pressed it down with the palm of her hand, sealing the two flaps together. She was about to rip the strip of tape against the serrated teeth when the last of it came off the spool. End of the roll.

She picked up the black marker and neatly wrote "Jake's Room." Then she stacked the box with the other two near his bedroom door. The room looked so empty, and still so full. She hoped the landlord didn't have a problem with the wallpaper. She couldn't resist it when she saw it in the store, a three-dimensional version of the cockpit of the Space Shuttle. She'd painted the wall black where the cockpit windows looked out into space, and affixed plastic stars that glowed in the dark. The first time Jake saw it he'd been struck dumb. Then he broke into a wide grin. "This is the best!" he told her.

She'd packed up his stuffed animals and cleaned out most of his closet. The Lego airplanes they had built together still hung by fishing wire from the four arms of the old-fashioned ceiling light. They flew when the fan was turned on. How was she going to pack those without breaking them? On his other walls were posters of his favorite athletes—Barry Bonds, of course, and ones she'd picked out for him: Joe Montana because he was gorgeous, and Muhammad Ali because she could tell Jake how Ali pursued his dreams.

She pushed strands of hair from her face and took a moment to pull it tight into a ponytail. She could get so much more accomplished with Jake and her mother out of the house than when he was underfoot, wanting her to play. And she needed to get a lot done. During the ten years that she'd rented the two-bedroom flat on the top floor of the converted Victorian, she and Jake had managed to accumulate enough possessions for a family of five. She'd have to get a lot more accomplished and a lot faster if she was going to be ready for the moving van Friday.

She sat on the edge of Jake's bed and felt the floor shake as the N-Judah streetcar rumbled past the front of the house. David's telephone call had been unexpected, but a sure sign, at least, that he was thinking of her, that perhaps they had a future together. The emotion welled in her eyes as she thought of him telling her to wait for him in Seattle, that he would find himself and be there. She only wished she could help him, even if only to comfort him. But he had never been that way. He had never been the comfort-seeking type.

He had no family. That thought continued to amaze her. It made what he had accomplished on his own all the more remarkable. It was startling that he would develop such a work ethic, become so driven—and yet that was what made him such a tragic figure. He had no one else. He had *nothing* else. Work was all he had. Being good at what he did was his only sense of accomplishment, the only reassurance that his life had purpose and meaning.

She stood from the bed and walked to the window, looking out from beneath the peaked roof. Parked at the curb in front of the walk was the police cruiser that Detective Gordon had insisted on. It was like leaving on a security light at night.

"Enough," she said, needing to get back to the task at hand. "Tape."

She walked down the narrow staircase to the tiny kitchen at the back of the apartment. Her new place had a kitchen twice the size, and granite instead of those tiny mosaic tiles, which were so hard to clean. She grabbed another roll of packing tape from the bag of supplies she had picked up from U-Haul, then opened the fridge for a Diet Coke. That was when it dawned on her. She turned her head to the right, looking over the top of the refrigerator door. The lock on the door to the back porch was vertical—unlocked. Living alone with a small child, she had become attuned to such things. She never left the door unlocked. Ever.

The hardwood floor in the hallway creaked. She felt the rush of adrenaline but fought the urge to panic. She bent over and reached into the fridge. The man came around the corner quickly. Just as fast, Tina straightened and fired the soda can as hard and straight as she'd ever thrown a baseball to Jake. Slow to react, the man took it flush in the face, momentarily halting his progress—enough time for her to get out the back door. She flew down the back porch multiple steps at a time. In an instant she was around the corner, racing down the alley between the clapboard siding and the neighbor's privacy fence.

"Help me!" she yelled, reaching the street and banging on the driver's-side window of the police cruiser. "Help me!"

The officer never moved.

She pulled open the car door. "Help me!" she started. The officer's body leaned to the left and tumbled out the door onto the street. Blood spattered the side of his face and the shoulder of his blue uniform.

She stumbled backward, unaware of the car that had stopped behind her, door open, or the man with the cloth. He cupped it tightly over her nose and mouth as he pulled her into the backseat.

64

TELL ME ABOUT the officer," Sloane said, saddened by the thought that another innocent person had died, and feeling some responsibility for it.

"Coop?" Molia took a deep breath and picked out a spot on the table, playing with a package of sugar as he spoke. "He was a good kid. Needed a break, but a decent kid. He was beat pretty bad—what would be expected in a high-impact crash." Molia looked up at Sloane.

"But you don't think so, do you?"

"No. Though I'm not at liberty to tell you why. What I will say is that the evidence is also inconclusive with regard to your brother-in . . . to Joe Branick." He picked up his mug in one hand and put his other arm across the back of the booth. "Now, tell me, why is a San Francisco attorney so interested in a homicide in West Virginia?"

"It's a long story, Detective."

Molia looked over his shoulder at the counter. "Merle? Two pieces of your apple pie. I'll take mine à la mode." He turned back to Sloane. "We got time, David, but give me the *Reader's Digest* version. I have a short attention span."

For the next thirty minutes Sloane ate pie, drank a second cup of tea, and explained what he could, trying to sound rational. The detective nearly spit out his tea when Sloane told him he had just spent the afternoon with Robert Peak.

"Holy Christ!" he said, then blessed himself as an afterthought.

Sloane took the page of telephone numbers from his jacket and handed it across the table. "The number that keeps repeating is hers, if the story is true."

Molia considered the page of numbers. "What do you think? You think Branick was banging her?"

Sloane put an arm along the back of the booth. "I suppose anything is possible, Detective, but I don't think so."

"Why not?"

"Something his sister said—that her brother always did the right thing. I didn't know the man, but from what I do know, he doesn't seem to be the type to do that to his family."

"According to Dr. Phil, we're *all* that type, David." Molia pressed a finger on the plate to get the last crumbs of pie. "But if you're right, then it's just an attempt to keep the family from pursuing this."

"I think so. His sister said her brother was a man of integrity. That was one of the reasons he decided to go home to Boston, to leave the CIA. He was tired of the politics; he thought they were dirty."

"I hope that didn't come as a revelation to him." Molia rubbed a hand over his bottom lip. "You think it's Madsen? You really think he's orchestrating this?"

"I'm not sure of anything, Detective. But he's the one who's been involved in this from the beginning, and with his background, he would have access to the men and the resources. And . . ." In his mind Sloane saw Madsen's eyes, as dark and threatening as storm clouds.

"And what?"

"Well, it's like your gut, you know? I have the same kind of innate ability, and I have this feeling that Madsen is involved in this, somehow."

Molia puffed out his cheeks before letting out a burst of air. "We'll need a hell of a lot more than what we have to storm the front door of the White House and accuse the chief of staff of conducting a military exercise on civilians."

"Which is why I think it's important we find this man, Charles Jenkins."

"You think he's friendly?"

"I wasn't sure, but yeah, I think so, and I think we need to find him sooner rather than later. I don't think we have a lot of time."

"Why's that?"

"Robert Peak said Charles Jenkins was dead. I know that isn't true, but he might not be alive much longer."

Molia picked up the sheet of paper with the telephone numbers, then picked up his cell phone. "Did I say these things have a way of coming back like a bad lunch? I hate being right all the time." He flipped open his phone. "Wish me luck; I'm about to really piss someone off."

65

~

J ENKINS STOOD ON the deck of Robert Hart's home, watching the storm clouds spot the sky black with pools of blood red.

"Have you seen the afternoon paper?" Alex continued to inch her way through traffic, her cell phone breaking up with static from the storm. "Big news from the White House. There's a story coming out of Mexico City that Alberto Castañeda made a statement at a press conference this afternoon and blew the lid on the negotiations. Peak is apparently going to address the nation this evening."

Jenkins considered the information. Castañeda had clearly stepped on Peak's toes. If he hadn't, they would have issued the statement together, likely shaking hands for the cameras on the White House lawn, which meant it was unlikely that the release of the information had been with the White House's approval. It had also been an unlikely slip. Castañeda could not afford to make a mistake if he was truly trying to cut Mexico a better deal than the predicament in which it currently found itself. That meant he, or someone, had orchestrated it. In doing so, he had left Peak no choice but to go on national television and embrace the deal unconditionally. If Peak did not, if he looked lukewarm or indecisive, it would fuel the growing criticism that Peak was a president who straddled the fence, unwilling to make the tough calls. The Arabs would perceive an opening, find a way to scuttle the deal, and make Peak look bad in the process, effectively ending his presidency. If Jenkins was right—and he had no reason to think he was not—Castañeda's next move would be to suggest a summit as early as possible, and Peak would accept it just as a man hanging from a cliff would accept a rope.

Was it coincidence that Joe had died the same week, working on the same issue, trying to find a man believed dead for thirty years?

"How far are you?" he asked.

"Twenty minutes, maybe half an hour."

He could hardly hear her. "You're breaking up."

"I can see the lights of the accident up ahead, but the weather isn't helping."

The first drops of rain fell onto the concrete deck, large drops that splattered on impact. "If we're going to stay here, we'll need some candles and matches," he said.

"You'll find candles in the dining room cupboard. My father kept matches on the fireplace."

The drops pinged off the deck surface and roof. Jenkins took cover inside, walking to the river-rock fireplace and finding a book of matches in one of the crevices. A gust of wind rushed at the house, rattling the windows, nearly masking the sound—nails pulling on hardwood. Jenkins dropped just before the shotgun blast shattered the floor-to-ceiling window in a shower of crystals.

"Charlie?"

He was rolling across the floor, hearing the pump action eject the shell, the shell hitting the floor, followed by the *click-click* sound of another shell being jacked in the pipe. He grabbed a fire poker as he rolled past the fireplace, knocking the set over with a crash, and continued toward the door. The second blast pounded the river rock, sending bits of stone and dust spraying into his face. Because he had just come off a commercial flight, he was unarmed, a target in a shooting gallery.

Alex's voice was screaming from the telephone. "Charlie? Charlie!"

He stumbled to his feet, rushing off balance down the darkened hallway, in and out of rooms, shoving doors closed behind him—a mouse trapped in a maze. He shouted into the phone. "Did your father keep guns? Guns! Did he have guns?"

The line was dead.

He kept moving, searching for an exit—the house was like a fortress with bars on the outside of the windows. He rolled into an ornate bedroom and pinned himself against the wall, hoping to surprise the man when he kicked in the door. Footsteps sounded down the hallway, then stopped. *Shit. Bad idea.* Jenkins bolted from the wall as the door to the room exploded, the blast removing a large chunk of the wall and door frame and showering him in fine white dust. *Third shot.*

The pump action ejected the cartridge and reloaded. The wall exploded in front of him. *Fourth shot.*

He retreated to an alternative exit. The weapon was a 12-gauge, pump-action combat shotgun, probably a Spas-12 or a Mossberg 500. Both were American military favorites. The problem was, the Mossberg carried five shots, but the

Spas carried seven shots in the tube and one in the pipe. Eight total. If the man wasn't reloading as he went—and Jenkins thought he was not—he either was down to his last shot or had a weapon still half full. Jenkins rolled underneath a pool table and out the other side, fumbling for a ball in one of the pockets. The room was as dark as night, the only window covered by a pulled shade. The door burst open. He hurled the ball, striking his target. The gun jolted upward, the blast blowing a hole through the ceiling. *Fifth shot.* Jenkins considered rushing the man, heard the pump action, and quickly dismissed it. The weapon was still loaded. His assailant had chosen the heavier Spas for the extra rounds. His luck.

He dived out of the room and rolled through a Jack-and-Jill bathroom and out the other side, into a large entertainment room with a high beamed ceiling and a wooden bar. Liquor bottles and glasses reflected in a mirrored wall beneath an old-fashioned Tiffany lamp hanging by chains from the ceiling. The only other exit from the room was out a sliding glass door onto the second-story deck, and he already knew there was nowhere to go from there but down.

Dead end.

66

∽

THEY STOPPED AT a supermarket so the detective could purchase milk, bread, and potatoes. He also bought a bag of cashews, which were now open on the front seat of the Chevy between them. The detective leaned forward, peering through the windshield at angry clouds rolling across a darkening sky, manifesting on currents of air as if someone had hit the fast-forward button on a video player.

"Thunderheads," he said, explaining the phenomenon of an East Coast thunderstorm to Sloane. "The persistent heat and humidity during the past week made it inevitable, sort of like boiling a kettle of water with the lid on, you know? The pressure builds until it blows. Just a matter of when and how much steam is gonna blow off. This looks like it could be a good one. Not like California—those are just showers compared to what we can get out here." He sat back. "I should just shut my yap. You're going to get a firsthand illustration. What's that thing about pictures being worth a thousand words?"

Dusk became night in a matter of minutes, punctuated by an arc of lightning that crackled across the sky, coloring the charcoal-gray cloud layer in a burst of purplish hue, like the colors of a healing bruise.

Molia counted out loud, "One thousand one, one thousand two—"

Thunder clapped and rumbled. He looked over at Sloane with noticeable pride; the storm had arrived, and it did not disappoint them. Rain fell like sheets of clear plastic. Molia turned on the car's headlights and turned the knob for the windshield wipers. The driver's-side blade never moved.

"It's the damn heat," he said, quickly rolling down the window. "Melts the rubber right to the glass." He reached out and gave the blade a quick jerk. It broke off in his hand. "Damn. That's a problem." As if on cue, lightning crackled again and the thunder roared. "We'll need to let this pass. I know a place close by—not much on atmosphere, but best bowl of gumbo you'll ever have."

Sloane was still full from the pie. "What about the pot roast?"

"Call this an appetizer."

Minutes later they turned off the highway onto a country road that cut through thick scrub and white ash, elm, and birch trees before widening at a small clearing. A dilapidated oblong wooden structure sat at one end of the lot, which was more dirt than gravel and had felled logs for parking curbs. The wind, blowing a gale, caused a hand-painted sign hanging at an angle over the screen door entrance to bang against the building like an unsecured shutter. Its red lettering, faded to a dull pink, read, "Herring Company Café & Bait Shop."

Outside the café were two vintage 1950s gasoline pumps.

Sloane pointed to a sign in the restaurant window between swipes of the blade and spoke over the rumble of thunder. "Closed. Looks permanent."

Molia looked genuinely perplexed. "Les and Earl have been threatening to retire the past ten years, but I never thought they'd do it." He turned to Sloane. "Two brothers. Fought like they were on opposite sides of the Civil War. Some say they were. Les ran the café and Earl managed the gas station. Had a thriving business for fifty years; every hunter and fisherman in the state started and finished his day here."

"Not today."

Molia shook his head. "Too bad. The gumbo was to die for."

The roar came from behind them. Not thunder or anything created by nature, but the manufactured sound of a car engine at high rpm, whining and revving. Sloane turned his head in time to see the battered white pickup truck slide across the dirt and gravel, the back end fishtailing as the driver corrected, causing the truck to tilt as though it might actually tip over before it bounced back on a course straight for them. The barrel of a large-caliber weapon extended out the passenger window.

"Don't think they came for the gumbo," Molia said. He pulled the Sig and tossed the Colt in Sloane's lap.

They rolled out the doors as the barrage of bullets peppered the metal body like hail banging on a tin roof.

67

~

JENKINS LEAPED OVER the top of the bar, frantically searching the shelves for anything he could use as a weapon—the fire poker wasn't much good unless he got in close, and that wasn't going to happen unless he survived three more shots. Not even a knife. He heard the door to the room open slowly, the man no longer worried that Jenkins might be armed, but still cautious in the dark. He was no doubt searching the room, eliminating potential areas of ambush, identifying the only two hiding places: on the deck or behind the bar.

Time. Jenkins needed time. He considered the liquor bottles beneath the bar—mostly good Scotch, the kind Robert Hart liked to drink when he smoked his pipe. The thought rushed to him. He grabbed a cocktail glass, threw it over the counter, and heard it shatter, drawing the sixth shot.

Precious seconds.

He grabbed a bottle of thirty-two-year-old Springbank from a shelf, unscrewed the top, and saturated a bar towel.

Pump action. The cartridge hit the ground. Click-click. The gun reloaded.

He stuffed an end of the towel into the top of the bottle.

The shotgun blast ripped a huge hole in the bar just to his right, splinters of the cheap wood laminate, shards of cocktail glasses, and alcohol spraying him and embedding in his skin like thistle needles.

Seven.

Jenkins curled into a fetal position. He wouldn't make it to eight. He rolled behind a small refrigerator, pulled the pack of matches from his pocket, and struck a match on the strike plate. It didn't light. He struck it again. Nothing.

Pump action. Final round.

He pulled another match.

Click-click—gun reloaded.

Jenkins struck the match. A small hiss, then a flame. The doused towel burst into a blaze. He threw another glass—a cheap trick that had little hope of working—stood, and hurled the most expensive Molotov cocktail ever made.

68

~

SLOANE LAY FACEDOWN in a puddle of muddy water, the rain pounding with such force that it looked to be rising from the ground. A tire on the Chevy exploded, a hollow, echoing ring that burst in Sloane's ears and, with the rush of wind and hail of bullets, deafened all sounds. At a lull in the attack Sloane rose to one knee, cupped his left hand under his right, and squeezed three well-placed rounds at the truck's windshield, blowing holes from left to right. He heard gunfire from the other side of the car, then Molia rolled over the hood, landing beside him in the muddy water. He pulled Sloane to a retreat behind the front bumper. They pressed low behind one of the tree trunks serving as a parking curb.

"You hit?" Molia yelled above the storm.

"If I am, I can't feel it." Sloane looked around the side of the car. The gun barrel reappeared out the window. He fired two more rounds. Three left. The other two clips were in the glove compartment of the rental car. "We are seriously outgunned."

Molia pointed. "We need to get into the woods. We can pick our shots in there. There's a creek runs north-south about three hundred yards back. Go. I'll find you."

Sloane shook his head. If he left, he knew that the detective had no cover to get into the woods. "Not leaving without you."

The barrel of the automatic extended out the window of the truck.

"No time to get heroic. I know these woods; you don't. I'll find you." He shoved Sloane in the direction of the scrub-and-tree line, turned, and squeezed two shots at the car windshield. It was all the cover he could afford.

SLOANE HEARD THE detective fire two shots as he hurdled a fallen tree at the edge of the forest. He dropped and took aim at the truck, which was at a ridiculous distance for a handgun. He fired twice anyway, leaving him just one bullet, and crawled into the thick brush. He moved as quickly as he could through the tightly knit trees, deflecting the low-hanging branches that scratched at his face and arms and tugged at his clothes.

Where the hell was the creek?

Lightning flashed, illuminating the forest in a quick burst, like something from a horror film. The thunder clapped damn near on top of him. The images blurred. He thought it was the rain. Then the pain shot daggers across his forehead, stabbing at him. He fell to one knee, holding his head between his hands as if it might split.

No.

He stood, staggering forward. Images pulsed in and out of focus. Black and white spots. The aura.

Migraine.

No.

His vision and balance deserted him. He stumbled

forward, blind, felt his bad ankle roll on uneven ground, his foot sliding, unable to stop his momentum. The wet blanket of leaves gave way like a rug on a freshly varnished floor. Sloane pitched to the side, head over heels down the hill, like a boulder. Stumps, trees, and rocks battered him until he came to a jarring stop against something solid and fixed in place. The wind howled. Lightning flashed another burst.

Men shouted. Smoke choked the air. Flames flickered colorful shadows and brilliant flashes of light that captured the woman on the floor in strobes of horror.

Sloane shook the thought. He kicked furiously, trying to keep from being pulled under, fighting to stay at the surface.

Outside he heard women and children wailing in pain, grief, and shrieks of confusion and horror.

"No!"

He pushed himself up, toward the light and the surface. He lay with his back against a tree, water continuing to pour from the branches overhead. Momentarily disoriented, he caught his breath, then struggled to his feet. He needed to find the creek. He needed to help Tom Molia. He put a hand against the tree trunk for balance. His vision remained blurred, but he could see where his sliding body had cut a swath down the hillside to the bottom of a ravine. He clawed and dug at the ground, gripping anything that did not pull from the earth—one step forward, sliding in the mud and leaves two steps back. The storm battered him with pellets of water. His head pounded a steady beat. His ankle ached.

When he reached the top he was out of breath and uncertain how many minutes had passed, but he didn't have time to stop and figure it out. Pinballing between the trees, he ducked beneath branches that pulled at his clothes.

Where the hell was the creek?

THE TRUCK RAMMED the back of the Chevy, pushing the front wheels up and over the log. The driver, the dark-haired man who had killed Bert Cooperman, swung the driver's door open, using it for cover, and fired a short burst from a fully automatic Uzi pistol as his partner, the bearded redhead, slid forward, gripping the handle of a 12-gauge Benelli tactical shotgun. They had watched Sloane flee into the woods but did not see the detective follow. Their orders were clear. Kill the detective, but bring Sloane back alive.

Red advanced, aiming inside the blown-out windows of the Chevy, his trained eyes scanning the interior. Empty. He slid forward, pointed the gun around the front fender. The detective wasn't there.

"They're in the woods!" he shouted back to his partner.

The dark-haired man moved forward, ripped the keys from the Chevy's ignition, and threw them into the brush. Then he stepped back and opened fire on the radio and car phone. He knew that the full assault had prevented the detective from radioing for backup—they had been monitoring the Charles Town police frequency—but this was a precaution in the event the detective had thoughts of doubling back to radio for help. They split up, his partner proceeding in a clockwise arc. He would move counter-clockwise, and they would meet at twelve o'clock. It was a military tactic to reduce the chances of shooting one's partner.

Once inside the forest, the dark-haired man moved from tree to tree, searching the shadows. The water cascaded from the leaves and branches. It was like looking through a waterfall. The wind howled at him. Tree limbs creaked and clattered. He worked his way through tall grass and scrub, crouching as he went, stopping to search for shadows that did not belong, his loins tingling with the thrill of the hunt and the anticipated kill. Overhead, lightning streaked. The woods pulsed a brilliant white, followed by the clatter and clang of thunder. A sudden pain stabbed his chest. He put the palm of his hand to his sternum. Lightning crackled, briefly illuminating the blood being washed from his palm and between his fingers. He raised his head in acknowledgment. The thunder boomed. And the second well-timed, well-placed shot hit him directly between the eyes.

69

∽

THE MAN SWUNG the barrel to deflect the ball of fire, shattering the bottle against the paneled wall, the ignited alcohol spraying him about the face and clothes. His final shot blew apart the Tiffany lamp hanging over Jenkins's head, showering him in green glass.

Empty barrel. Empty tube.

Jenkins vaulted the bar, fire poker in hand.

Well trained, the man dropped and rolled to extinguish the flames and rose to one knee, pistol in hand, but Jenkins was on him. He swung the fire poker like a baseball bat, sending the gun across the wood floor, and drew the poker back to strike again. The man reached up quickly, stopping the bar in midair—an amazing display of strength and tolerance for pain. Holding the bar overhead between them, at a stalemate, the man rose to his feet, a giant emerging from the ground, with shoulders like the bumper of a car. Jenkins kept his grip on the fire poker and drove a knee into the man's stomach. It was like hitting a wall. The man whipped his head forward, striking Jenkins in the forehead, knocking him backward. He held on to the poker and fell, using the momentum and his weight to pull the man with him. When he hit the ground, he drove a boot into the man's stomach, flipping him heels over head. Unfortunately, the poker went with him, ripped from Jenkins's grasp.

Jenkins scrambled to his feet and raised an arm to deflect the anticipated blow. Too slow. The poker smashed into his ribs, sending an electric shock pulsing through his body and driving him to one knee. He heard the whoosh of air as the man swung the iron overhead and brought it down like a lumberjack swinging an ax into a log. With no chance to stop it, Jenkins sprang forward, underneath the arc, absorbing the blow across his back as he drove his shoulders into the man's midsection, bull-rushing him backward into the flame-engulfed paneled wall. He brought his arms up inside the man's forearms and jarred the poker loose. The man shoved him back and pulled a six-inch blade from a sheath tied to his thigh, advancing, stabbing at the air. Jenkins circled and retreated, dodging the blade. He couldn't raise his right arm, and the warm and bitter taste of blood filled his mouth and nostrils, stifling his breathing. He felt his strength waning.

The man wiped at blood that flowed from a gash on his forehead, painting his face in a hideous red streak. "Your dogs," he said, the knife slashing and darting, "will make good fertilizer."

The pain and rage bled into one, rising from Jenkins's chest cavity and exploding in a guttural, primitive howl of blind anger. As the man stabbed, Jenkins leaped forward, grabbed his wrist, and struck the back of the man's elbow, hearing it snap like a chicken bone. The man cried out in agony. Still holding the wrist, Jenkins leaped and spun, his right cowboy boot whipping across the man's jaw. Then he spun again, whirling, the left leg following the right, each finding its target, driving the man backward until he stood listing on unsteady legs, a silhouette in the storm-darkened room. Jenkins gathered himself and rose again. He drove the heel of the boot into the man's chest, his leg unfurling like a loaded spring. The force of the kick propelled the man backward; the plate-glass door exploded with a percussive blast, and the man hurtled over the railing and was gone.

Jenkins dropped to his knees. "So will you," he whispered.

70

Tom Molia watched the dark-haired man drop to his knees and pitch face-forward into the brush.

"That's for Coop," he said.

He stood from beneath the pile of leaves and scrambled forward, taking the gun from the man's hand and shoving it into the waistband of his pants. He swore he'd never again complain about the humidity. The storm had been a blessing. The lightning gave him the illumination he needed to see, and the thunder covered the sound of his shots to keep from giving away his location. Molia could shoot a flea off the ass of a white-tailed deer with a rifle, but a handgun was not nearly as accurate. He had aimed for the center of the chest but thought he'd missed his mark when the man barely flinched. On the next streak of lightning he had counted a beat and fired his second shot with the clap of thunder. This time there was no mistake—he hit the man directly between the eyes.

It was time to find Sloane.

He started for the creek, moving quickly. When he reached it he dropped to one knee and slid down the muddied embankment into the water, searching the woods but not seeing Sloane or the redhead. Streams of water cascaded down the bank, swelling the creek. Molia waded downstream several hundred yards, then climbed back up the side, searching as he backtracked, hoping to find Sloane, hoping to get behind his red-haired pursuer. He continued from tree to tree until he had reached his point of origin, and his gut told him everything he needed to know.

If the man was not in front of him, he, too, had doubled back.

Molia turned.

Red stood ten feet behind him, the barrel of the shotgun lowered and ready to fire.

71

~⌒~

W HAT STRENGTH JENKINS'S anger summoned had dissipated, leaving him without resources, beaten and battered. Facedown, he slipped in and out of consciousness, struggling to stay alert, hallucinating. Around him the fires burned pockets of intense heat, sucking the oxygen from the room, the flames creeping closer, licking at his face, tasting his flesh, waiting for him to die, ready to devour him.

Charles Jenkins's mind urged him to move, to get up, to get out. His body would not listen. His head would not rise. His legs no longer pushed. His fingers no longer pawed, dragging his weight inches at a time.

So this was how he was to die. How it was to end.

He had wondered how it would happen, never truly believing he would make it to old age, to a peaceful life sitting in a rocking chair on a porch with a beautiful wife, grandchildren playing at his feet. That was not a life for him. They had taken that from him. He would not close his eyes with loved ones surrounding his bedside, watching him exhale his last gasp of air. He would die as he had lived, alone, with no one to miss him, no one to wonder about him, no one to care. They had taken that, too. He would vanish, the world unmarked by his presence—a cruel fate for having kept silent so many years.

He closed his eyes, feeling his will trickle from him like water down a bathtub drain.

Alex.

He wanted something beautiful as his last recollection.

Alex.

Her name teased his lips, and he envisioned her standing in the doorway of the caretaker's shack on Camano Island, her hair caressing her unblemished face, settling along her neck and shoulders, more beautiful than any silk shawl. He saw her magnificent blue eyes—her father's Scottish eyes, sparkling like diamonds. God had never created anything so beautiful.

He would have loved her. He would have loved her each moment of each day of what life he had left. He had wasted so many years brooding about the past, doing nothing about the future. He had stood on pride and principle, staying true to his own moral fabric. But in the end he had punished no one but himself.

He had lost. They had beaten him.

The room burned, awash in the colors of a distant sun: reds, oranges, and bursts of yellow. The flames inched closer, surrounding him, patiently waiting. He drifted off again, deeper into the darkness, and saw them come— angels descending from above, lifting him, carrying him, he hoped, to heaven.

72

~

"THROW THE GUN away, Detective."

Molia tossed the Sig onto the ground and raised his hands shoulder high. He had the automatic tucked in the small of his back, which wasn't much help at the moment, since he was staring down the barrel of a gun that could cut him in half before he ever reached it, but it was at least hope. Then hope went out the window.

"Take off your coat. Let it drop." Molia complied. "Turn slowly. Throw it on the ground."

The detective reached behind him and let the automatic fall into the dirt and leaves with his jacket. He braced for the burst of buckshot to hit him in the back.

"Turn around."

Why Red did not just shoot him when he had the chance, Molia did not know, but whatever the reason, every second was an opportunity to stay alive. And Tom Molia intended to stay alive.

"Who are you?" he asked.

"Does it matter?"

They shouted above the wind and rain, like deckhands on a boat in a storm.

"I'll need your name when I book you."

Red seemed to find that amusing. "I'll give it to you then." He looked about, wary, water pouring from his hair and beard, matting them like the coat of a stray dog. "Where's your friend, Detective?"

Sloane. That was why the man had not just shot him in the back. They wanted Sloane, or, more likely, the file Sloane had spoken of.

"Alerting the cavalry. This place will be swarming with a lot of people real soon, and they aren't going to like a cop killer too much. If I were you, I'd be leaving."

"Good advice. I intend to."

"You'll be going alone."

It was a stupid thing to say, but at the moment it gave Molia a perverse sense of satisfaction while he continued to consider his limited options. Could he jump into the stream? The burst of pellets would pick him off like a clay pigeon before he hit the water.

The man shrugged. "Casualties of war, Detective."

"Really? And here I thought declaring war was Congress's job. I'll have to brush up on my Constitution. Whose war are you fighting, soldier?"

"I could tell you, Detective, but then I'd have to kill you. Ironic, isn't it?"

"You can do better than that. That's a throwaway line from a bad movie. Tell me this. Give me some peace of mind to take to my grave. Are you the assholes who killed Cooperman?"

If he fell to the ground and rolled, he might be able to get to the gun, but he'd also have to get off an accurate shot, and that was not likely. If he was going to die, he preferred to do so standing, not writhing on the ground like a snake while Red stood over him, emptying a magazine.

"If you mean the police officer, yes."

"Then the score is at least even." He pushed away thoughts of Maggie and the children. He would not die. He would not allow it. *Turn your body. Don't give him a full-frontal target.* It didn't matter; the shotgun would still inflict mortal wounds.

"I don't keep score, Detective. This isn't personal. I take no pride in killing an officer of the law. I generally respect law enforcement personnel; you have a difficult job."

"I can't tell you how that warms my heart."

"The officer was an unexpected complication. We were left with little choice."

"I'll be sure to tell his wife and child when I see them."

"I'm afraid not," he said, and raised the Benelli.

THE WOODS thinned, leaving worn paths that led him to the edge of a small clearing—an outdoor amphitheater amid the dense trees and brush. Whether it had been cleared by man or nature, Sloane did not know, but its emptiness made them easier to detect, despite his blurred vision and the rain cascading from the leaves overhead. The problem was the distance. It wasn't likely he could hit his target with a pistol even under perfect conditions; trying to do so with his vision blurred by the migraine and the water made it a million-to-one shot. And that was all he had, one shot. He pressed his back against the trunk of a tree, his mind racing, no clear answer becoming readily apparent. He looked again.

At least a shot would draw both men's attention. That just might give the detective the time he needed. He took a deep breath and reached for the Colt in his waistband.

It wasn't there.

73

~⌒~

T HE PAIN WAS an intense burning. Charles Jenkins's bones ached. His muscles throbbed. His head felt as if it were about to explode. If his jaw didn't hurt so much, he would smile. He assumed dead men didn't feel pain, and what he felt at the moment was pure, unadulterated hurt.

A thin sheet draped him, but it weighed on his aching bones like a slab of lead. His mouth and tongue tingled as if coated with hair, and the air crackled with a strange static charge, like wool socks being pulled from the dryer. Each blink brought a stabbing pain behind his eyes. The last thing he remembered was the floor in Robert Hart's home, and the hazy recollection of floating above it, angels carrying him down a darkened tunnel toward an intense light—to what he assumed was the other side.

He lifted his head, the images undulating: a desk and chair, a television console, flowered wallpaper. If this was heaven, he was bitterly disappointed.

He fell back against the pillows and drifted again, unable to stay alert, wanting only to sleep, time passing in fuzzy, uncertain minutes.

"How do you feel?"

The voice reverberated, departed, then came back as a hollow ringing.

"Charlie?"

He turned his head. She stood in the doorway. Alex. Maybe this was heaven after all.

She approached the side of the bed. "How do you feel?"

"How—" He winced at the pain.

She helped him sit up and propped a pillow behind his back, then held out pills and a glass of water.

"No," he said, squinting at the light from a desk lamp.

"It's Motrin. Sorry I couldn't find any beer. You'll have to drink water."

He smiled and immediately regretted it. "Don't make me laugh. Hurts too much." He sounded like a villain in a cartoon.

She sat down on the edge of the bed, poured two capsules into the palm of his hand, and held the rim of the glass to his lips. It felt as if he were swallowing golf balls. He caught his reflection in a mirror above the desk and wished he hadn't. An ugly shade of purple encircled his eyes, giving him the appearance of a raccoon. The bridge of his nose was flattened like that of a boxer, the tip shooting off at a right angle.

"Is there any part of me that isn't supposed to hurt?"

"Well, let's see: bruised and broken ribs, possible broken collarbone, broken nose, a lot of bruises, a few cuts. You had glass embedded in your forearms and scalp. Oh, and a likely concussion, which is why we keep waking you." She leaned down and drew near his ear. "And you're still the best thing I've ever seen."

He felt the warmth of her hand cup his own, genuine and real. "You need to meet more guys," he said.

She sat back, smiling. "Tell me about it. I let you stay at my father's house, and you nearly burn it to the ground."

Now he smiled. "Call it even. Take it off the sales price?"

It brought them to the ultimate question. Alex was strong, but it was unlikely that she had reached her father's house that fast and had managed to drag his 240 pounds of deadweight up a staircase and out the door. "How did you get me out?"

She sat back and turned toward the doorway. A well-coiffed man in a blue pin-striped suit stood watching them.

74

〜

THUNDER NEARLY MASKED the sound—a twig snapping.

Red looked up instinctively and turned toward the sound. The shadow had leaped from the darkness like an animal on unsuspecting prey. Well timed, it hit him under the arm, knocking him backward and forcing the barrel of the Benelli up, discharging the round into the trees. Red flipped heels over head, landing in a crouch like a catcher behind home plate, the barrel again locked on Tom Molia.

The detective watched the barrel lower slowly, as if the man's strength to hold it were waning. Then the man teetered forward to his knees, eyes rolling to their whites in a death mask, and fell face-forward into the leaves.

Molia knelt on one knee, the Sig clasped in both hands, prepared to fire again. It would not be necessary. He stood, slid forward, and kicked the Benelli away. Then he reached and held the man's wrist, though that also was not necessary.

Molia holstered the Sig and walked to where Sloane lay in the leaves. After hitting Red, Sloane had continued over the top, his momentum propelling him just out of Tom Molia's line of fire. It was either an incredibly brave or stupid act. Either way, Molia knew, it was the only reason he was still alive, and he wasn't about to quibble with the result.

"Are you all right?" he asked, helping Sloane to his feet.

"Yeah. You're a blur. I can't see. It's a migraine."

"Is that why you didn't shoot?"

"Lost my gun. Charged what I thought to be the shotgun barrel. It was a guess."

"I'm glad you're telling me that now."

"Do me a favor—roll up his sleeve."

Molia bent down and pulled up the coat sleeve on the man's left arm.

"An eagle?" Sloane asked.

"Yeah," Tom Molia said. "An eagle."

THE STORM PASSED, leaving the sky streaked with a canvas of colors from pink to midnight blue. The air smelled like a cool stream. Birds, frogs, and insects came alive in a symphonic resonance to mix with the harsh crackle of police radios and the voices of a cavalry of state police stepping around muddy puddles as if they were land mines. Sloane watched the two ambulances leave the lot without sirens or flashing lights. There was no rush. The passengers were dead. Like the janitor, the two men would provide no answers.

The pain medication had dulled his migraine. His vision had cleared.

"You should get that x-rayed." The EMT attending to him had finished wrapping Sloane's ankle and helped him put his boot back on.

Sloane laced the final eyelets and pulled the strings snug, then hobbled to the cluster of unmarked patrol cars where Molia stood. At the moment the detective was taking a tongue-lashing from a petite man with wire-rimmed glasses, thinning hair, and a voice like a carnival barker.

"That must have been a miracle cure, Mole. An hour ago Banto tells me you're on your deathbed, and I find you running through the forest dodging bullets."

"I can explain it, Rayburn." Molia sounded tired and uninterested.

"Oh, you'll explain it—in writing. I want it on paper. Every detail. And I want it yesterday. I want to know what's going on, Mole. Gumbo? Is that some new flu remedy I'm not aware of?"

Sloane stepped forward. "Maybe I can explain."

The man looked up at him, one eye squinting as if holding a monocle in place. "Who the hell are you?"

"Earvin Johnson." Sloane held out his hand, but the man ignored it.

"J. Rayburn Franklin, Charles Town chief of police," Molia said, introducing Sloane.

"I'm afraid this is my fault, Chief Franklin."

Franklin arched an eyebrow. "*Your* fault?"

"I'm a friend of Tom's from California. I talked him into getting some of the gumbo he's been bragging about all these years. When we got here we found the place closed, got caught in that thunderstorm, and decided to wait it out. That was when those two men showed up, I assume to rob the restaurant. They came out, guns blazing. If it weren't for Tom's quick thinking, pushing me into the woods, I'd likely be dead right now. I owe him my life. He's a hero. Is everyone in West Virginia this crazy?"

Franklin peered up at him as if he were listening to a foreign language, then shook his head in disgust. "Both of you wait right here," he said. He walked in the direction of a forensic team poring over the Chevy and the truck.

"Not bad," Molia said. "I think he almost bought it. You lost him though on 'hero.' Got to know your audience. To Franklin I'm as close to being a hero as Schwarzenegger is to being a governor."

"Sorry about your car," Sloane said.

Molia looked at the bullet-riddled Chevy. "What the hell, maybe it's time I buy something with air-conditioning." He turned back to Sloane. "Earvin Johnson?"

Sloane shrugged. "Franklin doesn't look like a basketball kind of guy."

"He's not, but Magic Johnson is six foot eight and black. I don't think anyone would mistake you two for twins. Maybe you should have tried John Stockton."

"Stockton? Slow white guy. I'm a slow white guy. I like to dream, too."

Molia chuckled. "Maybe. But neither of us just dreamed what happened. Whatever you did or said today, you pushed some buttons. They were willing to kill me, but not before they knew where you were. That tells me their primary objective was to get back that package Joe Branick sent you. Any idea what would make them that nervous?"

"Not yet."

A second officer approached. Molia introduced Marty Banto.

Banto looked at his watch. "Hate to be you. Maggie isn't going to be happy about her pot roast."

"When I tell her I have to get rid of the Chevy she'll love me."

Banto reached into his shirt pocket and pulled out a slip of paper. "I traced that telephone number for you.

It's for an address in McLean, Virginia, a woman named Terri Lane."

"McLean?" Molia asked.

"Apparently she wasn't making fifty bucks a pop giving blow jobs in alleys, but don't bother driving out there."

"Dead?"

"Gone, and left in a hurry. McLean police took a ride for me. Said they found a half-full glass of wine on the table, the lights and stereo on, and a bath towel on the floor. A neighbor confirmed seeing Ms. Lane get into her Mercedes with a suitcase and drive off. So far her credit cards are clean, and probably will be for some time. I don't assume she was accepting Visa or Mastercard. She could hide forever."

"We're in the wrong line of business."

"Maybe, but I can't imagine anyone paying to have sex with either of us. The other name you asked me to check out—Charles Jenkins—no luck. Couldn't find anything about him anywhere. You sure he exists?"

Molia looked to Sloane.

"He exists," Sloane said, more certain than ever that Jenkins had been, or still was, CIA.

"Thanks for trying."

Banto nodded. "Ho get a hold of you?"

"Peter? No, why?"

"Called the station looking for you. I told him to try your cell. Didn't know someone was using you for target practice. He said that assistant U.S. attorney called him again and was more than a little upset about an unauthorized autopsy. What the hell did you do, Mole? . . . Mole?"

Tom Molia had started for the Chevy out of habit, stopped abruptly, and turned back to Banto, his hand extended like a panhandler's. "I need to borrow your car."

75

THE MOTRIN HAD dulled the pain enough so that he could sit up in the bed without every limb screaming. The fog in his head, as heavy as any that had blanketed his Camano farm, continued to clear, and the images in the room started to come in real time, no longer delayed like a B-grade Japanese movie. Alex sat in a chair at the side of the bed. The tall, lean man who stood in the doorway now paced a path at the foot of the bed. William Brewer, the director of the CIA, was impeccably dressed in a starched and fitted white tab-collar shirt, cuff links, and a navy-blue tie. A gold chain circled his right wrist. His salt-and-pepper hair matched the color of the pinstripes in his suit, the jacket of which now hung over the back of a chair. His beard was heavy, though the strong smell of cologne indicated that he had just shaved, perhaps following an afternoon workout. He had the physique of someone who played squash or racquetball regularly. His facial expression was of someone who had just paid a lot of money for a disappointing meal.

"I received a call from the Mexican Directorate of Intelligence wanting to know why we were interested in an organization that has been extinct for thirty years." Brewer paced the room as he spoke. "I had no idea what he was talking about, though I didn't tell him that. He said he got a call from the station chief in Mexico City, asking for information on a right-wing revolutionary group calling itself the Mexican Liberation Front, specifically on a man calling himself 'the Prophet.' That request apparently came from Joe Branick." Brewer stopped pacing and fixed Jenkins with his best bureaucratic stare. "You want to tell me what this is all about, Agent Jenkins?"

Despite the pain, Jenkins couldn't suppress a smile. "Mr. Brewer, I haven't been called 'agent' in thirty years."

Brewer nodded. "I know. I read your personnel file. You're supposed to be crazier than a loon." He looked to Alex. "But Agent Hart says it isn't so. She also says you're the best bet we have of finding out what's going on, and I believe her about both things." Brewer checked his watch. "The problem is, if something is going on, I need to know quickly. Because in about ten minutes the president is going to address the nation and confirm a report out of Mexico City of an agreement to substantially increase the amount of oil and natural gas this country purchases from Mexico. When he does, it's not going to make us many friends in the Mideast." Brewer swung the chair on which he'd draped his jacket backward and straddled it, settling in. "Agent Hart filled me in on Joe Branick's theory about a possible revival of this group, the Mexican Liberation Front. I want to hear what you have to say."

"It's not a theory."

"The director of Mexican intelligence thinks it is. He said they found nothing to indicate that organization continues to exist, and he did not hide his amusement that we would concern ourselves with an organization that has been extinct for thirty years. He said they have modern-day terrorists. They don't chase ghosts."

"They did in 1973," Jenkins said. "So did we."

"El Profeta?"

"That's right."

Brewer nodded to the round table behind him, on which a copy of the manila file lay open. "I read your file about him. But let me tell you, while you were drifting in and out of la-la land we pored through a considerable dossier maintained on that organization and that man. Every indication is that el Profeta either never existed or is dead. There hasn't been a rumor of him for three decades."

"The indications are wrong."

Brewer inhaled and exhaled deeply, eyeing him, not convinced but not willing to dismiss Jenkins outright. "All right. Tell me why."

"Because the Mexican oil market is sacrosanct. Castañeda is not about to enter into an agreement that will open the door for American oil companies to get back into the country."

Brewer picked up a copy of the afternoon *Post* so Jenkins could see the headline. A Mexico-U.S. oil summit in Washington, D.C., was said to be imminent.

"You're wrong. He already has. The president will confirm a summit day after tomorrow, starting with a ceremony Friday morning on the South Lawn."

Jenkins shook his head. "You're wrong. He's agreed to a summit. There will be no oil agreement."

"The negotiations are a done deal, Agent Jenkins. The summit is for show."

"It will be a show, all right—just not the show everyone is expecting."

"What do you mean?"

"He's orchestrating the summit."

"Castañeda?"

"Yes."

"You think he's el Profeta?"

"No. Too young. But I do think he's doing el Profeta's bidding."

"And el Profeta is orchestrating the agreement and the summit?"

"El Profeta is orchestrating the agreement because he knows Robert Peak. He knows what Peak promised the American public and how Peak intended to keep that promise. And he used that like bait to lure Peak into the negotiations."

"Why?"

"To get close to him. He nearly did in South America, but Branick's death changed that. So he had to change plans. He's resourceful. He's also persistent and patient. Why not? He's been waiting thirty years for this. So he tells Castañeda to go public with the negotiations, to force Peak's hand—which he knows will work because he knows Peak is an arrogant son of a bitch who only cares about his career. That necessitates a summit, and in a hurry."

Brewer shook his head. "You're asking me to believe that one of the most notorious terrorists in Mexico's history, a man believed dead for thirty years, is not only alive but is secretly orchestrating confidential negotiations?"

"What the hell." Jenkins shrugged. "I'm crazy."

Alex stood, trying to broker a compromise. "What the director is saying, Charlie, is that he's finding the statistical probability of something like that very difficult to swallow."

"I don't give a shit what the director is having difficulty swallowing." He turned his head back to Brewer. "What I know, Mr. Brewer, is that statistical probabilities do not apply to this man. I studied him. I tried to get in his head so I could figure out who he is: revolutionary, religious zealot, genius—likely all three. And what I learned is that sometimes fate and destiny can take precedence over mathematics and science, that the human spirit cannot be calculated, that what people are willing to do and how long they will wait to do it, when properly motivated, is often beyond human comprehension."

Brewer stood. "Maybe so, but I have to deal in realities."

"Well, make no mistake about it, he's very real."

Brewer rubbed his forehead. "Then tell me this. Based on everything I've read, including your file, this summit goes against everything that man believed in. Why would he do it?"

"Because, as I told you, there will be no agreement, and he knows that. What's motivating him is not politics and oil. It's something much more primal." He looked at Alex. "The kind of motivation one gets when people take from you everything you've ever loved, and you're unwilling or unable to forget."

"And what would that be?" Brewer asked.

Alex answered for him. "Revenge."

76

Tom Molia skidded the Jeep to a stop at a small staircase that led to a metal door at the back of the stucco-and-brick building. He left the keys in the ignition and pushed out of the car, pointing to a blue Chevy Blazer parked in the shade of a tree in the corner of the lot.

"That's Ho's car."

"That's good." Sloane jumped from the passenger seat and hurried around the car.

"No. It's after five. Ho doesn't work after five." Molia pulled on the door handle. Locked. "Shit. He also never locks this door."

He vaulted over the stair railing and sprinted up the alley, Sloane limping to keep up. At the front of the building he pulled open two glass doors and rushed down the hall to a door with a smoked-glass window. Stenciled letters identified it as the office of Peter Ho, Jefferson County medical examiner.

"Stay behind me."

Molia pulled the Sig and opened the door into an empty waiting area, crossed it, and opened an inner door that brought the nauseating odor of formaldehyde. The smell grew stronger as they crept down a darkened hallway and emerged in a room of tables that resembled large metal baking sheets. A bright light illuminated a dark green body bag on one of the tables. Sloane heard the hum of a motor, perhaps the air-conditioning. Otherwise, the room was deafeningly quiet.

Molia raised a hand, a signal to stop. He disappeared into a doorway that Sloane assumed was an office, emerged, shaking his head, and pointed to the rear of the room. They stepped past a large stainless steel box with multiple drawers and took up positions across a door frame at the back of the room. Sloane gripped the door handle, thinking of Melda's lifeless body, and waited for Molia to nod. Then he flung the door in. Molia swiveled inside, gun extended.

A bathroom. Empty.

They stood in a moment of uncertainty, Molia scanning the room, running a hand over the bristles of his hair until his eyes came to rest on the green body bag on the metal baking sheet. Sloane knew immediately what he was thinking. If the coroner had gone home, would he have left a body out? They started back across the room, eyes focused on the bag. The shadow appeared in his peripheral vision, creeping across the floor like spilled ink. A door on the stainless steel box had swung open, and the metal tray inside shot out like the tongue of some huge animal, knocking them both off balance. A body sat up, screaming.

The sheet fell away, the scream becoming laughter.

"You son of a bitch. I finally got you! After all . . ." The man sitting in the tray paled an ash white.

Molia was in a crouch, the barrel of the Sig locked on the man's forehead.

"Tom?"

Molia lowered the Sig and pulled the man from the tray by the collar of his shirt. His legs buckled, unsteady.

"Goddamn it, Peter, I nearly killed you. What the hell were you thinking?"

Peter Ho looked stunned, afraid. "It was a joke, Tom."

Molia turned from him, walking in circles like a caged zoo animal, spitting his words, making the sign of the cross repeatedly. "Jesus H. Christ, Peter! Jesus H. Christ! Goddamn it to hell! Shit!"

Ho looked to Sloane, but Sloane couldn't find any words. His stomach remained lodged in his throat.

Molia collapsed onto a wheeled stool like a fighter at the end of a round, physically and emotionally beaten. "I'm sorry, Peter. Shit. I'm sorry."

"What the hell happened, Tom?"

Molia slid back his chair and stood. "I need a drink. You still got that bottle of Stoli?"

Ho retrieved three sterilized glass test tubes from a cabinet, pulled a bottle of vodka from one of the drawers in the reefer, and poured them each a shot. They drank without hesitation. Ho refilled the tubes twice as Molia told him about the two men in the woods, and about Sloane's theory that Parker Madsen was behind much of what was happening.

"Banto said you called—something about Rivers Jones knowing about your autopsy. I half-expected to see you on one of your tables."

Ho looked stricken. "Yeah, he called."

"What exactly did Jones say?"

Ho shook his head. "He was ranting and raving, Tom, telling me he'd have my license, wanting to know why I'd disobeyed his direct order to cease and desist."

"Did he say how he found out?"

"Apparently their coroner detected my biopsy. I denied it, but I was also tired of listening to the little prick, Tom. I told him to go fuck himself. He can have this job. I'll go back to private practice and make a lot more money."

"Okay, Peter, okay," Molia said, trying to calm him.

"Jesus, Tom, do you think they'd really try to kill me?"

After what had just happened in the woods, Sloane knew that the answer to that question was a definite yes.

"Nobody is going to kill you, Peter. But right now I want you to think about taking a couple of days off—get away from here for a while. Take your family and go do something fun."

"I already considered that after I got the call from the sister."

"Whose sister?"

"Joe Branick's sister."

"Aileen Blair?" Sloane asked.

Ho turned to him. "That's the name."

"What did she want?" Sloane asked,

"She wanted to know the results of my autopsy. Maybe I was still pissed from talking with that asshole Jones, but I said some things I shouldn't have, Tom. I told her she should question the accuracy of any autopsy the government provides her, that I had reason to believe her brother did not kill himself. After I hung up and calmed down I decided maybe that wasn't too bright."

"Well, what's done is done," Molia said.

"They're going to kill me."

"Nobody is going to kill you, Peter. Where are you thinking of going?"

"The kids have been after me about taking them to Disney World ever since you preempted me last summer."

"A public place—good."

Ho looked suddenly scared. "I better call home."

Molia put a hand on his shoulder. "It's all right, Peter. I had a black-and-white dispatched to the house."

"That is going to scare the crap out of Liza. I better get home. Liza must be jumping out of her skin."

They helped him put the body on the tray back in the reefer. Then Ho walked into his office and emerged wearing a light blue windbreaker. Sloane and Molia followed him to the back door and down two flights of stairs, talking as they went.

"Why are you here this late, anyway?" Molia asked. "You never work after five."

"Paperwork is due to County at the end of the month. I always put it off until the last minute, then spend three nights of hell getting it done. With all the shit that's been going on, I got behind. That's why I didn't have the music on and I could hear your car drive up. I looked out the window and saw you get out and head for the back door. I figured you were coming to scare the crap out of me again." Ho reached the bottom landing. "I told you I was going to have Betty start locking this door."

"You've been telling me that for years. I didn't think she'd actually do it."

They emerged in the parking lot. Ho turned and used a key to lock a dead bolt. "Neither did I. But I'll tell you this, after getting in that box I've decided I want to be cremated."

"You almost had the chance."

"I did get you, though, didn't I?"

"Yeah, you got me, better than you'll ever know, Peter."

"Payback's a bitch."

Molia smiled. "I'll follow you."

Ho started across the lot to his Blazer. Molia slipped behind the steering wheel of Banto's Jeep. Sloane pulled open the passenger door. The thought came suddenly. He turned and looked at Peter Ho unlocking the door of his car. "I didn't tell her."

Molia leaned across the seat. "What's the matter?"

Sloane leaned down and spoke into the car. "I didn't tell Aileen Blair that Ho did an autopsy."

"What?"

"Aileen Blair, Joe Branick's sister—I didn't tell her Ho did an autopsy. She thought he didn't. She thought the Justice Department stepped in. She had no reason to call back for results."

Molia had already unsnapped his seat belt, getting out of the car, shouting Ho's name, but the Jefferson County coroner had slipped into the Blazer and slammed the door.

"Ho!"

77

~

B REWER REREAD the newspaper articles, the ones that had lingered with Charles Jenkins like a malignant tumor—treatable perhaps, but never completely gone. The newspapers had yellowed and faded with the years, crackling to the touch, but he recalled well the contents of two articles in particular.

Mexican Massacre

The Associated Press

OAXACA, Mexico—In what Mexican officials are describing as a bloodbath, at least 48 men, women, and children are reported to have been raped, beaten, and killed in a remote mountain settlement in the jungles of Oaxaca, Mexico.

Already being described as the worst massacre in Mexico's sometimes troubled and violent history, the Mexican newspaper *La Jornada* blamed the attack on a series of escalating battles between Mexico's indigenous poor, fighting for better living conditions, and government paramilitary forces.

Mexican military leaders have strongly denied any involvement in the attack or that any coordinated operations were under way to put down persistent revolutionary groups in Mexico's southern region, where the groups are suspected of using the rugged mountainous terrain and dense jungles to avoid government and paramilitary forces.

There are no reported survivors.

Brewer skipped the remainder of the article and turned the page to an equally faded clipping dated two weeks after the first article.

Mexican Massacre May Not Have Been Work of Military

The Associated Press

OAXACA, Mexico—Mexican officials are hinting at evidence that last month's attack on a village in the jungles of the southern Mexican state of Oaxaca was not perpetrated by government military units as widely suspected, but was instead carried out by a hard-line underground organization known as the Mexican Liberation Front, or MLF.

Considered to be one of Mexico's most violent revolutionary groups, the MLF and its leader, known only as *el Profeta,* the Prophet, has recently accepted responsibility for a series of attacks on government forces and government officials in the southern Mexican states. Mexico's military intelligence and CIA counterpart, CISEN, has had little success stopping the violence or identifying the organization's leaders.

A government official said heavily armed members of the MLF, dressed in black and gray uniforms commonly worn by a paramilitary force known as *los Halcones,* the Falcons, perpetrated the attack. The MLF's motivation is not yet clear, but officials said it was likely to inflame the passions of Mexico's middle class and 9 million indigenous peoples to take up arms against the Mexican government and military.

If the reports prove accurate, the act appears to have backfired badly. Mexican officials say it has hardened the government's resolve to hunt down the perpetrators in the rough and dense terrain, and that villagers once loyal to the group's leaders have already given up several suspected MLF leaders.

"It's a fairly common tactic," Jenkins said. "If you can't find the man, you try to turn those closest to him against him. The Israelis have done it, and we did it in Afghanistan."

Brewer removed his reading glasses, holding them in his hand. He looked stunned. "Peak did this?"

Jenkins nodded. "Peak gave the order. The attack was carried out by a group known as Talon Force."

"Ours?"

"Ours."

Brewer rubbed a hand across his jaw. "Jesus! Why?"

"The American people did not have the stomach for another war, Mr. Brewer, and Robert Peak was not about to allow Communism to set up shop in America's backyard, not at a time when the president was looking to Mexico for its oil. Peak always had political ambitions. His father made sure he had his eye on the ultimate prize at all times. Nothing was going to get in the way of that, especially not some peasant revolutionary stirring up trouble in the mountains. Peak needed to ensure the stability of the country in the event the Arabs didn't blink and called the president's bluff."

"But a village? Why women and children?"

"You commit an act so horrific it shocks the sensibilities of the country and the world; then you blame it on the organization you're trying to dismantle, and you get the people who've been protecting him to give him up. It worked to a degree. The problem was, nobody, except perhaps for a select few, knew el Profeta's identity. He was smart in that regard."

"And el Profeta intends to kill Robert Peak for this massacre?"

"Yes."

"How? Tell me how he could get close enough to do it."

"I've told you, we've invited him."

Brewer's face pinched. "The summit."

"Do you think he's been living in a hole for thirty years, Mr. Brewer? Alex said these negotiations were top secret. So to have pulled off what he's pulled off, el Profeta has to be a high-ranking member of either the Mexican military or the government. Either way he'll be part of the Mexican delegation. He'll be standing at the ceremony. He's waited thirty years for this opportunity. He won't let it pass now."

"But he has to know that security will be a bitch, even for the delegates. How does he get a weapon in?"

Jenkins shook his head. "That I don't know, which is why I assume Joe was trying to determine not how he was going to do it, but who he is."

"But that doesn't make any sense, either; if Joe was trying to determine this man's identity, to possibly save Robert Peak's life, why would Peak have him killed?"

"Because Peak didn't know that. What makes men like Robert Peak strong is also their biggest weakness. They have just one interest: themselves. When Peak learned that Branick had the file and was making these inquiries, he assumed Joe intended to expose him for what he did back in that village. To Peak there was no other reason to keep something like that unless it was to use it against him. And I assume that is why Peak kept inviting Branick back to work for him. It wasn't because of friendship; it was because Peak feared what Branick knew."

"Keep your friends close. Keep your enemies closer," Brewer said.

"Exactly. What Peak couldn't understand, because it is so completely foreign to his way of thinking, is that Joe Branick would never have betrayed him or breached his code of silence. Joe believed in his oath, and Joe always did the right thing."

"Then why *did* Joe dig up the file after so many years?" Brewer asked.

"I asked myself that very same question."

"And the answer?"

"Joe left it for me in the file. Get me in to see Robert Peak, and I'll tell you both."

78

~

THE FORCE OF the explosion shook the parking lot asphalt like an earthquake, knocking Sloane from his feet onto his back. Twisted metal and bits of glass rained from the sky, flames engulfing the Blazer like tentacles of a huge octopus. Plumes of black smoke billowed into the air, carrying the smell of burning rubber and an intense rush of heat.

Sloane sat up and watched Tom Molia stagger toward what remained of the car, jacket draped over his head. He scrambled to his feet to intervene, but Molia shoved him aside and continued forward, dropping low to the ground, disappearing momentarily in the black smoke. He emerged dragging Peter Ho's body. Sloane rushed forward and grabbed Ho by an arm—deadweight across the parking lot. They fell to the pavement, coughing violently, spitting up black gunk, struggling to breathe. The fire and smoke had blackened Ho's face, spotting it with patches of pink where the skin had been torn away. He was drenched in sweat. The force of the blast had literally blown him out of one of his brown loafers.

Molia cradled his friend's lifeless body to his own, rocking in agony, arms shaking, chest heaving in silent sobs.

Guilt gripped Sloane's chest like a kick to the sternum. The light in his head flashed, and he plummeted into darkness as if dropping into a hole. This time he landed in the arms of the woman. Warm and alive, she rocked him, humming softly as she caressed his hair. He felt the warmth of her breast, her hands comforting him, soothing him, and something he had never felt before, what he had missed all of his life, what he had longed for and never found: love. Pure, unconditional, unadulterated love.

He knew her.

"I don't know who they are," Molia said, looking up at him. "And I don't know how I'm going to find them, but I will. And when I do, I'm going to string them up by their balls."

SLOANE STOOD WITH three uniformed police officers on Tom Molia's front porch—young men milling uncomfortably like distant relatives at a family funeral, not knowing what to say. Their patrol cars waited in the street, headlights on and engines running. The swirling lights and screaming sirens that had brought the neighbors out onto their porches were now silent.

Molia knelt to hug and kiss his daughter. She wore a blue jacket with the words "Disney World" stitched across the back, and held the handle of a pink suitcase. The detective pulled her to him, inhaling the smell of her hair and kissing her cheek. Then he grabbed his son, T.J., who remained insistent on wearing his father's black and silver Oakland Raiders jacket though it extended past his knees. He, too, held a small suitcase, the arm of a toy sticking out from the zipper. Tears streamed down the boy's cheeks;

neither child was accustomed to seeing their father and mother so upset.

"You listen to your mom, and I'll meet you as soon as I can," Molia said, trying to calm his son.

"Why can't you come now, Daddy? I want you to come now."

"Of course I'm coming. I'm just coming later."

"I want you to come now," the boy insisted.

Molia pressed the boy to his chest. "I have work to do. I have to put you two through college, don't I?"

"I don't want to go to college. College is stupid."

"Don't say stupid. You'll want to go to college. There are pretty girls in college."

"I hate girls."

"I met your mom there."

T.J. rubbed his nose, perhaps never having considered his mother a pretty girl.

"Kiss Grandma for me," Molia said.

The boy made a face as if he'd sucked a lemon, looked up at his mother, who stood watching, arms folded, hands clutching crumpled Kleenex, then leaned forward to whisper in his father's ear, "She has bad breath."

Molia whispered back, "Kiss her on the cheek. And don't play with Grandpa's trains. You know how he can get."

He hugged both children again in a fierce embrace, then stood and turned to his wife. Maggie rubbed her forearms as if trying to warm them. "I'll call you."

She nodded, gathered both children, and started down the porch steps.

"Hey," Molia said softly.

Maggie ushered the children to Banto, who had met her halfway up the walk.

"Can we turn on the siren, Marty?" T.J. asked.

"Not a police car if you can't turn on the siren," Banto said, leading them down the path to the cars.

Maggie turned and rushed back up the steps, hugging her husband like a sailor returning from war. "Don't you make me raise those two kids alone, Tom Molia. Don't you do it; don't you dare do it."

"I won't," he whispered.

"If you die on me, I swear I'll kill you."

He released his grip, his cheeks saturated with his own tears and hers. "Then I won't die on you. Who loves you, babe?"

She closed her eyes as if struck by a pain. "Who loves *you*, babe?"

He wrapped an arm around her shoulder and walked her down the porch steps. The officers followed at a respectful distance, leaving Sloane alone to watch from the porch. Banto helped Maggie into the backseat, then shook his partner's hand.

"You sure you don't want my help?" Banto asked.

"I'm trusting you with my family, Marty. Don't let anything happen to them."

"Nothing will. You're a pain in my ass, but I can't take Franklin alone." Then Banto lowered himself into the car and shut the door.

The detective stood on the sidewalk watching the procession make its way down the street, their departure punctuated with two short blasts of the sirens to pacify his son. Then the cars turned right and were gone.

Tom Molia paused for a moment as if to gather his emotions, then wheeled and walked briskly back up the path, taking the porch in a leap. He pulled open the screen door. Sloane followed him inside and watched as the detective unlocked the dead bolt to a closet in the front room, pulled out a Kevlar vest and flung it on the couch, then brought out an assortment of handguns and rifles, as if taking inventory of a small gun shop.

"First we'll pay a visit to Rivers Jones." He laid out his weapons as he detailed how they would gather enough direct evidence to implicate Parker Madsen. With three dead men all bearing the same tattoo, they had enough to get the feds involved, but Molia wasn't interested in that at the moment.

"Going to the feds would be like blowing a shrill whistle in a crowded theater," he'd said. "We'd get everybody's attention, but not much else. All it would do is give Madsen, and whoever else is involved, a chance to get their defenses in order."

Sloane knew that would effectively end the investigation, and that would effectively end his quest to figure out his own identity. But he also knew that the detective's plan was born of anger and not reason. It would not work. Madsen was too well insulated. Rivers Jones was likely a pawn, a fall guy in the event anyone got close. They needed the Justice Department to cooperate, to say Joe Branick had killed himself. Jones was that guy. Sloane knew there was only one way they were going to get close to Peak or Madsen, and that was by using the file. That was what they wanted most. That was the bargaining chip. It was the only way to end it, however that might be. He needed to stop the killing.

As Molia discussed his plan and took inventory of his weapons, they heard an otherwise familiar sound that at the moment was so unexpected, it took them both time to determine what it was. The phone on Sloane's belt was ringing. He snatched it and flipped it open, expecting to see Tina's number on the lighted display. The caller ID was blocked.

"Hello?"

"Mr. Sloane."

A man's voice, somehow familiar, though Sloane could not place it in that instant. "Who is this?"

Molia stepped toward him, and Sloane hit the speaker button on the side of the phone.

"Who this is, is not important, Mr. Sloane. You have turned out to be a formidable adversary. The two men you disposed of were highly skilled and highly trained soldiers. So was the man in San Francisco. I commend you."

Sloane looked to Molia and mouthed the word "Madsen."

"Whatever they were, General, at the moment they're just dead."

The caller did not dispute his identity. "Yes, that's my understanding." It was Madsen.

"What do you want?"

"I have a proposition for you, Mr. Sloane, a *settlement* of sorts, to use a word that I'm sure you can appreciate."

"I'm listening."

"A meeting, just you and me, alone."

"Why would I do that?" Sloane asked, though it was exactly what he'd had in mind.

"Because you have a package, and I have a need for that package."

"I asked why *I* would meet with *you*, General, not why you would meet with me. It's readily apparent what you want."

"Very good. I would expect such a precise and reasoned response from an acclaimed trial lawyer such as yourself."

Madsen paused. "In order for there to be a successful negotiation, each side must have some leverage, something to bargain with, something the other side would want. Am I correct? Is that what you're getting at?"

"I assure you, Mr. Madsen, there is nothing in this world that you could have that I would want."

"I find that response very disappointing, Mr. Sloane. I must admit that I had been looking forward to meeting you, or should I say, meeting you again? That was quite an accomplishment, getting into the West Wing of the White House. I believe it to be unprecedented, and clearly indicative of someone highly intelligent, skilled, and composed. But if you think I would make such a statement without the ability to back it up, then I can only say that perhaps I have overestimated you, or you have underestimated my resolve."

"I haven't underestimated you at all, Mr. Madsen."

"Oh, I beg to differ."

"David?"

Molia pulled his face away at the unexpected sound. Sloane closed his eyes. His head slumped to his chest.

"Tina," he whispered.

"You will see, Mr. Sloane, that I am not a man who makes bold proclamations I cannot keep."

"Madsen, you son of a bitch. So help me God—"

"I'm glad to hear she is of as much importance to you as I suspected."

"Madsen, you listen to me—"

Madsen's voice hardened. "You are in no position to be making threats or demands, Mr. Sloane. Nor is there any need to make this personal. Consider it a business transaction. You have a package. I want it. You bring it to me, and I release the woman to you. Simple, neat, and clean."

"Where?"

"That information will be given to you at a later time. You are to come alone, Mr. Sloane. Do not bring the detective. Do not bring the police. If you are listening, Detective Molia—and I assume you are—then know this: I will kill the woman if I smell you within five miles. Mr. Sloane, I will contact you on this phone. Trying to contact me or to trace this number will be quite futile, I assure you. Your calls are also being monitored. If you call anyone while you are en route, I will know it. Understood?"

"Understood."

"Now, I'd suggest you get moving. You have two minutes before I call back with your next set of instructions. One hundred twenty seconds. If you are not moving, alone, the woman will die."

"Madsen . . ."

"Time is running. Precisely two minutes starting . . . now."

Sloane shouted, "Madsen!"

79

~

Tom Molia paced the hardwood floor near the front door, the keys to Banto's Jeep firmly in his grip. "No way. I can't let you do it, David."

Sloane looked at his watch. He had a minute and forty-five seconds to be on the move. "You heard him. He'll kill her."

"He'll kill her anyway, and he'll kill you. Madsen is a trained killer, David. You don't stand a chance, and there is no guarantee he will go alone."

"He'll go alone. His ego won't permit him to think he needs anyone else to get the job done. I've become a challenge for him. He wants the challenge."

"Which is exactly why you're not going alone, macho bullshit aside."

Sloane looked at his watch. He was under a minute and a half. "This isn't about macho bullshit."

"Then what *is* it about?"

"You don't understand, Tom, and I don't have time to explain it to you, but I cannot let her die. I can't sit by and watch another woman I love die. I've had to do that twice. If this is the only way to keep her alive, then I have to try. I have to do it."

"We can—"

"We don't have time," Sloane growled, adamant. "We don't have time to make plans. We don't have time to call in backup. Give me the keys."

"I'll follow you at a safe—"

He held out his hand. "Give me the keys to the car."

"I'll hide in the trunk."

"Jeeps have no trunks."

"Then I'll hide in the fucking backseat."

"You don't think he's thought of that? You don't think there's somebody outside right now, watching?" Sloane looked at his watch. Under a minute. "We're running out of time."

"I have a stake in this, too, David; they killed Cooperman and Peter Ho. This is not just your battle."

"Then give me the chance to do this for both of us. If you don't, Tina will die and we both will have lost. You have a family to think of. You have two small children who need their father, and a wife who needs her husband. I don't have anything in this world but Tina. She's it. If he kills her, I don't care whether I live or die."

Molia shook his head. "I'm sorry, David. I'm not going to let you commit suicide."

The detective turned his back and started for the door. Sloane grabbed the lamp off the side table and swung it like a bat, hitting Molia in the back of the head, knocking him to the floor. He dropped to one knee, put a hand just to the right of Molia's chin, and felt a steady pulse.

"And I wouldn't be much of a friend if I left your wife a widow and your children without a father." He took the keys to the Jeep from Molia's hand, quickly gathered what he needed, and pushed open the screen door as the cellular phone rang in his hand.

80

F ORTY MINUTES LATER, Tom Molia sat on the couch in his living room, holding an ice pack against the back of his head. Standing over him was a contingent of people, but his focus was on the large African-American man who looked as if he'd just gone twelve rounds with George Foreman in his prime and lost. Next to him was an equally tall, attractive woman.

"How did you get my name, Detective?" Charles Jenkins asked.

"Sloane said he was looking for you. He said you used to work with Joe Branick and you might be the key to telling us what the hell is going on."

Jenkins spoke to the woman. "He remembered me."

"He said he saw you in a dream," Molia said. "And don't ask me any more than that. Given the pounding in my head at the moment, I'm amazed I remembered your name."

Molia had awoken on the floor with the keys to the Jeep missing, Maggie's favorite lamp broken, and a headache that four Tylenol had not touched. He put out an all-points bulletin on Marty Banto's Jeep, giving strict instructions that anyone seeing it was to call in its location but otherwise to stand down. Then he took his only option: He dialed the number for Langley, provided his credentials, and said he had information on the death of Joe Branick. That got him to the first gatekeeper. Once there, he mentioned the name Charles Jenkins. That set off alarm bells that kept pushing him up the chain of command and did not stop until he was talking with William Brewer, the director of the CIA. Half an hour after hanging up the telephone with Brewer, Molia's neighbors got the second thrill of their evening when a helicopter touched down in the cul-de-sac and delivered the two people standing in his living room.

Jenkins filled in Molia about the village in the mountains of Oaxaca, and a massacre that had taken place there thirty years earlier.

"And you saved him?" he asked, referring to Sloane.

"I didn't save him, Detective. Fate saved him that day."

"Well, that's all well and good, Mr. Jenkins, but right now *we're* fate. If we don't find Sloane, he's dead. Madsen will kill him."

The telephone rang. Tom Molia snatched it from its cradle and spoke into the receiver, listened for a beat, then handed the phone to Jenkins.

Jenkins listened intently. When he hung up he told Alex Hart that Brewer reported that they had been unsuccessful in locating Parker Madsen.

The phone rang again. This time the call was for Tom Molia. "You're sure?" Molia asked the caller. "No. Nobody is to do anything," he said, hanging up. "We don't have much time."

"What is it?" Jenkins asked.

"They just spotted the Jeep. I know where they're going," Molia said, grabbing the Sig. "It seems our Mr. Madsen has a flair for the theatrical. He's bringing this full circle."

"Full circle?"

"Where we found Joe Branick's body."

"How far are we?" Jenkins asked.

"Too far, I'm afraid," Molia said.

81

~⌒~

Black Bear National Park,
West Virginia

SLOANE STOOD LOOKING up at a crescent moon
streaked by the contrail of a jet. Stars pierced the night
sky like pinholes in a children's theater canvas backdrop,
but offered little in the way of usable light. The hushed
sounds of a river flowing resonated with the symphony of
insects, and the air was heavy from the humidity of the
day. Thick brush and tall, slender trees, standing like atten-
tive soldiers waiting for the events they were about to witness, surrounded the clearing. Sloane knew from the
newspaper articles that Black Bear National Park was
where they had found Joe Branick's body, but he didn't
imagine that Parker Madsen chose their meeting place for
sentimental reasons. No, the general had chosen it for the
same reason it was chosen as the place to end Joe Branick's
life: It was remote, dark, and heavily wooded, which
allowed for the element of surprise, and a loud noise such
as a gunshot would echo on the still air in every direction,

making its precise location impossible to detect with any degree of accuracy.

Madsen's second call came as Sloane rushed down the front porch steps of Tom Molia's house, exactly two minutes after the first. The general provided directions to a public gas station, where a man emerged from the shadows, casually opened the passenger door, and searched the inside of the car, confirming that Sloane was alone and had the package. The fact that the man did not simply take the package indicated what Sloane had already figured out: It had become personal. Sloane had likely embarrassed the general. He wanted to handle the matter personally. He wanted the challenge of bringing matters to an end, and he didn't want to share his victory with anyone else. Sloane had sensed Madsen's character during their abrupt meeting in the Oval Office. A short pit bull of a man, Madsen exuded a wall of omnipotent arrogance that had prevented Sloane from getting behind the pinpoint eyes of hollow darkness but had not prevented Sloane from knowing exactly the type of man Madsen was. Men like Parker Madsen did not consider failure a possibility. Their egos were of such immensity, it was inconceivable that the outcome of any engagement would be anything but what they expected. Their arrogance put them in positions of power, but more often than not it also led to their demise. Sloane had met similar men in the military, and the nation had received a very public display of that arrogance in the White House. Richard Nixon and Bill Clinton came immediately to mind.

Beyond that, Sloane felt something else: fear. There was something about the impending confrontation with Parker Madsen that made his legs go weak and his stomach churn. It had nothing to do with the thought of dying.

It was something beyond that, something that told him Madsen was the predator that had stalked him, and that this would be the confrontation from which he had been running, and which he could no longer avoid. He and Madsen were like two lines running toward each other from a great distance, with their intersection at this very spot, the spot where Joe Branick had spent the final moments of his life.

After the initial checkpoint, Sloane was given a series of directions, likely designed to ensure that he was not being tailed, that ultimately ended on the flattop. That was twenty minutes ago. Madsen was now content to make him wait, to gain some psychological advantage while he observed Sloane from somewhere in the dark.

"Your training has served you well."

Sloane had not heard a sound before the staccato voice disrupted the beauty of nature. He turned, panning the darkness left, right, and back to dead center. He saw no one. Then, slowly, his eyes made out the imprecise outline against the darkened tree trunks and shrubbery. Parker Madsen appeared from the underbrush like a Bengal tiger emerging from thick jungle. He stood at the edge of the clearing, perhaps fifteen feet away, dressed in jungle camouflage fatigues that seemed to float a foot off the ground, presumably where they had been tucked into black infantry-style boots. His face was a streaked mixture of light and dark greasepaint.

The bulb in Sloane's mind flashed, followed by the percussive blast. He heard the heavy boots stamping into the room, felt the vibrations running through his body. He fought to stay in the present; Tina's survival depended on his staying in the present.

"You were a marine, were you not?"

Sloane opened his eyes. He had avoided falling into the black hole, but unlike in the past, this time he felt a compelling urgency to go there. "Why do you ask questions you already know the answers to, General?" He was counting on Madsen knowing much more than the branch of the military in which he had served. "I didn't come here to discuss my past. Where is she?"

Madsen stepped forward, stopping at a point perhaps ten feet from Sloane. With the dark of night, it was not possible for Madsen to see much of anything, but the general seemed unconcerned whether Sloane was carrying a weapon—part of whatever mind game Madsen was intent on playing, like a gunfighter on the dusty streets of an Old West town, daring the other to make the first move. "You enlisted at seventeen without parental consent, yet did not lie about your age."

"I got caught up in the commercials. You know: 'the few, the proud'? Let's cut the bullshit, General. Where is she? We had a deal."

"You managed to talk your way past the marine recruiter. By the time your age was determined you had already obtained the highest score that year on the Marine Corps aptitude test, not surprising given your IQ. Your commanding officers elevated you to platoon leader, First Marine Division, Second Battalion, Echo Company. You earned citations for marksmanship, saw action in Grenada, received the Silver Star for gallantry, and took a Cuban bullet in the shoulder for reasons far more puzzling to me."

Sloane knew that the reason he had given for taking off his flak jacket would intrigue a military man like Madsen, as would the reason postulated by the military psychiatrist they had required him to see. "I was young and stupid," he said, still struggling to stay in the present. His mind and body felt as if someone had tied a weighted rope around him and dropped it down a hole. It tugged at him, urging him to descend to that place where he had found Joe Branick and Charles Jenkins, and the woman he now knew had been his mother. Unlike in the past, however, it was an urging fraught not with peril but with the instinct for self-preservation.

"You're being modest, Mr. Sloane. But I am always curious when a soldier disregards his military training, and particularly so in this instance. You took off your flak jacket during a hostile engagement. Why would you do that?"

"I suspect you already know that answer as well, General." Sloane braced his legs, feeling as though, if he did not, he would be dragged backward across the ground and into the depths. He could not go. He needed to get Tina. He could not let her die.

"I am aware of what you told the military doctor who examined you, as well as the conclusions he drew from it—the act being indicative of someone with suicidal tendencies. It certainly fits the profile: a man without family in search of a place, and frustrated because he has not been able to find it. Was that not how he put it?"

"You'd know better than I, General."

"And yet you have evaded some of the finest-trained soldiers this country has ever produced. I know; I trained them." Madsen sounded almost impressed. "Why would a man seemingly without a burning desire to live do that? What are you fighting so hard for, soldier?"

"I'm not a soldier, General, and I have no desire to be one again. I didn't come here to engage in a philosophical exchange about the idiosyncrasies of men."

"Then answer a more basic question: How is it that you knew Joe Branick? I will admit that I have found no possible connection between the two of you that would justify his sending you a package about which you could have no knowledge."

"You should have asked him that question yourself before you had him killed."

"Oh, I did, but he was equally recalcitrant." Madsen sighed. "No matter. I assume we will get to the root of that problem imminently. You have the package?"

"Where is she?"

"If I am satisfied with its contents—"

"No. I'll show you the package when you show me Tina. Then we discuss the details of an exchange. I don't trust you any more than you trust me."

Madsen smiled. "A hardened negotiator. Fair enough."

Madsen stepped back, the darkness swallowing him. He emerged with one arm extended, his hand gripping Tina by the shoulder. Her mouth was taped shut, her hands bound in front, hair disheveled. Though it was difficult to see in the dark, she appeared to have sustained cuts and bruises on her face. At the sight of her, Sloane's legs came out from under him and he dropped, no longer able to fight gravity or the heavy weight pulling him into the depths. He landed at the bottom of the hole and found himself beneath the bed, wedged against the wall, unable to move. His mother sat on the floor, and now it pained him even more to see her battered, bruised, and violated. The man stood over her, shouting the words Sloane had, until that moment, refused to hear.

"*¿Dónde está el niño? ¿Dónde está el niño?*" (Where is the boy?)

They had come for him. Outside they were killing—killing everyone . . . because of him.

The words rang in his ears and struck a chord deep within him, a place as dark and desolate as the hole into which he had fallen. From beneath the bed he looked up at the face, a streaked reflection of light and dark—nondescript features concealed beneath the dark of night and the smear of grease-paint. The eyes, however, could not be concealed: white, shimmering pearls rimmed by red fires of hell, and in the center a black abyss of nothingness—the eyes of a predator intent on killing, and feeling no remorse for its act. Sloane saw them in his dreams, in the Oval Office, standing before him now. Unmistakable. Unforgettable.

Parker Madsen's eyes.

He would kill Tina.

He sprang to the surface, the need to be there breaking whatever barrier had confined him to the past or trapped him in the present, free to go between both worlds now, able to remember without pain, able to see. It had been Madsen.

"*You* killed her."

The eyes narrowed.

"You came that night. You came into the mountains, to the village. It was you and your men. You killed them. You killed them all."

Madsen studied him in silence.

"You beat and raped her. You slit her throat. I saw you do it that morning. I saw the darkness come. It was you."

"How could . . . ?" Madsen stopped, his voice a whisper of disbelief and devoid of bravado. He tilted his head and craned forward, as if intrigued but leery of what he might see. At that moment Parker Madsen's past and present collided, just as Sloane's had, and his mind solved his burning questions: why Sloane had no living relatives, why he seemed to have materialized out of nowhere, why Joe Branick would send him a package about events in which he could have had no involvement.

Because he *had* been involved.

Because he had been there.

Madsen laughed, but it was nervous, hesitant, and devoid of humor. "You're the boy," he said. "He saved you. Joe Branick saved you."

"Joe Branick may have taken me out of that village, but he didn't save me from what I saw that morning. I watched you do it. I watched you beat and rape her. I watched you hold her by her hair and slit her throat. I watched you kill my mother."

He remembered it now vividly, clearly, as if a tarp had been lifted. He remembered lying beneath the bed in the stillness of early morning, the light of day breaking into the room and bringing with it the horror. He told himself it was not real, that it was just a dream, that when he opened his eyes it would all be gone. He remembered hearing the men come into the room and felt the terror that surged through him all over again. He remembered holding his breath, trying not to make a sound, until he could no longer do so, and it escaped in a whimpered cry. He remembered the rush of air, the pressure against his chest suddenly relieved, and the blanket that had concealed him being pulled away. Charles Jenkins and Joe Branick stood over him in stunned silence.

The handgun materialized in Madsen's hand like a rabbit from a magician's sleeve—the trained soldier returning to the task at hand, setting aside the unexpected turn of events. "The package, Mr. Sloane."

Sloane unzipped the jacket he had taken from Tom Molia's closet, bulky and too large for his frame, and removed the file he'd stuffed inside. "Let her go."

Tina stood shaking her head, mumbling through the tape, eyes wide with fear.

"Throw it on the ground."

Sloane tossed the file on the ground.

"Who says you never get second chances in life?" Madsen said.

Then the smile disappeared, and he pulled the trigger.

82

〜

It was the cry of utter despair and anguish, of hope lost, and futures shattered. It exploded from Tina with such force that the tape tore from her cheek and flapped like a Band-Aid that had lost its grip.

"No!"

Her cry united with the explosion of the gun, a shimmering echo of violence that permeated the peace like a blast inside a metal drum, clattering and horrific. She watched as Sloane fell backward. Her legs collapsed as if broken from a fall from a great height, and she dropped to the ground, lifeless and languid, sobbing hysterically, unable and unwilling to move.

Then she felt Madsen's hand grip her by the hair, and the pain at her scalp as he yanked her to her knees, pulling the combat knife from the sheath on his belt.

Sloane lay on the ground, a throbbing pain radiating from his chest—a center-mass shot that left a gripping knot of agony pulsing through him. Thunder rang in his ears. Blood overpowered his taste buds. A burning fire consumed his being, leaving his limbs without life. He felt the cool dampness of dew and the sharp sting of the pebbles and rocks against the back of his head. Darkness unlike any he had ever experienced enveloped him. Had it not been for the ringing in his ears and the taste of bile in his mouth, he would have concluded that Madsen's shot had blown away his head.

His eyes fluttered open and closed, fighting the desire to drift away. He turned his head, watching. The woman lay on the ground, sobbing hysterically, her body convulsing in agony and torment. Her executioner reached down and grabbed her by a tuft of hair, pulling her to her knees as he unsheathed the blade from his belt.

"Your dreams may not be dreams. They may be real."

Tina.

Not a dream.

Real.

Madsen.

At that moment any remnant of the carefully crafted image of the politician disappeared, and the person within, the man who, during a military career of over thirty years, had become a hardened killer, escaped from whatever prison Madsen had locked him in. He burst free in a sardonic mask of evil and perverse enjoyment that came with the rush of absolute and unadulterated power. This was why General Parker Madsen had never left the fields of battle. This was why he never left the men he trained and led. This was why he never left Talon Force. It had nothing to do with loyalty to his soldiers or to duty and honor. It was a selfish, perverted fulfillment of his own desires. There was nothing that equaled the rush of war, the thrill of killing, having the power within one's hands to give and take life. It was omnipotent, the closest thing he could imagine to being almighty. It was intoxicating. His addiction. His weakness.

He grabbed the woman's hair with his right hand and pulled her from the ground to her knees. Then he reached across his body with his left hand and unsheathed the blade from his belt. Tonight he would finish the mission he had left unfinished in the mountains that morning thirty years ago. History would repeat itself. And in the end, Parker Madsen would stand on top, as always.

The woman no longer fought him, no longer struggled, shocked or resigned to her fate. Madsen raised the blade.

He heard the sound no soldier who had served in Vietnam would ever forget, the sound of salvation in the darkest of moments, distant but rapidly approaching—the whir and chopping sound of a helicopter coming at full speed. He looked up at the night sky, and in an instant his trained eyes distinguished the moving white lights amid the stationary stars.

"Too late!" he said out loud, nearly shouting his defiance. "You're too late."

83

❦

Tom Molia focused on the instrument panel, trying not to look out the window or think about how high they were off the ground. He felt chilled to the bone, as numb as the day he picked up the phone and heard his mother's voice tell him that his father had passed away. Perspiration rolled down his temples and under his arms. He kept talking, distracting himself with conversation, trying to avoid that moment when he knew the pilot would need him to look out the window and find the flattop where they had found the body of Joe Branick. He hoped he wouldn't faint.

Charles Jenkins had folded himself into the back next to Alex Hart, and the big man seemed to be in considerable pain. Brewer had assured him that more men would be sent, but none would arrive before him and Molia.

"How much longer?" Molia spoke into the mouthpiece of his headset, shouting above the whir of the blades and hum of the engine. He was fighting to hold it together. He had almost collapsed when Jenkins told him they'd have to take the helicopter.

The pilot checked his instrument gauges. "Maybe six minutes."

"Can this Mosquito go any faster?"

"Maybe four minutes."

"Do it."

Molia turned his attention back to Jenkins. "What I don't understand is why the CIA was so interested in a kid. How much power can a kid have? Hell, I can't even get my son to lead the dog outside to pee at night."

Jenkins responded in an amplified voice that sounded like someone driving with the windows down. "He was not just any kid, Detective. Some in the villages were convinced he was much more than that."

"Much more how?"

"Special. Someone who would lead Mexico's poor and indigenous peoples out of centuries of poverty and despair—a gift from God."

"A kid would do all that?"

"You weren't there. You can't understand the circumstances at that moment. You did not see it like I did. You didn't experience it. You didn't feel him inside your head and your chest."

Molia turned in his seat and looked at the large man. Despite his size, Jenkins had a soft quality to him, a sincerity and kindness. "Inside your head and chest? You believed it?"

"I don't know what I believed in the end." Jenkins touched his heart. It appeared an unconscious act. "It was like sitting in a soothing bath and having warm water flow over you, washing away your concerns until all you wanted was to hear his words. Did I believe it? I don't know. But I know that after what I witnessed in Vietnam I wanted to believe it. I wanted to feel the peace and comfort his voice seemed to give. And that was when I came to realize that what is important is not what is true, but what people believe is true and what they're willing to do for that belief. He could control that. Regardless of how he did it, it was an incredible gift. Our concern was not how he would use it, but how others would use him."

"And that's why Peak gave the order to kill him?"

Jenkins nodded. "Because of what I wrote in my reports. Because I convinced him that the boy was real, and that the threat that others, most notably el Profeta, were using him for the wrong reasons, was real."

"He figured that if you believed it, so would everybody else, and he had a potential revolution on his hands when he was supposed to be keeping the peace—bye-bye political career."

Jenkins nodded. "Exactly."

"And that's why you feel responsible for what happened to those people."

"I've thought about it every day for the last thirty years."

The pilot tapped Molia on the knee. It was time to look out the window and face a completely different kind of horror. He hoped he could do it, for Sloane's sake.

84

～

T HE SHOT ECHOED across the canyon, making it impossible to determine the direction it came from, but there was little doubt of the target. Parker Madsen had been staring up at the sky when the bullet pierced his chest just below the pit of his raised left arm. It bent him sharply to the side, as if snapping him in two, and he stumbled backward on legs no longer truly functioning as limbs but serving only as supports to keep his body erect. The bullet, a Remington Golden Saber brass-jacketed hollow point, entered the body subtly but continued on a path of heavy destruction. It passed between the ribs, tearing cartilage and muscle, boring its way through both lungs, until it exploded out the other side.

Madsen's right hand lost its grip on the tuft of hair, and Tina fell back to the ground. His left hand dropped the knife to reach across his body and feel the warm flow of his own blood soaking his fatigues. His face registered what his body already knew, what no man, no matter how well trained, could accept willingly. He had not just been hit; he had been mortally wounded. He cocked his head, searching for the source of his demise, as if almost amused at his circumstance.

Sloane sat on the ground, his left leg straight out in front of him, his right leg bent at the knee, hands shaking slightly, still clutching the Colt, locked on target.

"Too late," Madsen whispered again, blood now dribbling from his mouth, his hand reaching for his firearm.

"Not this time," Sloane said, and squeezed the trigger again.

85

H E CRAWLED TO her across the uneven ground, every part of his body screaming in pain. Tina sat slouched over, head slumped to the side, hands bound, shoulders heaving.

The second bullet had struck General Parker Madsen square in the chest, driving him backward like a sledge-hammer blow. He lay five feet behind her, the soles of his thick black combat boots visible in the grass. As Sloane reached out to Tina, her eyes widened in confusion and joy. She pawed at his face, caressing it, as if merely touching him would convince her that he was in fact alive, that her mind was not playing tricks on her.

He picked up the knife from the grass, gently cut her hands free, and pulled her to him, clutching her, feeling her tremble with life.

Alive. She was still alive.

"It's all right," he soothed, speaking the words as much for himself as for her. "It's all right. It's over now. It's over."

She looked up at him, her eyes disbelieving. "But how?" she asked, confused. "I watched him shoot you, David. I *saw* him shoot you."

Sloane grimaced and opened his shirt beneath Tom Molia's jacket. The detective's Kevlar vest had stopped the bullet, but the impact had been violent. His chest hurt with each breath. Maybe this was how it felt to be run over by a truck. Sloane had been unable to pierce Madsen's exterior, to truly know the man, but it had not been necessary. He knew men like Parker Madsen. Madsen didn't stop to consider for a moment that Sloane might wear a vest, because the general was relying on the psychiatrist's report in Sloane's file, the one that said Sloane had suicidal tendencies and was prone to making rash and spontaneous decisions. But what the psychiatrist did not know, what was nowhere to be found in his report, what no one except Sloane and a private first class named Ed Venditti would ever know, was the real reason Sloane took off his flak jacket that day in Grenada. It wasn't because of the oppressive heat. It wasn't because of a desire to move faster. And it wasn't because Sloane had a death wish. Venditti, a twenty-year-old husband and father of two, had, in the rush of combat, left his flak jacket on the helicopter that dropped them into battle. And when he realized what he had done, he looked to Sloane with the same fear that Sloane had seen that night in the faces of Tom Molia's relatives. It was the fear that they would never see their loved ones again, and the hollow emptiness of worrying that their family, their children, would be forced to go on without them. Sloane had pulled Venditti behind a rock cluster, taken off his own vest, and ordered him to wear it. Sloane didn't have the same fear of dying and leaving others behind. No one's life would have changed if he had died that day. After he got hit, Sloane knew the Marine Corps would court-marshal Venditti for his negligence—the military had no leniency for mistakes. Since Sloane had already decided that killing wasn't for him, being denied officer candidate school was a small price to pay.

He kissed the top of Tina's head and smelled the sweetness of her hair, soft against his cheek. "It's over, Tina. No one is going to hurt you. Not now. Not ever."

"What about you, David?" She spoke in a whisper, her head against his chest. "Is it over for you? Did you find what you needed to know?"

"Not entirely," he said. "But enough. I found you. I found that I love you and that I can still have a good life if I just keep focusing on that love."

"Then just keep focusing on it," she said, embracing him. "Just keep focusing on it."

They looked up at the sound of the helicopter. Sloane shielded her face and raised an arm to block the wind kicking up dirt and disturbing the grass like an oncoming storm. It touched down on the flattop. In the front seat, illuminated in blue by the glow of lights on the instrument panel, but still looking ghostly white, sat Tom Molia.

86

∽

THE TWO MEN stood in silence, content for the moment to look out over the water, decompressing after having faced their worst nightmares. The moon and stars glittered on the darkened surface as if a long school of fish were darting just beneath the surface. Sloane was struck by the beauty of nature and by the ugliness of men. In the span of a week this place had been marred with two killings.

"He could have killed you," Molia said. "Not exactly the smartest thing for a guy with your apparent IQ."

Sloane pressed the handkerchief to his mouth. The impact of the bullet had caused him to bite his tongue, and it continued to bleed. "I knew he'd take a center-mass shot. It's his training. Madsen couldn't deviate from his training."

Molia turned to him, chuckling. "Bet that gives you a lot of comfort now, huh?"

Sloane smiled and touched the blossoming red welt on his chest that was already becoming an ugly bruise. "Sorry about your jacket," he said, fingering a hole in the fabric.

Molia shrugged. "Never liked that jacket anyway. Maggie's mother gave it to me. I had to put it on once a year. Thought it made me look fat."

Sloane laughed. He'd chosen it for that very reason. Its bulk hid the vest.

"Besides, it's Maggie you're going to have to worry about. She's going to raise hell. That was her favorite lamp."

"Is it anything like when you ruin her pot roast?"

Molia put a hand on Sloane's shoulder. "That, my friend, is like comparing a cool summer breeze to a tempest."

They turned at the sound of approaching footsteps. Charles Jenkins was as Sloane remembered him: larger than life, though at the moment his arm was in a sling, and his face bandaged and bruised.

"I'll wait over by the Jeep," Molia said. "I'm not letting you leave without me this time, because I sure as shit am not getting on that helicopter again."

"But you did it: You faced your fears," Sloane said.

"Yeah, well," Molia said, looking over at the winged beast, "like I said, facing your fears is overrated."

Sloane looked up at Charles Jenkins. Two grown men, each with a lot of water under the bridge, forever linked by a single event—one that Sloane had been unwilling to remember, and Jenkins unable to forget. Maybe that would change for both of them now. Or maybe facing one's fears *was* overrated, as Tom Molia said.

"This is where they found him?" Sloane asked.

Jenkins nodded. "According to the detective, this is it."

"You knew him?"

Jenkins nodded. "Yeah, I knew him."

"What kind of man was he?"

Jenkins looked back out over the water, contemplative. "A good man. A family man. Honorable. The kind of man who'd lay down his life for another if he thought it the right thing to do. If you're feeling guilt, David, don't. Joe wouldn't want you to. I'm sure he felt great guilt over the years about what happened to you. We both did. He was just man enough to do something about it. That's why he kept the file. I struggled for a long time about why he would have, but I understand now. He couldn't keep you. That would put you in too much danger. And he couldn't visit you, for the same reason. But he wanted to keep you somehow, so that perhaps someday he might have the chance to find you, and explain to you what had happened and who you are."

Sloane felt a tear roll down the side of his face. He understood now that Joe Branick had done just that.

Jenkins handed Sloane a three-inch-thick file. "You'll find a note in the front. Joe meant for you to have this. Hopefully it will answer some of your questions."

Sloane took the file. "Can you tell me what happened?"

"You sure you want to hear this now?"

He turned and looked at Charles Jenkins. "I don't know if I'll ever be ready to hear it, Mr. Jenkins. But I don't have a choice. I have no idea who I am."

Jenkins knew the feeling. "Maybe we'll both find out," he said, and started.

He arrived at dusk, soaking wet from a rainstorm and sweating beneath a heavy wool poncho in the sweltering humidity. He fell in step with a group coming from the west, entered the village, and saw a crowd he quickly estimated to be 700, far larger than they had suspected. He looked for men carrying weapons, but if any of the crowd were soldiers, he could not detect them.

The village was truly in the middle of nowhere. The steep footpath had been scratched from the ocher soil and rocky foothills. The nearest drivable road was two miles away, and given its inhospitable condition—ten miles of potholes and rocks—the distance might as well have been two hundred. One-room mud huts with thatched roofs appeared randomly arranged in the midst of a thick and unforgiving jungle threatening to swallow them. Pigs, chickens, and malnourished dogs roamed the dirt roads with barefoot children. There were no sewers or piped-in water. No home had a sink, a bathroom, or electricity. There were no streetlights. No phones. A one-acre patch of land dug into the hillside produced corn, beans, chilies, squash, pumpkins, and gourds.

Jenkins took a seat at the back of the crowd, conscious of his height, and folded his legs underneath him, waiting—for what exactly, he did not know. After ten minutes, his knees, sore and bruised from banging beneath the dashboard of the Jeep on the potholed road, ached from a lack of circulation. His ass hurt just thinking about the ride home. As if to spite him, the rain started again, permeating every hole, every rip, every seam in his clothes. He pulled the hood tight around his face, seeing the world in front of him through a small slit. The crowd appeared unfazed. It was as if an electric current of anticipation ran through them, like a crowd awaiting the start of a sporting event or a critically acclaimed Broadway play.

Then a hushed silence fell over them, leaving only the distant howl of a dog, and their necks craned to see. Jenkins rose up over the rows of heads but initially saw nothing that could have drawn the crowd's interest.

And then he saw him.

He was lifted onto a large, flat stone and stood as if floating above them.

A boy.

He was just a boy—barefoot, soft angelic features, and a mop of dark hair.

Jenkins watched as he closed his eyes, stretched out his arms, and tilted back his head as if drinking the water falling from the leaves. His shirt, a white smock, caught the breeze and rippled like a sail.

"Levante sus ojos y mire del lugar donde usted es." (Raise your eyes and look from the place where you are.)

The crowd looked up as if in obedience to his command.

"Let the villages rejoice. Let the people of Mexico sing for joy; let them shout from the mountaintops. The Lord will march out like a mighty man; like a warrior he will stir up his zeal; with a shout he will raise the battle cry, and he will triumph over his enemies."

Jenkins pulled the poncho from his head. Those around him had closed their eyes, becoming rigid, silent statues, though their lips moved slightly. *Prayer.* They were praying. It was astonishing.

The words flowed from the boy like a stream over rocks, rolling over the crowd to where Charles Jenkins sat.

"For a long time I have kept silent; I have been quiet and held myself back. But now I cry out. I will lay waste the mountains and the hills and dry up all their vegetation; I will turn rivers into islands and dry up the pools. I will lead the blind by ways they have not known; along unfamiliar paths I will guide them; I will turn the darkness into light before them and make the rough places smooth. These are the things I will do."

The words were somehow familiar, but from where? It came to him as the boy continued speaking. What he thought he had forgotten in the Baptist churches had only lain dormant. The boy was reciting scripture, though it did not appear that way, not at all. He spoke the words as if saying them for the first time, as if they were his own. Ten minutes passed. Twenty. The crowd barely moved; tears of joy streamed down their faces.

My God, he thought.

The boy paused and fixed his eyes upon them with such intensity that those sitting in the front appeared to fall backward. His voice hardened. The words no longer flowed but stabbed at the crowd like the point of a blade. "We are Mexicans. Our ancestors called this land their home before others invaded it and took what was rightfully Mexico's. We are the descendants of a great race of warriors, a proud people."

A murmur of unrest swept through the crowd.

"We are Aztecs, Toltecs, Zapotecs, and Mixtecs. We lived free and independent for thousands of years. We built great civilizations. We relied on no one. We sought no help. We gave generously, but still they came for more. We did not ask for war, but war came to us. Hear me now. There can be no true Mexico unless it is a free Mexico."

And so it was true. Jenkins had hoped not. But it was true. This was the vortex of the unrest.

"There can be no true Mexico so long as we rely upon those in power, those who seek to keep the Mexican people in bondage, to elevate themselves to positions of power, to live in splendid mansions. Those who seek to destroy Mexico, to enslave her people, cannot be allowed to stay. Those who rape Mexico, steal her land and her treasures, cannot be allowed ever to come again. Only when the people of Mexico are truly independent will a nation flourish. Only then will we be again a proud race with honor."

The crowd stood suddenly around him, shouting its agreement, surging toward the rock. Jenkins lost sight of the boy, then watched as the crowd raised him overhead and he danced on their shoulders to the beating of drums. It was surreal, like a theatrical production unfolding on a stage or the back lot of a Hollywood studio. But these were not actors, and this was no play. This was real. This was happening.

Thunder clapped from an angry sky, a blast that shook the jungle with such ferocity that the ground trembled and the sky opened. The rain fell into the canopy in great sheets, running from the leaves like water from spigots. The crowd dispersed quickly to the huts or melted back into the surrounding jungle from which they came.

Charles Jenkins stood in the rain, alone.

"I filed a report after each visit," Jenkins said. He shook his head. "I'm sorry. I never intended for it to happen."

Sloane could see the pain in Charles Jenkins's eyes, a lifetime of agony and guilt. They were the same, he and Jenkins. They had spent much of their life not knowing who they were, and uncertain they wanted to find out. "What happened that morning wasn't your fault," he said. He rubbed a hand across his chin, thinking of Melda, and the young police officer with the newborn son, and the night security guard at his building—a new grandparent—and Peter Ho and his family.

He thought of Joe Branick.

He thought of the women and children in that village.

He thought of his mother.

The immensity of the loss—and the pain it brought— weighed on him so heavily he felt it suffocating him.

"I convinced them that the threat was real, that you were real," Jenkins said.

"No." Sloane shook his head. "*I* convinced *you.*" He looked up at him. "I convinced you because it was what I was taught to do, what I understood I had been born to do. Neither of us could control what happened. We were both too young, too trusting. What I don't understand is, why now? Why, after so many years, did Joe Branick dig this up again? He had the file. Why wait thirty years to expose Robert Peak?"

"Because Joe wasn't trying to expose Robert Peak, David. He was trying to save his life."

"I don't understand."

"No matter what he might have thought of Robert Peak when he learned the truth, when he confronted Peak and learned that the man he had served for much of his life was a murderer, Joe loved his country and would not want to see it suffer."

"So why did he need me?"

"Because you're the only one left who knows el Profeta's identity."

87

~

The White House,
Washington, D.C.

THE SOLARIUM ON the third floor of the White House had been used as a classroom to teach the children of presidents. It had also been used as a type of family room for gatherings over the holidays. Robert Peak's children were grown when he took office. He and his wife had used part of the budget given every president to decorate the White House to meet the family's particular tastes to turn the solarium into a den that was part family room and part monument to Robert Peak. The dark oak-paneled walls displayed photographs of a man and family at work and at play, and Robert Peak was at the center of it all—the son of an honored statesman who rose to become president of the United States. Leaded-glass cabinets contained hardback books, souvenirs, mementos, and accolades collected during his distinguished political career. They were displayed among the family photographs, all illuminated under the glow of soft lights. The only other light came from an antique table lamp—as if the room were kept purposefully dim so as not to cast further light that might reveal the secrets in Robert Peak's closet and otherwise disrupt his neatly crafted image.

Sloane sat in the muted light, the file open in his lap, reading the reports that Charles Jenkins had filed, the reports that had convinced Robert Peak to send Talon Force into the mountains to kill. Over the six months that Jenkins visited the village, the language of his reports describing the gatherings had become more ardent and persuasive. They started out with blatant cynicism, became cautious contemplation, and ended with conviction. Sloane reread one of the entries:

> The events I have witnessed must not be dismissed out of hand. The atmosphere surrounding these gatherings is one that I can only describe as electric—similar to witness accounts of paranormal events. This child does not just recite scripture; it pours from him like water from a faucet, as if written by him . . . or for him. The crowds that gather to hear him do not merely listen to his words. They absorb them, hypnotized by his very presence.

Sloane thought of the jurors and felt them even then, yearning to hear more about what he had to say.

> The child's "sermons," as those in the region refer to them, have become increasingly disturbing.

Though he continues to promote Mexican cultural ideals, the message he delivers is clearly antigovernment rhetoric. He advocates a return to the traditional principles upon which the Mexican revolution was fought—greater freedoms for the poor and indigenous, distribution of large land tracts to those who farm them, nationalization of Mexico's banks and natural resources, and government-subsidized housing and medical care. He has become increasingly critical of the Mexican government in power and the historical intervention of the United States into Mexico's political affairs. While not expressly advocating violence, he has, on more than one occasion, incited those present to a fevered response . . .

The influence of Marxist rebels who would seek to turn Mexico into another Vietnam cannot be disregarded. With the size of the crowds growing exponentially, it is likely that the boy's message will spread from the jungles and find a ready and more sophisticated audience in the students, laborers, and unions causing unrest in Mexico's cities. Should this occur, the child's message, delivered as I have witnessed, could have incalculable ramifications on the stability of the government in power.

The door to the room opened.

Robert Peak walked in, dressed casually in blue jeans, a cashmere sweater, and slippers. Ignoring Sloane, he walked to a glass cart near the window, pulled the stopper from a crystal decanter, and poured brandy into a wide-mouthed glass.

"What I did," he said, his back to Sloane, "I did because it was in the best interest of this country. Our armed forces were on worldwide alert, with the Middle East threatening to explode. Our fleets in the Indian Ocean and Persian Gulf were in danger of being put in maximum peril."

Peak turned from the window to face him. His casual demeanor and arrogance could not hide what his body revealed. His famous blue eyes appeared more tired than radiant, with dark bags beneath them. His skin sagged, and his cheeks were flushed from high blood pressure.

Sloane's bitterness and anger, deeply rooted, bloomed at the man's arrogance, and he felt it like a great ulcer in his being. He put the file aside and stood. "What you did," he said, his voice no louder than a whisper, "was slaughter innocent women and children."

Peak bit his lower lip, then continued. "I gave the order because the consequence of not giving it outweighed the consequence of giving it."

"You gave the order to save your political career."

"Innocent women and children could have died if a revolution broke out."

"Innocent women and children *did* die."

"There are times when a few must be sacrificed for the good of the country, for the good of the many. It's not my rule. I didn't make it. It was my job not to allow anything to come between us and access to Mexico's oil. I did my job."

Sloane heard himself uttering similar words to Emily Scott's mother, and he felt ashamed.

Peak circled behind a wingback chair, holding it as if to steady his balance. "I cannot change what happened thirty years ago, Mr. Sloane."

"No, I assure you, you can't. But you could have changed what happened this week."

"You don't know the things I know, the things I knew back then. You don't sit in my chair. You have no right to judge me."

"You're wrong," Sloane said. "Tonight I do sit in your chair. And tonight I do judge you."

Peak brought his hands to his mouth, bowing his head as if in thoughtful prayer. "These negotiations are bigger than what happened between us. We have an opportunity to reduce and potentially end this country's dependence on Middle East oil and all of the problems associated with it. It's a good deal."

"There is no deal, Mr. Peak. Your past has finally caught up to you, and this time you can't run, and your father can't save you. You can't give an order and save yourself. He's outsmarted you. You're committed. You've pissed off OPEC, and if you don't get the oil companies back into Mexico they'll hang you. You can't back out. You have to be at that summit or you'll be out of office. And right now that's the least of your problems."

Peak swallowed the last of the brandy. "The security for this will be the highest ever. There is no way that man gets within a mile of the White House."

"If you believed that, we wouldn't be having this conversation."

Peak's Adam's apple bobbed like a fishing cork. "And you know who this person is, el Profeta?"

Sloane did not answer.

"You want something for it."

"Not much, really. Not given what's at stake. You took my life. I'm going to take yours. There are times when a few must be sacrificed for the good of the country, for the good of the many. It's not my rule, either, Mr. Peak. You have my terms."

Peak shook his head. "I won't do it."

Sloane turned and walked toward the door. "Then you'll be dead by noon tomorrow."

88

⚭

A T 10 A.M. THE ROSE GARDEN warmed under a brilliant morning sun. Secret Service officers took up positions along the rooftops of nearby buildings and swarmed over the White House grounds with dogs trained to detect chemicals used in explosives. Workers set up chairs and put the finishing touches on an elevated platform on which the dignitaries would stand. Cars parked within six blocks were towed; manhole covers were sealed with torches. Press credentials for the estimated 250 journalists were meticulously scrutinized.

Across town, Miguel Ibarón emerged from a secured lobby in a classified hotel and hobbled down a concrete walk toward a waiting car. Despite not having slept, he felt alert and calm. As he sat back against the leather, memories flooded him, a lifetime coming and going. He thought of that moment, thirty years earlier, when he separated the dense foliage and returned to find them all slaughtered, and how he had vowed that day, upon their blood, that he would live long enough to exact revenge on the man who had done it.

Today was that day.

Today Robert Peak would die.

He had kept his word.

Sensing the passage of time, Ibarón shook the memories and looked at his watch. Thirty minutes had passed since they left the hotel—sufficient time to arrive at the White House, even with the anticipated security checks. He looked out the window, but the scenery did not look familiar. He leaned forward, pressed the intercom, and spoke to the wall of glass that separated him from his driver.

"Why is it taking so long?"

The driver did not respond.

Ibarón depressed the button again. "Driver, why is it taking so long?"

No answer.

He tapped gently with the handle of his cane.

The driver did not acknowledge him. The limousine merged onto a different highway.

Ibarón freed himself from his seat belt and rapped on the glass with greater force. Still it brought no response. He reached for the door handle; it could not be unlocked from the inside. He flipped the switch to lower the window. The glass did not move. He felt the rush of anxiety.

What was this?

He beat the gold handle on the glass. It flexed but did not break.

"Where are we?" he demanded. "Answer me! I am expected at the ceremony. They will look for me."

The intercom clicked. "You are not expected at the ceremony," the driver said, his voice calm and impassive. "And they will not look for you."

"I demand that you take me to the White House."

"You are in no position to make demands."

A pain gripped his chest, restricting his breathing. He loosened his tie and undid the top button of his shirt, thoughts rushing through his head. He thought of Ruíz and his concern because the CIA had made inquiries into the Mexican Liberation Front. Someone had been looking for him. But who? This man Joe Branick? Why? Who was he? How could he have possibly known he was el Profeta?

He began to cough, a spasmodic wheezing that took away his breath and left him sucking for air and spitting phlegm into his handkerchief. When he looked up he noticed the driver's eyes in the rearview mirror.

"They will search for the limousine," he said, calmly wiping his mouth. "The ceremony will not go forward without me. They will find and punish you, whoever you are."

"They will not search for you, because you are reported to be too sick to attend the ceremony. They will not look for the limousine, because your car and driver were canceled. And they will not find me, because I am already dead."

Ibarón sat back against the seat, his mind working more furiously with each passing minute. Already dead? The man was crazy, but if his intent was to kill Ibarón, he was sorely mistaken. The cane, the instrument that God had placed in his hands to support him during his crippling illness, would be the instrument to get him through security. Brilliantly modified, the inner cylinder of high-quality steel was capable of handling and firing three .44-caliber bullets; the trigger was a small release in the gold handle.

The driver turned onto a dirt road, and the car bounced and pitched up a narrow incline, each bump sending daggers of pain shooting through Ibarón's ravaged bones. Then, just as unexpectedly, it came to a rolling stop and the driver turned off the engine. Ibarón leaned forward to look out the windows. "Where are we? Why have you stopped here?"

The driver disengaged the locks with a pop, opened his door, and stepped out. Ibarón clutched the handle of his cane, prepared to attack, when the back door opened, but the man made no advance toward the car. He walked off and stood on a bluff, hands in his pockets as if admiring the view.

What kind of game was this?

Ibarón struggled with the weight of the door. He held it open with the cane as he stepped out and used the cane to navigate the uneven ground, picking his spots carefully. He stopped six feet behind the driver. "Who are you? What game is this you play? Face me."

Sloane turned. The face was not like the one he remembered. It was no longer richly handsome with prominent, angular features and a head of black hair. It had become narrow, with sunken cheekbones, the chin pointed, the hair thin and white—the face of a man critically ill and without long to live. The eyes, however, remained the same: pools of dark chocolate that radiated power. It was the eyes that Sloane remembered and that had allowed him to pick Ibarón from the photographs of the Mexican delegation.

Though the bitterness and anger that Sloane felt for Robert Peak called out for revenge—thirsted for it—Charles Jenkins was right. Joe Branick realized that the assassination of Robert Peak was not the answer, and Sloane knew that he could not allow his own hatred to undo the reason why Joe Branick had died. The demands he gave William Brewer were modest. He wanted Aileen Blair flown to Washington, D.C. He wanted the chance to meet Robert Peak and let him know that whatever decision Sloane made, it would be for

Joe Branick and had nothing to do with saving Robert Peak, and he wanted to meet el Profeta alone.

When he had left Peak in the solarium, Aileen Blair sat quietly in a chair, patiently waiting. Nothing would save Robert Peak from Aileen Blair.

"Do you not know me?" Sloane asked Ibarón. "Many years have passed between us. The last time we saw each other I was just a boy."

Sloane watched as the old man's eyes peeled away the years like peeling the skin of an onion, his expression changing with each layer removed. Like Charles Jenkins's reports, Ibarón progressed from confusion to disbelief and, finally, to shock.

"Chuy," he whispered. He said the word as if unable to comprehend it, walking closer, studying him. "What trick is this?"

Sloane shook his head. "It is no trick, Father."

"You are dead."

Sloane nodded. "Yes. The boy you remember died that day, Father."

He seemed to contemplate this for a moment, considering how it all fit together. "How? How did this happen?"

"You, Father, you are the reason this happened. You taught me the things to say. You taught me how to say them. You sent me out to preach the things I had no business preaching. You brought the soldiers that night."

"No."

"You used me, and your abuse killed my mother and all those people in the village that night, and it may just as well have killed me, because for the past thirty years I might as well have been dead."

"No. You had the power."

"I was your son. You were supposed to be my father. You were supposed to protect me, to take care of me. But you used me. You used me to pursue your hatred and politics."

"God gave you a gift, a powerful gift."

"Yes, he did."

"God sent you to the people."

"*You* sent me to the people."

"Because you were the instrument to bring the people out of centuries of oppression and poverty. You were to deliver the Mexican people from so much misery, so much pain and suffering."

"And instead I've only caused them more."

Ibarón grew more adamant. "How can you say these things to me? I have spent thirty years planning for this day, for what they did to your mother and everyone in that village. I vowed to avenge their deaths, and your death. I have not rested one minute of one day. Now it is time. Take me to the White House and I will show you my commitment to her and to those who died that day. Take me to the White House so that I may finish it."

"It is finished. Not as you imagined, but as it will be. No more people will die because of me, Father. Today I do what you and Robert Peak and Parker Madsen and everyone else involved cannot or will not do. Today I end the killing. It started because of me. It will end because of me." Sloane pulled the limousine keys from his pocket.

"What are you doing?"

Sloane swung his arm backward, then suddenly forward, like a slingshot.

Ibarón lunged in horror. "No!"

The keys arced high against the blue sky, lingering for a moment as if floating on a rising current of air, catching the glint of the sun before falling, and disappearing into the thick brush at the bottom of the embankment.

Ibarón stood motionless, as if watching his life pass before his very eyes.

"I'm sorry, Father," Sloane said. "I wish things could have been different between us."

The old man wheeled, his body rising up like some great beast awakened from slumber, his back straightening, giving him height. The muscles of his arms and legs, so crippled an instant before, seemed to swell in size and power. He forced the tip of the cane into Sloane's chest with enough force to send him backward a step.

"No. It is you who are mistaken. It *will* be as I imagined. You are not my son. I refuse to believe it."

Sloane knew—how he knew, he was not sure—but in that instant he knew that the cane was the instrument of death that would have allowed Ibarón to get past security and kill Robert Peak. Yet he felt no fear. He did not relish the prospect of dying. For the first time in his life he saw a future for himself, one that included Tina and Jake— something to live for, someone to live for. But he could not do that until he had closed this chapter in his life, and if that meant dying to do the right thing, as Joe Branick had been so willing to do, then it would be so. He needed to know that he wasn't a person like Robert Peak and Parker Madsen, a person who did his job without concern for the consequences. He needed to prove he would not be like his father, filled with a thirst for revenge, bitter and angry at the world, and consumed by hatred. He had not come to this bluff to save Robert Peak. He had come to find himself. Because in the end, he realized, he needed to know not just who he was, but what kind of person he was.

"You cannot kill me, Father. That boy is already dead."

The tip of the cane shook, a tapping against Sloane's chest that became more violent, as if an electric current were passing through the old man's body and increasing in intensity, until a jolt sent Ibarón tumbling backward and off balance. His body, no longer empowered by hatred and conviction, crumpled, and he collapsed where he stood, a frail old man in whom a burning fire had been extinguished.

Sloane could not help but wonder what part of that man was a part of him. He wanted to know what shaped him as a person, but he also knew that time had long since passed and he could not change it. He would not be defined by others but by his own acts and deeds. He could change the future.

He touched the old man's shoulder as he passed, leaving him alone on the flattop, peering to the heavens, babbling incoherently. And as he walked past the car and started down the dirt and gravel road, a small wind kicked up as if to usher him away, rustling the leaves of the trees standing like an honor guard along the fire trail, silent witnesses to history. Behind him he heard the hushed flow of the river, a reminder, like the steady beat of the waves that crashed outside his sliding glass door, of time passing. He kept to his path, never turning back, his pace never slowing, not even at the sound of the gunshot, the fourth in little more than a week to echo across the canyon to points unknown, and beyond.

Epilogue

∽

Seattle,
Washington

SLOANE OPENED HIS black binder, removed the envelope he had stuffed in the front pocket as he rushed
out the door to court, and pulled out the photograph:
Charles Jenkins knelt in a vegetable garden, Mount
Rainier looming in the distance. Beside him stood Alex
Hart, arms draped around his neck, her head on his shoulder. At their feet, tongue hanging out the side of its mouth,
exhausted, was Joe Branick's dog, Sam.

Having learned of Jenkins's loss, Sloane had asked
Aileen Blair for the dog. She gave it gladly. For himself,
Sloane had asked for nothing, but it arrived two weeks
later by special delivery anyway—the cardboard cutout of
Larry Bird, the one her brother had loved. It now stood in
the entry to their house, watching over all who came and
went. Tina never complained.

Sloane had sold the apartment building, feeling that it
was an appropriate way to bury his memory of Melda. He

could no longer live there. He missed her terribly and knew he always would.

In the days following the summit, Aileen Blair spoke with Sloane frequently about her private meetings with Robert Peak. Ultimately the family had decided to let the investigation into her brother's death end quietly, comforted by the knowledge that he had not taken his own life. She told Sloane that despite her own anger and desire that Peak be punished, she, too, knew that her brother loved his country and would not have wanted a national scandal to rip it apart. Even in death Joe Branick had done the right thing.

The United States returned Miguel Ibarón's body to Mexico. The official pronouncement of the cause of death was that the senior statesman had died of complications associated with his cancer, but with the knowledge that he had served Mexico with dignity and honor. It was said that he received a statesman's burial.

Parker Madsen was not as fortunate. His body was recovered from the burned-out hull of his car. An autopsy revealed that the White House chief of staff had been legally drunk when he drove his car off a steep embankment and crashed into a tree. His image would also not survive. Weeks after Madsen's death the *Washington Post* cited confidential sources reporting that Madsen's death was likely a suicide, and that he had taken his own life when word leaked that he had commanded an ultrasecret paramilitary force suspected of perpetrating atrocities on civilians in Vietnam and perhaps in other countries. Shortly after that report, the front page became the forum for President Robert Peak's stunning decision to resign the presidency because of unspecified family concerns.

Political analysts said it was a mere formality, given the United States–Mexico oil agreement he had negotiated. Peak's staunchest supporters, the oil and car industries, were livid. Analysts called it political suicide.

Alberto Castañeda returned to Mexico a hero of the Mexican people. They likened his bold actions in securing the agreement to Lázaro Cárdenas's nationalization of the Mexican oil industry some sixty years before. Mexican newspapers said Castañeda returned emboldened, and predicted he would do great things for the Mexican people with his country's newfound wealth.

Tom Molia had discovered the power of e-mail, writing to Sloane often, usually to send him a joke. He continued to work as a detective, telling Sloane he didn't know what he would do with himself if he didn't have J. Rayburn Franklin busting his balls. He had sent Sloane a photograph, now held by magnets on Sloane's refrigerator door, of the detective standing next to a green 1969 Chevy. On the back he wrote, "Does not have air conditioning."

Sloane slid the photograph of Charles Jenkins and Alex Hart into the pocket of his blue blazer and stood as the bailiff called the proceedings to order. Judge Brian Wilbur entered the courtroom. A balding man with angular features and the athletic build of an All-American college basketball player, Judge Wilbur took his seat atop the bench beneath the seal of the great state of Washington, arranged a stack of papers, and looked down at Sloane.

"Counsel, are you prepared to give an opening statement?"

"I am, Your Honor."

Sloane pushed back his chair, stood, and buttoned his jacket. Then he unsnapped the binder and removed the pages of his opening statement, smiled at the act, and put them back. As he started from counsel's table his client reached out and squeezed his hand. He paused briefly to lean down and whisper reassurance in her ear.

"*Volverá bien*" (It will be all right), he said.

Then he turned and approached the jury.

"Good morning, ladies and gentlemen. My name is David Sloane, and I represent the plaintiff."

About the Author

❧

ROBERT DUGONI has practiced as a civil litigator in San Francisco and Seattle for nineteen years. He has a degree in journalism from Stanford University and worked as a reporter for the *Los Angeles Times* before attending the UCLA School of Law. In 1999 he left his full-time legal practice to write, and authored the award-winning exposé *The Cyanide Canary*. Dugoni lives in the Pacific Northwest.

Enjoy a sneak peek at Robert Dugoni's
blockbuster new thriller!

Please turn this page
for a preview of

Damage Control

Available in hardcover.

1

〜

D<small>R. FRANK PILGRIM</small> adjusted the flexible lamp clipped to the edge of his cluttered metal desk, but the additional illumination did not keep the typewritten words on the page from blurring. He set his wire-framed glasses above his bushy gray eyebrows and pinched the bridge of his nose. His eyes had reached their limit; they could no longer take the strain of a night reading small print.

Pilgrim glanced across the room, the details a blur. It wasn't too long ago he could watch the television screen atop the military-green filing cabinets without glasses. Now he could barely make out the cabinets, even with prescription help. His cataracts were getting worse. It didn't matter. With all the reality-TV crap being broadcast, he had long since relegated the television to background noise. It kept him company at night. He liked to listen to the Mariner baseball games, though the team continued to disappoint him. At seventy-eight, he didn't have many years left to experience a World Series in Seattle.

The telephone on his desk rang at precisely ten p.m., as it had every night for the past forty-eight years. "I'm just finishing up," he said, speaking into the old-fashioned handset. He rocked in his chair, bumping against floor-to-ceiling shelving cluttered with a lifetime of books and knickknacks from his and his wife's trips around the world. Their next stop would be China in the summer. "Just a couple more minutes and I'll be done, dear."

His wife told him to be careful walking to his car, reminding him that he was an old man with a cane and an artificial hip and no longer the starting wingback at the U-Dub. "I'm as young as you are, beautiful," he said. "And as long as I still feel like I'm eighteen, I intend to act that way."

He told her he loved her and hung up, looking out through the wood-shuttered window of his ground-floor office. His fifteen-year-old BMW sat parked in its customary spot beneath the floodlights' tapered orange glow. When he'd opened his practice, the lot had been surrounded by cedar and dogwood trees, but that was a good many years ago, when getting to Redmond required taking a ferry from Seattle across Lake Washington. With the construction of the 520 and I-90 bridges, the population on the east side of the lake had exploded. Office complexes and high-rise condominiums now shadowed his medical building.

Pilgrim closed the file, rolled back his chair, and carried the file to the cabinet, pulling open the drawer to the file he'd angled as a marker and sliding it back in place. Then, as was also his routine—rain or shine—he slipped on his raincoat and hat that at he used to think made him look like Humphrey Bogart in *Casablanca,* and reached to shut off the television. He hesitated at the lead news story.

"Robert Meyers was at the Washington State Convention and Trade Center in downtown Seattle today to give the keynote address at a conference on global warming."

Pilgrim turned up the volume and watched the charismatic young senator enter the convention center, shaking hands with some of the attendees.

"Meyers took the opportunity to continue his attacks on the current Republican administration's record on the environment."

The broadcast cut to a shot of Meyers standing at a podium behind a throng of microphones. "This is an issue whose time has come," he told the audience. "The people of the Pacific Northwest know this as well as any in the United States. The current administration's continued disregard for the environment is a further demonstration that it is out of touch with issues that will affect the future generations of this great country."

The story ended, and Pilgrim switched off the television. Curious, he raised his glasses back onto the perch above his eyebrows and used his finger to trace the faded letters on the white cards on the front of the file drawers. His daughter remained determined to modernize the practice, which was now hers, but to him the computer screens, hard drives, and printers throughout the rest of the office made it look like the control room of a spaceship. Not so in the sanctity of his four walls. All he needed were cabinets and the twenty-six letters of the alphabet—a filing system that had worked just fine before Bill Gates and computers. His daughter had relented, but only after he agreed to separate his active from his inactive files. In exchange, she promised not to ship any of his files to storage. His cabinets would leave his office with his body.

He stepped to the cabinet containing his closed files and slid open the third drawer down, thumbing through the manila files and straining to read the faded ink on the raised tabs. He still had the file. He pulled it from the crowded drawer and raised the next in sequence to mark its place, then walked to his desk. Sitting, he heard the familiar sound of the bells indicating the front door had opened. At this time of night, he locked the front door, though the janitor had a key, and Emily occasionally came back to do paperwork after putting her two children to bed. She had her father's gene for long hours.

Pilgrim stood and pulled open his office door. "Emily, is that you?" The well-dressed man in the dark suit and raincoat stood like a giant amid the miniature chairs and tables. More curious than concerned, Pilgrim asked, "Can I help you?"

"Dr. Frank Pilgrim?"

"Yes. How did you get in?"

The man closed the outer door, locking it. "I brought a key."

"Where did you get a key?"

The man approached. He did not answer.

"What is it you want?" Pilgrim asked. "I have no money here, or anything that would even remotely be considered a narcotic."

The man reached into the pocket of his raincoat, pulled out a syringe, and removed the stopper at the end of the needle. "That's okay, Dr. Pilgrim. I've brought my own."

Pilgrim's eyes narrowed. He balled his fists. "My daughter is here. She's . . . she's in the office right over there." He called out. "Emily'. Emily, there's a man here. Call the police."

The intruder stepped forward, displaying no concern. Pilgrim stumbled into his office and closed the door, but the man caught the edge and pushed it open, knocking Pilgrim backward. He closed the door behind him. Pilgrim scrambled for the telephone, but his momentum abruptly stopped, and he felt himself being pulled back by his collar. Instinctively, he turned. The man grabbed him by the throat and jabbed the hypodermic needle into Pilgrim's chest, depressing the plunger. A burning sensation spread quickly across pilgrim's shoulders and down his arms and legs. Pain gripped him, constricting the flow of air to his lungs. He righted himself, then fell backward into the filing cabinet, shoving closed the file drawer. The images blurred, distorted and unrecognizable. He lurched for the telephone and managed to grasp the receiver, but the strength in his legs dissolved and he collapsed across the desk, sliding to the floor, his arms pulling forty-eight years of clutter on top of him.

2

Seattle, Washington

HER KNUCKLES FELT thick and swollen, and her skin was as chilled as if she were working outside in a numbing-cold rain. Dana Hill fumbled with the button and missed the hole of her silk blouse. The button slipped from her grasp. She flexed her fingers and noticed the tremors. She could not steady her hand. She chastised herself, grabbed the stubborn button again, adjusted her blouse, and pushed the bead through the slit. Then she worked her way down the row and tucked the shirttail into her wool skirt. Sweat trickled from beneath her arms— the radiologist had advised that the aluminum in deodorant could interfere with the images.

She sat in one of the chairs and pulled a binder from her briefcase, flipping it open to her presentation. She read three sentences, made a note in the margin, then closed the binder and set it on an adjacent chair, considering the room. The pastel colors and floral wallpaper contrasted sharply with the vinyl table in the center. The sheet of white paper covering it always made her feel like a slab of meat being weighed at the butcher shop. A colored diagram of the interior of the female body hung on the wall, the fallopian tubes a bright red, the ovaries blue, the uterus green. She considered her watch. How long had she been kept waiting? At Strong & Thurmond, she billed her clients in six-minute increments; few would tolerate being kept waiting. Every fifteen minutes was a .25 on Dana's billing sheet, which translated into $62.50, based on her $250-an-hour billing rate. The numbers caused her to reconsider the statistics she'd read in the articles from the Internet. Who said too much information was a good thing? Did she need to know that one of every seven women in the United States develops breast cancer, that a new case is diagnosed every three minutes, or that a woman dies of the disease every twelve minutes?

One every twelve minutes. A .20 on her time sheet.

Her cell phone beeped, mercifully interrupting her train of thought. She retrieved it from her briefcase and noted that she had missed a call from her brother, James. She was not surprised; she'd read that twins could have an almost innate sense about each other. Her brother always seemed to know when she was troubled. Sadly, she had either not inherited the same gene or had never managed to cultivate it. She returned his call.

He answered on the first ring. "Dana? How come you didn't answer your phone?"

"I've had the ringer off."

"*You* had the ringer turned off?" His voice rose with incredulity.

"Very funny. I'm at the doctor's."

"I know; your secretary told me. Is everything okay?"

"Everything is fine," she said, trying to sound convincing. "Just annual checkup stuff."

He didn't buy it. "You don't sound fine. You sound anxious."

She debated over what to tell him and decided on the truth. "I found a small lump in my breast in the shower the other morning. I'm just here to have it checked out. I'm sure it's nothing."

"What did the doctor say?"

She noted the alarm in his voice. "I don't know; I'm waiting to talk with the radiologist." She sat in the chair. "I'm sure I'm fine." Seeking to change the subject, she asked, "Why did you call?"

He sighed, then asked, "Why don't you ever listen to your messages?"

"Because it takes too long. Do you know how many messages I get? It's quicker to just call back. Did you call to gloat again about how much more you love teaching the law than practicing it?"

He didn't answer her.

"James, that was a joke."

"I know . . . Listen, this can wait. I'll call you later."

"It's fine. I'm just sitting here waiting for the doctor. You know how that goes. I could be here until tomorrow. Is anything wrong?"

Again he paused. "I have a problem. I'm not sure how to handle it."

"What about?"

"It's complicated. I'd rather not talk to you about it over the phone. Can we have lunch? I could meet you downtown."

She shut her eyes. It seemed she never had time. She rubbed her forehead, feeling the onset of a headache. "I can't today. I have to give a presentation this afternoon.

What about tonight? Grant is picking up Molly. I could meet you after work."

"I can't tonight," he said. "I have a late class and forty legal briefs on the Erie Doctrine and federal jurisdiction to read."

"So teaching isn't all peaches and cream after all?"

"What about tomorrow?" he asked.

"You're not sick, are you?"

"No, nothing like that."

"I don't have my calendar with me. Call Linda and make sure I'm free."

The door to the room pushed open. A tall woman wearing a white smock over a beige shirt and blue cotton pants stepped in holding two X-rays. "James, I have to go. The doctor just walked in."

He rushed the next sentence. "Okay, but call and tell me what the doctor says."

"I've got to go."

"Dana?"

"I'll call you. I'll call you." She disconnected and shoved the phone into her briefcase. "Sorry about that."

"Not a problem. I'm Dr. Bridgett Neal. I'm sorry to have kept you waiting." Dr. Neal's white smock seemed a size too large. It came to her knees and hung from her shoulders as if she'd borrowed it from a big sister. "The mammogram went all right?" Neal wore no jewelry or discernible makeup. She had dark hair with a curl and fair skin. Dana guessed Irish, maybe Scandinavian.

"As well as having my breast flattened like a pancake can go." Dana mustered a smile. Her conversation with James had distracted her. Now anxiety seeped back into her joints, making her restless.

Neal smiled. "I tell my husband every man should have a similar experience with their testicles to appreciate it fully."

Dana chuckled. "And you haven't had any volunteers?"

"Imagine that." Neal flipped on the light box and snapped three X-rays in place. "We've located the lump." She pointed the end of a red-capped pen at a subfusc gray dot the size of a pea. "When was your last exam? I didn't find any notation in your file."

"About a year ago, I asked my doctor to have the files sent over."

Neal sat on a rolling stool and adjusted the height. "I have them. I'd like to talk with you about the incident in high school." She reviewed notes Dana assumed had been made by the nurse during their earlier conversation. "You indicated there was no mammogram taken?"

"I don't think so. Dr. Watkins described it as hard tissue that became inflamed when I had my period."

Neal grimaced. "It's too bad they didn't do a mammogram, but they didn't always do them back then. It would have been a useful baseline to compare with these images." She pointed back at the mammogram. "How old was your mother when she had her mastectomy?"

"My age—thirty-four." Dana's stomach flipped. She brushed strands of hair from her face, pulling it back off her forehead and readjusting the clip, then she wrapped her arms across her chest. She wished she'd brought a sweater. Why did they always keep these rooms so cold?

Neal put down the pen. "Lumps are not uncommon in younger women. They can come and go with your menstrual cycle."

"I'm on the pill."

Neal picked the pen back up. "Lumps are still not uncommon How long have you been on the pill?"

"Since my daughter was born, almost three years . . . and four years before that. I've wanted to stop, but my husband refuses to wear a condom."

Neal finished making a note, and slipped it into the front pocket of her white coat. She stood. "Will you open your blouse for me?"

"Again?" Something was wrong.

Neal looked calm. "I'd like to feel the nodule."

Dana got up from the chair and sat on the edge of the examination table. The buttons were decidedly easier to undo. She unclasped her bra and raised her right arm over her head. Neal probed with her fingers, looking past Dana at the diagram on the wall. "Do you have any pain in that area?"

"No."

Neal wrote some additional notes in the chart. Dana reclasped her bra. "Hold on." Neal looked up. "As long as you're here, I'd like to do a fine-needle aspiration. "

The words hit Dana like a blow to the chest. "What? Why?"

Neal pointed to the X-rays. "The bump you found appears to have an irregular edge, and it's hard."

"Oh, shit," Dana said.

Neal raised a hand to calm her. "That doesn't mean it's cancerous."

"Then why the aspiration?"

"Without another mammogram to compare it to, I don't know how long it's been there or if it's changed shape. A fine-needle aspiration allows me to have some tissue examined under the microscope."

Anger began to replace Dana's fear. Her mother had lost a breast thirty years ago, and it seemed nothing had changed. "How long will it take? I have an important presentation to give today." She thought it sounded like an excuse.

"Just a few minutes. It will save you the trouble of having to come back. I can give you the results over the telephone. If it's fluid, we'll know immediately. If it is a mass, I'll obtain some cells and send it down to the lab. Depending on how backed up they are, they should have the results in a few days. The alternative is to schedule you for a biopsy in the surgery clinic downstairs."

Dana sat again. Neal opened and closed drawers, removing a needle and syringe. Dana said, "You know, when I was seventeen, I never thought anything about it. I remember being embarrassed because my mom was freaking out in front of the doctor. Now I know exactly how she feels. I'm most concerned about my daughter."

Neal snapped on latex gloves. "How old is your daughter?"

"Three. I read that breast cancer can be genetic."

"Let's take it one step at a time. We'll do the aspiration today, and I'll give you some written information to take home to read. I'll call you with the results as soon as I get them. In the interim, try to find something else to focus on."

Dana nodded, though she was unable to think of anything at that moment.